THE PAST IS A DANGEROUS PLACE

Evelyn Turner

THE PAST IS A DANGEROUS PLACE

Copyright © 2024 by Evelyn Turner

All Rights Reserved

No part of this publication may be reproduced, stored in a retrieval system, or transmitted, in any form or by any means, electronic, mechanical, photocopying, recording or otherwise, without the express written permission of the author.

The story, all names, characters, and incidents portrayed in this production are fictitious. No identification with actual persons (living or deceased), places, buildings, and products is intended or should be inferred.

Acknowledgment

My sister Monika, and my nieces and nephews. Award-winning anchor Tiffany Murphy. My Godchildren: Tony and Sarah. Great producer, Arthur Sarkissiam. Ryan and Stephen.

My dear Rose, Rosann, and Shawn, so close to my heart. Cathy Laramore. Marj Gallace. My aunt Jane, cousins Denise, Patty, Marybeth, Grandparents, aunts, uncles, and my father: Collette, Carrie Duffy, Michele Defere, Hostetelers, Brights, Ed, Rod, Travis, Greg, Colleen. My readers.

Robin M, Jeannie S , Caroline and Ron, Gail S. Margie K. All the great Editors that helped me thorough this process. In memory of all those who have died and suffered during war. To rid our world of antisemitism.

I thank all those who told me the stories and gave me journals of a time long ago, to learn from, those who have gone through my life giving me the experience and events to write about in this fiction based on some facts in my life.

I would also like to thank Nick Difonzo for his input.

Table of Contents

THE PAST IS A DANGEROUS PLACE

Chapter 1

1960-1965, Paris, France

The door creaked open at the back of the church, and Father Damien looked up, recognizing Hans standing in the doorway. He motioned to Hans to stay where he was and slipped out of the pew, patting Katarina's hand as she sat and clenched her tissues. Father Damien strode to the back of the church and greeted Hans with a sad look in his eyes. He glanced back at Katarina as he spoke in hushed tones. Katarina appeared lost as her black dress hung from her bones; she'd lost so much weight. Her hair was lank, her face was devoid of makeup, and her skin was alabaster.

"I have suggested she see a therapist," Father Damien said. "She says she will think about seeing one, but as of right now, she tells me the memories that surface, keep her awake all night, and her thoughts retreat into a dark place with her memories. They are always right there at the cusp in her mind."

Hans sighed and rubbed his temples. "Father, I need to take her back to Berlin. For a very long time, Anthony was the only one who could talk to her, help her, and get her to stop drinking at night. She tells me it's her way of falling asleep. I think she needs to be back with her family, not stay in Paris any longer."

Father Damien looked at Katarina again. "Hans, I won't be here for more than a few weeks. They have assigned me to a parish in Chartres in the Loire Valley. As Anthony called it, the 'land of castles and dreams.' Your brother always dreamed of being near the Basilica and having a parish in the area of Loire Valley."

There was a moment of silence as they looked at Katarina, her eyes still swollen and red from crying.

Father Damien hesitated. He knew what he needed to mention was a sensitive topic. "Only one person could talk to her if you called him here."

Hans shook his head. "I won't bring him back into her life at this point. He has moved on."

Father Damien sighed. "I'm afraid they will never move on from one another. He stood at the graveside in the distance and watched her at Anthony's funeral. The sorrow was written on his face. Hans, you must realize your war was different from ours. You were in the military in Africa. Many of us still live with the trauma we endured, and it will not let us live in peace. It will always manifest itself in depression, anxiety, and nightmares at various points in our lives. It's part of us, etched into our hearts. Anthony and I had God to turn to, but many others just live with these memories. Some block the memories out of their minds, but they always resurface." he glanced at his watch. "I really must go."

They shook hands, and Father Damien strode out of the church. Hans walked down the aisle and slid next to his sister. The wooden bench showed decades of hard use. *How many have knelt here and prayed?* he thought. Katarina tilted her head slightly as his hand reached for hers, clenched in her lap.

"Katarina, it's time. Come home. Anthony is in our hearts and our memories… But not here."

Her complexion was pale, and her face so drawn, dark circles encapsulated her big violet eyes, behind them years of pain. She had not had a good night's sleep since Anthony died. Elvie was the one who called Berlin and told Katarina's parents someone needed to help her. Hans came as soon as possible; he had promised Anthony he would always care for their sister.

The morning sun showed its presence through the glass-stained windows. The church felt cold, and the dampness crept through their bones. Katarina shivered, and Hans took off his coat to warm her. Her voice was now a whisper. He touched her face gently and moved a stray blond hair away from her face.

"Let me help you, Katarina. Let's go home."

"Where is home?" she took several deep breaths as tears welled in her eyes. She glanced over her shoulder. She thought she saw a shadow of someone, but that wasn't new. She always felt as if someone was nearby. It was just paranoia; it was all in her mind. If it was not fear, it was wishing that Anthony or Gregory would walk through the door.

Hans sat with her for a few more minutes and took her hand to rise. She reluctantly stood as he urged her to go with him. He led her out of the pew. She stood at the back of the church, and as she wistfully looked back, he wrapped his arm around her thin shoulders.

"Hans, how often have we stood in this church waiting for Anthony to finish Mass? How often have I waited for him… waited for him just to make me feel safe?"

Hans chewed his lower lip. Everyone who knew Anthony had been devastated when he died of heart failure, but Katarina had taken it the hardest. "Katarina, Anthony was a savior to all of us. He had a gift in the darkest times to ease fear, sorrow, and pain. Peter said he was our conscience. He can't ever be replaced." he took Katarina's cold hand in his. "I will always look out for you. I'm here for you." he moved Katarina to the door and pushed the heavily worn oak church door open to the clear, chilly morning sunlight.

They walked in silence toward their family's apartment. It was early spring, birds were abounding in their chirping, and tulips were emerging.

"I don't want to go back to the apartment right now," Katarina said. "It's still early. Let's just take our time and visit our favorite café for a little coffee. Anthony so loved the café. Remember, it was the last place we ate with him. I go there frequently. I just sit and remember."

They walked a few blocks till they came to the café. Entering was like having ghosts swirl around from the past. Countless hours were spent in this tranquil cafe with Anthony and, during the war, with their other brother Heinz and friend Gregory. Hans and Katarina had a little conversation between them, listening to the sweet sounds of Edith Piaf, their favorite singer from France, playing on the radio in the distance. They listened to the haunting sound of "Non, Je ne regretto rien" and the beginning of "Mon Dieu." Kat and Hans got lost in their thoughts as they recalled how Edith Piaf was Anthony's favorite singer. Anthony had become good friends with her, and now they were both gone. A truck backfired, and Katarina jumped.

"It's just a truck," Hans said, his voice reassuring.

Their order arrived; quiche Lorraine and Ile Flottante, meringue floating in vanilla crème and coquettes. Color slowly returned to

Katarina's cheeks as they sipped their strong coffee.

Kat pulled her sweater closer as a cold breeze came in with the next guest who walked through the café's door. The café owner came to their table and addressed Hans. "Monsieur Rahmel, it is so good to see you. I'm so sorry about Father Anthony. Please stay longer so we can talk."

The owner's eyes glistened with tears, and Hans understood why. Anthony, Father Damien, and Father Julian had hidden him and his family and three others when they got word that they would be included in the next roundup of Jews in Paris. They hid for three years in the church through the war. The sisters fed them what little rations they had in the convent. Occasionally, the sisters dressed them as priests and nuns so they could go outside and feel the sunshine on their faces in the back of the church garden. When waves of Gestapo or SS entered the church to search every inch, they were never found. When the war ended, this man could reclaim his café after others had taken it over. Anthony fought hard for them to have their property rightfully returned to them.

A small burst of pride swelled in Hans's chest, as it always did when someone reminded him of his brother's heroism. "Thank you, but we really must go. We are leaving tomorrow. The late breakfast was outstanding as always." Hans shook hands as he rose to leave.

Hans and Katarina walked the long way back to the apartment, enjoying the rush of people passing, the cafés filled with people, flower stands in abundance filling the air with their fragrance. They both loved Paris. The day was perfect; the sun was out, and yummy scents of baked goods wafted into the streets from cafés that dotted their walk. It was nearly noon before they arrived at the apartment. Before entering the beautiful seventeenth-century building, Hans stopped Katarina at the heavy oak door. He pulled her by the elbow. She turned to face him, and they waited as a rush of children ran past.

Hans reluctantly brought up the subject of Katarina's daughter, Natalie, who had been living with him and his wife, Gertrude. Katarina's husband, John, had been asking about the child. "When we get upstairs, can we sit and talk about Natalie? John spoke with Gertrude. He needs you all to return to the States. He wants you to bring back Natalie. It might be good for you to go back to the States and try to start over. I know John loves you. But Gertrude will be devastated if Natalie leaves."

Irritation prickled down Katarina's spine. The last thing she wanted to talk about was her estranged husband. She'd borne him a child without his knowledge when she was still married to someone else, and he hadn't taken it well when she'd finally told him about the child whom she'd given up for adoption. Now, he was trying to heal the rift in their marriage by dragging her and Natalie all the way to the States, whom she barely knew,

"Yes, he tells me in every letter how much he loves Natalie and wants to start fresh with me." her voice had a sharp edge. "You and Gertrude do a lot of talking with him." her hand was on the door as she turned. "We can talk about it later."

Hans sighed. "Our lawyers notified him to see if we could adopt Natalie. If she leaves, it will be difficult on all of us, especially Mother and Father and Gertrude."

Katarina stared at him. When she spoke, her voice was ice.

"I really don't care if you want Natalie, but John would never let you adopt her. I realize she has this unexpected charisma for a child in which you all seem to be caught. She needs to return to the States."

she looked at Hans impassively, her eyes hard. Hans let out another long sigh and shook his head.

"Kat, the child has never done anything to you. Why do you resent her and Alexandra so much? If you felt so strongly about not having children, you should have given them up long ago."

She glared at him. "Can we discuss this elsewhere, please? I don't like my children. What else can I tell you? They were always a burden. If I had not been eight months pregnant with Alex, I might have been able to escape the Gestapo. I blame the pregnancy."

Katarina sighed and rubbed her temples as if she didn't want to continue the conversation. She gave Hans a weary look. "Natalie was an accident, so soon after the child, I gave up for adoption. I'm here in Europe because John found out about our first child being put up for adoption, which I blame on Francis. He assured me the child would be adopted by wealthy, kind people, which I know the child has been. It's not like I just put her in an orphanage, but John is still trying to find her." Katarina sighed again. Her ex-husband, Francis, was a never-ending source of irritation. He'd kept their son, Douglas, with him in Hawaii, telling the boy that his mother had died in a car crash.

"I'm not sure the fracture in our marriage can be mended. This was a betrayal too great for John to overcome. Then to find out fourteen months later I was pregnant again…" she drew in a shaky breath. "I didn't want Natalie, but there I was dealing with another pregnancy. I have no regrets about giving up Douglas and then John's child. Alex has turned out to be a good child, and so has Natalie, so they turned out well despite me being their mother. Even Gregory ensured Benjamin was in a happy home, being raised the right way, away from me. I know I'm not mother material."

Hans shook his head. Five children and Katarina had pushed them all away. First Alexandra, then Douglas, then a child whose name they'd never know, then Benjamin, and now Natalie. He fought to keep a growl out of his voice.

"It was no one's fault but yours, Katarina. You made all the choices in life. There was a time in your life when you wanted children. Anthony told me how you tried to save two children during the war."

Ignoring him, Katarina heaved open the heavy door and moved up the old, worn stairs.

"Hans, I was much younger. I knew nothing about the cruelty of this world. We learn to survive. You know yourself how a single act can affect our lives and those around us for years. I made some heart-wrenching choices, but I have no regrets."

Hans walked behind as they climbed the three flights of stairs in silence. They entered the apartment, and Hans could tell Katarina was still agitated. In the hallway, as they entered, they heard voices. They saw their late brother Heinz's wife, Elvie, walking into the living room from the hallway. She stopped and gave them a warm smile.

"Join us! My brothers are here. You left so early this morning that I had no time to tell you they would visit. It's been years, Katarina, since you saw them. Come, they would love to see you again. You had just returned to Berlin when they were here last. I'll fetch more wine glasses."

She served cakes and red wine to Louis and Henri, and both men rose and embraced Hans. He'd just met with Louis a month ago on their contract of the vineyard they owned in partnership. The vineyard had been in their family since the twelfth century.

Louis

Louis took a deep breath, staring at Katarina, where she stood at the entrance to the living room. This was Katarina, whom he saw so many years ago. Now a little older but just as beautiful. Her beauty remained, though her eyes had changed. There was a lostness in them, but from what he knew of what she went through, it was no wonder.

Louis was the first to stand, walk over to her, and take her hand. "Hello, Katarina, it's been a long time. Last time I saw you was at Simon's and on the road in France, where we took out a few Nazis."

She smiled at him, and he could tell she recalled him immediately. He was thinner, his brown hair graying at the temples and his eyes as deep blue as Elvie's.

"I never thanked your family for getting Elvie out of France to Switzerland," he said. "She would have ended up in a concentration camp." Louis directed her to the chair opposite where he'd been sitting. He and Elvie had looked long and hard after the war for each other, always just missing one another. He hadn't known she'd remarried.

It was a chance meeting in 1958 as Louis was visiting church for Mass, and Anthony was also on a visit. It was Anthony who told him that Elvie still went to the Paris apartment and lived in Berlin but spent a great deal of time in the Villa in Italy. She had married Dietric years after the war, and they had become close; she loved Dietric, but her first love would always remain Heinz. Dietric was so close to the family, he was like another brother to all of them. He helped raise Heinz and her daughter. He loved Sarah.

Louis and Anthony became the best of friends, having dinner

every week when Louis was in town. They would spend time fishing and twice went to England to visit Anthony's cousin Peter. Peter remained with MI6 and knew Louis as Louis was in French intelligence.

Louis was now looking intently at Katarina. She bore the same scars as he and Henri did. They'd been betrayed at the end of the war, both caught by the Gestapo. In 1944, the brothers had been present when the Gestapo shot Heinz for not divulging his family's whereabouts or the resistance he was working with. The Gestapo didn't care that he was a decorated Luftwaffe pilot. The resistance could not reach him in time to warn him. They watched, helpless, as he was murdered.

Louis would never forget the look in Heinz's eyes as he turned toward the resistance group who were hiding and could not get to him. It was as if he saw Louis, Heinz's crystal blue eyes directly looking at him, then the shot to the back of the head. Louis and the others watched his body slump, the blood seeping into the ground before the Gestapo kicked him into the ditch. Louis and the others waited until nightfall to take his body to the church. They could not chance being seen, and it had taken everything to hold Heinz's cousin Peter back when the shot rang out. They sat for a long time till darkness descended upon them. Only then could they recover their friend, lying in a ditch, his life that had such promises, gone. Louis and Gregory would never forget the Gestapo's faces and vowed they would find them all, those who shot him and those in the car, were indented on their memory.

Louis loved where he lived now in Haut Morais. He was close enough to see Elvie and Henri. Anthony had brought Louis back to the church but not Henri. Henri had stopped believing after what he saw, and not even Anthony could convince him to return to faith.

Louis was now only partially listening to Henri as he kept looking at Katarina, his memory going back to when he first saw her at Simon's. Finally, Katarina's voice brought him back to the present. Katarina was asking Henri what he was doing now. Henri was not much for giving personal information, but he gladly told her of the children he had now.

Henri took a long sip of wine and said, "You know, Katarina, if it had not been for Gregory that day, I, too, would have been lying next to my wife and child and the unknown child she was trying to rescue. Did you know she was three months pregnant? The Nazis shot her like a dog, and my boy, I could only watch, then they just threw them on a truck like garbage. Gregory followed me that day. He caught up with me right before I turned the corner. My brother here found out the Gestapo had issued a warrant for my clinic and family to be investigated. Unfortunately for Gabriella, she was not going to give up the little Jewish boy when they demanded to see papers on him."

Louis interjected into the conversation.

"Katarina, the reality of that day was difficult. We were fortunate that Gregory caught up with Henri. He came back with Henri and told us. It wasn't easy to see. He was almost caught that day also as the two Nazi soldiers stopped him and asked for papers. Gregory told us he didn't have time to deal with these two soldiers, and in the end, they could have had him arrested on any charge they wanted, so he took it upon himself. He sliced open both of their necks, hid them in an alley, and continued to find Henri. Henri joined the resistance with us full-time. Now, though, he has a good life, correct Henri? Henri teaches art and works as a doctor two days a week. He has three beautiful children."

Gregory and his brother Nicholas had taken the Von Rahmel family to their heart. Katarina would become the love of his life, but war changes everything. On the day he saved Henri, Gregory had spotted him by pure luck, leaving a bakery a block away from his clinic. Henri jumped as Gregory grabbed his elbow and pulled him to the side of the building, hoping not to see any more Germans. Not understanding the danger he was in, he turned the corner just in time to see the Gestapo shoot his wife and child. Gregory had to use all his strength to hold onto Henri so he wouldn't rush out and meet the same fate.

Henri cleared his throat, turned back to the bar and poured another glass of wine. Wobbling back to the Queen Anne chair, he leaned closer in so Katarina could hear him. "I spent the rest of the war wondering where the Germans had taken my family. After the war, I learned they had been burnt with others like trash outside of the city. I went to the site. Anthony came with me, and we searched for any token, any small proof of his family's existence. Finally, he spotted something sparkling like a star on the ground. I picked it up. It was a wedding ring, but not Gabriella's. I set it reverently back on the ground with a small wish that a family member of the ring's owner might find it and take some small solace in having it. I did find a teddy bear that belonged to my son. It was torn and battered, but I kept it." he leaned his head back.

The thoughts were dark like thunderclouds in this beautiful, newly decorated room. The old dark leather and dark curtains were gone. The room was lovely with its cheerful deep blues and peach colors on the furniture, unlike the war years. Elvie and Heinz's mother, Lisa, took it upon themselves to make it bright after the war.

Such dark conversation for such a beautiful room Elvie thought..

Elvie poured the wine into La Rochere crystal glasses that dated back one hundred years and survived two wars. She had brought them back from their estate along with several vases. Elvie set down a cheese plate with crackers. Louis handed Katarina a glass of wine, and his fingers briefly touched her hand.

Henri was now telling Katarina how little he had seen Louis lately. Louis shot him a warning glance, which Henri ignored. All the wine had made him talkative.

"Katarina, I'm sorry for the morbid conversation. I used to have Anthony to talk this out with, as we would talk weekly as he visited while I painted or had dinner. I will say I miss him, I long for those conversations with him. I hope you realize he spoke of you often."

Louis rose and went to the window as he stretched. He looked down at the active street of people. The streets were back to the living after the war. With vibrant music, abundant food, and farms back in production, the City of Lights is alive again. He watched the birds hop from branch to branch and thought how free they were. During the war, even the birds seemed to disappear.

Henri spoke louder, which made Louis turn. He was now intently looking at Katarina, who just sat and listened.

Henri stood and walked over to the fireplace, looking at family pictures that Elvie had placed on the mantel. It was as if Henri was now talking to the pictures, but his voice could be heard. He walked back to where Hans had just sat in silence all this time.

"Your brothers Anthony and Peter helped find us at the war's end. Did he tell you?" Henri said and tapped Hans on the knee.

Louis cleared his throat. They knew the events already. Everyone had suffered. He turned from the window, fresh air filtering through the lace curtains that moved like angels in the breeze, the sounds from the street filtering up to the balcony. "Henri, we don't want to rehash the memory."

"Such a long time ago," Hans answered.

A look of annoyance crossed Henri's face. "It's been a long time, but it's burnt into our memories. It took Louis and me months to recover just like all of you."

Louis looked right at Katarina; he knew what she had gone through. He'd been in a concentration camp, too. Elvie tried to turn the conversation, but Henri leaned forward and spoke in almost a whisper, his eyes glistening.

"I remember the time in Neuengamme we kept every SS man in our memory. We will find every one of them."

Louis came back to the chair and sat down. "Henri, leave it be." his voice sounded weary as he rubbed his hand through his hair.

Henri looked surprised. "No, I will not. You told me how Anthony and others managed to get rid of an SS man that Katarina saw. When she visited a few years back, why not talk and say we will find all of them and have them pay for their crimes? I know you have found some of them. You remember the rectory story with that bastard Nazi."

Louis cleared his throat, and his voice got stronger. "We testified against the SS, all mighty Sicherheitsdienst, the security Service of Schuttzsaffel, Paramilitary, the most feared."

Henri shook his head. "Listen, all of you. I saw the doctor who murdered children after the experimentation on them. The SS established the Neuengamma subcamp of Sachesenhausen on the banks of Dove Elba. One hundred and four thousand German nationals, 13,500 were women and Soviets, Poles, French, Dutch, Danes, Belgians, and always Jews. They were always the first to be moved to Auschwitz. They killed them by whim. SS physician Kurt Heissmayer killed twenty Jewish children. Knowing I was a doctor, they forced me to watch and attend to those in the camps who were dying, and I tried to save them. Will never forget those in the camp or on the ship, watching my wife and child, their blood seeping into the ground as no one helped them, not one neighbor, no one. Their fear of the Germans was greater than helping one of their own French citizens." his voice was bitter as he spoke, his voice cracking with the heartache that he carried all the time. From what I was told, it was a history lesson he was explaining to Hans and Katarina, which he would speak a lot when he drank.

As Henri was about to pour himself and others another glass of wine, Louis took the bottle out of his hand. Henri lowered his head and shook it slowly as if to remove the cobwebs of that horrible time.

Louis came and sat next to Henri and gestured to Katarina and Hans. "Henri, they know of all the horrible things. They, too, lived through them."

Henri's reply was almost a whisper. "Do you all know how we escaped off the ship at the end of the war? We were moved from the concentration camp to a ship. We ended up there because we were all betrayed by one individual, and we will hunt him down. He was a traitor to the resistance. On the ship the *Thielbek,* two thousand prisoners were killed by mistake because the British were unaware that the *Cap Arcona* and the *Thielbek* had British, American, and

French prisoners."

Louis now had his eyes fixated on Katarina. She was uneasy listening. She had her horrors to deal with, and he could tell she didn't want to listen to the past.

Henri slammed his fist on the table.

"That is where we ended up at the end of the war."

Elvie was pale, and her hands were clenched. She turned to Kat and Hans and gave them a pleading look. Henri turned and looked at Katarina.

"Louis told me that Peter and Gregory found the two Gestapo men who killed Heinz, and they were taken care of a few months back." Louis watched Katarina's head shoot up.

"My brother here and Gregory have made it their life mission to track and find the Nazi killers," Louis said. "Some come to justice, some are just never heard from again. I admire their tenacity."

"You have talked with Gregory?" Katarina said, her eyes fixated on Louis. Despite her marriages, she'd never stopped thinking about—and loving—Gregory. She knew he was taking good care of their son, Benjamin, but she never stopped aching for word from him.

"Many times."

"How many times, Louis?" she asked, her eyes coming alive.

Henri spoke first. "Gregory and Louis are as thick as thieves. Didn't you know they are in the same line of work? My brother here works with the General Directorate for External Security—DSGE. They say it's like MI6. Louis spends a lot of time in other countries."

Louis stood and took the wine out of Henri's hand that he had repoured, then turned to Elvie.

"I think it's time we say goodbye. We can talk again over dinner sometime without rehashing the past." Hans and Katarina had rehashed enough times how Heinz died, and they knew Gregory sought out those who hurt the Jews or meant harm now.

Hans and Katarina looked at each other, and Louis knew they had questions about Heinz and how Peter and Gregory found the individuals. They wanted the details of the find and what happened to the men once Gregory and Louis found them. They had rehashed how Heinz died too many times to be repeated now. Lisa and Jona Von Rahmel sat in silence as the death of their son was told to them of the how and where. It was late in the evening that night. As Elvie came downstairs, she saw Jona holding Lisa in the library as she sobbed into his arms. Elvie cried so many tears she told Lisa it could fill a lake.

Louis convinced Henri it was time for him to go home as his speech was slurring from too much wine. Louis could see the tears on Elvie's lashes. Louis turned to Hans at the door before shuffling Henri down the stairs. He turned to Hans who had walked them to the door.

"I should have warned you that once Henri drinks, he speaks too much. He still lives with the memories." Louis looked at those brilliant eyes of Katarina who was now standing next to Hans and thought to himself that he now understood what Gregory's Achilles heel was. Katarina had not changed much since the days of war. He knew now what haunted his friend. He kissed his Elvie goodbye and promised to have dinner with her. He was putting Henri into a cab when he felt a hand on his shoulder. Instinctively, he reached for his weapon until he turned and met Katarina's eyes. A gust of wind sprang up, tearing at Katarina's pulled-back hair.

"Louis, you know we first encountered each other in Lyon." The cab pulled away from the curb. He turned and centered his attention now on her.

His eyes roamed over her. He recalled her very well. How could he forget her? He grabbed her hand and yanked her down the street.

"Where are we going?" she asked.

"Just follow me." he took her to a little café he'd frequented with Anthony and Elvie. Everyone greeted him as he entered the door, and he moved Katarina inside and found a little table in a corner.

Katarina looked around. She had passed this café but never gone in. Louis narrowed his eyes on her, and she waited for him to talk. She couldn't stand the silence as he stared into the distance, so she spoke softly, tapping her well-manicured fingers on the table. Leaning forward, she spoke in a whisper. Simon is a person one of the resistance fighters and he married Amelia.

"I remember you very well. We were all there the last time I was in France. We had left Simon's, Simon is a person, and we went to the safe house, waiting for transportation, then again to a church, waiting to leave. Peter, Gregory, Anthony, and I watched you pull the telephone wire from the wall in Lyon when we entered the room. The wine merchant was working with the Nazis. I recall everything that night, including how you strangled him to death with the telephone wire."

Louis took a deep breath. "Katarina, we have had many seasons of love lost, memories lost, too many seasons to deal with." she sat opposite him, her violet eyes as big as saucers topped with long fringed lashes, that perfect face that saved her from death. She sat there in black slacks and a black sweater with a strand of pearls showcasing her long, slender neck. Her blond hair fell around her face. She looked pale, which made her eyes shine even brighter. He ordered two glasses of wine, and they waited until the wine arrived. He put his hand over hers and spoke in a deliberate, slow tone.

"If I hadn't killed him, none of us would be here today. You saw the risk we took. We were able to warn the other resistance fighters and those operating the transmission devices. Only a few of us went to the safe house they had set up for us. He was not expecting us so soon, he was trying to set us up for a later time to be caught. We knew he was a traitor, and we dealt with him. It was the only justice then, maybe even now. There were a lot of mistakes that night. We lost a lot of good resistance fighters and British operatives that Peter had put in place, even with all our warnings."

He sat in silence, looking out in the café. Even now, he wished not to speak loudly as he moved closer to her as his tone was lower. He cleared his throat.

"When Elvie and I had the chance to catch up, she wanted to know how Heinz died. It was hard to tell her, but she wanted to know the truth; it was the first thing she asked when we found each other. We waited for hours to bring Heinz out of the ditch. German soldiers were crawling all over the place. Knowing your family would have wanted him back in Berlin, it was an agonizing choice for Peter and all of us to bring him back to Paris. But we knew all of you were gone also, and there was no way even to conceive how to get him back to Germany. Father Julian buried him behind the church in Paris, and then Anthony moved him back to Berlin after the war, but you were already in the States at that point."

He shifted in his seat. "That last year in Lyon was the hardest for all of us. We fought hard in Lyon and Paris, and we also had betrayal. We still want those who betrayed us to be found. Most have fled France or changed their names. Many live in South America. Some even made it to the States."

He gently took Katarina's hands. "Katarina, I know what Peter and Hans are asking of you, I have been aware of their movements as I, too, have worked with them. Of course, Gregory is with the Mossad and on a different mission to rectify what was done to his people. I ask you to go back to the States. Staying here or Germany is not good for you. Elvie told me that your husband wants you and your daughter back there. Europe can be dangerous for you." he hesitated, hating to give Katarina more to worry about, but she needed to know the details.

"East Berlin might be aware of you and your whereabouts since the rescues in the tunnels," he said. "They and the Russians know of Hans and Peter, but we don't believe they know us by face except for Hans. He was so vocal on television and in newspapers about what faced those on the other side of the Berlin Wall that he made himself a target. They might only have a description of you so far, but it is hard to hide when you look like you do. We have not determined if Frederick was actually killed, but at the time, he was working with the KGB, so there is another threat for you if he managed to stay alive after the last encounter in East Berlin."

A chill ran through Katarina's body at the mention of her ex-husband, Frederick Spitz, and she pulled her trembling hand into her lap so Louis would not notice. Her breathing was shallow. Louis shifted in his chair, leaned back, and closed his eyes momentarily. In his mind, it was 1942. That year and the years that followed were never far from his mind.

Between the war and now, he spent his life in danger. He still wanted revenge and, with the British, sought information about the perpetrators who deported Jews, especially many of the resistance fighters to Neuengamme. He was constantly confronting the past. Looking at Katarina, the past rushed in once again. He hadn't expected to see her today. He'd caught a glimpse of her in all black with her face covered at Anthony's funeral. He'd stood in the background and saw Gregory watching in the distance. But this was the first real encounter he had with her, he had heard enough about East Berlin through intelligence with the Rahmel family. Gregory and Peter sometimes mentioned her name, but he never forgot her the first day he saw her at Simon's in Lyon.

He had been in Berlin several times since the wall went up, and he knew the Von Rahmels were smuggling people out of the east side of the city. It was no secret; it seemed the four powers in Berlin knew of their clandestine activities. There were more intelligence operatives in this small part of Germany than anywhere in the world.

It was a constant battle of truth between the Soviets and East German agents; constant kidnappings, and on the East German side, the Stasi were always kidnapping. Anthony had been on their list before he died, as well as Peter. Even though they were in Paris and London, the secret police from the East were everywhere with their double spies.

Sitting here in his silence, Louis tried to gather his thoughts, but he knew the world of the KGB, and Stasi was the headquarters of St. Antonius Hospital in the Kurlshorst district of East Berlin. Louis himself, at one point, met up with Gregory on this 160-acre compound that was well patrolled by Stasi guards a few months before Anthony's death. The KGB in East Germany were ruthless; they tortured people for any cause. Fear ran rampant in the East. They spied on neighbors, murdered innocent citizens, and took their personal belongings after they were murdered. They used Hitler's playbook as they took every belonging from the Jews, including their businesses and homes.

Gregory, Louis, and Peter were there a year ago to find information on what the KGB knew of the US and NATO military presence in Western Europe and how much they had found out.

The Russians were constantly causing issues. French intelligence had enough of the KGB when two Soviet MIG-15 fighters attacked an Air France plane as it approached Berlin, wounding two passengers. Next, a British bomber was shot down on a routine mission between Frankfurt and Berlin. Then they shot at a US plane.

Louis turned a few KGB agents into informers when he went to Berlin. One in particular worked for him and Peter, and they pushed off the information to Gregory. They encountered the KGB agent when he met Peter and Gregory in East Berlin at Café Warsaw. It was the main place to exchange secrets before the wall went up. Everyone knew it was like a Western movie or *Casablanca*. Everyone was suspected; everyone had secrets for the right price.

Louis thought back to Lyon as he looked at Katarina, watching her sip her wine slowly as she nibbled on the cheese plate the waiter had just brought over. Katarina knew of betrayal as well as he did. His first wife was betrayed. He'd loved Carlie from the first moment he saw her. He was in Lyon when Peter came to him during the war, in a submarine with Carlie, her unmistakable Irish lilt, green eyes, and flaming red hair against her alabaster skin and perfect full lips. The moment he saw her, he fell in love. She was handed over to him to be placed in the best position to be a wireless operator. She organized drops of arms and made sure they were equipped with plastic explosives, fuses, detonators, and Colt pistols. She worked tirelessly, moving agents all over France and sending the British a wealth of information.

Father Julian secretly married them in Paris a year later. A year after that, the Nazis caught and tortured Carlie before sending her to a concentration camp, where she died. Louis swore no woman would ever capture his heart again. He now looked at Katarina and this feeling entered the pit of his stomach. The same feeling he felt with Carlie. He'd tried to be in a relationship again, but Sabina couldn't handle his job, even though they'd met at work. She knew his division because she filed most of the reports, but she still couldn't bear his disappearing for days at a time. She left with just a note to him one morning at his apartment.

Katarina snapped her fingers. "Hello, come back."

Louis blinked, dragging himself back to the present. "I'm sorry, I was thinking when I first saw you."

Katarina leaned back, her eyes fixed on his. "I remember it clearly." Louis leaned in and touched her long, slender fingers on the table. She let his hand linger, enjoying the warmth of his skin against hers.

"I remember it was Paris," Louis said, "during my introduction to Anthony's activities there. Anthony had learned from Father Julian what happened to my wife, and we were introduced. I was instructed to help Anthony in any way possible, so we found him the best forger in Paris." Louis smiled, remembering how authentic the identification papers the forger made so they could help people escape

Berlin. Those papers helped Katarina's brother Heinz get out of Berlin, when he'd come to move a downed British flier out of the city. Katarina's mother hid the pilot until Heinz and Anthony could get him out.

Katarina's eyes bore into him, and she had to ask the question that had been on her mind since the apartment. "Louis, I know you know where Gregory is. I can't call his house because his wife hangs up on me. Could you reach him?"

He leaned forward in his chair and looked right into those brilliant eyes. "He's in South America." Katarina's eyes widened, but the waiter appeared before she could say anything. Louis ordered appetizers from memory, and they sat silently until the waiter left.

The frown on her face amused him. It seemed she wasn't getting her way, so she was pouting.

She was aware of him staring at her. He was intrigued that there was a sudden change in her. She was the Katarina he recalled in Paris and saw once in Berlin as she was helping people come through tunnels from the east; the French sector wasn't pleased with their work. He saw her waiting outside the tunnels as she put blankets around those who were emerging. She was the brave one, the fighter, the one who captured men's hearts. He knew she could also easily destroy a man. She had destroyed his friend Gregory's heart and left a scar that wouldn't heal. Her file showed her marriage to Francis Lee and John. They, too, were faced with her demons.

Katarina was now equally intrigued with getting to know this man better. She already saw he wasn't hard on the eyes. He had Elvie's eyes, large and blue, deep in color like the ocean. He had a rough, unshaven look and small lines around the eyes.

He leaned back in his chair. Her tension was dissolving, and her smile could give solace with little effort.

"Katarina, go back to the States. Leave your memories here in Europe. Place them in a hidden box in your brain. And leave Gregory behind. He has a life now."

She leaned forward so close he could have kissed her lips, which he had a sudden desire to do.

"Why do you think you know my relationship with Gregory or my life in the States?"

"I know you very well. I spent many a night in some godforsaken part of the world, sitting with Gregory. I saw what he went through, trying to forget you. He loved you the first moment he saw you in Berlin. He tortured himself for not being able to save you from the concentration camp. It killed him when he couldn't save his brother or his family. He was tortured by every resistance fighter who died next to him. He drove himself into dangerous situations, which would be insane for a normal agent. He wanted to forget you left for the States. He had hoped you would return to him after your first divorce, but you married John. He couldn't understand, but he moved on, Katarina, as you know. He has the child you bore him, and he's married."

One corner of Katarina's mouth twisted up. "I guess you do know more than I thought. No secrets to keep from you."

He smiled. "There are always secrets we don't let others into in the soul. We're almost finished with our plates. Afterward, we can take a walk and talk some more, or you can come back to my place for a while. It's not far. I seldom have a day off like this."

She said nothing for a few moments. He leaned over, moved a

stray hair from her cheek, and placed it behind her ear. "Let's take some time and just walk the streets of Paris. It's a lovely late afternoon. Let's just act like normal people who do not live with terrible memories." he paid the waiter, and they left the café.

They walked for about an hour, stopping at bookshops, galleries, and parks. There was a blush of sunset over Paris. Louis hadn't realized so much time had passed.

They silently walked and crossed the short bridge connecting Notre Dame and Ile Saint Louis. He hailed a cab and ordered the driver to drive to La Petite Chaise, the oldest restaurant in Paris that dated to Louis XIV.

The minute they got out of the cab, he was recognized again as in the previous café. No reservations are needed. The host led them to a small corner table and immediately brought Chateau Haut Brion 1961 from the Bordeaux region, a fine wine from a family-owned vineyard dating to the sixteenth century. Louis closed his eyes as he sipped. The wine was velvety, sumptuous, harmonious, suave, and complex. He described it in detail after the waiter asked how it was.

Kat laughed at him. "Do you think I need to eat again? I'm not sure I can get any more food down me. I have been eating all day."

He looked at her up and down in amusement. "I think you can put on a few pounds."

Kat sat in amusement at this sudden role reversal. He went from wanting her to go back to the States to café-hopping because he wanted her to stay with him. She was suddenly interested in this man, especially since he was clearly the person Gregory had told all his secrets to.

During dinner, they only made small talk. After dinner, Louis hailed another cab. When it arrived, Louis hesitated.

"Do you want to venture to my place, or would you rather I order the cab to take you home?"

Katarina took his hand. "I would love to see your place."

He smiled. "Okay then. Just off Rue de Sully, there's an area in the heart of the Le Marais. It's one of my favorite places, and I want to take you there."

Her eyes widened. "Are you sure? It's getting late."

"I'm sure." he was silent in the cab, then suddenly turned to face her.

"I want to apologize for Henri earlier. He was a brilliant doctor in Paris and still is. He worked hard saving lives as well as spending hours transmitting to the British and us. He worked as hard as my wife."

Louis cleared his throat.

"Henri met his wife in Lyon, where she was already a resistance member. Together, they watched out for the Jewish families and brought them food. When the Germans entered Paris, Gabriella thought she could keep helping Henri by acting as the dutiful wife. She slowed down her activities but kept up transmitting information to the resistance. When they had their firstborn, most of her attention was centered on their child. But she loved children, and she knew that if the SS took the Jewish children, their fate would be death that day. Henri will never get over seeing her and their child shot as well as the children she was trying to save."

Katarina reached over and took his hand. "We all tried to save someone." her smile told him she understood. He also saw her irresistible charm; it made him feel unnerved as he suddenly felt drawn to her. He saw why Gregory was tied to her emotionally. He understood now, and Peter once told him about her bravery in East Germany, getting people through the tunnels and how she worked in Berlin during the war. How she used all those tools to stay alive, her looks, her charm. She could manipulate men to do her bidding.

He saw tonight as they entered each café how everyone they passed gave her a second look. He watched her intently in the cab as it crept through the streets. Tourists were abounding now in France, especially in Paris. The cab stopped, and he helped her out of it.

"Let's walk a little. My apartment isn't far," he said. "I want to show you something. Soon, the lights of Paris will start to click on one after the other, and it will be like the city before the war."

They were walking in the Fifth Arrondissement after being let out by the cab. He wanted to show her a new bookstore that opened.

"I visit this area frequently. As you can see, it is filled with local cafés, old and new, with bookstores sprinkled throughout the neighborhood. I visit the Jardin des Plantes; it's popular with botanists. Before the war, I wanted to attend school and become a botanist."

She laughed. "I just can't picture you as a botanist."

He shrugged. "We all had different dreams before the war. We still own our home in Reims, and I garden there. We have fruit trees, rose bushes, and lots of growing vines for wine, enough so, I hope to retire someday and make a living with my little wine business. Your brother Hans has partnered with me since your family has the facilities. The cuttings of the vines are old and from my parents' time. We hope to merge them with your family's."

"It seems all of you have been very busy. Hans never mentioned you. He never talks business with me. I have not heard of any of these plans. Why should I? I'm not interested in the family business." she saw a book in the window about doctors in the war. As she turned to Louis, the smile was a memory.

"I thought Henri would always remain a doctor, and now he seems more interested in painting as he sits at the Sacre Coeur with his brushes and paint, only seeing patients two days a week," he said while looking at the book.

"I don't blame him for not wanting to practice any longer, Louis. Sounds and smells can bring back memories. It's a strange reaction, but when I poke a fireplace and see ashes, it brings me back to another time of cleaning ashes."

His voice changed to understanding as he simply answered, "I'm sorry."

They kept walking, and she couldn't help but notice he was always looking behind him or to the side, his head on a swivel. He pointed out new stores and cafés. The night was growing dark, and the moon had risen as he hailed the cab again to his apartment. They arrived within minutes. He opened the front door to his building slowly, and they headed to the third floor.

The apartment was immaculate, inviting, and cozy. The hallway led to the kitchen, which was spacious compared to most Paris apartments. Farther down the hallway was a large living room with a balcony, the French doors leading out to it covered with heavy, beige curtains. To the side stood the bedroom, which was also dark green and light brown. He had soft beige sofas and chairs; the walls were covered with books that filled old cabinets. The rooms had large paintings with Henri's signature at the bottom; his paintings aligned with old Renoir paintings. The wood floor was oak. In the center a large antique maroon color rug filled the room. It was worn but meant a lot to him—the rug had belonged to his parents.

He motioned for her to sit as he went back to the kitchen. She couldn't help but think a woman helped him decorate. The colors matched too well, and everything had its place.

He returned with another bottle of wine. She was amused by how seriously he took himself trying to get the cheese and sausage to look nice on the platter he had brought with the wine. She covered her mouth so as not to laugh.

She took the wine with a smile that could melt an iceberg. She looked the same as she had in 1941 when he met her in Paris at the reception with Heinz and Anthony. "Kat, you haven't changed since I first saw you."

A sad smile crossed her face. "I'm older. I have made some terrible mistakes and seem to keep making them. There is no Anthony to pull me out of the darkness."

"The war changed all of us," Louis answered.

A car backfired. She jumped, and he tensed.

"Well, we make a fine pair," he said.

"I jump out of fear, and you jump to kill to avoid being killed."

Louis didn't respond but got up to close the balcony door as he stood looking out.

"Have you been to Cote de Azur?" he asked.

"Not lately. Why do you want to take me?"

"I have tickets for a long weekend." his answer sounded so matter of fact, it caught him by surprise to have offered. "You, my dear woman, could be trouble for me."

She walked over to him and leaned against him.

"Where have you been?" she said.

He walked back to the sofa, poured another glass of wine, and this time drank it quickly as he let it slide down his throat. His thoughts drifted. He knew her life was full of scars; they both had given up hope so many times. He knew threads of insanity coursed through both their veins when they recalled memories of the past. She left a trail of broken pieces, but her smile and beauty left many with hope. He asked her if she recalled August 14, 1942. She nodded.

"What do *you* remember?" she asked.

He thought for a moment, closed his eyes, and spoke. "I'm sure we both recall the same experience… Katarina, the past was a dangerous place. The secrets, the lies, the loves lost. It's a place I try to avoid going." he took a deep breath. "I try not to think of the past as I would hope you would, but I know you don't. It's a part of our history. It sits at the edge of our memory, coaxing us to recall things we don't want to."

He cleared his throat. "Katarina, so long ago, when I first encountered you, you and Anthony were in Paris seeing Heinz." his memory went back, standing looking at the lights of Paris now. Katarina joined him.

Chapter 2

1941-1945

The memories swirled across Louis's mind.

A beautiful woman walked across the room in a black satin dress with small silver stars of crystals. The dress was heart-shaped on the top with small flutter sleeves, exposing her long neck and long arms. Her hair was swept above into a twist in the back with diamond-studded pins that glistened in her blond locks. This must be Katarina, he thought. She was exactly as she'd been described.

She walked arm-in-arm with his sister Elvie, who was now walking towards Heinz. Heinz and Elvie looked at each other like no one else was in the room. Elvie looked so demure next to Katarina, with her dark pink empire dress that covered her neck with a delicate ruffle.

They were at the Le Meurice Luxury Hotel. France was in two sections after Germany invaded. Vichy France was free from the Axis military presence. On June 14, 1940, the Parisians awoke to the sound of German accents and loudspeakers as troops entered Paris, and a curfew was set. Their hell and darkness had begun.

Anthony and Katarina were visiting Heinz almost a year later, under the pretence of just visiting siblings, while Anthony received documents moving between France and Berlin.

Military commander Carl-Heinrich Von Stulpnagel asked Heinz to include them as he had seen Katarina perform in Berlin. Heinz mentioned that he could not attend the dinner reception because his brother was visiting, setting the stage for his commander to order him to bring Anthony and Katarina. Then, Anthony had made friends with Stulpnagel to throw off any suspicions of being in Paris.

Anthony tried to guide Stulpnagel several times, but once the soul is tainted with evil, you can't come back until you confess and believe again. Stulpnagel was able to reconcile his military task and conscience with ideology. He claimed he didn't want to be part of the Einsatzgruppen, but he did nothing to stop the horror of the mass murder of Jews. Toward the end of the war, Hitler had Stulpnagel executed, and Anthony was saddened he had not been able to save the man's soul.

Anthony's first visit with Stulpnagel was at the dinner reception through his old friend, the Bishop of France, who had invited Anthony to Paris. Anthony was also in Paris at that time to pick up fake passports and false ration cards to give to the Jews; hence, he was moving to Germany. He had always wanted to be a teacher in France at the religious universities. He loved France and knew his fellow priests there would help him procure the necessary papers for those in need; it was too dangerous to make them in Germany. The French priests had a forger so good that even a trained eye couldn't tell the false papers from the real.

So, when the general who knew Heinz asked if he would invite Katarina, the famous ballerina, she travelled with Anthony to Paris, where Gregory, Louis, and Elvie were already part of the resistance.

Louis still recalled Stulpnagel telling Anthony about the Final Solution and how it was to be handled. Anthony, in turn, told the resistance of the fate of the Jews and how they would seek out the resistance. Stulpnagel, of course, carried out all orders, even though he knew of the extreme aspects and the promotion of racial and national fear. He claimed he struggled with it ideologically, but Anthony didn't believe him. Ultimately, he could not come up with excuses for why he participated in so much killing. With all of Stulpnagel's sins, it was difficult for Anthony to forgive him. The man knew that what he was doing was evil. Anthony prayed to be forgiven for his lack of forgiveness, but he never felt any sympathy for anyone who followed Hitler.

It was many years after the war when he would meet Louis for their monthly dinner. Anthony grew melancholy and told Louis intimate details of his sins. He said he didn't think he could be forgiven but asked God daily regardless. He told Louis of his dinners with Stulpnagel and the people Anthony himself killed to protect the innocent, especially children. With tears in his eyes, he told Louis how he killed two Nazis to save twenty children in an orphanage. The two Nazis were going to shoot them all. Anthony begged for forgiveness, but he could not let twenty children be executed.

It was at this particular dinner that Stulpnagel invited Heinz to the dinner party because of his iron crosses as a pilot; he was showing him off to the rest of the officers what a fine man Hitler trained. Heinz was reluctant, but orders had to be followed. He invited Anthony and Katarina as asked and let the resistance know of the large dinner party with many generals and lieutenants. He and the Resistance, at this point, made the arrangements for what followed. Louis dressed as Heinz's secretary of notes. Anthony was not regarded well because of being a priest, and his attendance at this party rubbed some people the wrong way. To Hitler, the Catholic and Lutheran churches were the enemies. Anthony, who was warned not to go to this party, went regardless because to say no could raise questions since he was told to come by direct request of the general.

They had been mingling for about forty-five minutes, everyone's eyes on Katarina, many wanting to know what it was like to be in Hitler's company. After she performed, Katarina was the one who received all the attention, not Heinz. Peter, Gregory and Nicholas were all serving as waiters. Nicholas had slipped into one of the generals' rooms at the hotel and was to exit and meet them in the alley with a car. Suddenly, Peter stood next to Anthony, offering him a drink and telling him they needed to leave immediately.

"Take Katarina and Elvie down the sidesteps," He said. "Nicholas is waiting there."

Katarina and Elvie said their goodbyes, Katarina declaring that she had a terrible headache.

Heinz came alongside Anthony as Peter moved away, but not before he whispered in his ear to follow instructions. Anthony saw the worried look on Peter's face, and Heinz ordered Anthony to follow. Heinz led Katarina and Elvie to a side door down the steps that opened to the street, and Anthony slowly followed, looking back at Peter.

After ushering them down the steps to a waiting black car with German flags, Heinz turned and returned to the reception to rejoin Louis. People would start asking questions if he disappeared from the party. Gregory and Nicholas ushered Katarina, Elvie, and Anthony into the car. They saw the explosion; the windows were blown out, and they sped away in the car as quickly as they could as debris came raining down on them. The SS coming at the last minute was not planned, but the explosion was. The resistance had planted a bomb earlier that evening.

Elvie looked at Anthony, her eyes wide with horror. "Heinz and Louis and Peter," She said. "They stayed behind." Elvie grabbed Katarina's hand, which was ice cold.

Someone had tipped off the SS that the resistance was at this party. Peter and the others showed up at the party in waiter uniforms that four real waiters had been killed for. They didn't want to give them up and tried to make their way to the reception hall to tell the general there were resistance fighters in the room. The resistance executed them and left their bodies in a trash bin.

Katarina, Elvie, and Anthony needed to leave when it was nearly time for the bomb to go off. Peter had been told by another worker that someone had betrayed them. The SS were on their way, and the resistance needed to leave. Heinz and Louis knew the time of the bombing but did not expect the SS and soldiers to suddenly be coming up the stairs just as they got Anthony, Katarina, and Elvie out the back.

Fortunately, the SS didn't know about the explosive planted under the bar. They were only there to find resistance fighters. Their informer had told them that resistance fighters were going to kidnap the general. In actuality, the resistance wanted to *kill* the general, along with as many other Nazis as they could take out. The bomb would have to go off sooner, so it was time to get everyone out who needed to move.

Peter scurried outside as the bomb went off. A resistance fighter who didn't make it out had handed him a message that he needed to get to Lyon. A Lysander would pick him up to return him to

England. Too many agents were being lost, so Peter had ordered back.

Gregory looked at Anthony as they had all parked in one location where they agreed to meet Peter. Heinz and Louis joined them, covered in debris. Heinz's uniform was singed. He and Louis had narrowly avoided the explosion; they'd reached the stairs just as the bomb went off and made it down the steps after they delivered Elvie and Katarina downstairs. The explosion had blown out windows and heavily damaged the room, but not enough to kill everyone inside.

Now, the street was crawling with SS, who stopped Heinz and Louis for questioning since they were the first ones to come outside. Heinz had made prior arrangements for a staff car to meet him outside, but with a driver who was one of them. When they stopped him, his voice ringing with authority, he told the officers he had to return to his hotel for a meeting he could not miss. He was only to stay at this party for a few minutes. They were welcome to follow him and question him there. So many people were now staggering out of the building, bleeding and coughing, that the SS let him go.

Heinz drove to where they had all arranged a meeting. Nicholas first saw the other car blinking its lights, and they blinked in return as both cars emerged on the same street near Notre Dame. Gregory turned to Anthony, who was leaning his head out of the window.

"You and Katarina need to get back to Berlin now." He handed Anthony envelopes stuffed with food rations and identification cards.

Anthony heard Gregory tell Peter he also needed to leave, but Peter insisted he wouldn't leave until everyone was safe. They all needed to fall into their respective places. Peter explained he told one of his SOE agents to send a message to England that he would come later; situations were unfolding that he had to deal with. Peter had met with a new agent named Lisa two days ago. She was a brilliant woman who spoke fluent French without an accent. Peter knew only a few women who could face the challenge of this new life of risk besides Louis's wife, Carlie. It was a challenge, mentally and physically. Any slip-up could lead to capture, torture, or execution.

As Peter now shed his waiter's coat, he winced.

"What's wrong?" Elvie asked. "I saw you limping in at the party."

Peter ignored her as Nicholas helped him take off the jacket. Peter leaned into the car to speak with Anthony.

Elvie asked again, "Why are you limping and in pain?"

Peter sighed. "Long story short, I was arrested by the Gestapo. About a month ago they found me and another agent transmitting from Lyon. They waited until I came out of the building and started to pull me into the car. I twisted my ankle and banged my shoulder on the doorframe when they tried to wrestle me in. But the dumbasses didn't search me first. I delivered four rounds—all headshots—with my .38. I drove the car into the woods and left it there for the Gestapo to rot."

Gregory never took his eyes off Katarina as she quietly listened to Peter's harrowing tale. He tried not to picture something like that happening to her. Louis knew there and then that Gregory was in love with Katarina. Any fool could see it. He and his brother Nicholas promised Anthony they would look after her and the family, if needed, should something happen to him or Heinz.

They had to get back to Berlin. They needed to get the forged documents to the people who needed to be moved. Time was of the essence for those in hiding. Nicholas and Gregory proved to be their best help in Berlin as they slipped in and out to Paris and Italy.

Nicholas and Gregory spent three months in England in 1940, learning the fine art of explosives, maps, and transmitters. They learned to fire their guns from every conceivable position. Hungarians and Czechs were also sent back to Europe to fight the Germans in their countries. When Gregory and Nicholas first approached Anthony in a bar, they didn't think they would be so connected to this family and stay with them for the rest of their lives. The killing came easily to Gregory after he watched the Nazis kill his parents and sister and almost his entire small town.

Gregory seemed to have ice running through his veins. The rest said he was the master, always in control, skilled at killing silently without weapons. Gregory now looked over at Anthony, whose eyes closed as he fingered his rosary in silent prayer.

Peter saw it, too, and rolled his eyes. "Anthony, put the beads away for another time. We've got to get going." He turned to Gregory. "Let's get these cars moving before anyone sees us."

Peter worried when Gregory was around Katarina. She distracted him. Peter could see in his cousin's eyes that he was in love with the woman, and Peter worried she'd make Gregory unfocused. For his part, Gregory knew Kat was elusive to him. No one could make a future in a war; maybe he could have approached her in a different time and place. Before the war, he came from a good family. His parents were Jewish, and both were university professors. Very few women went to the university like his mother did. He had completed a university degree in science, and Nicholas and his sister were to follow. His mother was so proud that Gregory had finished because of her three children, she felt he was the strongest and the smartest.

Peter turned to Nicholas. "Did you get the information from upstairs? We saw you one moment, and then you were gone. We hoped you got upstairs to the general's office."

Nicholas handed Peter a heavy canvas sack. "I found pictures and letters and a camera with film in it. Hopefully it's got more pictures in it that we can develop. God only knows what, though. It was in a bag labelled to be sent to Berlin for Himmler's eyes only. Unfortunately, there's a dead body in a closet in that room." He hesitated. "She came out of the bedroom and started to scream. It would have meant the end to all of us. I had to…" He swallowed hard. Killing women was difficult for him.

"I wanted to get more, but time was limited," Nicholas continued. "You're not going to like what you see as it is. I was almost sick while I was gathering them up. I also took more pictures I found in the files and snapped photos of the general's calendar."

Peter was getting anxious. They couldn't just sit here any longer; they needed to split up and go in different directions. Meet up again outside of Paris. He, Gregory, and Nicholas were going to Lyon. Heinz had managed to have German flags and insignia on the car given to them.

Nicholas turned to Anthony and Peter before getting into the driver's seat. "Von Stulpnagel might not like Hitler, but he isn't going to disobey rounding up Jews," He muttered as he said goodbye. "There are not enough prayers that can save this man's soul."

"Did you notice anything else, Nicholas?" Heinz asked before they went separate ways.

Nicholas nodded. "July sixteenth was circled on his calendar. There was a name, Jacques Jaujard, and a note that he was going to be arrested and questioned. Stulpnagel wanted to know who helped him move out art treasures before the Germans arrived."

Peter let out a long grunt. Heinz began to give instructions.

"Okay, Anthony, you get in the car with me, Katarina, and Elvie. Nicholas, you drive until you reach the outskirts." He embraced and passionately kissed Elvie. "I will see you soon, my sweet woman."

After rolling along for a few minutes, Anthony spoke up. "I don't think we need to worry about the German officer Jaujard. Count Franz Wolf Metternich wore the Nazi uniform but was not in the same mindset. He helped with the art protection and managed to help Jaujard save Europe's art from Nazi plunder. He is working side by side with Jacques Jaujard and Elvie and has gotten resistance fighters special paperwork for travel permits he's signed. I have met both men through Father Julian. Metternich is no fan of Hitler. We need to tell Peter that Metternich will be shot if he's caught."

They arrived at the outskirts of Paris, at their designated address quickly relayed to Peter. They moved into a dark forest area outside of Paris, and all climbed out of the cars.

"This is not a good time for me to return to England," Peter said, banging on the side of the car with his fist. "Not with everything up in the air."

Anthony tried to reassure Peter. He understood Peter's frustration but wanted his cousin back in England, out of danger.

"If you go, you can come back with even more help," Anthony said. "I will try to speak with the cardinals and send by courier to my Pope to make them open their eyes to what is being done right now. France has the most active priests. They are going against Vatican protocol; I will try my best to have many on board."

Peter didn't look reassured as he glanced over at Louis and Gregory.

Anthony continued, "Peter, understand that many priests, other clergy, farmers, those with true power, they are hiding airmen, Jews, anyone who the SS and Gestapo want to arrest. They're after a few priests also, and we try to move them as quickly as we can when Edwin learns of them. We see many arrested here and in Germany. Many from Germany have been sent to a concentration camp: Lawyers, judges, professors and anyone else they suspect is against Hitler or has said any words against Hitler. I'm surprised I have not been arrested more than once."

Anthony closed his eyes. He was tired of all the death, destruction, and fear. He took a deep breath.

"I'm good friends with a Lutheran pastor named Dietric Bonhoeffer. I first met him when he was preaching his theology in Berlin; he's anti-Nazi. He was a lecturer at Berlin University, and two days after Adolf Hitler became chancellor, Dietric took to the radio, denouncing the Nazi Fuhrerprinzip, which was already known to be a dictatorship. He was cut off before he could finish his radio broadcast.

"When I met him in London, he was a pastor of a German congregation and supported the church movement in Europe and Germany. He refused to allow the churches and clergy to be controlled or co-opted by the Nazi government for propagandistic purposes. He then returned to Berlin in 1935, when I met him again. Once again, he restarted the church they had closed in 1937. He pulled me into the German resistance movement after they tried to silence him and would not allow him to lecture in public. I worry about him, as well as all of you. I do not worry about my fate; it's in

God's hands. I have only known to do God's work, which is part of it."

They all caught the bitterness in Anthony's voice. "Everyone who does not go along or agree with Hitler, who doesn't even respect the Geneva Convention, is in danger," Elvie said. "Hitler, as they say, is an equal opportunity killer without regard for any human life."

Peter handed Anthony a small box he removed from his bag. Heinz had caught up to them, and Peter also handed him a small box.

"Use this if ever you need to get out of any situation," Peter said. "I meant to give this to you sooner. We all have some. Just put it into the Nazis' coffee cups, if you can, and they will head for the bathrooms immediately. It helped me in Avignon, buying me enough time to leave a café." He grinned. "The waitress let me pour it into the coffee and beer."

Silently, Elvie and Katarina clasped each other's icy, shaking hands.

Heinz had arrived only to give them their baggage. He had to return to the hotel to avoid falling under suspicion, but he wanted to ensure Elvie was okay. They loaded the luggage into another car as Peter bellowed out instructions once more.

"Elvie, you'll ride with Gregory," He said. "He'll take you and Louis to Saint Ann's Church. The rest of us will follow."

Katarina sighed slightly, knowing Gregory would not be escorting them. She felt safe with him, but he was needed in France.

Gregory, who had been silent up to now, said in a clear voice, "We hope the blast got enough of the police since they collaborate with the Gestapo, even against their people. At the beginning of the resistance, the resistance fighters found out too late. We can only hope when this war ends, justice will fall upon them."

Louis's voice cracked as he let out a long sigh.

"The Germans would have never known the labyrinth of Paris without help from collaborators and the police," Elvie said. "Even Vichy will not be spared. We, the resistance, will keep them in their minds forever."

Heinz said goodbye, and Peter had his head back, and eyes closed as they climbed back in the car.

"I truly believe they won't bother him," Peter said. "He's a decorated pilot. Even though Hitler doesn't completely trust the military, he sees them as ideologically similar to social conservatism. He respects his pilots for now. They help him conquer."

They reached a desolate, dark area again way out from Paris. There were no lights, but they could just make out the shape of another car waiting. They pulled into a wooded area so as not to be seen. Katarina rummaged through her bags for clothing and pulled out a high-collar grey sweater, black slacks and boots with a long black coat. Elvie dressed in a dark-green sweater that had seen better days and grey slacks with chunky boots and a scarf for her hair. She and Katarina laughed over dressing outside a car, but they couldn't stay in their evening gowns.

Kat saw the intensity in Gregory's eyes as she came around the car. There was always such intensity when he looked at her. Nicholas laid a warm hand on her shoulder and guided her to the other car. She turned back to Gregory.

"Gregory, please be safe."

Her words momentarily took him aback. "I will, Katarina. Just let Nicholas take care of you, and for goodness' sake, don't talk to anyone." He kept his head down and shifted from foot to foot because she always made him nervous. The fog was now leaving her with a grey, shadowy vision. Leaves swirled around their feet, and a cold blast of icy air hit them.

She kissed his cheek and whispered, "Please be careful." The softness of her skin next to him nearly stopped him from breathing.

Peter put his hand on Anthony's shoulder. "Anthony, you will be met by Father Benedict. Before you reach Lyon, let him give you more paperwork. Father Daniel Pezeril at St. Etienna Dumont did an excellent job this time with false certificates of baptism for Jews and others. He has already recruited other Jesuit priests to work underground. You were right when you told us to seek him out. Your name carries a lot of weight."

Peter looked away for a moment. It saddened him to involve his cousin; he loved this man as his brother, and Anthony took such a risk as Edwin and Heinz. Hans was on better terms with Rommel in the tanks and knew nothing of their activity.

"Anthony," Peter continued, "remember to always be on your guard. The SS and Gestapo are out to get anyone they suspect. Father Julian has found hiding places all over France, especially for the Jewish children, in peasant houses, churches, and hospitals. He works with Father Theomir Devauy, who is adept at finding hiding places."

They all drove their own ways. Elvie returned with Gregory, and Louis went elsewhere to meet up with resistance.

When they all arrived at their designated areas, Anthony recognized Father Timothy pacing in front of the car, and it dawned on him that this was helping them with the extra car. He wore a German soldier's uniform like an official driver would.

Father Timothy motioned for them to hurry as he stood before Anthony and Nicholas.

"I will be your driver briefly," He explained. "Then Nicholas will take over as I will meet up with others. We won't be bothered; the Germans won't stop what they think is a military vehicle. But first, we must drive to Clermont-Ferrand before going to Lyon. A priest will meet us at the L'Assumption Cathedral. He has helped get aviators and the resistance to Lisbon or Spain. He'll help the three of you get to Berlin."

Their headlights moved through a cruel shaft of fog as Elvie and Gregory started the engine, and they killed the lights immediately. Soon, Father Timothy was in deep discussion with Peter, and they agreed that they had to change plans once they arrived in Clermont-Ferrand. They had followed Father Tim's car, and they would change roads until Father Tim stopped when Peter blinked his lights. Father Tim explained they all had to separate because Germans patrols were looking for resistance fighters and were stopping anyone they could find.

They agreed that Kat and Nicholas would go in a different direction when they reached Clermont. Kat and Nicholas would now travel alone in a small Citroën. They had all the paper to move across France to the train station and then to Berlin. Anthony would follow later. Peter and Father Timothy needed Anthony to stay a few more days.

"Kat, you and Nicholas will go to Berlin," Anthony explained. "Peter and I need to meet with Helena Marzellier."

Kat turned to Peter. "You need to get back to England, and Anthony needs to come home with me." Her voice shook. "He has a better chance coming with Nicholas and me. A priest travelling alone would be in danger, regardless of the paperwork he has on him. It makes more sense for him to be with me." Her voice was filled with anxiety.

Peter shook his head. "Kat, listen. Anthony knows the churches and priests better than I ever will. He has been here in and out for years. I promise he will come home to you safely."

"You can't promise that, Peter. This is a time when no one can promise anything." Tears now rolled across her cheeks. Louis knew what Peter and Anthony were up to as he thought of them, reflecting further on that time. Standing now next to Katarina, both just looking now at the vibrancy of Paris, he remembered even more.

Anthony and Peter

Nicholas took Katarina's cold hand. "They'll be okay. This woman gets prior notice of arrests. She can warn Peter and Anthony. I'm sure Louis will join them. Helena and her colleague, Jeannette Caillardt, have always given us accurate information through many liaisons. I promise, Katarina, we are getting very good at this. We've organized Jews to pass freely through the free zone. We've moved aviators with Portiers. Trust me."

Kat looked at Anthony and saw a different side to her brother that she'd never seen. "How long have you been doing this, Anthony?"

For a moment, the only sound was a lone owl calling in his loneliness. When Anthony finally spoke, his voice was low, his eyes downcast.

"Since before Hitler even took power, going back to 1933," he said. "I have made so many friends on this long journey. Recently, I befriended Roger Braun, who works at an internment camp in Southern France, along with Rabbi Henri Schilli. The rabbi works with Rabbi Leo Cohen, who works with French Jewish Scotse—the EIF—and sets up escape routes and finds guides from southern France to Spain. He's also working with Father Braun to move as many women and children as possible. Louis introduced me and then Elvie. As you know, she keeps tabs on all the stolen art and jewels. She hides artwork and jewels that were stolen from those deported. She hopes to one day return some of it."

Nicholas looked at the paperwork Anthony gave him. "These papers are amazing, Anthony," He said, his burly hands riffling through the pages. "Thank you. They'll get twenty families out of Berlin. I promise I will deliver them and take good care of Katarina on her return to Berlin."

Katarina's hair was now covered with the evening dew, and she placed a black scarf over her head.

"Anthony, please come back to Berlin!" She said, her voice raspy and shaky. "Don't stay here. They will question where you are in Berlin." She began to cry again.

Anthony looked at Nicholas. He had faith in this burly bear of a man. Nicholas had the tender side that his brother Gregory lacked. Nicholas had been out hunting when his parents and sisters were murdered, so he didn't have to watch helplessly as they were cut down like Gregory did. Now, Gregory was unmerciful and had ice running through his veins. Killing someone was his revenge for what the Germans did to his family, and he was fighting—as they all were—for what was right.

Peter, his leg now throbbing, leaned against the car. "Maybe Kat is right," He said to Anthony. "You can't fall under suspicion in Berlin."

Anthony laid his hand on Peter's shoulder. "Peter, if anyone should make their way home to their country, it's you. You need to see your wife and children and speak with those who need to hear the real story and why it's imperative for more supplies to reach Lyon."

Peter sighed. Anthony had won, as he usually did.

They all got into their respective cars and began to drive; staying out in the open too long was dangerous. They didn't speak as they bounced along the bumpy side roads, passing abandoned farms. Suitcases were strewn along the side of the road, marking places where people had given up on their attempt to escape from the Germans. During the day, circling buzzards made it clear where people, often the elderly, had died along the way. Food was scarce because the Nazis would rob the farms of their livestock and burn the fields. The group just looked at the devastation in the darkness of the full moon as they passed through clear areas, then back into the fog as they travelled through what used to be beautiful France. They each sat in their thoughts till they reached their first destination, where Nicholas and Katarina got into a separate car. Katarina held on to Anthony as long as she could with her hugs as well as Peter.

Katarina and Nicholas looked back to see their car disappear into the cruel fog with Peter and Anthony. It was like a bad dream; suddenly, they were all gone, like ghosts swirling and disappearing before your eyes.

When Peter and Anthony arrived in Clermont, they were told it was best for Peter and Anthony to drive to a different meeting place as Father Timothy continued with them. They watched the sun spread its morning fingers over the volcanic Chaine des Puys mountains, and last night seemed so long ago. They were going to the Gothic Notre Dame-do L'Assomption constructed from lava stone. It was all part of the Auvergne-Rhone-Alps. You entered the city with the church at the center, high above its residents. But they were on their way to Puy de Dome.

Suddenly, a car pulled up alongside them. Peter pulled out his Colt .45. A Jesuit priest waved them over. He got out of the car with his hands up. He was a small man, nearly bald and slightly pudgy, but had a generous smile. They rolled the window down, and Anthony immediately recognized his friend, Father Jules.

"Ah, Anthony, so it is true. We had been told you were coming." Father Jules had them pile out of the car and then ordered Peter to push it down the side of the cliff they had been driving. It was on the Gestapo's radar, so it had to be disposed of. They watched it disappear, ending in an earth-shattering crash at the bottom. They climbed into the priest's very old car, and as they started again down the road, it sounded as if the wheels were coming off. The car was so small they figured this was how sardines felt caught.

"Little sisters of the poor are waiting for all of you." Father Jules looked at Anthony. "If all goes well, we'll have you on a train home tomorrow. Louis arrived a few hours ago. Katarina and Nicholas had to be detoured as well, along with Louis. Louis had heard that the SS were looking for someone on the same train they were to board in Lyon. He met them at the train station. We had to be sure they were not looking for them. It was best they be moved here. When we arrived at the train station, police were all over. We suspect the free zone is not so free, as we could see some were SS in civilian clothing."

He rolled his eyes. "You can't miss the look. We are sorry. The sisters made sure they were hidden. Anthony, your sister Katarina is wearing a nun's habit." A smile twitched the corners of his mouth, and Anthony chuckled.

They arrived and drove to a side alley, where Father Jules climbed out of the car. He looked around, then ordered them to hurry into the church and make for the altar. The door was heavy and groaned as it opened. Inside, the church was cold and smelled musty. Some of the pews had been taken for firewood to keep people warm. A single candle burned on the altar.

Behind the altar was a large crucifix and several wood panels with various saints carved into them. Father Jules walked up to one panel and pushed on the tip of St. Francis's nose. The panel swung open on hidden hinges. Eyes wide, everyone followed him into a room with three cots, a table and chairs, and lots of weapons. Simon and Richard—two SOE agents Peter had trained—waited inside the hideaway.

"Peter, we are glad to see you," Richard said as they approached him with a hearty handshake. "We heard chatter and were told we needed to come here. It took us a week to avoid the Germans, hiding in every old barn that had been abandoned. We didn't know who among the farmers we could trust. We came to the church when we got here and hid in the confessional booths till we saw the priest. At first, we thought he might shoot us. We thought at first he was going to shoot us. He hides a gun under that cassock."

"Hard to believe he is a priest," Peter said in a low voice.

Simon answered, "Once one of the bravest priests we know." He cleared his voice. "He has gotten many of our aviators out to Spain."

The table in the room had food and wine. It was sparse but filling. They had some warm broth with sliced onions, some cheese sprinkled on top, and slices of dark bread. Not the onion soup they were used to, but it filled their stomachs. They were getting used to going hungry.

"Now, not to worry, my friends," Father Jules said as they ate. "Katarina is safe, and so are all of us. The sisters will take good care of her and provide us with food. Even priests and nuns have to be careful. The Nazis don't hold back shooting one of us, but so far we are okay. The villagers are all working for the same goal."

Peter walked over to a large box and whistled when he looked inside. He turned back to the group.

"Well, we have an inventory of a Browning .30-caliber machine gun to be mounted on a truck along with Springfield rifles, several Colt .35s, and demolition kits."

Father Jules smiled wickedly, a twinkle in his eyes. "I thought you would like the inventory we have gathered. We wish we could do more. We'll gather as many weapons as possible because I just know God will not let this evil prevail. It will be defeated." He patted Peter's shoulder, excused himself, and scurried from the room.

Simon shook his head. "So sad for my country. We need more help from England and pray the Americans might deliver us. Driving here, I saw all the abandoned farms, animals, and homes sitting empty. People abandoned their lives out of fear or were killed in cold blood by the Nazis. Many sought refuge from Paris. Even the rich are gone. The SS have carte blanche to kill and arrest, unlike the military.

"We do have a top Russian aristocrat who hates the SS," Simon continued. "He's working hard to keep the SS and Gestapo on their heels and off ours. We've met with him several times and sent information to Peter. He's receiving information straight from General Gerd von Rundstedt's office which reports to the sadist General Knochen. He will give Henri and Gregory an update in a day or two. Then later, they will tell Peter what they learned." Simon chuckled as Anthony asked if they would be safe.

"Can't get much safer than a whorehouse and living in a commune in the celebrated chabanais," Simon said.

Peter always liked Simon; that's why he'd trained him in England. He didn't fall under suspicion. He was a wealthy wine merchant living in a twenty-five-room chateau passed down through generations, with large tracts of land on the outskirts of Lyon. He made friends with the Gestapo and Vichy police. He had dinner with them while he hid English airmen in the basement. It was through family business that Anthony was also aware of Simon and the secret he held of Simon's family, his secret as well.

He also provided the best medications to kill Nazis or was then called upon to help bury them. Simon didn't wear the defeated look so many French people had. He refused to have a moral breakdown. He made many hazardous trips through France carrying information. He had secret passageways and rooms in his home and parts of Lyon and Avignon. If need be, he'd die for his country. His wife had taken their children to Switzerland and then returned alone to Paris. Simon worried for her safety as he could not find out where she was. Amelia was the love of his life.

He always carried small medical tablets to hand out and advised anyone who was captured and knew they were going to be tortured and killed to take one. The pills made sure the Gestapo and SS didn't get the satisfaction of taking their lives.

They sat in silence as they ate cheese and bread and drank wine. Anthony sat next to Simon.

"Simon," Anthony said, showing him the packet of papers in envelopes, "I need to get these to Father Jules. Will he be back soon? In confusion, I forgot to deliver documents to him."

"I wouldn't go out there. I'm sure Father will be back," Peter commented.

Anthony shook his head. "There have been so many setbacks already. I was told he needs them tonight."

Simon gestured to him. "Follow me and do not speak with anyone, regardless of how perfect your French is. As you said, time is of the essence, and Father Jules can deliver the documents tonight to the parties who need them."

Peter took Anthony's arm. "Don't go, Anthony."

Anthony yanked out of his cousin's grip. "He needs these. People are depending on them."

Simon and Anthony moved silently through the streets until they arrived at the convent. Katarina sat inside, helping the nuns peel small potatoes and old, shrivelled onions. Anthony bit back a chuckle at the sight of Katarina in a nun's habit.

When Katarina saw Anthony, she jumped up and almost knocked over the table. Simon knew immediately that the nun's outfit wouldn't make her inconspicuous. She was stunning to look at.

Father Jules was in deep discussion with one of the sisters when he looked up and saw Anthony.

"Why did you leave the church?" He said, striding up to him and

Simon. "It's dangerous!"

Anthony handed him the packet. "I was afraid that if something happened to me, these would be lost to those who needed them. Katarina and Nicholas needed to return to Berlin. They, too, are carrying some documents. Staying in the nun's garment might be better. Do you have an extra collar and black jacket that would fit Nicholas?"

Katarina looked at Anthony. "You can't be serious. This habit itches like crazy on my head."

"It also hides your blond hair and body," Anthony answered.

A young priest motioned Father Jules to the other room and whispered in his ear. Father Jules let out a long sigh.

"Anthony, you and Peter will stay here a while longer. Peter's Lysander could not land and won't be back for another week. It seems the Gestapo arrested, tortured, and shot two of England's agents."

Fury rose in Simon's eyes. "Let's get back to the others."

Father Jules promised to return in the morning and would have more transportation and weapons for them to go back to Lyon.

Making their way back to the hiding spot, they moved in silence and arrived unseen at the church. Simon explained to Peter what happened.

Peter looked at Anthony. "What the hell did you two think you were doing, going out in the streets? You were gone so long I was worried sick."

Anthony was amused since Peter usually never displayed an outward sign of worry. "Looks like you will stay here for a while and help me with your language skills," Peter said, sighing. "We could use you for just a little while."

Anthony shook his head. "I can't stay away from my parish that long without someone asking where I am. We have this Gestapo named Frederick Spitz snooping around already. He's taken a liking to Katarina, and I fear she might be falling for some of his false charm. I can feel the evil coming out of him."

Simon kept silent as Peter was swaying him to stay for longer than the week. They were short of people to help until more agents were dropped in. He knew Heinz had already moved a pilot out of Berlin with the family's help. Anthony sat and bowed his head in thought.

"Peter, I pray all the false papers will be used and come in handy for all of us."

"We have it done," Simon spoke up. "Plus, you can say you are also asking your brother for help in estate matters for your parents, who are leaving most of it to Hitler, as required."

"I'm not sure if we should involve Heinz," Anthony replied.

"Not to worry," Simon said. "Elvie and Heinz are already known on Baker Street in England. Heinz wanted to tell you when he visited you in Berlin, but he felt the less you knew, the less information they could get out of you if you were caught."

He patted Anthony's shoulder. "Your lineage and the medals Heinz has received will protect him from questioning. And Elvie, Louis, and Henri return to the House of Bourbon, the French European Dynasty. They can trace their family back to the Capetian Dynasty. Hitler wants them on his side. He won't suspect them because the Germans think the wealthy would never risk their wealth and position."

Peter sat in silence, nibbling on a piece of cheese. He was glad Louis was there with them now. Louis was still looking in the boxes as Simon spoke.

"Unfortunately, the Germans realize that besides Paris, Lyon is now the centre for Allied transmissions and resistance fighters," Simon continued. "If caught, they were shot or languished at Perigueoy in Southern France. It was literally a dungeon of water coursing down the walls in prison."

He turned to Peter. "While we are on the subject, we had thought you would be gone, but since you're staying until the next aeroplane can take you out, would you like to help with a prison escape? When we return to Lyon, I was to meet at the Grand Hotel Nouvel to receive instructions for it."

Peter looked at Anthony. "You can stay at Simon's chateau when we go back. I'll go with Simon for now."

The night was growing short as they decided they all needed to rest up for tomorrow. Morning arrived quickly, and Father Jules woke them with some very bad black coffee and hard bread with only jam. There was a bucket of water for washing up, and new clothing was brought in for each of them. Once dressed, they all gathered their weapons.

Father Jules arrived with the car keys to the Citroën while a driver in a German uniform drove them. Father Jules again reassured an anxious Anthony that all would be good with Katarina.

Nicholas and Katarina received travel papers back to Berlin and would leave later.

Peter, Anthony, Simon, and Louis changed their journey, travelling first to Simon's chateau as they realized they could use

Anthony for the next few days. He needed to freshen up, especially his priestly garments that he would wear, along with the letters necessary to allow him into the prison to say prayers and hear confessions. It was his way in. The prison held many of the British and others, but they still had inside information they could give, and Anthony was the perfect person. He would hear confessions.

They waited three days at Simon's before they went to the hotel and received all the necessary documents in Lyon that they needed to help those in prison. Anthony's first visit to the prison made him sick. He went into deep prayer to overcome what he saw, from the injured and beaten to the darkness of the cells and nearly nonexistent food. Those who died were meals for the rats. The Mauzac prison was hell. The trip was long, going back and forth from Lyon.

He took in black-market groceries. In each jar was a tool, anything from wire cutters to tiny files. Anthony was never asked to show his items as long as Simon gave him enough food and money to bribe the guards. Other instructions he carried in his Bible with most of the pages covered. The top was in Latin. He only had to peel the top off carefully to give to those who were to escape. Peter and Simon were organizing their escape over the Pyrenees to Spain. The papers were finished for them to use.

Anthony had gained enough information from those captured to give back to Peter. He let London know of newly built explosives factories. Those in prison could hear the explosions of the RAF bombers nightly. Fortunately, the bombers never hit the prison. The information was right on target about the factory.

Peter had to be careful not to put Simon in the Gestapo's sights. If Simon were seen with him for even a second, they might pull him for questioning. Since his plane couldn't land, Peter got his room at the hotel. This was the third time he'd tried to get an aircraft back to London. The first time, the city was covered with fog, and the second time, the whole flight was aborted because Gestapo agents might have learned about a drop.

The night after the failed attempt of the flight, Anthony and Peter were walking back to the hotel when they both sensed they were being followed. Soon, they spotted a figure in the darkness. Peter reached for his Colt revolver, and he and Anthony whipped around a corner and pressed against the wall.

Footsteps stopped and started again. Suddenly, the figure loomed in front of them with his weapon trained on them. With no hesitation, Peter jumped on the man. He clapped his hand over the man's mouth as he got behind him, and the gun fell to the ground. Peter yelled at Anthony to run.

Keeping the man in a vice-like grip, Peter smashed the man's head against the wall. Blood spurted against the cement wall and onto the alley pavement. Peter heard the crunch of the stranger's nose breaking, and more blood hit the pavement. Peter throttled the man's throat and soon heard the gurgle of a breath as the man tried to loosen Peter's grip. They crashed to the ground. Knowing he had to end this, Peter wrapped his legs around the man's waist and held onto his neck. He twisted as hard as he could and heard the man's neck snap and the last breath leave his body. The man's eyes now stared blankly at the black sky, and Peter kicked him for good measure.

Anthony walked a few steps but turned back; he couldn't abandon Peter. He arrived just in time to hear Peter snap the man's neck and to witness the body convulsing.

Peter let the man go and had his revolver ready. He hadn't wanted to use it on the man following them because it would have drawn too much attention. An explosion rang out in the distance, and a car screeched to a halt beside them. For a moment, Anthony thought this was the end, that this was the Gestapo. Then Simon poked his head out the window.

"Get in, you two!"

Relieved, Peter and Anthony lurched into the car.

"Can't you two stay out of trouble?" Simon said, smirking.

Peter looked so controlled as Anthony glanced down at his shaking hands.

Simon turned to Peter. "I'm going to leave you both at a friend's, let this chaos calm down, and come back for you. I need to go back and have the body disposed of. The Gestapo are all around, and we're not sure why. You should hide till we find out what they are up to."

They pulled into an alleyway at an open door, and a well-rounded woman motioned for them to hurry. She wore a short dress, lots of makeup, and a top that showed what God gave her. She had deep blue eyes lined in black. She wore high heels with black stockings, her face was round, and her long black hair pulled back. Her tone was strong, reminding Anthony of a schoolteacher giving a lecture.

Peter saw the horrified look on Anthony's face as soon as they entered the hallway. Anthony wrinkled his brow, trying to understand the sounds he heard coming from the rooms on either side. When it clicked, he stopped dead.

"Peter, I can't do this, in the name of God."

Peter put his hand on his shoulder. "Cousin, God will tell you, under the circumstances, it's all forgiven."

The woman motioned to them each to go into a room. Anthony hesitated until Peter nudged him.

"Go, for God's sake, you will be safe here," Peter said.

The madam called loudly, "Girls, two men in uniform need your service. Be good to them."

Peter whispered to Anthony, "This is Madam Bridgette. She and the girls work for us. All you have to do is sit and talk. Try to even sleep for a little while."

Peter gave Madam Bridgette a soft kiss on the forehead. She looked at Peter and Anthony. "You both do as the girls instruct you to. The Gestapo has been through the house once this week. Before they left, they demanded favours from the girls." Her face radiated rage. "The Gestapo are such pigs. We wished we could have cut out their hearts."

Peter went into his own room, and Anthony reluctantly sat on the bed in his. He was saying silent prayers when a petite young girl entered. Her features were like a small, dainty pixie, but her green eyes were fierce. Her makeup was minimal. He thought she didn't need much; she was an exceptionally pretty girl, no older than twenty. But she wore very little clothing. As Anthony averted his eyes, his brow furrowed in concern.

She sat next to him. "Father, you must take off your shirt, collar and cross. I have a safe place here under the floorboard."

Anthony reluctantly removed them, and the girl meticulously folded his shirt, placing his items under the floorboard. They just sat there for what felt like an endless amount of time before boots and a commotion echoed in the hall.

"It's showtime!" the girl said. She kicked off her shoes and shoved him backwards onto the bed. She lay on top of him, placing a kiss on his lips as the door swung open. She had undone her top as she stood up, out of the bed and stared down the Gestapo soldier who burst in.

"Excuse me," She said, "but this gentleman paid. If you want part of this, you must talk to madam." She stared unblinking into the Gestapo's eyes as he studied her nakedness. He strode into the room and looked over her shoulder at Anthony, who had pulled up the covers to his waist. The Gestapo grabbed the girl's breast.

"I will make sure you are on my next visit," He said, letting his hands linger on her breast.

"I hope to see you soon, then, mein Herr."

The Gestapo stood another minute, looking at Anthony.

Anthony knew the soldier must be hurting the girl; he gripped her breast so hard his knuckles were white.

"Where are you from?" He suddenly asked Anthony. In perfect French, Anthony gave the address for an abandoned farmhouse that he'd memorized in case he was stopped. The Gestapo twisted the girl's breast until she whimpered. Then he left, chuckling.

The girl stood there for a moment, telling Anthony not to move. When the Gestapo's footfalls faded down the hall, her composure crumbled. Anthony rose and placed a blanket around her shaking shoulders, directing her to sit next to him on the edge of the bed.

"I hate them, Father." Her mouth trembled, and tears fell. He put his arms around her, and they both said a prayer. Eventually, her head fell on his shoulder, and he let her cry. He told her he would help her to get out of this business after the war.

An hour must have passed with them just sitting there before Madam, and Peter came through a secret door. Madam motioned to Anthony as the girl gathered Anthony's belongings. Peter whispered something to the young girl, and Anthony thanked her and told her he would pray for her.

They entered a different alley where Simon was waiting. "Peter, I'm taking you to the airfield," He said. "We received word tonight that you should be able to get out."

Peter turned to Anthony, who had gone pale. "There was no other way we could have hidden. I'm sorry for putting you in that position."

Anthony shook his head. "It had to be done."

They drove in silence, Peter radiating anxiety. As much as he didn't want to leave France, it would be good to return to England briefly. He could explain exactly what was needed and how they were doing, considering how many agents they lost.

Simon parked the car. After a long drive in a hidden spot, they saw the eight hundred yards of open field. Both sides were lined with trees. In the distance were two men. He thought that Simon gestured for Peter and Anthony to stop; their men would not come out in the open. They heard the soft droning of an aircraft. Peter flashed a code with his flashlight, hoping not to be seen by any Germans. When he didn't receive an answer, he tried again. Still nothing. His stomach rolled.

"Simon, I don't like this," He whispered.

The two men headed their way as Simon, Peter, and Anthony crouched behind some large, green bushes. The three of them were almost directly in the men's sights. They overheard the first German asking the other where he thought the flash was coming from.

"I don't see the plane either," the other said, his voice laced with frustration.

This wasn't good. Simon, Peter, and Anthony moved farther behind the brush and trees. They had to get back to the car undetected. They all could feel this situation was different, foreboding.

They ran as fast as they could, hearing the aircraft overhead and footsteps behind them. Simon and Peter pulled their weapons at the same time—the place was suddenly crawling with Germans. Someone had betrayed them, and they'd walked right into a trap.

Suddenly, the footsteps stopped, and something thudded on the ground behind them. They looked back, and Simon recognized two men from the resistance. They must have heard about the trap and rushed over. They'd taken out three Germans.

Simon, Peter, and Anthony pushed the car a good distance before they started the engine. New footsteps now sounded like they were going away from them, in a different direction towards the airfield. They heard the aircraft lifting higher and disappearing; Peter's last chance for a while to return to England.

Anthony cleared his throat. "I prefer we not revisit our last hideaway."

Peter laughed as Simon assured him they would be taken to a much safer place, a convent, while he kept his promise of a dinner party to the Gestapo and Vichy police while his chateau was being prepared. If he arrived late, he'd say he was out looking at his wine collection on the estate.

Simon looked over at Peter. "We need to get you to Toulouse. We can't take the chance of Marseille. Agents were arrested as they tried to escape by boat. We did move two aviators out of Cannes."

Peter nodded. "How did the Germans know the aircraft was coming?"

"They must have picked up a transmitted message," Simon said, rubbing his temples. "They're driving all over Lyon with antennas, trying to pick up messages being sent and received. Peter, I think you might be the one they want to catch. The Funkabwehr, the German counterintelligence, are working hard to track you down with your radio. Heinz told me last month that the Germans were installing sophisticated radar equipment, and we would deliver eighty grey-green detonator jammers. Heinz told Louis about it in Paris, too."

Anthony interjected, "Are they no longer under suspicion?"

"No, they've been cleared," Simon said. "And we should have told you that we received a message from Louis. Your sister has arrived safely in Berlin."

Anthony let out a sigh of relief. "How did Heinz receive the information?" He asked Simon, who looked away from the road.

"Your brother Edwin." Simon almost went into a ditch as he got the vehicle back under control.

Anthony shook his head. "My brothers are putting themselves in great danger."

They all agreed.

Peter was going over the next steps in his mind as he spoke to Simon.

"I have to get over the Alps for many missed flights, and Anthony needs to get back to Berlin, but first, let me go back to my room. I have papers and the transmitter there that I can't let fall into the wrong hands."

Simon nodded. "All right, but you must hurry. The sisters can't keep their gates open very long." He waited in the car as Anthony and Peter ran up the steps.

Peter put up his hand and placed a finger on his lips as he heard shuffling inside. He pulled his revolver as he silently opened the door. Heinz and Elvie were sitting in the chairs at the dining room table. Heinz shifted nervously in the chair as it kept making creaking noises. He, too, stood up, not knowing who was coming through the door.

"Good God, I could have shot you both," Peter said. "How did you know to come here? It's not safe."

Heinz let out a little chuckle. "Collette in Paris told us. She, too, thought you were on your way back to England and asked us to sweep the room. If the Gestapo showed up, I could have told them I was renting the room for the night, and they wouldn't have searched."

Elvie took Anthony's hand as she sat next to him. "I'm so glad you're safe." She looked up. "Peter, we had hoped you could get out. Louis is trying to track down who could possibly have betrayed us."

Anger flashed in Peter's eyes. "We heard a transmission that the aircraft was able to abort. I'll have to go through Spain or Switzerland to get a plane back to England."

Anthony walked over to the window where Heinz was standing. They dared not open the shade. Heinz turned to him.

"I heard Nicholas and Katarina got back without any difficulty. The forged papers indicating they are from the Vatican serve us well in moving people and priests being able to use them." He looked at Anthony, who sat down wearily in a chair. He had grown thin and looked exhausted. As with everyone, the war was taking a toll on him.

Heinz was still dressed in his full Luftwaffe uniform. It was a lifesaver and most likely the reason he was not stopped. He had a bag with him and handed it to Peter. "Here are more items you might need. I brought it from Paris for Simon. There are false medical records, ration cards for the Jews, transmitters, and the locations of more weapons. Edwin informed me that the Germans had perfected the radio direction-finding. They're increasing the mobile D/F units that are disguised as commercial vans with antennas mounted on the roof. You can't miss that part, so be aware. I was told that anyone who gets caught will most likely be shot on the spot."

Heinz handed Anthony a billfold of new identity documents for people moving out of Berlin. "We had someone else in mind to take them to Berlin to be handed over to you, but since you're here, you might as well take them."

There was a soft knock on the door. Elvie opened it as the rest of them stepped into the kitchen. It was Simon.

He looked at the guns aimed at him through the kitchen. "That would have made a lot of noise," He said, shaking his head. "Everyone in the building will hear it if you fire shots. Not a smart move on any of your parts."

Peter lowered his weapon, "Not with this, Welrod. We had these air dropped a month ago. It's designed for close assassinations. It's extremely quiet when fired; its effective range is short—not more than ten yards—but I don't mind seeing the Gestapo's eyes when I shoot him in the head."

Heinz and Anthony winced. They knew their cousin loved them, but it was still difficult for him as the Germans were bombing and killing his people in England.

Peter gave Simon three guns from his bag that he had stashed behind the wall where the stove was. He had to get these guns out of the room, lest the Germans find them. He still could kick himself for being sloppy and leaving items that could have identified them somehow.

"Give one to Louis and Gregory and keep one for yourself. Heinz, I'm unsure what would happen if you were caught with one."

"It's easy," Heinz said. "I tell them I got one from the Gestapo as they captured a few British."

Peter shrugged. "Okay, then, here you are. We still have the preferred way of killing after the weapon, knives, ropes." He motioned to Simon. "You need to get back to Lyon."

Simon smiled. "And I want you to get back to safety. A car is waiting around the corner to take you to the rectory. The nuns will let you in for the night. Tomorrow you make your way to Savoy Annecy. It's on the northwest border of Lake Annezy, twenty-five miles from Geneva. We have you staying there for two nights. It's booked in Hotel de la Pase. You are no longer Peter. You are now Gustuv Marsac. My cousin will pick you up at St. Anne's church."

Peter looked at his identification papers.

Heinz cleared his throat. "Simon, that's the other reason we came here. Louis and the others felt it would be easier if I helped Peter and Anthony get through the countryside to the border. We're going with him. It's my few days of leave. I'll make sure we glide through any checkpoints or some who might stop the car. You and Anthony have a good night's sleep. We'll be back at the convent by six a.m." He turned to Anthony. "We have all the papers to get you into Switzerland. You need to get back to Berlin. Edwin says Frederic Spits is circling the family, especially Katarina. He's pretending to be interested in her, but we know that's not true. He's up to something."

Simon looked at his watch and jumped. "Oh my God, I have to return to the chateau," He said. "There are only thirty minutes left before our arrival. But I have to ask. Heinz, did you forward the information we intercepted to Gregory and Louis? They've made it back to Paris."

Peter looked at Heinz. "What information?"

"We have someone travelling to Paris to let them know they are under no circumstances to meet at a café. Maurice, we transmitted also. We believe there's a woman who needs to be eliminated sooner than later."

Elvie took Simon's arm, "What happens when they encounter her?"

"They kill her, of course. If any of us were found out because they captured Gregory or Louis, we would all be running for our lives, and two years of operation goes down the drain."

"How did you find out about her?" Peter asked.

"Edwin found out. One woman was placed in France to act as a Parisian, and two more were placed in London. We can't find the two in London, but we've identified the one in Paris. She is pretending to know Louis through a messenger. Her name is Michelle, and she's working for the Germans. She asked to meet with him, and we're sure it's a trap to kill us all, or she wants a lot of information. We also know now the messenger is a traitor. We will deal with him as well as Michelle."

After goodbyes, they went their separate ways until morning.

Simon had a long night with the Gestapo. They drank his best wine and ate like kings, but they gave him several useful bits of information in their drunken stupors. The fools thought Simon was the best French man they could have ever made friends with.

The next morning, a slightly hungover Simon came to find Anthony and Peter to drive them to where Heinz was waiting. The journey was unnerving to them all as they left St. Anne's.

The rest got to their destination, went directly to the hotel, and waited for three days for the aeroplane. Finally, the courier brought the message to arrive on time. They received the coded message and managed to intercept an airdrop of supplies without mishap with word of Peter's pickup.

Heinz and Elvie said goodbye to Peter as they had spent their days in the small village with him. They were on their way back to Paris, and because of Heinz, they flew through any stops or questions by the Germans going and coming back to Paris. They were concerned about Louis and Gregory. Heinz could say he needed to stay and meet with doctors in Paris because of his injuries from the last mission when the British shot into his aircraft, and he limped back to France with a shoulder wound. They arranged to meet Louis at the Champs-Elysees on a side street, where he still held an apartment. As far as the Nazis knew, he worked for Simon, bringing back the wines to the generals and others. They didn't know his family lineage and his connection to Elvie.

Heinz had additional information to give to Louis before they left. Edwin knew who the traitor was and what she looked like. Their first appointment had not happened, so she sent through transmission for Louis to meet her again. The Nazis were also looking into Henri. Henri and Louis were quietly working in Henri's health clinic, managing to get the Jews and children out of Paris.

At this point, no one had been suspicious of Henri. They hadn't bothered him because he was also taking care of Germans who visited him for various ailments. Henri was also handling a captain who had come down with diseases from visiting the whore houses. The captain respected Henri and seemed to keep the Nazis from trying to inspect his clinic.

When Elvie and Heinz returned to Paris, Heinz immediately had to go back to his office and seek out the medical doctor for his wounds. He hoped he wasn't going to be sent back to fly immediately. Elvie finished up her work at the museum, and Louis met her outside after work.

Louis asked Elvie to approach the café first. She saw the woman called Michelle pass a note to one of the waiters. Elvie took out her lipstick, the signal to the others that Michelle was there.

Michelle was a pretty blonde with big blue eyes and a fair complexion. A waiter, who they knew was also working with the Gestapo, whispered something in Michelle's ear, then disappeared back into the café. The other staff pulled him out into the alley as he entered the kitchen. They'd been informed that he was a traitor to France. Once in the alley, two men asked him to follow them. The waiter did not cry for help as he walked with a gun at his back. The men asked one of the other waiters to have Michelle come through the kitchen to the alleyway, which she obliged, thinking she was going to meet with Louis. Neither the waiter nor Michelle were ever seen again.

Heinz's time was ending in Paris, and he didn't want to leave Elvie. His thoughts went back to the first time he saw her. It was early on, right after Germany walked into Paris. He didn't believe in love at first sight, but it happened to him. So much water under the dam since they came together. When he thought of her, his head still spun like a schoolboy, and his heart throbbed when she walked towards him. He relished every kiss from her. It didn't seem reasonable that his heart hurt and ached for her every moment he was apart from her. How could love hurt when it was such ecstasy?

Chapter 3

1941

Heinz knew the minute he saw Elvie at a bakery that he wanted to be with her. Those few moments stirred a longing in him. He was always being approached by women and for a time being, was even engaged to a sweet girl in Switzerland. His parents were delighted. While that didn't work out, he knew he was longing for the same feelings of love his brother Edwin had for his wife, Rita. He watched them, and it was a love so deep it could never be undone, not by living or death in the concentration camp.

Elvie was standing in line with her ration cards, tapping her foot in irritation. The line was so long she hadn't even made it inside the bakery yet, and she was already late for work. The captain would be angry, but her tardiness was due to his own order. French people could no longer use all the tables and chairs; many were reserved for German soldiers.

Annoyed, Elvie turned and saw Heinz. Her breath caught, and she immediately looked away. He wore a German Luftwaffe uniform, which meant he was the enemy. She forced her breathing to slow as she peeked at him again. He was glancing down the street as if he were waiting for someone. She tried to look away from his crystal blue eyes, his strong square jaw, and high cheekbones. He wasn't pasty white like the rest of the German soldiers. Instead, he had a golden tan, wide-set eyes, and sandy brown hair that was a little longer than allowed. She spotted the emblems on his uniform. Suddenly, a Catholic priest was embracing him. The priest whispered something to this handsome pilot, then stood back, and Elvie could see the worry in his eyes. A chill ran down her back.

Heinz noticed the woman immediately and also spotted the Nazi soldiers watching her like hawks looking for prey. Church bells tolled in the distance. While Anthony was talking to Heinz, Heinz's eyes didn't leave this woman, her skin alabaster white, with a bit of lip stick. Her cheeks pulled in because of how thin she was, like so many women in Paris. Her hair was jet black, and her large, blue eyes were fringed with long lashes. Her clothing, though, looked refined and rich. She wore a light blue suit, a cream-colour sweater underneath, and a little hat with her hair trailing in a long braid down her back.

Heinz watched a Nazi who looked as if he had too much to drink walking towards her. Too many women couldn't put up a fight and just had to give in. Even though the soldiers were told they could not take advantage of the French woman, they didn't listen. Too many of the women had to live with the torment and shame or become part of them. A soldier was walking toward this beautiful French woman, his beady eyes ogling her.

Heinz stepped over to the woman and slipped his arm around her waist. She flinched, but Anthony stood at her other side. The Nazi swaggered over.

"You with her?" He said, his breath stinking of beer. "If not, she can come with me. There's a good alleyway behind the bakery."

Heinz and Anthony pulled her into the bakery with them, jumping her forward in line several spaces. No one objected because

Heinz was in uniform, and the tension of another ugly situation brewing was evident. Most other shoppers moved with their ration cards to the side of the bakery wall.

The Nazi from outside stumbled into the bakery and grabbed Elvie's arm. "Fraulein, you come with me."

Heinz thought this young soldier must be insane to challenge a top Luftwaffe pilot. What was wrong with him? Heinz removed his hand from the woman's arm and gave the soldier a rough push. The man crashed into the table where two others sat. Heinz stood over the drunken Nazi, whose eyes finally focused on the Knights Cross and Iron Cross on Heinz's uniform. He leaned over the drunken, belligerent soldier while the other two started to leave the bakery.

"Shall I have you arrested? It's in my power," Heinz said. The Nazi wisely stayed silent, so Heinz turned back to the woman. "You must trust me and my brother."

She nodded; her hands were shaking as she swallowed hard. Heinz walked outside with her after she received her rations. The drunken soldiers were still outside, one of them leaning over, getting sick in the gulley.

"All of you need to move along and never come near my wife again. I will make sure all three of you rot in prison," Heinz barked, and the three men went white. Two of them apologized and ran off like dogs with their tails between their legs. The one who accosted Elvie glared at Heinz with hate.

Heinz turned his attention to Elvie as he and Anthony offered to walk her back where she needed to be.

Elvie hesitated. Could this stranger be laying a trap? Did he know of her resistance and her brothers' clandestine activities? This could be dangerous, but she was so careful. And the priest looked honest.

She took a deep breath as she walked beside them with her limited amount of bread and butter, plus one item for her Nazi captain employer, back at the museum. He had a standing order the bakery had to bake just for him.

"Let me introduce myself," Heinz said. "I'm Heinz Von Rahmel, and this is my brother, Anthony." The priest was older and a bit taller but had the same eyes and rugged features. "Let us walk you back to where you need to go. I don't need those three suddenly reappearing." Heinz smiled down at her.

"You can trust us," He continued. "We can take you to the church where my brother is staying. They can vouch for us."

Elvie suddenly started to laugh. Heinz shifted back and forth, looking nervous. She glanced down the street, and her laughter died on her lips. This was not the Paris she loved. People had their heads down, the streets were bare, and German propaganda was on every corner. It was safe to talk with the priest, but others looked at her suspiciously as she was now talking to a German military man.

Elvie knew immediately there was something in his eyes she could trust.

Anthony cleared his throat and rubbed his forehead. "My brother here is usually not so forward," He said. "I can vouch for him."

Elvie stared. Why was this priest familiar to her? She had seen him somewhere but couldn't recall. Perhaps Lyon? His eyes widened, and she knew he also noticed a familiarity in her.

She had to laugh again. It had been a long time since someone made her laugh. Life was so depressing in Paris, the city of lights, cafes, the music… It was all gone now.

"You both speak French as if you are French," She said. Several people were beginning to stare, so Anthony took her elbow and moved her along.

"Let me walk beside you and Heinz next to me. It might not bring as much attention."

Anthony now moved her elbow gently. She looked up at him.

"Have we met in Lyon? I swear I have seen you."

"Where can we walk you to, Mademoiselle?"

"I work at the Louvre. I'm taking inventory of the art and jewels that the Germans are taking, some items are from wealthy Jewish homes. Some are from art leaving the museum and Lyon."

Heinz and Anthony immediately heard her voice change to a tone of bitterness. She was testing them to see their reaction.

"We are truly sorry; you must be very well versed in the art world to be able to take on this work," Heinz said. He asked where she had studied, and she immediately noticed his question was sincere.

"I studied at 31 Rue du Dragon in the Sixth Arrondissement." She stopped and looked at the two of them. "Would you like to hear how it's done?" There was a question in her eyes about how they would respond. Heinz took her elbow and moved her along again.

"I would like to know, and maybe there is something we can do to help you."

She stopped again and cocked her head. "Help? I doubt." Anthony put his hand on her shoulder, also unsure if they could trust her.

She studied them for a moment. The priest might be safe, but the pilot could have her shot on the spot. She pulled Anthony to the side, knowing for certain now that she had seen him in Lyon talking to her brother Louis.

"Father, do you know someone in Lyon named Louis?"

Anthony exhaled. "Yes, I last saw him at Simon's house."

"Which priest is at the church you visit in Lyon?" She was breathing deeply, afraid she was making a mistake talking so openly to him. What if he was the enemy? But something in his eyes made her reach further into the questions.

"Father Julian," He said, giving her a smile filled with sadness.

Elvie smiled, too, and a deep sigh of relief came out of her chest. "Well, I guess I can trust you."

"My child, it's hard to trust anyone."

She pointed to a bench not far from the museum and told them to follow her. They sat as she paced in front of them, watching the eyes of those who passed. Most looked down at their feet; no one wanted to make eye contact in France any longer. Everyone was too terrified.

Anthony took her hand and stopped her. "What's on your mind? We mean you no harm. We only want you to return to the museum safely."

She decided to trust them. For the rest of her life, she would not understand why, but it was the best decision in her life. This priest knew Father Julian, and she was confident she had seen Father Anthony at Simon's.

She blurted out, "So far, we have had to move out two hundred and three vehicles from the museum. Somewhere around a thousand marked cases were sent to Chateau de Chambord. A yellow circle for valuable pieces, green for major works, red for world treasures…all moved. Mona Lisa moved to Chambord. We have art stashed all over in abbeys, churches, and castles. Almost two hundred thousand boxes, nearly thirty-seven hundred paintings, and thousands of statues." She paused and shook her head. The numbers were mind-boggling. "I work with Jaujard and Metternich, who are good men. They hate Hitler and the Nazis as much as the French do. Many in the art world knew what was to happen and moved much art to Geneva before Hitler entered Paris. They Nazis came to look at empty frames." A smile came to her lips as she recalled one of those days.

She looked at her watch, stood suddenly from the bench where she had sat, and beckoned for the men to follow her. She began to walk with long strides, biting her lip. Her head spun. Were these men the enemy? Was she stupid to say anything about the movement? What in the world had gotten into her?

Heinz was serious as he gave her a slight smile. He wanted this woman's company but felt it would be a tough sell. He never in the past had any issues with women, even the few around the Luftwaffee base. They mostly approached him with advances. Some even told him boldly that they wanted to have a serious relationship with him. He now ached for intimacy. She was exquisitely beautiful, and he yearned to know her better.

Elvie saw the starved look in his eyes as they continued walking. They were now standing at the Louvre.

She wanted nothing more than to hate Heinz. But as much as she tried, she just couldn't, not like she had hated other Germans she met.

Heinz was looking down at his shoes. He was afraid she would leave, and he would never see her again. Anthony took her arm.

"Mademoiselle, do you go back and forth to Lyon?" Elvie immediately stiffened. "Mademoiselle, if you travel back, would you be so kind as to leave a verbal message for Father Julian at the Lady of Sorrows church and let him know I will be in Paris for a while?"

Elvie arched one eyebrow. "You know him well, Father?"

"I instructed Father Julian when he was in seminary, and he has remained my faithful friend."

She moved her foot back and forth, crumbling flowers on the sidewalk like Paris crumbling under the Germans. She knew her brothers Louis and Henri worked with several Jesuit Priests. Could Father Anthony be one of them?

"Father, I'm not sure when I will be travelling back, but I will let him know. When the time comes, shall I reach out to you?"

Anthony's shoulders dropped in relief. "Tell him I will be here for as long as he needs me, but there is some urgency to the matter."

She was ready to ask him questions when all three were startled by a voice behind them.

"Oui, bonjour, mademoiselle. You are running late. We need the inventory catalogued quickly."

With cold eyes, the captain turned his attention to Heinz. He didn't outrank Heinz, so Heinz did not speak up but stepped forward. His status was far more important than this captain's.

"I will escort her in. She is a bit shaken since a drunken soldier tried to take advantage of her… She is very important to me."

Heinz spoke quickly in French to Elvie. It was evident the captain did not know the language.

Heinz informed her he would be back after she finished work. Anthony would be with them if she wanted dinner, so she wouldn't feel awkward being with a German. "We will dine at the Ritz Hotel. It's occupied by the Germans." He shrugged. "I hope it won't be too awkward."

She hastily bid goodbye and informed them she would be finished at five. Heinz saw the trembling hands again and fear in her eyes.

The captain hurriedly escorted her into the museum and looked at her with contempt.

Once inside his office, she gave him the macaroons he had on order at the bakery every week. She was going to speak up, regardless of who he was.

"I stood in line minding my own business when two of your soldiers tried to move me out of the bakery and suggested they take me into an alley. He grabbed me. The two men you just met saved me from a likely terrible event and escorted me back here. Thank goodness they had come along and recognized me as their friend from previous years. I was concerned I would be followed. I didn't much appreciate the suggestion from your German soldiers."

She swallowed hard; she was not going to waiver in her demeanour. She looked the captain straight in the eyes while one hand held onto the desk.

Once again, he slowly looked her up and down. His eyes a pale blue, his face a pasty white, and his blond hair short. His face had scars, and his stomach protruded over the waistband of his pants. He was taller than Elvie, but not by much.

"You are a beautiful woman; it is no wonder you attract attention. I have seen the way men look at you."

Elvie clenched her teeth. She wanted to slap him. Her hands were now furled into fists along her skirt.

He came next to her and put his arm around her waist, holding it too tightly as he escorted her out of the room. His hand was now slightly on her waist as he led her to the end of the hall where her office was.

"Thank you, Captain," She said as she abruptly turned to him. She opened the door and prayed he would not follow her in as he had done before.

She wished she had a gun and could get away with shooting him. She had visions of killing him. She closed the door and leaned against the wall. She saw another art piece on her desk. Thank God they managed to remove ninety per cent of the art from Paris. There were always items that arrived in crates from private homes, personal items of art and jewellery. She would hold them in her hands and cry, knowing they were from Jewish families or families who stood up to the Germans.

She managed to hide a few pieces of jewellery and always wrote down where they came from. She knew there would come a day when she would return the pieces to their owners, even the wedding rings. The most magnificent piece she hid inside the Louvre was a tulip encrusted with diamonds and emeralds; the leaves were solid gold. She knew the jewellery store it was stolen from belonged to a third-generation Jewish family. She wished so many times that she could remove the paintings. Once, she managed a five by ten. Employees were always searched before leaving the Louvre, so she found places to hide the pieces within the walls and floorboards.

She shuddered when she heard the heavy boots and the barking voices outside on her street or building. She wrote down every family and every French family who immediately took the bigger apartments and ransacked their belongings. She would not forget those who stood by and even turned some families in. Her eyes welled with tears as she recalled her neighbour begging to leave her children with them as they were separated into two different vans.

She took the piece off her desk, took the painting down to be catalogued, and placed it in boxes. She secretly took pictures with a camera of all the boxes. She would hand over the film for safekeeping to her brother in the resistance. In between, she thought of Heinz and Father Anthony. She knew Father Julian well—he worked his magic with false papers, ration cards, baptism names and records for the children they moved and hid. These two men must be part of the resistance. The priest, anyway. Maybe not the Luftwaffe pilot.

She was so deep in thought as she had walked to another room to place the crate of pictures and had not realized the hours that had gone by when the captain shouted behind her.

"Your gentleman officer is downstairs. So, you found yourself a fighter pilot with a Knight's Cross and an Iron Cross."

He followed her back to the office, where she retrieved her jacket. He tried to help her with her jacket like he always did while his hands slipped slightly to where they shouldn't.

"Good night, Captain, I will see you tomorrow." She smiled

sweetly as he stood in the doorway now. He lifted her chin as she squeezed by him, and their bodies touched.

"He will leave you behind, but I will be here. We will take up where I left off, and you will do as I say." She squeezed by him as the front of her touched his chest, and he moved her hips into him with a hard slam. He grabbed her buttocks and held her tight as he slipped his hand down her blouse and rubbed hard with a sinister smile. There was nothing she could do. If she did not oblige, he could have her killed or sent to a concentration camp. That was the situation many French women were facing. When he let her go, she walked down the stairs, and the lyrics of Edith Piaf came to her lips as she sang them silently to herself. "Mon Coeur est au coin de la rue… My heart is around the corner."

When Heinz entered the building, he was met with hostility from the captain, who had now followed Elvie down to the steps and onto the street. Heinz moved back outside and waited curbside for her with the car adorned with German flags. She hurried to the car and climbed in, her stomach in her throat like it was every day when she left. It was always the same ritual; some days could be worse as she had to submit to him.

Her jaw dropped when she saw who was already in the car. "Oh my God, what in God's earth are you doing here, Louis?" She turned to Heinz who was sitting next to her, and looked at both with confusion on her face.

Heinz smiled. "Anthony put two and two together. He knew Louis and spoke of you and what you looked like. Once you were at the Louvre, he went back to the church and had a message sent. Hence why we are here now."

"What do you do for us?" Elvie asked Heinz. Clearly, she'd been right to trust him earlier.

"I'm helping my cousin Peter, who is with the British OSE. I pass him information about drops that could be compromised or buildings that might be targeted. My brother in Berlin, Edwin, sends us coded messages of arrests coming or those who are put on trains."

Elvie's eyes widened. "They will hang you if you're found out!"

Heinz winced and touched his neck. "It's a risk I've willingly taken. I didn't join the military to kill innocent people in bombings or watch children being led away in trains. My sister-in-law is Jewish. That's how I became involved. Anthony asked me to bring back papers that changed her birth and religion."

"It's a little hard to believe you would betray your country," Elvie said.

Heinz flinched because her tone was so cold.

"There are a few Germans who don't agree with what Hitler is doing, and Hitler doesn't respect the Military. My family works hard. My brother Edwin forwards us information, and my sister takes pictures of the British. We are all taking the risk of death if found out."

There was a question on Elvie's lips. She had so many more questions she wanted to ask, but Louis interrupted her.

"Elvie, we need to make a quick stop. You can't go to dinner in a suit. You have to start playing a part with Heinz. Don't worry. I trust these two men, and you, too, can trust them with your life."

They circled the neighbourhood a few times before stopping two blocks away, then walked to a worn-out building. Heinz and

Anthony stayed behind. Too much travelling at this time of night could cause anyone to report them.

Elvie and Louis walked into a dark and cold basement apartment. The air smelled thick and mouldy as they moved down hallways filled with doors, and he guided her to a room. The door stood ajar, and she heard a sound that nearly didn't sound human; it lingered between life and death. She abruptly stopped and looked through the half-open door. Gregory was there. There was no emotion on his face. She and Louis exchanged glances.

"Louis, Gregory is torturing that man! Look at all the blood on the table," She whispered.

Louis moved her forward into the room. "Yes, he is, but that man is the reason six of our fighters were caught and murdered. He deserves much more than torture; he is a French collaborationist."

Elvie looked at Gregory. "He is a Gestapo. I have seen him many times speaking with Gaspard Neveu at the Louvre."

She could see the man was desperate to die from the torture, and she realized she didn't have an ounce of sympathy for him. She knew he was capable of horribly unspeakable things inflicted on the innocent.

Gregory washed up over the sink, blood draining off his hands in a swirl. He spoke without looking at the man.

"This man is known in Lyon for his barbaric tortures. He killed two British agents in Toulouse and sent two priests to a concentration camp, but not before torturing them savagely."

Elvie didn't look at the man tied up; she kept her eye on Gregory.

"I understand. I had heard of and met him once when they had a party at the Louvre for all the art they had acquired from Jewish homes. He was bragging. I sketched a picture of him from memory. I saw Peter in Lyon and gave it to him so he could be on the lookout."

Gregory growled. "I wish I had known it was him living with resistance fighters. Suppose I had only given Peter his picture sooner. We might have saved the six men!"

Elvie walked over and looked at Gestapo's face. His eyes were swollen, his lip bleeding, his arms turning blue from one long bruise, and his hands burned from matches.

"This is nothing compared to what you will feel in hell," she spat. "That's where you are going." She walked out and listened to him, begging Gregory to be killed.

Elvie and Louis heard a large thump as they closed the door behind them. They continued down the dark, damp hallway filled with peeling wallpaper.

The next room they entered felt warmer and was filled with three men working on transmitters, pounding out codes. Louis walked over to the closet and rummaged through it until he found the dress.

"Here, dear sister. I believe you left this in Lyon. Isn't it one of your favourites?"

"I can't wear this. Chanel is at the Ritz, living with a General. She's a traitor. I left this behind because of this exact reason."

"Yes, you can. It will look like you sympathize with her and will fit in with the rest of the women who have whored themselves to the Germans living there. We need you to listen closely to all conversations. Meeting Heinz is a godsend."

They looked at the gown, with its layers of chiffon, deep green and tulle with a large cucumber-coloured band around the waist, thin straps from the heart-shaped top, and small stars strewn into the material.

"Elvie, this is a good thing having dinner there. You can mingle and listen to conversations."

She looked down again at the gown and went back and rummaged through the closet, where she found two green slippers to wear with the dress. They weren't in the best shape, but the long dress would partially cover them. She found a black shawl that had also seen better days. She removed the little brooch on her suit and placed it over a hole in the shawl. She reluctantly put on the gown and let her hair fall in curls around her face. She found some old lipstick in her bag and applied the pink hue to her lips.

The three men working on the transmitters whistled when she came back out into the room.

"Louis, I guess you conveniently just went into my closet at home." She gave him a smile.

Louis grinned. "I brought them here in case we needed them like we do now. I'll go and tell Heinz you're ready, and he can bring the car to the last block."

"No! It's too dangerous. Anyone could be watching. Put an old blanket around me, and I can walk to where they are parked. You stay here. I will be fine."

Heinz saw her first as she came around the corner. He couldn't take his eyes off her as he helped her into the car. She felt anxious to be seen with so many Germans in one room as they arrived at the Ritz. She didn't know who knew what and who was friend or foe.

She clutched Heinz's hand as they entered the restaurant and dance area. Women, mostly speaking French, were with the German men as the champagne flowed. Some of the women were part of the echelon of Paris and high society. Baron Von Behr immediately approached them.

"You, Heinz Von Rahmel, our best of the best. We are honoured to have an ace fighter pilot join us tonight."

Baron Von Behr then stared strangely hard at Elvie as if he knew her. Heinz saw the look and spoke immediately.

"This is my fiancée, Mademoiselle Elvie Rousette."

Elvie stiffened as Heinz gave her a slight kiss on her temple.

The baron congratulated Heinz, and the server came by with glasses of French champagne. Elvie immediately took one, hoping a few sips would calm her nerves.

The server came over to Heinz with more food and, through clenched teeth, said, "Do not stay long. We are trying to find a way to remove several who were just caught sending transmissions before they are moved to Buchenwald." Heinz kept his face neutral and merely smiled and said thank you.

Elvie just smiled as she took the champagne and handed it to Heinz, who now turned his back to her as he spoke to a general and his girlfriend. Elvie saw Coco Chanel sitting in a corner, smiling and sipping champagne.

She wanted to walk over and slap her and every woman in the room. Traitors, she thought. They were all nice and fat with good food, nice dresses, and jewellery. If they only knew how many of the Germans had wives sitting back home in Germany.

Elvie and Heinz danced as the music took over the room, and he held her tight. He didn't want to stop dancing with her. Her perfume, ever so light, smelled of vanilla, and her skin was so soft as he touched her arm.

She was whispering to him. Did he understand the message the server told him? He nodded yes, and he excused himself. She took a seat at a table for dinner. She could barely eat what was in front of her, knowing how many of her neighbours were hungry at that moment.

When Heinz returned, he looked uneasy.

"What happened?" She asked, noticing his knuckles were scraped.

"I have what I need. In my hat, there is a special lining for documents. We were exchanging in the alleyway, and someone approached us. A French police officer, we had to remove him…. He was placed in the trash bin by the kitchen with all the other rotten smells."

"You killed him?"

"We had to."

A young officer with his girlfriend asked if they could join them at the table. Heinz asked them to take a seat. Elvie listened to the tales of the young officer's conquest in his war effort while in Rome. He didn't seem to mind just talking about himself.

Elvie and Heinz finished their meal and apologised because Elvie had to rise early for work.

The car was brought around.

In the car, she leaned her head into his shoulder as she whispered,

"Why do you have to be German and our enemy?"

He looked down at her face; her eyes were closed.

"This German will protect you the best I can, and I will protect your family and my own. I know the Germans are determined to arrest as many resistance fighters as they can, but know that you all are doing a hell of a job with attacks on railways, trucks, and factories."

She turned to look at the back seat for her work clothing, but she immediately noticed the car following them. They pulled over, and the car pulled behind them. When the driver lit a cigarette, Elvie could see his face illuminated by the flare from his match. Her blood ran cold. It was the captain.

"Why would he follow us?" She asked.

"Because you have rejected him at work and now you are with a German but not him. I'm afraid he will cause a problem at work for you." Heinz opened the door to walk back and talk to him, but before he could reach the car, three figures jumped into the man's vehicle, and suddenly, blood spurted from the man's head. A stranger approached Heinz from behind. He was unsure which side this man was on.

"Just take her home," an unknown voice said. "We'll make it look like he committed suicide. He was starting to dig into her family and you. We aren't sure what he was looking for, but it couldn't have been good for any of us in the long run. He needed to disappear."

Heinz didn't know who he had spoken with, but it was obvious they knew a lot more than he or Elvie did.

When he got back into the car, he noticed Elvie was pale, and her hands were trembling. The driver, one of them, slowly moved the car out into the street.

"Elvie, go to work as usual tomorrow," Heinz said. "If the Gestapo show up and ask about the captain, tell them nothing. You only took orders from him. Make yourself look busy as they talk to you. Tell them the last time you saw him, he was leaving with a French girl. If they ask you to sketch her, which they will, just make someone up."

"What about you? They will certainly know we were at dinner at the Ritz."

"That's good. We *were* there. We do not know anything about the captain. Tell them we have been engaged for a month if it comes out. We met through my brother at the church while he was visiting last month. You attend mass at Saint Anna's. It was a whirlwind romance."

They pulled in front of her apartment building, which had been in Elvie's family for generations. He leaned over and kissed her on the lips ever so gently.

"I will see you tomorrow."

She walked up to the apartment, leaned against the door, and closed her eyes. She just wanted to sleep.

There was a knock on Heinz's window. He jumped and went for his pistol.

"Good God, I could have shot you, Peter. Get in the car."

"I would hope not," Peter said. "Being shot by a Luftwaffe pilot, of all people. I'm wearing this general's uniform, which I hope he won't miss. Did you get the information tonight?"

Heinz took his hat, unzipped the inner lining and handed its contents to Peter.

"Must be important?" He asked.

"It is Heinz. Lyon is a mess right now. With this information, we are one step ahead of Vichy and the Gestapo."

They moved the car onto the street with the limited moving traffic.

"Did you know what happened with the captain?" Heinz asked.

Peter nodded. "We were afraid he would have gotten into a confrontation with you or gone up to her apartment. Either way, it was not a good scenario. They will take him to his apartment, leave him in the car, and place the gun in his hand. It doesn't matter what they try to find for a reason. You don't have to worry about Elvie. She has been in tighter situations."

They pulled in front of the apartment that the Von Rahmel family had owned for years.

"Are you coming in, Peter?"

"No. One of the cars behind us is for me. Anthony is upstairs. We left him there several hours ago."

Peter disappeared as the vehicle pulled up next to them. Heinz walked up the three flights of stairs, feeling weary and worried for Elvie.

Anthony was sitting by the window as he entered the living room. Heinz sat back in his soft favourite chair as Anthony handed him a glass of wine from their estate that they managed to get out before the Nazis took over their childhood home in Munich. Living in Berlin was not their family's favourite place, but the factories they owned were there, and they had a small home in Grunewald, in the middle of a forest, with a barn for their horses. The estate was left to the family, but no one knew for how long. They were told to hand over property to the Germans' newly installed government. So far, they have not been approached because of their operation factories.

The saving grace was that Anthony was in Berlin with his church, and the family divided their time between the Berlin apartment and the estate. Father managed to move his horses to Berlin along with some of his books and art. They had also been able to hide Mother's jewellery and quilts. She was determined not to leave it to the Nazis. Mother's sister Helena lived in Berlin, but their heartache was missing their sister Martha in England. Martha, Peter's mother, had married a British man with a great deal of wealth and title. Peter's father went on hunting expeditions with the upper ruling class.

Their estate home in Berlin was beautiful. Eighteen rooms, four bathrooms, a guest house, and state-of-the-art stables that his father insisted on. When he arrived in Berlin, Hans hired people to work in the still-standing factories before he was sent off and was a Tank Commander, and they brought all their help from Munich. They were not left behind to face an unknown fate. They were like family. Dietric was like their brothers as he was raised with the siblings and treated like one of their own. His parents were killed in a car accident in the Alps when he was just four years old. He was always helping Anthony in Berlin, moving papers to people who needed to get out of Germany or ration cards to the Jews who needed food or money. The journey to leave Munich at that time and go to the estate in Italy was not an option. Jona was a vet and needed to stay with his horses and help at the Berlin Zoo. The animals were being hurt and stressed during the war and bombings, and Jona knew in his heart that the animals would not survive the war, but he would help the zoo and farmers around him as best he could. He dreamed of returning to Munich. He missed his Alps, the fresh air, and his way of life.

Anthony was weary of going back and forth from France to Berlin, and the toll was evident on his face. But he had no choice since some of the best-forged papers were in Paris, and he desperately needed them. There was a knock on the door, and Heinz and Anthony looked at each other as concern shone in their eyes. It was awfully late for visitors. Heinz walked back to the door and looked through the peephole, relieved to see only Peter. Heinz let him in.

"I thought you were on your way to Lyon," He said as he followed Peter into the living room.

Peter saw the wine and immediately poured himself a glass, then sat opposite Anthony.

"It's dangerous to go back tonight to the Heights of Fourviere. The Gestapo are watching Lyon for any transmissions. You can't miss the fools in their black Citroens."

Anthony leaned forward, "Peter, you have got to get back to London. It's becoming too dangerous here for you."

Peter leaned his head back and slowly let the wine slide down his throat. "We have fewer safe houses now. Our agents don't seem to last more than three months here in France."

Heinz was standing looking out the window. "Peter, I promise, I will let you know any hint of safe house captures."

"Heinz, I know. I also understand how you feel. It's your country you are betraying."

Heinz turned and looked at the two men.

"I'm also protecting my family and wanting this lunatic's war to end. I can't understand the apathy of so many. They are letting the Nazis move their neighbours out in box cars."

Peter looked down into his glass.

"Heinz, there will come a time when we must move you and others to the escape line. It's not easy going over the Pyrenees to Barcelona. We have guides that we trust. We call them the passeurs. They have been rebels of the Catalan Republican Army, and they hate Hitler as much as we do.

Peter stood up. "I really need to rest. Do you mind if I take the first bedroom?"

Anthony stood as well and put his arm around Peter's shoulder. "I also need sleep," He said.

Peter looked back at Heinz, who had turned back to the window. "Anthony, you're my family. It hurts in ways I cannot explain. If they suspect Heinz, I'm not sure what would happen to him. Likely prison or execution."

No task was too great or favour too big to ask, Peter thought as he lay down on the bed, thinking of the German side of his family, especially Heinz. His family. Integrity was always tied to humanity. Peter knew it was vital for Heinz to get back to the Luftwaffe in Juvincourt. He himself needed to move on to Lyon tomorrow, but first, he had one more meeting with one of the best engravers in Paris at the passage de l'Hotel-Dieu. His papers were able to fool even the best. Peter had to check on the escape lines and radio operators. He was in awe of those who were there, especially Virginia Hall, a Baltimore socialite who was amazing at getting things done. She recruited more people and chipped away at the Vichy government. It took some convincing that Heinz was one of them, but he saved them more than once with information.

The next morning, the grey sky had a filter of dawn sunlight coming through the windows. Peter once again dressed in a general's uniform. As he left the apartment, he told Heinz and Anthony to have a safe journey. Heinz and Anthony went to Mass and then to the Louvre to check on Elvie. They were worried about her being questioned after the captain was found dead.

Elvie's heart beat faster when she saw Heinz enter the hallway to her office. Her mind had spun all night with thoughts of him. He'd stirred up desires in her that she wasn't even aware of having. She kept telling herself not to get involved; she was crazy to think of him. Heinz himself was disturbed over such instant feelings for her. They were intense. Heinz jumped at the voice behind him.

"Good God, man, I thought you were on your way to Lyon?"

"Peter, why are you here?"

"I can't leave right away," Peter said. "SS are crawling all over Paris looking for someone. I'll just stay here in a general's uniform. I won't be questioned."

Elvie walked towards them until they met in the middle of the hallway. Enough time to move to one of the exits if needed.

"Elvie, have the Gestapo been here to question you on anything?" Heinz asked.

She shook her head. Heinz was glad they hadn't told her about making the captain's death look like suicide, though. The less she knew, the better. Heinz took her hand.

"I have to return to Juvincourt tomorrow. I will find you if you move on to Lyon." There was almost a pleading in his eyes.

"Heinz, I will see you. I need to make a trip to Reims, where my father lives. It's not that far from you, maybe thirty minutes. Meet me there in a week." She gave him a piece of paper where she had already written down the address.

Peter was watching the exits with a nervous look. Elvie followed them to the door as she said goodbye. She reached up to Heinz as her lips lingered on his. She watched them walk down the street, empty as usual. The Germans had sucked the life out of Paris, causing millions to flee on June 14. She returned to the second floor to start a new day of cataloguing looted paintings and jewellery. A chill ran down her spine as she passed the captain's office.

"Halt."

She stopped and turned and saw two Gestapos. She thought they could hear her heart pounding. She kept telling herself not to panic, to stay calm. After all, she worked here.

"Mademoiselle, have you seen the captain?" A trick question since they already knew he was dead.

"Not since he left yesterday."

The Gestapo's voice was harsh, his eyes giving off a dead, beady look. His face was pale and marked with deep indentations. The other looked like a bulldog. They walked around the room, observing the art on the floor. They looked at the paperwork on her desk as she stood in the doorway, not wanting to enter the room with the two of them.

"Where have you been since you left yesterday?" the pale one asked. "Were you back at your place before curfew?"

She looked at him and stiffened her shoulders back. "No, I was not. I—"

The Gestapo raised his hand and cut her short. She stood in silence, heart pounding when she suddenly sensed Heinz and Gregory behind her. Heinz came forward and stepped in front of her.

"Why are you questioning my fiancée?" He demanded. "She was with me last night at the Ritz. You may verify my presence." Heinz felt an urge just to shoot both officers.

The Gestapo looked at Heinz with contempt. Then their eyes shifted to Gregory, who had his hand on his pistol. He was dressed in a warrant officer uniform. The Gestapo turned his attention again to Elvie.

"Mademoiselle, you say the captain did not show up for work today?"

"I did not say that. I told you I saw him last night as my fiancé came for me."

They now turned to Heinz, their eyes cold and menacing.

"Why are you in Paris and here right now?"

Heinz moved forward till he was within inches of the Gestapo's face.

"I'm here to meet with Hermann Göring. Would you like to join me and have him tell you why I'm here? Otherwise, I would suggest you leave, or Göring might think you would serve well on the Russian front."

A tense silence settled over the room. The Gestapo gave them each a long look and turned and left.

All three let out a long breath. Elvie leaned against the wall and stared at the ceiling, trying to keep the tears of fear from cascading down her face. She grabbed Heinz's arm. "They can double-check on Göring, and you must be here."

Heinz smiled. "Relax. When I got to the office to pack my items, I was asked to return here. Göring is making a surprise visit. I already met with him upstairs, where he is still looking at paintings. I told him I would look for you before I left and informed him of our relationship. Do not forget we are engaged to be married. Here, I have something for you." He reached into his pocket and produced a diamond with emeralds cut on the side, and Elvie gasped. He slid it onto her ring finger. "Now, it's not a lie." He and Elvie stared into each other's eyes for so long that Gregory cleared his throat.

"We need to leave; they might return to be belligerent."

Elvie turned to Gregory, still stunned. She didn't have words when the ring was placed on her finger. She looked at her ring again. "How did you find a ring? There are no jewellers open."

"I didn't," Heinz said. "It belonged to my mother. She gave it to me long ago to give to a woman if I ever found the right one."

"How do you know I'm the right one?"

He took her by the shoulders. Gregory was now pacing,

"I feel it. It's love at first sight."

Elvie stammered, "I'm not sure I can wear this."

"You can. If it doesn't work out or I'm killed, just give it to Peter or Anthony."

Tears filled her eyes. She placed both arms around his neck; her lips kissed his neck, then his face and then his lips. "You won my heart but restored something inside of me that I thought was gone. You fill the room with light. Real love is what I see."

"Wear the ring, Elvie. I want you to see me next week, every week, month, and year after this! I had an immediate connection with you. I have never experienced this feeling before. It's as if love goes to the far depths of the ocean with you. I don't think I have ever loved anyone as I love you right now."

"Come on, Heinz." Gregory was becoming anxious as his pacing became more hurried.

Heinz suddenly felt he couldn't leave Elvie. He took her hand. "Grab your coat and bag. Let's just leave right now."

Elvie quickly gathered her belongings in her office and left a note on her desk that she wasn't feeling well and had to leave.

She left with them as they walked with her in the middle for a few blocks to where the Citroen was waiting for them. She saw Louis behind the wheel. They drove in silence till they reached the Eighth Arrondissement.

"Where are we going?" She asked. They pulled into an alley and walked three more blocks until the reached a small building, which they entered from the side.

She was now in their shadow world, a small apartment. Peter was at a small desk; two other men were placing guns into the ceiling crawl space. This was different from the other one, where she changed clothing. There was an envelope with a map of the Underground, identification cards, small weapons being handed to several men, and the transmitter being used by an individual.

Heinz moved over to Peter. "This is all you wanted with the

weapons?"

"Yes. Your brother Edwin did well to let us know when the weapons were to be delivered. Anthony managed to move the information to us. I'm sorry, Heinz, but we also received information on the V2Rocket."

Heinz closed his eyes. "I pray Edwin does not get caught. What he is doing outside of Berlin headquarters is so dangerous. He puts the whole family in danger."

"He is careful. It's Katarina we're worried about. She is young and impressionable to this Gestapo agent who is trying to court her. The family is trying to keep him away, but she thinks she might be in love."

Gregory's head shot up. "I pray not," he interjected. "He is as evil as they come. No good will come out of it."

Elvie turned to Louis. "Has the entire Rahmel family been part of the resistance?"

He nodded. "They have been since Anthony saw the first Jew beaten."

Heinz came over to her side. "I'm sorry I moved you so quickly out of the Louvre. I just felt the farther you were from any Gestapo, the better. Now is the time if you don't want the ring or my hastily unromantic proposal."

She watched him shuffle his feet like a little boy as he looked down. "It's forever, Heinz." She took both his hands. "I'm not sure how it happened or why, but the universe and angels brought us together."

Louis came over and interrupted them.

"I think it's better to stay in Paris for now, Elvie. It will look odd if you just disappear right after the captain's death. It would draw suspicion if they come looking for you and can't find you."

"You're right. I'll go back, and if anyone saw the note, I'll just say I felt better and came back."

They looked at Peter, who was rubbing the deep lines etched on his face. "They didn't get my man out in time. He was caught and is on his way to Sachsenhausen concentration camp."

Louis patted Peter's shoulder. "I'm sorry so few of us are fighting this battle against Hitler. How France capitulated to the Germans, I will never understand. We, of course, can infiltrate better and hide better because we are the Bourgeois Catholics of our family. We are not doing too badly, I believe so far. We have had one hundred fifty acts of sabotage. I just wish we could have saved some of the Jewish children taken."

Peter shook his head. "Louis, France was still reeling after losing more than six hundred thousand of their sons in World War One. I can see why they are unenthusiastic about confronting Hitler. They didn't realise the gathering of darkness that descended upon France and other countries."

Heinz came over to Louis and Peter. "I will take Elvie back to the Louvre. She is safe with me. Walking these streets, we will take several catacombs to avoid needless attention. I still must pick up my suitcase. I have one more meeting with Dietric Von Choltitz, our military governor. It's easier to take her first, then I will return to Hotel La Meurice to meet Cholititz."

Elvie kissed her brother and the others goodbye as she and Heinz returned to the Louvre.

She grew anxious when she saw so many uniforms outside the museum, but they slipped in unnoticed.

Heinz stood at the door as she entered her office and saw the letter was still in the same spot. Thankfully, it didn't seem that anyone had seen the note saying she was sick.

"I'll be okay, Heinz. You just come back safe yourself."

"Elvie, marry me." He walked over to her and kissed her gently. She didn't resist. The taste lingered on his lips. He leaned his head into her hair and took in the smell of lavender.

"You have to get back to your Luftwaffe and Berlin. We can marry when you return. Just please return to me." She moved back from him. "It will be dangerous for us. So many will judge me for marrying a German without knowing the full story. We must keep a low profile."

It was like a sword twisted in his heart.

"Elvie, my family is different, you know this." He knew his eyes radiated pain. "We can keep it a secret."

"Heinz, it's the resistance, your missions; you could be shot down. There only needs to be one weak link, and my brothers and I could be killed. This is carelessness."

Tears welled in her eyes just thinking of the obstacles they could face. She never believed in love at first sight, but here he stood, a love entering her life so quickly.

"Let's go and see Father Duboudin. His church is not far from here. He is a family friend and one of the resistance fighters, and he will marry us." He pulled her close, "I can extend my time here by saying Dietric Von Choltitz wanted me to stay for a few more days.

He'll arrange it. I'm one of his favourites."

This was insane, she thought as she nodded her head yes.

Chapter 4

Heinz left and was back by sunset to find Elvie still at her desk. No one stopped them or asked any questions as they left. They arrived at the church, and Father Duboudin opened the door cautiously. When he saw it was Heinz, a big smile crossed his face, and he swung the door wide open and pulled them in.

"Ah, my boy, come in."

He was much older than Elvie expected, maybe in his late seventies. A shock of white hair, tall in stature, he moved slowly with a slight limp. His eyes twinkled as he grasped Heinz by the shoulders and gave him a large bear hug.

"This man, young lady, is my godchild. I have known him since he was born." He motioned for them to sit.

"Father, we are here because I want to marry her," Heinz said. "It must be in the church. I have the paperwork I need from my German commander, but it must be with you in the eyes of God."

There was silence as the priest looked at them and then the paperwork. He arched one eyebrow and levelled his gaze on Heinz.

"Does she know?"

"Yes, she's Louis's sister and is heavily involved."

"Heinz, do you feel joy in this union, in a hopeless world right now?"

"I know God will grace us again. He will not allow evil to persist. Satan only has so much power."

"But do you feel this is wise?"

Heinz took Elvie's hand. "Father, this is the most insane thing I have ever done. I can't describe how much love I have for her. After the war, we will move to Switzerland. There won't be judgment."

The priest rose slowly and hobbled across the room to get his Bible. Worry creased Heinz's brow.

"Father, your leg. Is there something we can do to help?" Heinz stood to help him.

"No worries. Your brother Anthony and I got into a bit of trouble before we left Lyon. The bullet has been removed. We couldn't get the British SOE agent out in time, but right now, the world is fragile; lies, truth, trust, extremism, left, right, and democracy are on the brink, but in all of this, we have our champions to keep it right."

He motioned for them to follow him into the church. He woke one of the sisters in the building to witness the union.

The dark church felt cold and musty. Two candles were lit at the altar. Elvie stopped momentarily as she was walking over to the altar. Was she crazy after only knowing this man for a few weeks? A German no less. "God," she prayed silently, "give me grace." She turned and saw Heinz staring at her.

He put his arm around her shoulder. "I promise you a grand wedding with a white gown, flowers, and music one day. I promise."

She nodded as they made their way to the altar and saw a nun scampering from the back of the church, adjusting her habit as she ran. Her face was angelic as she stood beside Elvie and Father performing a short ceremony.

The words spoken were tender as they recited vows of marriage. The priest looked at them, their faces so full of hope as he read:

Roman 4:20-21

Yet he (Abraham) did not waver through unbelief regarding the promise of God but was strengthened in his faith and gave glory to God, being fully persuaded that God had power to do what he had promised.

Father Duboudin wished them happiness as he finished and had Heinz and Elvie sign the marriage certificate.

He and the sister watched them leave the church. Father Duboudin hung his head low as he said his own private prayer for their safety, but a chill came down his back.

Heinz gave Elvie a long kiss outside the church, the darkness of the street providing them cover.

"Elvie, we'll go back to my apartment. Fewer people to talk to and judge. There are too many peering eyes at your apartment."

She was stunned when she entered. The apartment was full of luxury, every room eloquently decorated. She entered each, checking how many rooms were on this floor. In the distance, she saw the Eiffel Tower. How beautiful it would be all lit up.

She sat on a soft sofa and put her feet up on the ottoman. The sofa was a light peach with beautiful green Queen Anne chairs facing her. The oriental rug almost covered the whole living room. Heinz had disappeared after telling her he would be right back.

She leaned her head back and closed her eyes. She heard him return, and he brought in a tray filled with cheese, fresh rolls, and red wine, a luxury. She almost felt guilty knowing how many were standing in line with ration cards, including herself. She smuggled bread and old tea bags to friends who were Jewish and hadn't been given ration cards.

"Heinz, may I take a few pieces of cheese to give to my neighbour tomorrow?"

"You may take anything you want in this apartment except my father's old books and this rug."

She laughed softly. "I promise only food."

"Elvie, before I leave, I will make sure you have a basket of food to fill your cabinet. But may I suggest you stay here?" He poured the wine into the crystal glasses, held it up, and looked at the colour as he swirled it into the crystal glass. "From our estate in Italy. I can't wait to take you there. Between the olives and the smell of fresh lemons, it is heaven. We might even think of settling there, and I can help my parents with the wine business. I thought Switzerland, but I think the sun in Italy would be good for both of us."

He saw she was flushed and quiet. "Regretting this, Elvie? I promise I will take care of you. I love you forever."

She swallowed hard as tears rolled down her face.

He took her hand and kissed the soft skin. He stood. "Come, Elvie."

The tenderness he showed was like no other man she had encountered. This was what she'd been waiting for. He was her first. He slowly unbuttoned her blouse as he kissed her exposed shoulders. He led her to the bedroom with a large, four-poster bed with expensive quilts. The sheets smelled like fresh spring flowers. He helped her out of her clothing, and she helped him out of the uniforms. His hands were so strong but so gentle as he touched her intimately. She felt so much love and joy, as if she was floating. As he kissed each part of her body, it was an awakening with fresh thrills. Through the night, he whispered every second he could that he loved her.

Afterwards, she lay in his arms as if they had known each other for years. She had her head on his chest, and he placed his hands around her.

"Elvie, I've loved you since the moment I saw you in the bakery. I know it sounds absurd."

"I felt the same way, but I tried to fight it. You won me over with those eyes."

They slept till they heard the birds chirping. She woke slowly and just lay there and whispered.

"Heinz, I need to go to work, so there is no suspicion." She stared into his eyes. "You know, I dreamt I found you." She kissed him swiftly on the lips and got out of bed.

"Come back here after work," Heinz said. "My sister Katarina is the same size as you. She has a full wardrobe, and you can find some things to wear for the week." He changed into his uniform so he could walk her to work.

The walk was a little tense, with Elvie receiving dirty looks for being with a German. When they heard the shouting, they were ready to part ways at the Louvre. A woman was clutching her children as they were being pushed into a van. Elvie stifled her cry. She had seen this play out too many times. She hated the sign of the yellow star on their clothing. Heinz pulled her closer as he saw her face go pale. Her eyes swelled with tears. The first roundup was her butcher two doors from her. Every roundup, her heart shattered.

Their first involvement was when Louis heard that the bookshop in his neighbourhood would be raided and the owners taken. He watched France change, his Paris turn dark, and they began their work. He quickly moved the shop owners to Lyon with identification papers. It seemed an eternity ago. What made it more sickening to all of them was the fact that most of the French police were in on it.

Elvie shook her head trying to remove the cobwebs of when it all started. She watched Heinz make the sign of the cross as he turned her away from the scene.

So many bakeries, butchers, and beautiful flower shops shuttered… All because the owners were Jewish or had Jewish blood lines.

The hate came in full force by the resistance when, in 1941, la rafle du Vel' d'Hiv' roundup began. Jewish children under sixteen years old, along with some non-Jews, were violently arrested. It was then they started to move those they could. Then, the Jesuit priest entered the picture, and the sisters hid as many children as they could. Anthony, too, was moving Jews and others out of Berlin. They met him on the journey with Father Julian when they were moving children to a convent outside of Lyon. In 1940, Anthony had managed to move Jews to France as refugees, never thinking it would come to this. In Saint Georges, France, Henri and Gabriella moved dozens of children with new identifications into a network known as Circuit Garel.

It was the first time Elvie became involved with moving identification papers in art pieces or hiding art and jewellery.

They worked with Anthony as Elvie took identification papers to Lyon for Henri so they could save an entire family before they were rounded up. She hadn't yet met Anthony, and she quickly grew to love this gentle, unwavering man. They had received a great deal of information regarding who was to be sent to a concentration camp called Venissieur. Anthony was working with Father Alexandre Glasberg of the Amitie Chretienne organization. Peter thought Elvie was the perfect fit to go back and forth because of the art dealings when she met them. She was fluent in several languages, and she was stunning to look at. She moved identification papers for Jews and agents of the SOE for Allied pilots in hiding.

Many children were moved to Catholic boarding schools, homes, and orphanages. Many, if not all, were baptized Catholic or Lutheran. The trauma of losing their parents and siblings was difficult for many. She watched Louis, Anthony, and Father Julian holding the children many times in their arms, giving comfort. So many parents, in their despair, knew that handing their children over was the only answer. So many would lose their identity for life and never know of their Jewish heritage because they were adopted and had baptismal papers.

It was on one of those visits to Lyon where Elvie met the beautiful Katarina. She was helping to smuggle papers to the Federation of Jewish Societies of France (Federation des Societes Juives de Franco, established in 1913).

The FSJS leaders thought it best to leave occupied France for unoccupied Southern France. It was only now, in 1942, being set up as an absorption center in the part of France occupied by Italy where Jews were protected from Nazi and French authorities.

In Le Chambron Surlignon, pastors felt it was their Christian obligation to save Jewish children. It was at this time Elvie met Gregory, Anthony, and Katarina. There had been a large sweep of almost 13,000 Jews at once. To Anthony's dismay, Switzerland forced many Jews back to France. In fact, some 10,000 returned to France and to their deaths.

It was always a horror to see the belongings left behind: clothing, jewellery, homes filled with memories, livestock, along with many pets. They tried to get them as many ration cards as possible for those not yet arrested. They had no meat, milk, bread, or warm clothing.

Elvie's journey seemed a lifetime ago. Under her desk, the floorboard was nailed down, hiding jewellery with the addresses and names for returning it. As she sat in the cold office, she wished Heinz had not left. She put her head on the desk, and tears fell on the hard mahogany wood.

She sat up after a good cry at her desk, her head in her hands, and thought back to her beginnings with the resistance. It was when Henri and Gabriella came to her in her office. It seemed a lifetime ago. Her memory cast deeply in her mind.

The first few years with Elvie and the Resistance

Elvie met Gabriella and Henri who came to her office and sat on the sofa with a nervous look.

"We have two infants," Henri said, "a two-year-old and a three-month-old now at our home. We need to move them to Lyon, from there, Louis and his friends will help."

"Who are the children?" Elvie recalled asking, wondering how they'd come to have children who weren't theirs.

Henri sighed. "Their parents were rounded up as they went

looking for food. They'd left the children in the next apartment for safe keeping. When they returned to their apartment, the Gestapo was waiting."

"Henri, how will I ever explain what I am doing with two children?"

"You can say you took them because your sister-in-law was sick. It was important for you to deliver some jewellery to one of the museums. We have the paperwork ready for you to move them."

Elvie stared at the floor, trying to process what they were asking of her. Gabriella's voice cut into her thoughts.

"You know their parents will likely not survive. If they do, they can come back to their children. We must move them out of Paris. We are not sure how much the Gestapo knows about the children in the neighbourhood. The neighbour will not say a word. She is a devout Catholic and fears hell more than the Gestapo."

From the corner of her eye, Elvie saw two French policemen approaching the office door. She motioned to Henri and Gabriella to stand up and study the paintings on her desk as well as the ones against the wall that were stacked and had not been catalogued yet.

The policemen came into the office area. Two little fat men with bloated faces and dirty uniforms. They looked around and motioned to Henri to come closer.

"What's your business here?" One of them asked, and before Henri could answer, they heard a voice behind them. The captain suddenly appeared.

"You two, out of this office. You will make an appointment the next time you enter this building with me."

One of the officers had the nerve to talk back. "We are checking the papers of everyone working in established museums."

"I have her papers. You two out." He motioned them to leave. They left like dogs with tails between their legs.

The captain now turned his attention to the three of them. He pointed to Henri and Gabriella. "Who are they?" Elvie's insides trembled.

"My brother," Elvie said, fighting to keep her voice from shaking. "He's a doctor here in Paris, and he was checking on me because I told him I felt sick yesterday." She smiled and shook her head. "He always looks after his little sister. I had only a slight fever. Come see what they also brought with them, Captain." She motioned toward her desk. "They have donated a small painting of Frederick Bazille from Montpellier. It's from the same time he did the *Pink Dress* in 1864. He was only twenty-three years old with so much talent."

The captain's eyebrows shot up. "Would it be something Göring would like?" He stepped forward and studied the painting on the floor next to her desk.

"I believe he might." It was a lie, of course, telling him the painting was his brother's. He studied her.

"Why have they donated it? Elvie, you are part of the Bourgeoisie Marquis de Lafayette very few of the wealthy have given up anything. Do you not trace your family back to the twelfth century? You come from the house of Bourbons, from the last king of France. Your family-owned chateau still has exquisite chandeliers, beautiful rugs, and plenty of works in the gardens, designed with beautiful pavilions and grand stables perched on a hill. The generals occupying it now say it is just grand. So, I must ask, why would you all give up a painting from your home?"

Henri stepped forward. "We are not giving it up, Captain. We were told if we had paintings of value to bring them here." The captain stared at them. Then he walked over to the desk and looked at the uncatalogued paintings. He stared straight at Elvie as he shouted.

"All right, I think you and your wife should leave now."

Elvie could feel his breath on her neck as he was now standing behind her.

"I will make sure the right people know of your generosity. Now go. I have unfinished business here."

They hesitated to leave but Henri saw the look in Elvie's eyes and knew it was best.

"We were hoping to find favour with the German government," Henri spoke up. "There are times I need more medications at my clinic, and many of your soldiers have given me a visit because of unclean prostitutes. I run low on medicine."

"I will make a note, Doctor."

As Henri and Gabriella left, they looked back several times.

"Elvie, show me this painting that arrived today," the captain said. She bent over the desk to bring up the painting. He caught her by the waist and pressed his body against hers. He put his lips on her neck. She froze as his hand brushed the side of her, coming down to her thigh as he pulled up her skirt and reached for her private parts. She closed her eyes and wanted it to be over. He turned her around to face him, his sloppy lips now on hers as he groped every part of her and would not let his lips leave her. He had now unbuttoned her blouse as he laid his hands on her. She knew she couldn't pull back. All the while wishing she could kill him.

He pulled her down to the floor, and she closed her eyes as he unbuttoned his trousers and pulled up her skirt. Suddenly, footsteps came down the hall, and a voice called for him. Elvie closed her eyes as he got off her and pulled her up by the arm. She stood in front of him as he ran his hands down her one more time.

"Make yourself presentable, mademoiselle."

She curled her hand around the letter opener, wishing she could plunge it through his heart.

"There you are, Captain," a young soldier said, appearing in the doorway. "We have been looking for you. You must come and see the new shipment. The Jews in this house had a fortune in paintings, jewellery, and very good rugs."

Elvie turned her back to the soldier as she buttoned her blouse and pretended to be looking at the paperwork.

"I will be right down." He turned to Elvie. "Next time, Elvie, you will be more receptive. Admit it to me now that you liked it."

She swallowed hard. "Yes, next time, Captain."

"There is a cocktail party I want you to attend this weekend."

Elvie nearly gagged. She thought fast for an excuse. "Captain, I promised my elderly father I would visit. I'm sure you understand. You've often mentioned that you wish you could see your parents in Germany." She prayed this would work.

He walked back and yelled for the soldier to leave. Her heart sank. He wasn't satisfied with her answer. He put his hands on her waist and kissed her harder than last time.

"I have a few minutes left," He said, pulling her to the sofa and pushing her down. This time, she wasn't lucky. He touched her all over, kissed her hard on the lips, then down every inch of exposed skin. She shivered with disgust but would not cry. If she objected, he could have her sent to a work camp. She kept her eyes closed till he was done. He repeated this several times a week, and she would only cry when he left. He never consummated the act, always staying on the outside, leaving her untouched by a man.

"I will allow it this time for you to leave. But don't refuse me next time." He left the office.

She immediately dressed herself, wiping off anything that felt like his saliva or his manhood. She put on her coat and left the building, her whole body shaking as she kept wiping the memory of him off her lips. This was the worst among the times he had approached her, but what was she going to do? She didn't want him to touch her again, but she had to stay in this position. She was helping those who did not have any help.

She stopped to vomit as she stepped into an alley. She wanted revenge, but how?

She met with Henri and Gabriella at 31 Rue De Cambon First Arrondissement, where they had told her they'd be waiting. Together, they backtracked to Angelina's tearoom. Gabriella clutched her hand, and she could feel Elvie trembling and saw the paleness in her face. She squeezed her hand, wanting Elvie to know she understood.

The owner knew them and moved them to a back room away from the German officers. He brought his famous pudding over and promised to bring them hot chocolate. They closed their eyes as they took small spoonfuls. Dressed in a powder-blue suit, Coco Channel sat at table ten with Baron Hans Gunther Von Dincklage and one other officer. The Germans left this place to themselves because of the refined, elegant mosaic floors. It was a glorious place; the décor was Belle Epoque, and it had marble-topped tables.

Hemingway used to frequent here before the war and before the shadow of evil came upon them with propaganda stickers plastered over beautiful buildings. The lights were out in Paris, replaced with fear, hunger, and hate.

"This is a little obvious for Henri to come, but he had delivered the owner's babies at birth, and they were friends. It was like sitting here in the middle of a viper's nest," Gabriella said. Elvie heard one French woman complain the chocolate was not up to par on the meringue.

Elvie clenched her fist as she looked at the woman eating with a German. She prostitutes herself for food and a better life right now, but it will not be forgotten. She was no different than the girls who worked the brothel or herself, she thought, as she had to let the captain have his way to survive.

"Henri, who are you looking for?" She asked. Gabriella just looked nervous.

"I was hoping Louis would come. He had a German Luftwaffe pilot who was to join us, who was part of the resistance. It would be a good connection for you."

Elvie frowned. "Henri, can you trust him."

"If Louis does, I will also."

"Why worry about me meeting him?" Elvie asked

"He is a German Luftwaffe Pilot but working with our resistance. He was able to get the Baron Buren to give us more medical supplies."

"Did he manage to give you poison so they can die in their misery?"

She looked at Gabriella, so quiet and pale and thin. Her big blue eyes stood out against her dark brown hair. She and Henri had been together since he met her in Lyon, working at a hospital. She was a nurse, and Henri was a good surgeon. They fell in love, got married, and decided to work with the resistance. Once the Germans entered Paris, they had one child, a three-year-old.

Henri works in private practice now. His home and clinic on Avenue Foch had not been requisitioned, and he worked a lot with an American doctor, helping POWs who were languishing in prisons. Henri was a gentle soul, but Elvie knew that he, Gabrielle, and Louis were bitter that not one shot was fired as the Germans entered Paris. So many Parisians left with as many personal belongings as possible. They let their pets go or killed them, not knowing what their fate would be if the Nazis got them. Clothing and other belongings were strewed on the streets and the forest on their way out.

They were fighting in their own way now. Father Julian and Henri made sure those who needed to leave had the proper identification papers. Henri would move them to the church, where Father Anthony or Gregory was there to take them to the border of Spain or Switzerland.

Elvie had not met Anthony; she was anxious to have an encounter with him.

The owner brought the hot chocolate and placed it in front of them.

"Henri, we can't afford this," Gabriella whispered.

"It's all good, Gabriella. Louis took care of it and paid before being called away." The Germans only knew Louis as one of the Paris police officers.

They sipped slowly as they cherished the sweet taste. They'd almost forgotten how good hot chocolate was.

Elvie looked over her cup and murmured, "Why am I here?"

"We need you to take an infant and two-year-old to Lyon," Henri said. "Gregory will go with you and pretend to be the father."

"Why?" She whispered.

"Their parents were taken. Luckily, the children were with a neighbor. The Gestapo and SS were removing Jews who had any influence or wealth, and both the Gerons were bankers. They were out to dinner and were arrested when they returned home. The neighbour watched from the window. The next morning, she went to the church, and the information got through to us." Henri sighed. "When you reach Lyon, Gregory and Anthony's sister Katarina will continue the journey until they get to Geneva. If it seems they can't move them, they will leave them in the town of Kreisau with the church.

"You are the most obvious pick to take them because you can always say you were picking up art or taking art to Lyon. We have two priests to help you. We just moved twenty-five Jews to Le Chambon sur Lignon to be hidden. Father Julian and Pastor Andre Trocme are risking their lives."

Elvie saw the sorrow on Gabriella's face.

Father Anthony and Father Julian were already in Lyon waiting for the children. They were working with several Jesuit priests and the French resistance, and they didn't feel guilty if they needed to resort to protecting the innocent. Father Anthony and Father Julian were engaged in a spiritual and theological understanding of how to fight anti-Nazi activities. They both hated anti-Semitism; they agreed it was incompatible with Christianity, and they were not going to follow the Vichy and Marshal Petain's Government.

Most priests and Protestant clergy did not fall in line and went without the papal decree. The courage from pastor Marc Boegner, president of the Federation Protestant, was the first to raise the alarm to go against the Vichy anti-Jewish platform. Then followed the Jesuits, nuns, and those who pretended to be friends with the Vichy as they hid Jews in their homes.

Can we leave some of this for a history lesson Fwith Henri slowly sipped the chocolate "Elvie, you need to know this. I will always remember Father Anthony's voice as he said in his church, 'When one member of the human race suffers, the entire body suffers with him.' The Gestapo were standing at the back of his church when he spoke. From that point on, they were watched." Henri took another sip of his chocolate. "Elvie, tell me, you will consider."

Elvie had moved children for the resistance before. Now, her head came up as she wiped off the tears she had shed recalling that first day.

Henri and Gabriella could not leave Paris. A doctor leaving his practice would be too suspicious. So, it was up to Elvie, Heinz, and Anthony.

Elvie arranged to be off from work by telling the captain she was going to Lyon to look at some paintings that had arrived at one of the churches and wanted to bring back. She asked with a smile, knowing he wouldn't decline her request; the more artwork he could give to Hitler, the better the chances of him being recognized.

Elvie added, "If you would like to join me," praying he would say no. His eyes lifted until she told him she was going to take her nephew with her to give her brother a little break. He decided not to. This time, she was able to leave his office without his abuse. He hadn't bothered her since her involvement with Heinz.

The captain arranged her travel papers and made her come to the office to receive them. He came from around the desk before she could reach for the signed paperwork, and the same dance began. He whispered he would miss her and was grateful she would bring back the art while sliding his hands over her body. He kissed her hard on the mouth while pinning her down on his sofa. She closed her eyes until he finished, as he asked her repeatedly if her young pilot touched her in the same way.

She left with tears falling freely down her cheeks. *One day*, she thought. *His day will come, but not today.*

She went to church the next morning as she slept poorly through the night. Heinz had to leave Paris, and she had not heard from him. She left the apartment at dawn, keeping the travel papers close to her inside her coat pocket.

The children were waiting for her at the church. She heard the cry of the baby and looked down into that precious face. He was too thin, she thought. She picked up the older child and kissed him gently on the cheek while telling him she was his Mommy for the next couple of days. They both had wide, large blue eyes. They looked like little angels, and she wanted to cry, thinking they would never know their parents. If, by some miracle the parents survived, they knew where to come to find out the information. But in her heart, she knew the children would never see them. Their identity, their heritage, their religion would be wiped away overnight. But they would live.

The Citroën was available to them. Gregory moved the stroller to the car, and Elvie sat with the baby on her lap in the front and made a small bed for the older one in the back. The Gestapo stopped them once and looked through their paperwork over and over before asking them to get out of the car. They woke the baby up as they searched the car. The Gestapo's demeanour changed as he looked at the baby, and he tucked the blanket around the child, telling her to go back to sleep.

Maybe he had a heart, Elvie thought. Having the travel documents from the captain explaining the reason for their journey added an extra layer of security.

Finally, they arrived at Simon's, where Peter, Anthony and Katarina were waiting. Simon pulled the carriage out and immediately looked for the hidden compartments.

The children were taken into the back bedroom and tucked in for sleep. Katarina and Anthony were in the kitchen making coffee. It was weak but a luxury to them all, as Simon still had unwavering inroads with the Gestapo. Elvie watched Gregory, his eyes staring at Katarina; it was a longing she had seen in a man deeply in love.

Peter came in with the paperwork. "Everything that we need is here. The forger did a fantastic job." He turned to Katarina and Anthony. "You won't have an ounce of trouble travelling with these documents."

As Anthony and Gregory studied the documents, Peter shook his head.

"I need to get back to London. This war is moving into a brutal phase, and we need more operatives and transmitters. It seems no one lasts more than four months over here before being caught or going into hiding. We worry all the time. There might be a double agent in our midst in Paris. I think now is the time to escape over the Pyrenees into Spain. One of our agents and two fliers that bailed need to be moved. We're moving the agent who gave us the information about the double agent because he was caught up with a woman. He was sleeping with her, and she was working for the Germans.

"He almost gave her our agents, but there was something that made him wake up and realize who she was, and he told us. She had already sent the names of some and got four of our agents shot. She also got some French resistance fighters caught and shot. She got caught sleeping with another agent when she mentioned him to our present agent, and thankfully, he put two and two together.

"As of right now, we are good, especially here at Simon's. Last week, we were concerned. We were all hiding when he invited the Gestapo and some of the Vichy officers for dinner. They sat up there and had a meal and wine. We had them here, thinking we could keep this place away from suspicion. We could hear one of the Gestapo, who had drunk a lot of wine, yelling at the others that spies were going back and forth from Lyon to Paris and all over France. They needed to be sought and killed.

"We set up our own Machiavellian scheme. We had this same officer fall for one of our agents. He's an alcoholic, so it wasn't hard to get him to drink. She would take the keys and go into his locked desk, pull the files, and transmit the information of where they had blockades, what agents were caught and who they were looking for."

"My Agent S made sure I received the information so we would send it to London and make sure not to drop transmitters or agents at certain times and places. We also found the identity of the Paris double agent with whom Ryan had been. Her name is Lola Chattee. She's a traitor of the worst kind. We hunted her down and executed her. Ryan, in the meantime, needs to get out of France because we don't need the Gestapo figuring it out."

Louis turned to Elvie. "When you return to Paris, change your route every day when going to and from work."

Katarina turned and whispered to Anthony, "I need to get back to Berlin also." Katarina was only there because Heinz had invited Anthony and her. She'd perform in a small dance for the higher-ups, which she accomplished before they left for Lyon. This was her first visit to Paris and Lyon. She'd had been in Paris many times at their apartment in happier times. "They will question the Ballet Meister about where I am. Frederick has already questioned the fact I did not see him for eight days. I told him I was very sick in bed. This time, I told him Heinz invited us to join him to meet the higher-ups, which is the truth."

Simon came back into the kitchen with bread and cheese that he had hidden in his basement. The Gestapo had a habit of going through his kitchen, looking for more wine and food when they came, and they drank too much. Simon now hid what he had. The cabinets looked almost barren. He managed to find more food for a favor from the Gestapo. Dinners were always sumptuous, taken from some poor farmer, most likely or baker in town.

The baby cried, and Katarina left the room to see what the

problem was. The poor thing was most likely scared and confused about where its mother was. Katarina brought the infant back into the kitchen, and they found milk to give her.

Anthony was sewing the papers he needed to return with into his frock. Some were for Edwin's wife and brother and her parents to get them to Switzerland and his own parents. They knew it was becoming more dangerous for both brothers Edwin and Heinz.

Anthony, pacing and rubbing his eyes, motioned to Peter to sit.

"Peter, sit. You are making yourself a nervous wreck."

"I know. It's been difficult keeping the network together from here to the coast and the Swiss border."

Anthony opened a new envelope. It was from Father Julian, asking him to give the included fake ration cards to a pastor who would meet them at his rectory when he returned to Berlin.

Julian's note told Anthony to be safe, and God be with him. Another priest was arrested and he was taken to the Perigueor jail. Anthony shuddered. The devil was working overtime, he thought. The prison was the devil's torture chamber.

Elvie was sitting next to Peter, and she laid her hand on his. "Peter, be safe! I pray we all will survive." Her eyes were deep in worry. "Henri and Gabriella are taking so many chances. Louis is filled with so much hate; he's on a mission to kill as many Germans as he can. His conflict is deep with Anthony and Heinz as his friend, which I can identify with."

Peter patted her hand. "We have no guarantees of the outcome of the resistance, Elvie. We can only try to defeat evil."

Elvie looked over at Anthony and Katarina. The baby in her arms had made little fists and kicked her tiny legs. She had the biggest smile on her face as she made cute baby noises. She was so thin, she didn't have the rosy cheeks most babies had. Elvie just wanted to sit and cry as she watched Katarina and Anthony talk to the little one.

Gregory watched Katarina with longing, Elvie thought as she looked at him. She knew he was in love with this girl. Who wouldn't be? Katarina was breathtaking; her pale skin with those large violet eyes, long lashes, high cheekbones, and incredibly long, silver-blond hair fell to her waist and tied simply with a bow. She was even thinner than the average dancer; her collarbones stuck out under the sweater. Her beauty was not something anyone could describe. It was captivating and unique. "Katarina, let me take the baby for a while and have some food," Elvie suggested.

Katarina handed the baby over, but not before planting a kiss on her cheek. Gregory walked over and sat next to her.

"Katarina, are you still ok with the plans tomorrow? Our paperwork says, husband and wife." She smiled sweetly. "Of course, it could change, and Nicholas will take you."

"Are you not the lucky one to have been married in twenty-four hours to two different women?"

He ran his fingers against her soft cheek. "You're the only one that matters, Katarina."

Katarina blushed and kissed him softly on his lips. "I'm honoured to be the second wife."

Elvie and Peter watched Gregory's reaction. His eyes were suddenly filled with anguish and worry. Peter went to talk to Anthony, who was in deep discussion with Simon. Peter caught bits and pieces as Simon explained that his wife was working in Paris with the resistance for a time but now he hoped she had made her way to Switzerland. He hadn't heard from her; his daughter and son were in boarding school in Switzerland. He couldn't get his wife Amelia to leave, so they compromised to have his daughter stay in Switzerland. The Germans thought his wife was also in Switzerland.

Anthony looked momentarily startled. Peter and Elvie didn't understand the look of sudden despair on his face. They only heard Anthony say to Simon that he knew a woman named Amelia once, long ago when he was just entering the seminary. His eyes had this faraway look as he recalled that time so long ago. It was a common name. What were the chances?

Chapter 5

Elvie sat next to Anthony as he leaned his head back in the Queen Anne chair and closed his eyes. He took her hand.

"Bless you, Elvie, for doing this. I know many of us have a spiritual resistance whenever we realize there is a great need to fight this evil that has descended upon us." He studied her troubled expression. "What is it?"

"Father, the fact we are saving children is a good thing. But at the same time, they will never know their true heritage since we are changing their names and their religion, making them Lutheran and Catholic. Will they ever know the truth?"

Anthony sighed. "I doubt it. Many of their family members are dead. They have nowhere to go. We can't send them all to Palestine or the United States. They need to be saved now. They will have loving families that will raise them."

They saw Simon pulling in one of the resistance fighters, Jacques, in the dining room as Peter followed. Elvie jumped as the wind scraped the tree branches against the window. The moon was bright, and she pulled her sweater tighter around her. She and Anthony watched as Simon, Peter, and Jacques discussed deeply. Peter returned to the living room and grabbed his backpack from the corner.

Anthony stood, took quick strides, and asked him what was happening.

"I must leave now," Peter said. "You and Gregory go with Simon. Our plans have been delayed by a day. Katarina and Elvia will stay here with the babies. We might have Nicholas drive with the two of you later instead of Gregory."

Simon cleared his throat. Anthony, they are under my protection here. The Nazis like their wine and food too much to dare come here without me here. Back at the Louvre, we will make sure of it. Elvie will give them an excuse that she is not feeling well and needs an extra few extra days off. A message will be sent."

They heard the front door slam as the strong winds from outside swept leaves into the parlour. Heinz entered, and Elvie's heart skipped a beat as she rushed over to him. He walked to the fireplace and warmed his hands, taking Elvie's in his own. Katarina immediately went to the kitchen and brought him a hot cup of coffee.

Heinz asked Peter and Simon to wait.

"I was on my way back to Paris when I heard one of our officers say they suspected the resistance to become stronger out of Lyon. I'll take Elvie back to Paris with me. She doesn't need to raise suspicion by being gone too long. We'll prepare our own story." Heinz looked at Anthony. "All of you need to leave for Berlin now. Get the babies where they need to be. Any delay might bring all of you under scrutiny. Edwin sent me a message that even now, he worries about his activity in Berlin. Anthony, you need to get back to your parish."

Heinz knew he was putting himself in danger just by being here in Lyon and not going straight back to Paris.

Simon came forward. "He's right. We need to change plans. The journey will be safe, Anthony. We will make sure of it. But first, we must move to Grenoble, then on to some business in Avignon. The Jesuits are under Nazi scrutiny in Avignon. They need our help with some false documents." He saw the worry etched into Peter's forehead and slapped him on the back. "Relax, my friend, we have a great collaborative group of rescuers who are helping me in Berlin and Munich. Anthony will be fine."

Peter looked at Anthony, who was in deep discussion with Heinz.

"Simon, my cousin, is theological and spiritually against Hitler and his evil manic followers. He started against them in 1939 and has been on their radar since. The Nazis hate the Dominicans and the Jesuits since they've had the loudest objections. Simon, Anthony is like my brother, even closer than the rest of the family. You can trust him with your life."

Gregory joined them in the parlour and spoke to Peter. "Anthony needs to take it down a few notches. He's becoming too visible in Berlin. The Gestapo Frederick Spitz is up to no good, trust me."

Anthony cleared his throat. They turned to see him with a sheepish grin on his face. "I promise I'll lay low for a while. You are right; we have one Gestapo in Berlin who is part of Satan's followers. Frederick Spitz is trying to get to us by wooing Katarina."

Gregory's face appeared like stone granite, and his eyes focused on her in the other room.

Anthony turned to Simon. "We might not be blowing up the bridges right now, but we will display our civil disobedience regardless of the consequences. What we are seeing is unbearable. Many of us are not part of the Catholic hierarchy or in bed with Petain. Too many in the Vatican allowed the Jews to be stripped of jobs and their freedom of movement. They have disappeared on trains and been murdered. We have voices that speak out as Roland de Pury, who spoke out for his church. Many are braver here in France, like Pastor March Boegner. The President of the Federation Protestant spoke out brilliantly against Vichy's anti-Jewish legislation. That is when many nuns and priests in Germany and Berlin started to help even more. It's a lot harder in Berlin since we are trying without a papal decree."

Peter cleared his throat. "Why are we all standing here? Let's go back into the living room, get our things together, and plan an exit."

They sat in the living room, where they could notice if headlights came up the long path. From this vantage point, if they saw lights, that would give them enough time to hide. The secret door that opened into another room was next to the fireplace. They could hide in there if they needed to. The hidden room was filled with weapons, fake uniforms, and explosives. They had a printer and transmitter, ration cards, and documents ready to use. The car was just one of their resistance fighters ready to move them as he had acquired an official car, stolen, of course.

Anthony had all the paperwork he needed to use in Berlin, and Peter had all the false papers he needed to help flyers and himself. At great risk, Anthony worked with one of the finest German theology and philosophy teachers in the Jesuit school at Fourviere. He had managed, in his own demanding and reserved way, to have Father Henri de Lubac and other theologians from Fourviere to help by printing the theological opposition to Nazism. Anthony was proud to distribute the information in Berlin and Munich. Anthony and Father Pierre Chaillet were close friends. He had admired him since 1930 as he taught classes that Anthony took part in as well in Austria and Rome. He saw early on that Nazism would be a Satan. He had spoken often with Anthony in 1940, especially when Anthony was in Poland and saw the many arrests. He told Anthony he must act against the internment of all people and those who oppose Hitler. He must act against the Jews being arrested. It had to be his calling. He had to help and could not look the other way as priests and pastors. He had a responsibility to stand up as others' rights were threatened. Anthony took this to heart, and his mission started.

Peter cleared his throat. "Anthony, this was one reason they were going to Grenoble. Father Aube, Jesuit Chaplain, wants us to pick up other clandestine documents for her churches." Peter lowered his head. "He also has information on where we need to blow up a bridge and how to bring ammunition into France via a certain railway. Father Julian will meet up with us enroute to de Limoges. His fellow priest friend, Father Jean Fleury, will deliver to us a Jewish scientist with the help of Rabbi Elie Blocch who knows the scientist. We need to move him back to Britain. The Germans want to force him to keep developing weapons and radar.

"Helen Marzellier is a senior clerk at the prefecture. She gives us information as she has prior knowledge of shipments, plans of fighters that will be arrested, and the Jews she has worked with. She knows he needs to move; he has information on a V2 rocket development and radar development. Father Fleury will help us move him through a path to allow Jews to pass through the Free Zone, the same escape route we are using in Spain for allied aviators."

Anthony looked like he was about to interrupt, but Peter held up a hand. "We have safe houses along the way to hide. In fact, many of the peasants help us at farms along the way. Father Roger Braun moved him once, as he is working diligently with Chief Rabbi

Abraham Deutsch in Limoges. They are also moving children to Switzerland and Spain, some to Portugal."

Heinz was leaning against the fireplace and started to pace back and forth. "Peter, be careful. The Gestapo have already heard of the 'Trap of Saint Mary of the Desert." It's a haven for Jews and non-Jews alike. They are moving them into convents and hospitals. Bishop Mgr. Jules-Geraud Saliege is helping to facilitate the passage of allied fliers and others to Spain. I heard he might be on the Radar of the Gestapo." Peter spoke

"We have the professor waiting for us," Peter said. "We must move him to the College of Saint Joseph in Avignon, where he can be hidden for a while. Father Jean Roche will hide him till we arrive. He makes his office available to all of us as drop mailboxes. He helps distribute the newspaper La Voix du Vatican; they take the Voice of the Vatican and reproduce it into French with their own take on the interpretation."

Peter looked at all of them. Each would be going their own way.

"It's time, Peter," Simon said. "We must move at dawn. There's a bridge that needs to be blown up. Let's get a few hours of sleep. The next few days will be a matter of life and death."

Dawn came and Simon was packing ammunition into large bags. He gave his first bag to Heinz to give to Henri in Paris. "You can leave the bag at Fathers of Notre Dame de Sion, and Sisters of the Visitations will pick it up."

"Our priests are walking a tight rope," Henri said. "Many have been arrested, sent to camps, or executed on the spot."

Simon put his hand on his shoulder. "Between you and me, you also must concentrate on getting your family out of Berlin. Especially

Edwin's wife. I don't think the false baptismal papers will help her. I'm telling you, Fredrick Spitz is the evil circling your family."

Chills ran down Heinz's back, and he grabbed Simon's hand. "Have you heard something?"

Simon looked at Heinz's face with sadness. "It's just a rumour, but Frederick Spitz is aiming for your family. He's courting your sister. Katarina seems in many ways to be a very naïve young woman."

Heinz nodded. "Edwin should be able to warn us if there is impending doom."

Simon cleared his throat and looked down at the floor. "Be careful about your own safety, too. I know Anthony thinks there will be this Christian reawakening because of the activities of all of us in France, but it's naïve to think this war is over. Most of our priests are outside of the Vatican's thinking. There is no clear voice from the Vatican regarding whom to protect or outrage what is happening. I think those of us, along with Anthony and other priests are on their own making decisions. We can't wait for the bishops, cardinals, and the Pope to decide to save people."

Heinz ran his hand through his hair and stopped for a moment as he moved items into bags. "Simon, you know us well enough that our family does not believe in the Nazi ideology. We are trying, I promise, to get as many people as possible out of these horrible circumstances."

They heard the rustle of the others coming from the kitchen. Katarina and the babies would stay for an additional day as they prepared to leave.

Heinz, Anthony, and Elvie walked out of the car. They both hugged each other as Heinz told Anthony to be careful. Sadness lingered on all their faces; Elvie had tears welling in her eyes. They watched the vehicle drive off, and Elvie waved to all of them.

She leaned back in the seat and closed her eyes as the sun began peeking through the trees. She turned and looked at Heinz and saw the worry etched on his face. She whispered to him, "Back to the darkness of Paris that was once full of lights."

"I will be there for a little while; I will make sure you are protected, and I promise nothing will happen to Louis or Henri." Heinz took her hand and gently kissed her soft skin.

Anthony walked back into the kitchen as Simon and the others discussed deeply. Katarina was feeding the little ones.

Anthony looked at Katarina, caring so deeply for the two children, making them smile as she played with them. Anthony took a seat opposite her now.

"Katarina, you will be okay. If anyone asks, the story is that you are visiting and waiting for your ride back to Berlin. I will have my diplomatic plates and flag by then to move us home safely. We will take the children to Switzerland, and then we will move back to Berlin. The driver and housekeeper all work with Simon. If anything, there is a safe room where they won't even hear the babies cry. When I return, we will make our way home."

Behind them, Peter cleared his throat. "Change of plans. You and Katarina must leave now. We just delivered the plates and flags to the car. Too many Vichy are roaming around Lyon, and they could come here. It's too risky for Katarina to stay and for you to come with us. Both of you need to get back to Berlin. You've been away too long. Gregory won't be going with Katarina. We need him here, but Nicholas will be with her."

Katarina nodded. "I'll go pack my bag. The babies and I have enough food, Anthony." She rushed out the door.

Within minutes, all were ready to leave in their own direction.

Anthony had a driver; one of the resistance fighters with Vatican papers was to travel a certain distance with them. They all pulled out of the long driveway. Nicholas would be there to switch as the driver as the resistance fighter only went a short distance with them and was to meet up with another group.

Anthony watched as Louis, Simon, Gregory, and Peter moved hastily out of view. They followed twenty-five minutes later.

Louis took the back roads. They were to meet in the Beaujolais region in twenty-five minutes to pick up an SOE agent, then backtrack to Grenoble, where they were to meet up with others in Saint Etienne, just Southwest of Lyon railroad and freight yards. Louis looked at his map as he spoke to Peter, "Our communication from London says to get the agent out. We will blow up the bridges and let the train fall into the river after we get the agent out."

They parked in parts of the woods that not many Germans crossed, left the car, and covered it with brush as best they could. They needed to get to the church as soon as possible, so they moved into the vineyards; the church was just at the edge.

They saw a priest at the steps. In silence, Peter moved as the priest motioned for him and the others to follow. The priest took Peter to the confessional booth and opened the door where two men were waiting, a flier and the SOE agent. Peter recognized them immediately and stared in horror. They both looked like skeletons, and the flier's arm was bloody.

"Jesus, Bradley," Peter said to the agent. "What the hell?"

Bradley sat now in the pew with the flier. They came out of the small confession booth.

"Peter, I thought the word would never get to you. I had received a message to rescue our boy here because the Nazis were looking for him. I suddenly heard footsteps coming up the stairs just after I received the message in Lyon. I climbed out of the window. I have the transmitter. We were betrayed, and now I know by whom. You told us this was the church to make our way to if something happened."

"How long have you been out here?" Peter asked. "We just found out a few days ago."

"We've been hiding for thirteen days. I dared not use the transmitter. We met up here at the church, knowing this was one safe place."

"So, if we go back to Lyon, do you know where we can find the traitor?"

Bradley nodded. "He's on the floor directly below where I was. We trusted him."

"Can you move with your injuries?" Peter asked the RAF flier.

"I can still give a good punch with the arm."

"That's good, my friend. But we are going to have to leave you with a friend until we get rid of our traitor. We do not need additional troubles. We hate the idea of moving you both back to Lyon, but we can't leave you here any longer."

Peter also couldn't leave the traitor living any longer. He had a wireless transmitter that some of the resistance had to confiscate, along with all material relating to resistance fighters. They hurried back to the man's home on the outskirts of Lyon and slipped into his living room as he was reading. Peter came from behind and shot him dead. In the man's paperwork, they found the name of the Gestapo officer he'd given information to. They quickly made their way to the Gestapo's apartment and took care of him, too.

Peter moved the flier to the brothel, and once again, Madam and her girls came to their rescue. Once back in Lyon, they silently worked their way twenty minutes from the city centre at 68 rue Henri Dechaud. They knew this could be the end of them. Citroëns were moving through the streets. Anyone who looked at them could suspect they were resistant and try to stop them. It took longer than they had anticipated to arrive.

Louis, Gregory, and Bradley moved silently to the second floor while Peter waited in the alley in the car. They opened the door to an empty living room. They saw papers on the dining table and gathered them up for good measure as they worked their way to the bedroom. As they neared, they heard faint snoring.

This man was responsible for agents being turned into the prison in Périgueux. They had their Colts drawn. Gregory stopped and glanced before gathering the rest of the paperwork. This man sleeping in the next room was the embodiment of a sociopathic, sadistic killer. Gregory saw on the paper that this horrible human had circled a family with two babies to be killed.

Bringing his finger to his lips, Gregory pointed for them to retreat to the door and whispered to Louis, "We don't want guns to be heard. Let me do it my way."

Peering in the bedroom, Gregory saw a woman sleeping next to this psycho, but it didn't matter. To him, she was in the same league as the devil. If they let her go, she'd most likely get on the phone and call for help. The woman and man opened their eyes at the same time, and before they could get a word out, Gregory sliced their throats and watched their blood flow out of them, flooding the sheets beneath their now lifeless bodies. This pure evil had been taken care of; he wouldn't be killing any more people. He took no joy in killing anyone, but it was necessary.

They left as silently as they arrived and made their way to the car. Once inside, Gregory gave Peter the papers and transmitter. Peter's eyes widened.

"My God! He helped with the massacres of Oradour-sur-glane! The entire village was razed. Nine thousand police rounded up 12,762 men, women, and children. He himself threw two babies out of the windows as he wrote to his superiors here because the parents were fighting him to let go of their children. Wasn't Father Julian's family in this city?" No one knew.

They drove the car as quickly as possible, returning to the brothel to pick up their flier. They left the car a good distance away at an old farmhouse with the farmer's help. After they stopped and picked up the flier, they made their way to where they knew trains were coming in with soldiers and ammunition.

They made their way to the tracks and a few rail cars that were waiting to move. They were underneath the train, placing explosives, when five soldiers stopped directly in front of their rail car and decided to have a long conversation. They all held their breath, praying the soldiers would move on without looking under the train. An eternity later, the soldiers left.

With the explosives in place, they made their way back to the car, keeping a watchful eye on the bridge. Seemingly on cue, the train exploded, taking the bridge with it. German soldiers rushed around; some were even on fire. And they didn't feel an ounce of sympathy. Several cars fell into the deep gorge, exploding at the bottom.

Chapter 6

Anthony and Katarina were feeling anxious as Marcel, their driver, slowed to a stop. They were the last to leave Simon's. Nicholas had to leave ahead of them to take forged papers to another group and would meet up with them later. The children sat between Katarina and Anthony. Three German soldiers stopped their cars and demanded the windows be rolled down. The first soldier peered into the back seat. He was horrid looking, with pale skin with pock marks, white lashes, and eyes that seemed to disappear into the white pigment of his face. Katarina shivered, and Anthony took her hand.

"Anthony, I wish they had left Gregory or Nicholas with us," She whispered.

Nearly screaming, the terrifying soldier ordered them out of the vehicle with their paperwork. One of the babies was asleep on the floor and thankfully stayed asleep.

Marcel was ordered out as well. They gave the paperwork to the first Nazi as the other soldier walked to the other side. The car was on an embankment's edge that dropped several hundred feet. He had difficulties walking around as he watched gravel roll down the embankment. A gusting wind shook their vehicle. Katarina didn't move quickly enough, and the soldier pulled her out of the car. She fell to the ground, and when Marcel jumped to help her, he felt the end of a rifle in his ribs. The soldier snapped at him to stay on the driver's side and mind his business. The Nazis noticed the decal of the Papal decal and the Swiss embassy.

Anthony sensed that they didn't really care about the diplomatic papers or plates, and anger started growing in his bones.

"Take the children out of the car," one of the Nazis demanded.

Katarina narrowed her eyes and responded with a cold and determined voice. "They are sleeping. I don't want to wake them."

The atrocious-looking man came closer. "I'm telling you to take them out of the car."

She looked at him defiantly. "I'm not going to wake them."

The one Nazi pushed Katarina against the car as he grabbed her arm and started to pull her toward their vehicle. The other two pointed their weapons at Anthony and Marcel. Katarina tried to pull away, but he was too strong. He grabbed her around the waist and threw her in the back of their car.

"I saw your children. Do you want them to live?"

He was leaning over her, and she spat in his face. "Do not touch my children!"

He wiped the spittle, and for a moment, she was frozen. She would rather die than let him have his way. She kicked hard, right in his stomach, and pushed him away from her, but just as quickly, he was looming over her, his hands touching her as she fought back. She swore this was not going to happen to her.

The other two Nazis ignored what was going on. They continued to read through the papers of diplomatic reference to their travel. Panic grew in Marcel and Anthony. Suddenly, the Nazi looked like he had seen a ghost. He read their names, learning who this woman's husband was. These papers said she was married to a flier who was killed in Britain, and she was being escorted back to Switzerland by her brother, a priest who was stationed in the Vatican.

He peered at the children in the car, then back to Anthony and the children again. They were now wide awake, their blue eyes shining brightly amid their alabaster complexions. He paid no attention to what was happening in the car with Katarina, but fear etched on his brow, even though he could see her feet dangling out of the side of the car. He couldn't hear Katarina's muffled cry because her attacker now had his hand over her mouth. Suddenly he heard the Nazi scream. Katarina bit into his hand as he unbuttoned her blouse. At the same time, his other hand was feeling her breast and was jerking at her belt, trying to take it off.

The Nazi asked Anthony to explain again who Katarina was married to. Anthony shifted uneasily, his gaze on the Nazis' car. He knew he had to do something. Marcel was inching closer to the second soldier. There was now silence from the other car as the Nazi kept asking Anthony questions, but his brain couldn't answer. He had to get to Katarina.

Marcel moved close to the Nazi, who had just stomach-butted him with the end of the rifle as Marcel moved closer to bring the Nazi's attention back to him.

"I don't feel I need to answer you," Anthony said. "The information is all on paper. You, my man, are part of Germany's problem. Hitler has turned you all into psychopathic racist killers."

The two Nazis pulled their weapon now to Anthony's throat. Marcel saw the shadow coming over the embankment. The wind howled loudly, and it was hard to hear, but Marcel saw what was about to happen. The two Nazis had their guns aimed at Anthony.

Gregory came over the embankment separately from the others. He yanked the Nazi out of the car and slit his throat with wire. The movement caught the attention of the other two soldiers. Anthony threw himself to the ground just as Louis and Nicholas appeared from the forest on the other side. They aimed and fired, and just like that, their perfect shots killed the two Nazis. Blood spewed over the car and the ground, splattering Anthony's shoes. The soldiers lay in a pool of their own blood as it slowly seeped into the earth. Anthony got up, dusted himself off, and walked over to give them the sign of the cross.

In silence, Louis and Peter dragged both bodies into the Nazis' car with the one on the ground. Anthony ran to Katarina, who was now kicking the dead man on the ground. She kept kicking him and cursing.

Gregory had to pick her up by the waist to move her away. He saw the bruise on her neck as he helped her button her blouse. They pushed the car over the embankment, but not before they removed the soldiers' uniforms. Those could come in handy in the future.

Anthony reached Katarina and gathered her in his arms. "Did he hurt you?"

Gregory watched in silence.

"No," Katarina said. "I managed to kick him in the stomach, bite him in the hand and then gouge at his eyes." Even though he had not gotten any further with her, they saw her shoulders trembling.

Louis walked over to Anthony. "Father, what did you say? When we saw the gun at your throat, we thought it was the end."

"I told him he was a psychopath."

Louis pinched the bridge of his nose. "Well, that will do it, Anthony."

Anthony turned to Peter. "How did you find us?" He asked.

"We had an uneasy feeling about you taking this route," Peter said. "We found some papers on our traitor, and he'd marked some patrols on this highway. We finished our business and then caught up to you. We saw it all unfold, so we acted fast." The babies were now crying as they heard the commotion

Gregory helped Katarina back into the car while Marcel took instructions from Louis. He was given a gun and a different route to take.

Gregory walked over to Katarina. He held her for a moment, whispering in her ear, "I'm glad you are safe."

She looked up at the most intense eyes and saw a sudden tenderness she had seen only a few times. She wrapped her arms around him and placed her lips on his neck, making his skin shiver.

"Thank you for rescuing me," she whispered. She let go of him and walked back to the babies. The little ones had large tears trailing their cheeks.

Gregory had been with many women, but Katarina was the only one he wanted now. He longed for intimacy with her and to build a life. But they were in the middle of a war, and there was no time for romance. He didn't even know if she would want him. Her being pursued by Frederick Spitz also made it difficult.

She gave him a brief smile as she lifted one of the crying children and cradled her in her arms.

Anthony was concerned about the rest of the trip, but Marcel assured him they would be fine on this new route. When they arrived, they would leave the children with the sisters in a convent, where they would receive new identification, be baptized into the Catholic Church, and be moved to an orphanage or new parents.

They were making their way to Grenoble as they followed the Isere River, the oldest part of the city, cramped between the rivers and mountains.

Katarina was looking down at the sleeping child. She looked so angelic, Katarina thought.

"Anthony, are you sure they will be safe here? I had hoped we could have gotten them to Switzerland."

"I think we need to stay low," Anthony said. "I'm sure the Gestapo will be looking for those who blew up the tracks, and if they find the dead Nazis, they'll be on the hunt. So yes, I know they will be safe where we are going. The children will have no memory of these days. Starting now, they have a new life and a new story. Their parents will not survive, but the sisters will find them good homes."

Anthony leaned over to Marcel. "How are you doing? I'm sorry we went through that ordeal back there. I just don't understand. Monsignor Roncalli has given these papers before. Something the Nazi saw made him suspicious; they should have let us pass immediately. We need to reread, see if we missed a detail."

"Father, not to worry. It was just bad timing. Usually, the papal diplomatic papers work."

The fog had rolled in, and Marcel had to peer hard at the road. He hit the brakes as a deer darted in front of them, and Anthony saw how Marcel's hands shook. "Father, I'm surprised there are no more deer, as people are hunting them for food."

"Father," Marcel said in a low voice, "I heard Peter say the scientist might have to be moved through the Pyrenees to San Sebastian, Spain. We are waiting to see how sturdy in mind and body he is before we decide on that route."

They moved slowly through the streets to the church and climbed out of the vehicle with the babies. The nuns scurried out and quickly took the children out of Anthony's and Katarina's arms, along with the paperwork. Katarina had tears running down her face as she kissed the babies on the forehead before handing them over. Then, just as quickly as they had arrived, the nuns disappeared with the children.

The Jesuit priest quickly moved Anthony, Katarina, and Marcel into the church and took them to the back, where the rectory stood. He offered them fresh beds to rest, food, and drink and moved Anthony and Marcel to a different area. A sister came and fetched Katarina to follow her.

It seemed hours since their heads hit the pillows, and the sisters awoke Katarina. Father Ottavighi was in the kitchen with Anthony and Marcel as she walked in. Another priest had joined them, a large, six-foot-three hulk of a man with broad shoulders, red hair, and blue eyes. He was an Irish priest who hadn't been able to return to Ireland after the Germans invaded. He worked hard with the resistance outside of the University of Grenoble, working on clandestine operations. He was whispering to them now in a very low voice, saying that Katarina and Anthony would be leaving and the rest of them were in a safe house where they were still working on the extraction of the scientist. Katarina would have to leave alone, while Anthony would be staying. Katarina was horrified that he would stay behind. She feared there would be questions of his whereabouts in his parish.

The priests gave Katarina a black coat to wear. In the seams, there were documents to be delivered. She was now traveling under the protection of the Geneva ambassador. If stopped, she was to keep to the story that she had been visiting her brothers Heinz and Anthony in Paris. The Gestapo were more apparent in their stoppings because they knew of "secret smugglers," as they called them. So far, Peter had moved one of these small groups, who had microfilm that needed to get to the Embassy in Switzerland. The best place at this time to smuggle anyone across was at the Risoux forest in the Vallee de Jour, known as "passeurs." They helped resistance fighters, SOE agents, and others, and it was here they were going to move the scientist and Allied pilot and hopefully Peter.

Katarina was taken to a black sedan. The driver said nothing as Anthony and the Irish priest kissed her goodbye. She looked back several times and prayed Anthony would make it back to Berlin. She had to return. She was supposed to dance in front of Hitler at a performance for his upper officers and their wives. Frederick Spitz would also be at the performance. She closed her eyes, but it wasn't Frederick who came to her thoughts.

It was Gregory.

His eyes penetrated her, his hands holding her tight as they trembled. She knew his brother Nicholas would be in Berlin to follow her later, helping the resistance there. She shook her head; Frederick Spitz should come to her thoughts, not Gregory. Frederick was the one who spoke gentle and loving words to her despite her family's objections, especially Anthony's and Edwin's. She didn't see his evil, but they told her it would eventually appear. He could only hide it for so long. She leaned her head back for the long journey.

Meantime, Peter and Louis

Louis and Gregory slipped through the town silently. They knew the scientist was in a safe house. It took a few moments to locate it, and when they did, they knocked softly on the door. On the other side, a voice said, "Who's there?"

They gave the code word.

Maria opened the door immediately and pulled them in as she quickly looked right and left down the street. She kissed them both on the cheeks. Maria was married to an influential businessman whom she had not seen for several months since he had left to help the resistance. When it was late at night, when she was hiding someone, she demanded a code before she opened the door.

She ushered them into the living room, offering them wine in a glass cut from beautiful crystal. She was just getting ready to speak when there was an insistent knock at the door. She motioned for Gregory and Peter to move into the closet, then clicked the hinge that opened to another room for hiding. There was a small hole in the wall to see what was happening.

The local police commissioner stood where the men had been only moments earlier. He was short with a mustache that seemed to take up his whole face. His sparse hair was slicked back. He looked around with envy as Maria showed him into the room with its beautiful floor-to-ceiling windows, brocade curtains, the floors polished to a gleam, and the long hallway to the living room covered with famous artists' hangings and pictures of her and her husband. The floors were covered with Persian rugs. She had the influence to keep the house and everything in it.

The commissioner's eyes narrowed to slits. "I was driving by, and I thought I saw a man in your window. I'm just looking out for your safety since your husband is still gone."

An amused smile played on Maria's lips as she invited him to sit. She had black hair that fell in ringlets down her back, dark green eyes, and flawless skin. She wore no makeup, but her cheeks always had a hint of color. She was thin but endowed with well-proportioned hips and bust and long legs.

"I do hope you are not entertaining men while your husband is gone."

She was sitting in the chair opposite him. She leaned over and patted his hand. "Not to worry. If I were to entertain, I would ensure you were the first on my list."

His jawline tensed.

"Let me offer you some watered-down wine from our family's vineyards."

The commissioner stood and straightened his bow tie as a sliver of his sparse hair fell, and he moved it back in agitation. She had walked over to the setee with the wine poured and returned and offered him a glass. He took several sips, never taking his eyes off her. He placed the unfinished wine on the small table next to the chair with its fine crystal bowl. He envied the man who was married to this woman. This house had all the finer things in life, but he dared not make waves. He knew the general made visits here.

"I hope to see you soon, Mademoiselle when the night is not so late."

She walked him to the door, and he kissed her on the cheek. He placed his one hand on her waist and let it travel to her buttocks, lingering there for a moment before he stepped away with an evil smile.

'I must take care of the women in my town without husbands," He said. "I hope you come around to my suggestions."

Maria quickly closed the door while simultaneously wiping the residue off her cheek. She double-bolted the doors.

"Merde," She whispered. Louis was now standing behind her, and he put both hands on her shoulder as the coolness of his hands rubbed the tension out.

"Good job, Maria," He whispered in her ear.

They both went back to the living room, where Gregory looked anxious.

"He won't bother me," Maria said. "I'll go straight to the Nazi commander. We understand; he comes over, eats and drinks well, and has the luxury of my bed. I don't worry. Even if he suspects, he won't bring anyone back. He's become accustomed to our nights."

Louis was pacing. "We're sorry you've had to put yourself in this position."

She looked at him with a slight smile. So many years ago, she had lain in his arms. The two were in love. It seemed like a lifetime ago, but her family told her she was obligated to keep the vineyards and wealth in the family. Even though Louis and his family had their own wealth, the fact they were Catholic and her family was Greek Orthodox caused an issue. So, she married Paul, whom her parents approved of. But as the years moved on, she did not forget Louis. She'd heard he had married, and the Nazis killed his wife when they discovered she was a British spy. Paul was a good husband, but he had to disappear a while ago. He'd promised to return, but that was two years ago, and Maria had no idea as to his fate. And now, here stood Louis, the man she had wanted to marry. He'd come to her and asked for her help as she had a good understanding with the Gestapo in the village and they needed to go through this area and needed information. She slept with a German colonel and moved people under his nose. She did anything to help the resistance, so now, she would help Louis.

She smiled at him. "Let's go meet the scientist. And you two need to eat and rest for an hour or so. I heard about bridges and a coal mine being blown up. I won't ask, but I know who is responsible. Come down to the basement to meet the scientist, Herr Francois Rubenstein, before you relax. He's anxious to leave. The Jesuits moved him here. They were worried the church would be searched and believed my home was a better choice."

They slowly made their way down to a basement full of wine bottles. Maria opened one of the shelves as they rattled, and there stood Herr Rubenstein. Louis and Gregory did not speak immediately. Instead, they motioned for the man to follow. They reviewed a few items with the scientist and took time to rest before leaving.

It was dawn now as Maria woke them. She reluctantly woke Louis as he was in her arms. The Renault was outside. Anthony, Peter, the pilot, and Bradley were already waiting in a separate Renault, while Herr Rubenstein was placed in the truck just a short distance away. The truck had a false floor that Herr Rubenstein lay on while they covered him.

Louis held Maria in his arms for a long time as tears streamed down her cheek, and the two said goodbyes.

"Louis, look out for yourself and the others. If you meet up with my husband, tell him I love him."

The moon was disappearing as the convoy made its way through the streets of Grenoble. They returned to the church one more time to get more papers and ammunition. They moved without issues through two checkpoints, and the Germans never knew they had just passed through some of the best saboteurs. When they were able, they pulled the scientist off the floor so he could sit in the back with them. He kept repeating how grateful he was to them. He looked forward to leaving for England, then, hopefully, America.

"Herr Rubenstein, what happened to your wife?" Peter asked.

He lowered his head.

"She was British. She worked for the consulate in Switzerland. When she came to bring me back to Switzerland, as I was only visiting a fellow scientist here in France, she knew the Germans were looking for me. I have developed a few things that could change the course of the war, and someone in her office betrayed her. I watched them arrest her, and they made me watch as they tortured her, as they wanted to know why she was in France visiting me. She whispered to me before we heard the steps of the Gestapo, not to say a word, not to admit I was a scientist or that I was her husband. Why they demanded I watch, I would never understand. To them I was just a friend at that moment. I already had been given false papers from my wife, so there was no association, but it did not matter to them, I was just a schoolteacher on paper."

"She sat and didn't make noise. She kept shaking her head for me not to say anything. She refused to give up what I knew or what I was working on. She wouldn't even admit that I was her husband—she never uttered the word as they tried to force her to say it. She kept repeating she was visiting me, and I was her cousin, they wanted me to come to Switzerland to teach in a private school. She passed out several times. The floor was full of her blood. They then told me to leave. I'm not sure why. I think it was a ploy to see where I would go. I managed to lose them, and I was going to have the consulate demand her release. A Gestapo car picked me up, and someone pulled me in. They drove for a few blocks, then told me to walk several blocks as they dropped me off with instructions. It was obvious we foiled the Gestapo who had been following me. I went straight to the church with their instructions. They hid me and told me later that they had tortured her to death, but she would not tell them anything about me, only that I was a schoolteacher. There was a point I wanted to give myself up to save her, but the priest advised me not to because he knew they would still kill her regardless."

Herr Rubenstein was openly crying now, his shoulders stooped and his hands in front of his face, sorrow etched deeply.

Peter and the others had no words. After some silence, Peter was the first to speak. "We are truly sorry. She was a brave woman. She knew how valuable you are to us."

Herr Rubenstein looked up, his dark brown eyes red-rimmed. "These are evil men. Father Claus came to me every day while I was in hiding. He'd visited the prison where they held her, and he was fatigued seeing the suffering. But he told me at the end she said how much she loved me... She died in 'hell,' as he called it."

The scientist took a deep breath and continued, "There is a saying, 'He who had not eaten his bread in tears, he who has not sat up weeping upon his bed through the night of despair.' I believe it was Goethe. It was my motto: my faith knows he sees all, and he above has his reasons. We will come out of this darkness. There has to be a light. The Jewish people will survive. We are God's promised people, are we not?"

When they reached their destination, they quickly gave Herr Rubenstein, Bradley, and the pilot over to handlers who would help them get to Spain. They said their goodbyes. They knew it would be a hard journey, but Peter felt good about them making it. They were strong, and Anthony blessed each one before they left. Peter again refused to join them; he still had work to do.

They all climbed back into their vehicles and made their way to one more bridge that needed to be taken out. They were now heading north of Le Puy. Around midnight the following day, the small group put felling trees across the tracks. Another unit of fighters joined them. When the train stopped, they jumped the driver and pulled him out. Gregory and Peter removed the trees from the tracks and then made the locomotive move at maximum speed before jumping off onto the hill's side. They watched the train speed ahead and then plow off the bridge filled with explosives. The blast put the entire train down the ravine along with the ammunition and soldiers who had been asleep. Their fate was now in the hands of God to forgive them. This was their second success, with the trains exploding. They were sure they were being sought all over France now.

They were in constant motion for the next few weeks, destroying communications centers, trains, and bridges. They were always in camouflage positions and when they accomplished what they wanted, they vanished like ghosts.

They were notified not to make their way back to Lyon because the sinister Klaus Barbie was on the rampage. Looking and finding resistance fighters, as well as those in Montluc prison, they were being executed. But it did not stop Peter and the others as they continued their direct attacks on the convoys. The Germans considered the resistance fighters to be de Gaulles and underground annihilators.

It was the last involvement for Anthony. He needed to return to Berlin before he was scrutinized or his family was questioned. He was already concerned that Frederick Spitz was becoming more prevalent in Katarina's life.

Louis and Anthony were on the verge of saying goodbye. They had all returned to Paris, and Peter was on the radio when word came to them that one of the resistance wives was taken and put in prison with several other French women. They were all at Avenue Foch, but not for long before they would be moved. They were desperate to save the women. They didn't want anyone else to have to watch their family be executed like Henri had.

Jews were being told to sell their homes, or they would be taken. Anthony was moving people out as quickly as he could in Germany. Many of his Jewish friends came to him for help. He was able to move some to Palestine and some to South America. A few went to the United States, but that country had Jewish quotas. Anthony needed to return to Berlin; he knew many needed him. He decided first to help Peter and then leave.

The Jews had their stores taken—as the Germans called it, the "Aryanized stores." So many professionals had their licenses taken: doctors, lawyers, university professors, and even a judge. They couldn't practice and were forced to leave and find work elsewhere. How did Germany and France ever agree to the Nazi policies? As a priest, Anthony was told to shun his rabbi friend. Germans were not allowed to be friends with Jews, Italians, or French. So many were just silent.

Anthony watched and knew the terror as the Gestapo, or as they were known in Germany, the "Brown Shirts." The daily life of Jews was incomprehensible to everyone. Every day, another piece of life was torn away from many in Europe. His parents bought a home for their long-time neighbor Rita's parents. Deutsche Bank was calling in loans on non-Germans. They paid off their home loan so they could stay, and the bank could not take it from them. It was no different here in France, except they had a strong resistance and worked with the British.

Louis and Anthony first made their way to the safe house, where they met up with others, including Nicholas and Dietric, who had traveled back from Berlin to help Anthony. They enthusiastically greeted Anthony. They planned and went to find the woman arrested before they could be tortured for information. No one knew how any of the women could withstand the torture, and any information given out could destroy parts of the resistance. If they couldn't find the woman, their future was sealed. They would be tortured to death or put on a train to a concentration camp, most likely Ravensbrück, just outside Berlin. Anthony insisted on going with them.

They managed to get into the building where they were told the women were being held. They swiftly moved to the upper floor before anyone could stop them, and Gregory and Peter silently executed the guards. They saw the anguish on Anthony's face as each was killed. They pushed Anthony forward. They had made their way back downstairs while freeing four French resisters when Anthony froze. He heard her voice faintly singing in French Richard Tauber's "You Are My Heart's Delight." It was *the* voice.

He grabbed Peter's arm and pulled him back to the door. It was the last two verses, "The dreams of mine may at last come true and I shall hear you whisper I love you." They forced the door open, taking the two Germans by surprise. Peter shot them instantly. Amelia was tied to a chair; he knew the face and that body intimately, even though she was nearly unrecognizable because they had beaten her so badly. Her eye was swollen, and they had begun to remove her nails. She looked up at Anthony, startled to see him. Then, a faint smile. They heard the Germans trying to break down the door to the hallway that they had barricaded. One had broken the glass, and they felt the bullet whiz by their ear. Another shot almost hit Anthony in the leg. Peter was pulling at Anthony; there was no time. She looked almost dead to both of them. She only said a few words. They heard the foot steps now coming down the hall, and they had no time to untie her and move her out.

"Find Hanna. She is yours."

They rushed out of the building and to underground catacombs. They were able to move a few women. The others would either survive Ravensbrück or die there.

They got back to the safe house, and everyone was quiet. Anthony sat on the sofa, his hands burying his face, his suffering chiseled deep now in lines on his face. His voice was raw as he looked at Peter. He let out a howl as a man who had lost everything.

"Peter, it was Amelia! You have got to find her. I must leave. My parish needs me and my family. I have got to help those in Berlin, but please let me know what you find out. Try to find her. Promise me you will find her."

Peter promised he would try to find out where they took Amelia. Peter had visited Anthony the summer when Anthony was eighteen and met Amelia. She was also eighteen, and her parents and Anthony's were discussing a merger of their vinieries. It was a warm summer at their home in Italy. It was supposed to be Anthony's last summer before he entered his second year in the seminary.

Anthony put his head back in the chair, tears running down his face. "I have to find her," He muttered to himself. His thoughts went back to that summer.

Chapter 7

Thoughts of the past

Anthony first saw Amelia in the olive grove, walking slowly. Her violet cotton dress was thin enough to see through. When she faced the sun, he could see the outline of her long, shapely legs. She walked toward him with a broad smile and chestnut curls falling down the back of her straw hat. She now stood before him, a wide smile with deep blue eyes, her cheeks touched by the sun, her lips beautifully full. Her nose was perfectly elongated against her high cheekbones. She was about five feet eight, her long legs adorned with sandals, and the rest of her body was sun-kissed with a healthy glow.

She had walked down from the villa. The home stood out, perched on a beautiful hill overlooking vast groves of lemons, olives, and grapevines as far as the eye could see. The other side of the house looked upon the blue of the Mediterranean Sea with coves of small inlets of beaches.

His mother and their long-time help attended. The oatmeal-colored stone home was filled with roses and flowers. Inside were oak beams and cool tile floors with oriental rugs of light blue and greens. From the distance, you could see the terracotta roof. The walkways were lined with Italian cypresses, and tall evergreens dotted the property.

As soon as Amelia saw Anthony, she thought he was the most

beautiful man she had ever seen. She gave him her hand.

"Hello, I'm Amelia. I'm visiting the Von Rahmel family with my parents and my two very bad brothers. Do you know them?"

He thought her voice was like a beautiful song as he stammered a response.

"Yes, I know them." He had to turn away from her as he heard her laugh. Anthony was feeling speechless, and he turned back to her.

"I'm Anthony Von Rahmel."

She gave him a raised eyebrow. Even her eyebrows were perfectly shaped. She moved towards him, smirking.

"Well, Anthony, shall we take a little walk before we go back to the adults?"

"Where would you like to walk to?"

"Let's walk to the village. I have some money for a cold drink or maybe a nice glass of wine."

Anthony stopped. "How old are you?"

"Eighteen. Old enough to drink, if that's what you're thinking. Why? How old are you?"

"I'm eighteen, and I, too, am old enough to drink."

She laughed.

They were walking through some of the fruit trees, and he plucked an apple off one of the trees and offered it to her. The soil was rich, and everything dug deep into the ground, sprouting healthy, nutrient-dense roots. He whispered, "Le viti di Lisa, Questo e il vigneto di Von Rhamel." Amelia looked at him.

"You are saying these are Lisa's vines and the von Rahmels' vineyards?"

"I have grown up in vineyards and wine-making all my life, as I'm sure you have. It's not a big deal."

She took his hand and started to pull him in the direction of the village. She whirled around to say something as her foot caught on a stone, and she stumbled. But Anthony grabbed hold of her small waist and pulled her to him. They were face to face; his lips could nearly kiss hers. His pulse was increasing. He stepped back and cleared his throat.

"Do your parents know you are out here on your own?" He asked, and she laughed heartily.

"Yes, they know. I even told them I might walk to the village and be back for dinner. As you know, it stays lighter out now in the summer. We were also here last month. You were not here, but your other three brothers were, and they came and left."

"My dear girl, now you are teasing me."

She stopped and looked him square in the face. So handsome, she thought that his dark blond hair, blue oxford shirt, khaki pants and boots of fine leather all together fit his body perfectly... All six feet of him.

"I don't tease." She pulled him down the grove towards the road. Her hat came off with the wind, and her long blond hair with darker blond streaks came tumbling down.

She almost looked vulnerable and fragile, but not her eyes. They were determined and focused. Something happened at that moment when she took his hand as he was trying to catch the hat. He touched the softness of her arm.

She stopped and looked at him. She felt as if she had known him all her life. He gently brushed her hair back from her face as the breeze caught her hair and swirled it about. His need to be with her was overwhelming. His intense, crystal-blue eyes stood out against his tanned face and high cheekbones. She shivered as he moved her hair from her face and placed her straw hat back on her head.

He quickly looked back at the groves where they had a shed.

"Amelia, there is a shed up at the end of the grove where we have bicycles. It's much too far to walk to the village."

They ran to the shed, pulled the bicycles out and peddled to the village.

They promptly went to the café where they ordered lemonade and chocolate torte. Everyone greeted Anthony; the villagers had known the Von Rahmel boys since they were all toddlers. Her laughter was infectious. Amelia explained in French to Anthony how coming here was so exciting and different from Paris. The sun and the water were wonderful. She said that she hoped to take over her parents' business and be the first woman to run a winery. Her brothers were still too young to understand the importance of keeping it in the family.

He just listened to her talk. She seemed so much older than eighteen. She had so many goals she wanted to accomplish. They must have wandered the village for an hour before deciding it was best to return to the villa.

They found both sets of parents sitting on the front porch overlooking the beautiful Mediterranean. The aromas of roses and lemons floated in the breeze as they enjoyed cheese and wine.

Amelia's father saw her first. He was a short, stout man with jolly red cheeks, a long mustache that curled, and deep brown eyes. Amelia's mother was more like her—tall and tan with blue eyes and blond hair. The two seemed like such an odd pair, Anthony thought. Amelia had her father's broad smile, while her mother looked more pensive and tired.

"Ah, Amelia! We were starting to worry," Amelia's father said. He looked at Anthony following behind her.

Anthony introduced himself. He went and kissed his mother on the cheek and then excused himself, telling them he would freshen up for dinner. His mother was right behind him as he walked out of the veranda and into the large living room. The walls were a soft yellow with bright blue sofas and chairs. The tables were full of pictures and little lace napkins, and the larger tables had vases filled with flowers. The French doors opened wide to let the air fill the room. They could hear the clattering of dishes being placed in the dining room for dinner.

"Anthony, stop." His mother was right on his heels as he headed for the stairs. "You cannot go out with this young woman again! She is our guest, and her parents were worried where she had disappeared. We were about to look for her and see you with her... I can see it in your eyes, Anthony. Keep your distance."

"Mother." He put his hand on her shoulder and looked into her eyes, clear blue, like his. Her petite frame was strong, and her eyes usually twinkled as she saw her sons and Katarina. This time, they looked worried.

"Did you tell her you are going to become a priest?"

"The subject didn't come up." Anthony let out a sigh as he looked out to the veranda and saw her lying on the chaise lounge, her skirt pulled up a little higher, her long legs catching the summer sun. He let out a sigh, and his mother followed his eyes.

"Anthony, you can't. You must stay away."

"Mother, stop worrying. How many priests do we know who have women friends? She's a charming young woman, and I like having her company while I'm here."

"Then you must tell her you will return to the seminary."

Anthony sighed again. "I will tell her if the subject comes up. But let's not bring it up. Just let me enjoy the summer. Going back will be intense, and it will be a while until I see this villa or Munich."

His mother looked pensive. She gazed out at the veranda. Anthony knew how much she loved coming here in the summer. This villa was his father's honeymoon present. They started with the vineyards to have the best reds, and they grew for the best whites in Germany. Then, they ventured into olives and making olive oil.

"Mother, remember 1 Corinthians 2:9. 'No eye has seen, no ear has heard, no mind has conceived what God has prepared for those who love him.' Stop worrying. I promised myself to God."

"Yes, but I saw a look in your eye when you looked at her that I have never seen from you, even when you dated."

He kissed her cheek and headed up the stairs. She turned and walked toward the dining room and kitchen to check on the dinner being made. Anthony glanced one more time back at Amelia. She caught his eye and smiled as he walked slowly back to his room.

He was late arriving at the dinner table. He wore a white shirt and let his chest peek through the top where the buttons were left undone. He had blue slacks and sandals, his cross tucked in his shirt.

He was seated next to Amelia, and everyone at the table enjoyed a dinner of baked chicken in a sweet tomato sauce with bowls of pasta with lots of sausages and a cream sauce of capers and mushrooms. Anthony tried not to pay attention to Amelia, but it proved increasingly difficult. She had changed into a long, pink skirt with a short-sleeve button-down yellow blouse that amply showed the outline of her upper body and her tanned arms. Her hair was pulled up in a bun, showing her long, slender neck. A whiff of citrus flowed from her. After dinner, they all made their way to the veranda, but Amelia pulled Anthony back. There was a lower veranda, much smaller but still with a view of the ocean. She sat on the outside of a swing chair and motioned for him to sit beside her.

He sank down next to her. Her presence was intoxicating. They sat in silence as the breeze floated with all the smells of the wonderment of the flowers and a slight dampness from the sea. She shivered for a moment as he placed his arm around her, pulling her closer to him. His warmth chased away the shiver. He closed his eyes as he smelled the freshness of her hair and skin. He suddenly felt her lips brush his.

"Anthony, kiss me." Her lips were still on his as she whispered to him, her tongue now grazing the inside of his mouth, which he took willingly. She pulled him to her and took his hand to her upper chest.

He moved his hand away. "Amelia, it's late." They heard Amelia's mother calling for her from the upper veranda.

She stood as he did, and he kissed her on the top of her head. She called out to her mother that she was on her way. Then she turned to Anthony.

"We'll finish this conversation tomorrow." She slipped her arms around his waist. "Hold me for a moment." She nuzzled into his neck. When she stood on her tiptoes, her lips could reach his neck.

She let go and went inside. His breathing was quick as he sat back down, shaking his head. His mother was right—this was a temptation he needed to avoid. He couldn't think logically at this moment.

He went into the library, where there was brandy on the table next to the floral Queen Anne chair. He admired the pink and yellow design and matching sofa for a moment, then dropped into the chair. He let the brandy slide down his throat as he put his head against the chair and looked up at the ceiling.

What was he doing? God was the only one he could love. The only other time he'd felt such instant love was the day Katarina was born. He was just fifteen and had immediately sworn to protect his little sister. It was different than any love he felt for his parents and brothers. But now, standing here as an eighteen-year-old man on the cusp of becoming a priest, this gorgeous eighteen-year-old girl made him feel this same intense love.

He needed to leave sooner and go back to Rome, and he thought as he poured two more shots of brandy. He must have fallen asleep because the next thing he noticed was his father's hand on his arm.

"Son, go upstairs and sleep. Whatever worries are on your mind, you will work them out."

"I think I need to go back to Rome sooner."

His father put his hand on his son's shoulder. "Whatever you need to do."

"Before I go back, I'll spend some time with my friend in

Radicondoli. Do you mind? It's less time with you and Mother. I know I promised to go over the last grape inventory."

His father shook his head. "Son, the grapes this year will be the best. The traditional native grapes will make the best voila sciacchetra. I also feel the olive return will be the best. The Monterosso soil and hill sides are perfect this year. In fact, one of these days, Monterosso will be discovered by tourists. Then, I will need to expand our business. I believe we have one of the best vineyards in the Tuscany and Cinque Terre area."

"Father, between the Munich vineyards and these, you have more than you can handle." He looked at his father, thinking how much he and his father loved the land. He remembered them putting their hands into the soil together when he was about five years old. His father marveled at the soil and the minerals he knew to be in it. For years, they worked side-by-side in the vineyards in Italy and Germany. They received more rewards every year. Yes, this would remain in his blood, but now a person in his blood burnt heavily in his veins. Amelia… How to expunge her?

The next day, he left early and made a short visit to his friend. He got back to the villa around midnight. He let the sweet smell of the vineyards and lemons drift into the living room through the window. He always wanted this scent in his memory. He stood at the window for a long time, taking a deep breath. The air smelled sweet as the full moon peeked through the lace curtains. When he left the living room, he stopped in front of Amelia's door. He lifted his hand to knock and abruptly changed his mind before going down the hall to his own room.

In her room, Amelia had heard his footsteps. She pulled on a robe and silently walked down the hall. Leaning her ear to Anthony's door, she heard nothing and didn't see any light. She went back to her room and lay in bed, taking deep breaths as she thought of Anthony.

The next day, Anthony awoke at sunrise, leaving a written message for his parents. The only one up was Katarina, who was bouncing on the helper's lap, her face covered with the stains of strawberries and cream. She saw Anthony and slid off the helper's lap and ran toward him on her little chubby legs. As she ran, her long blond hair came out of the ribbon. He gathered her in his arms. "How is my sweet girl?" He kissed her face a dozen times, making her laugh as she placed her arms around his neck, "I love you, Anthony." Her large violet eyes filled with innocence.

"I love you too! As much as if we went to the stars and back."

"You can't go to the stars."

"For you, I can."

She giggled as he placed her back down, taking a cloth from the kitchen table to wipe off the thick cream on her face.

"I have to leave, sweet girl, but will be back soon."

He didn't see Amelia standing at the doorway, watching in amazement at this love being shown to this little girl. Love, like the child, was his own, even though Katarina was his sister.

Anthony deliberately went alone into the village to a village priest for breakfast. A man he had confided in for years growing up, he was the person Anthony had told about wanting to enter the priesthood. A waiter set warm bread with homemade jam, fresh local butter and strawberries in front of them. This was Heaven, Anthony thought. He spent most of the day helping the priest give the church a badly needed coat of paint. He stayed way past dinner time and slipped back into his home around midnight. When he headed toward the living room for a brandy, he heard Amelia call out to him.

"Anthony, did you try to avoid me today?" She was waiting in the living room for him. He didn't answer immediately as he walked over to her. She bit down on her bottom lip; her hair was tousled by the sudden breeze that came through the open living room door for fresh air.

"Amelia, you are only eighteen. There are complications."

"What complications?" She was almost eye-level with him now, her eyes piercing into his. "We're the same age. I have friends who married at seventeen. Our own mothers were only sixteen. We're attracted to each other. I can see it in your eyes. There is always this pervasive acceptance that people as young as us can't fall in love at first sight."

Anthony closed his eyes. "Amelia, you're dangerous to me. You're tempting."

Her lips quivered, and an expression of intense vulnerability came over her. He immediately gathered her into his arms, holding her as tightly as he could, as if he wanted her to be one with him. He finally forced himself to release her, cupping her chin to look at him, her eyes misty with tears.

"Amelia, let's just have a wonderful week. Let us just live for tomorrow and the next day. I promise, we will have a grand week. I promise, but I must visit Lucca tomorrow." He couldn't resist as she stared at him. Her robe was open, and he could see her bra and underwear. As her head tilted up, he brushed her soft lips with his. He wanted more and pulled her in again, feeling her body on his. He pulled her in harder as she reached for his lips, slipping her tongue in his mouth. He didn't want to let go as he could feel her heart against him. Her breasts heaved against him, and he reached and kissed the top of her head as he moved back down to her neck and then back to her mouth. His hand now reached under her robe to feel the skin on her waist as he closed his eyes and held her. He languished in each kiss as they became more heated. She moved his hand to her breast as his breathing, and hers became thicker. He moved her to the sofa, and they fell onto it. He lay there, kissing every inch of her. But he finally had to pull away. She pulled him back.

"Don't stop."

"I can't." He held her arms and looked her in the eyes. "I promise, after tomorrow, we can talk, but I need to go upstairs now. It's just not right. Not here, not now."

"When will it be the right time?" She asked as she stood and faced him. When he didn't answer, she shook her head in frustration. "I'll go first." She turned and walked up the steps to her room. He saw her legs coming through her open robe. The temptation to follow her was deep. He truly had fallen in love with her.

He stayed downstairs for a long time and poured himself a glass of red wine. He sat on the veranda, looking at the stars and sipping the drink. What was he doing? This was insanity. All he ever wanted was to be a priest, but then Amelia showed up, and now, for the first time in his life, he was confused about the direction his life should take.

He and his father had a short trip to Lucca. Even in those few hours, all he wanted was to go back and be with Amelia. It was a lovely ride in the morning, sunny with a fresh breeze. They had a chance to talk man-to-man as they looked for gifts for Anthony's mother and sister. Anthony slipped into a jewelry shop at one point, but his father thought nothing of it. He knew Lisa had given Anthony a necklace, and Anthony wanted to have the chain shortened. Afterward, they got wine and pizza at the local pizza café. They chatted about the future of the business. His father hoped he would stay involved with the family business even after he finished seminary and became a priest.

Hans, Heinz, and Edwin were interested in continuing the family business but couldn't do it alone. Anthony was better at going through the fields, picking and tasting. Anthony agreed he'd continue to play a role in the business, even after entering the priesthood. He knew his father needed to hear that his sons would take over. They stayed overnight in the small hotel, met with longtime friends, and had a fabulous dinner.

After they walked around Lucca and visited their old friends for breakfast, they caught the early train home. They left Tuscany and Lucca behind as the sun was rising. There was nowhere on Earth like the Tuscan hills, peppered with small villages. Anthony's best friend lived in Radicondolo. They went to school together and entered the seminary together. However, after just a few months, Carl decided it wasn't for him and left. His calling was not strong enough. Anthony enjoyed his visits with him as much as possible. Carl had married at twenty and had a young baby of one year old. He ran his father's tool shop. Anthony thought of his friend as their visit was short the other day, but he knew Carl had made the right decision.

Anthony prayed his calling was strong enough. His friend, the priest in the village, told him that everyone had temptation. Occasionally, before becoming a priest, a man had someone enter his life in temptation. It was up to him which path he wanted to take.

There was no sin in questioning which path. He just needed to pray and think about it.

Upon arriving home from Lucca, Anthony immediately changed into his bathing suit and made his way to the veranda and the pool. He stopped in the kitchen and asked the cook to make a picnic basket. Not a word was asked, but the cook had known him since he was a baby and knew this would not end well. Anthony had no business taking a young girl on a picnic as he was going to enter the priesthood. The housekeeper and cook shook their heads and wagged their fingers at him, but he just laughed.

He found Amelia on the lower veranda reading *Wuthering Heights*, tears running down her face. She was in her bathing suit with a gauzy cover-up over the top.

"What's wrong, Amelia?" He took a spot on the chaise longue next to her and kissed her hand.

"Anthony, have you read this? Love lost and wasted years. *Wuthering Heights* has to be one of the saddest love stories."

He kissed her cheek. "It's just a book. Come, I have a surprise for you." He gave her his hand as he pulled her up from the lounge chair. The breeze swept her hair around her face, and her thin skirt swirled around her legs, revealing her bathing suit underneath.

He took her hand as they picked up the picnic basket through the kitchen. He took a little wagon to pull as they worked their way down to the beach below. It was not a short distance, and it took a fair amount of time to work their way down and through the village, finding the perfect spot in a private cove.

He spread out the blanket and started unpacking the basket, pulling out a variety of cheese, sausage, grapes, and fresh bread that smelled heavenly.

Amelia unwrapped her skirt and sat there in her suit. He, too, removed the extra clothing he was wearing and donned only his bathing suit trunks. They didn't speak much except for describing his visit to Lucca. He was now fumbling in his pants pocket he'd laid next to him as he pulled out a box and shyly handed it to Amelia.

She looked at him long and hard before opening the velvet-covered box. The jewelry inside was breathtaking: a pure sapphire heart pendant surrounded with diamonds and matching earrings.

Her breath caught. "Anthony, it must have cost a fortune," She said, never taking her eyes off the necklace.

Anthony smiled and reached over. "Let me put it on you. I just had the necklace made shorter. My mother gave it to me, telling me to give it to someone special some day. I had thought in years to come, I would give it to Katarina. I didn't know I would find someone like you. And now it is yours."

Amelia turned so he could place the necklace around her neck. He caught his breath as he put the clasp on and moved her hair to the side. He kissed the back of her neck as he buried his head in her hair, holding a handful of her locks. He turned her head to catch her lips.

"Amelia, I love you. Please know that I will always love you."

She pulled him to her in reply. The next hour was never to be forgotten. They loved each other. Their kisses spoke of young love and the passion for first love. It was unmanageable. He wanted her as no other. He had been with others, but he had never been consumed with a feeling that filled his soul. They both had a contentment they had never felt before.

After that magical day on the beach, they never spoke of when they would have to part ways. They spent the week, just the two of them, hiking the hills. He took her to every inch of the property, showing her the grapes cuttings and where they were processed. They took long walks to the village and had private dinners. They made love every day. His mother was anxious, while Amelia's family felt this was wonderful. Two families of wealth combining. Their daughter and the most eligible von Rahmel boy. They, too, were unaware that Anthony was going into the priesthood.

Lisa tried to have Jona talk to their son, but Jona only told her that it was his life and that he would decide for himself. But deep inside, Jona feared the outcome. They saw the necklace and earrings and were grateful it was not a ring.

On the next to last day of Amelia's visit, she clung to Anthony in tears. His strong hands held her head to his shoulder, his crystal eyes stark against her tanned face. He just wanted to hold her longer, wanted to hold her his whole life. He let out a long sigh, knowing he was saying goodbye.

"I don't want to leave you, Anthony, but we must return to Paris. Promise me you won't be far behind. I have a birthday next week. Please come. You love me, don't you?"

"Amelia, you are the only one I will ever love. Besides you, I have no other love but for my baby sister. I just need to explain something, and it's not fair I didn't tell you weeks ago."

She started to back away. She didn't want to hear what he had to say. "Are you promised to someone else?"

"No, Amelia, only you." He hesitated. "Amelia, I was your first, but your parents mentioned someone in Paris?"

"Anthony, not to worry. I did have a young man interested in me, but once again, it was all about business deals with my parents so our family could have a bigger fortune. His name is Simon, and he's a very nice person, but he's not you." She smiled and trailed a finger down his chest. "Write me a beautiful letter for me to read on my way back to Paris."

He let out a long sigh. "I will write you a long letter and write one every day of my life."

"Anthony, that is so silly. We'll be together for the rest of our lives. You promised me on the beach. You know I'd never get over you."

The next two days were mingled with sadness and love-making as Amelia prepared to leave.

Amelia's parents signed a contract with the Von Rahmel family that was lucrative for both families and their wine business.

Amelia Bushreal left in tears, and her parents asked for the Von Rahmels to visit as soon as possible. She reluctantly took out the letter Anthony gave her. She knew she'd never forget how he held her, and she had the awful odd feeling that he was saying goodbye.

My Dear Amelia, my love, my life,

I write this with a heavy heart.

Amelia placed the letter in her lap and didn't want to read any further. She already knew. Tears spilled from her eyes as she forced herself to pick the letter up again.

Amelia, my secret has never been about anyone, but instead, another love that runs deeper than any human emotion. I failed to tell you that I will be entering into my second year of seminary life to be a priest.

I wanted to stay away from you, but I fell in love with you and will always love you. I want you to know that I will go through my life looking for you in every space where the sky meets the ocean. I will hear your voice in whispers as the breeze floats through the trees. I will have you on every edge of my dreams. When I hear rain, I will think of your voice. Every rainbow my eyes see, I will think of you. I will live remembering your laughter. Nothing on Earth can separate you from my mind, not time, not space, not even death. I will recall your cool hands on my brow and the touch of your fingers on my face. I will hear you in the whisper of the leaves. You, my love, are the fragrance of life itself. I will go through life craving you. Every dawn will be disrupted with thoughts of you. I will always be thankful for the light you have given me and will remain restless as the sea because of missing you. But my obligation is of another life that I give freely too. You would become weary of me if I left my God for you. Then, my heart would also have this same empty feeling. You would soon tire of me trying to serve two people.

My dream will be touching you, kissing your sweet lips, and smelling your skin. You will never be far from my thoughts; I will carry you always in my heart. In some small way, I hope I will also be at the edge of your dreams.

I want you to be happy and have a wonderful life filled with someone who loves you and gives you a good home and children. I will never forgive myself for the pain I'm inflicting upon you right now as you read this.

She let the letter flutter to the floor as she leaned her head against the window, silently weeping as she clutched her stomach and rubbed the life inside of her. She silently cursed his church and his beliefs. She didn't curse him because she loved him and always would. She knew she couldn't compete against God.

Her fingers went to her neck as she touched the necklace. She would never give the necklace away; it would stay with her. She gathered up the letter and folded it to be safeguarded as she would reread it many times in her life. She read it to Hanna the day she was born.

The Present

Anthony shook his head the long-ago memory as the thoughts of her caused a pain in his chest he had never had; it was an ache that never left him from the day he last saw her. There was no day he did not love or pray for or think of her.

The arm was now pulling Anthony. His thoughts only focused on one voice. He had to find a way to find her. He could only think of the love they first shared.

"Move, Anthony!" Peter said. "We can't save anyone else, not even Amelia. They will either kill her or send her to a concentration camp."

They made it back to the safe house. Anthony sat in silence; he couldn't get Amelia's bruised face or pleading eyes out of his mind. For the first time ever, there was a burning in his soul. It was the first time he wanted to kill those who hurt her. The sadist psychopaths. He hated every one of them and wanted revenge. *God forgive me*, he thought. He wanted revenge, and he wanted to kill them.

"Anthony, it's time for you to move on and get back to Berlin," Peter said.

Anthony shook his head. "I can't. I have to find Amelia, and I have to find who she said is mine."

Then they came into the room where Claude was.

"Father, Peter, they didn't kill her; she is on a train to Ravensbrück with another French woman. We believe the information is correct."

Anthony clenched his fists, and anger was building inside him. Peter sat opposite him and saw the anger and hurt growing.

"Anthony, she was one of us, an operative. She is married to Simon. She tried to help us save Simon's sister. Amelia took care of the SS colonel who had brutally beaten his sister. The man is sure to have risen from hell. He plunged our resistance fighters, especially the women, into cold baths, holding them under. He slashed their feet with razors and used soldering irons on their bodies, and raped them. Amelia found him herself, and she had him tortured. She made sure he was dead, but when she got back to Henri's, one of the soldiers who was being treated recognized her somehow as being around the dead colonel. He turned her in with Henri's wife and children. The same day, Gabriella was trying to help two children. I promise you, Anthony, we will try to find her. But right now, we need you back in Berlin."

Nicholas and Dietric went with Anthony. Nicholas drove as they put Anthony into a cardinal's outfit and transformed the others into priests as they made their way to the train station. They were saying goodbye to Father Julian in the church when they heard someone shout at them to halt. Two Gestapos were walking up the church aisle. Stepping into the shadows behind the large pillars were Nicholas and Gregory.

The Gestapo raised their hands and said, "Heil Hitler." Father Julian and Anthony made the sign of the cross. A fury crossed the Gestapos' faces.

"Priests, raise your hands."

Julian spoke first. "We raise our hands only to God."

The Gestapo pulled out his weapon. "We came to question you, but we see maybe it's better you spill your blood at your own altar. Your priest defies us on every corner we turn. But before we shoot you, you will tell us where Father McFarland, the Irish priest, is. He was last seen here in this church."

Julian smiled as he looked into their lifeless eyes with no soul, just evil.

"Sorry, we do not know who you speak of. An Irish man would certainly be noticeable." A smirk played on Father Julian's lips.

Before Anthony and Father Julian could react, the one Gestapo struck Father Julian in the face with the butt of his gun. A gash split open on Father Julian's forehead and began seeping blood. Before the Gestapo could point their guns, Nicholas and Gregory moved swiftly behind them, grabbing them by the necks and pulling them down to the ground. While they struggled to breath, the gun dropped, but not before Gregory placed the guns into the first Gestapo's mouth and pulled the trigger. The other Gestapo watched in horror, but only briefly, as Nicholas reached down and snapped his neck. The last sight as they took their last breath was staring at these two priests before they entered Hell.

They pulled the bodies between two pews. Footsteps approached, and Nicholas and Gregory pulled their guns.

"Don't shoot! It's us." Louis, Peter and Dietric rushed from the side door.

Peter looked at the dead bodies and arched his eyebrows as he turned to Gregory. "Good job."

"What do we do with them?" Father Julian asked.

Suddenly, three nuns appeared with sheets, plastic, and a bucket of water.

"Sisters, what are you doing here?" Father Julian asked.

"We were coming into the church to light some candles when we saw the Gestapo strike you," a stern-faced sister said. "We knew it was not going to go well, so we rushed back and got these items in the back of the church and hoped we could do something. We, too, are tired of the erroneous regulations, strict censorship, incessant propaganda, and nightly curfews. We're tired of living in this atmosphere of fear and repression without adequate food for our orphans. They continue to repeat the same lines that anyone who is caught should be shot. Well, we showed them, didn't we? They don't intimidate us any longer."

As the group of men stared into these angelic faces, one of the sisters pulled out a gun from her pocket, then another. This gun-wielding nun had two Berettas.

Gregory looked in disbelief like the others. "Sisters, are they loaded?"

The sisters started to laugh.

"Of course they are! Why have an empty gun?" Sister Anna answered.

Two of the sisters were already walking towards the bodies. One of them shuddered. They all worked quickly to fold the bodies into the plastic and carry them out the side door, hoping at this time of night, the streets were empty. Fortunately, Claude had waited and not left them as they had asked him to. He immediately pulled up to the alley side door of the church, placed the bodies in the car, and told the group that he would take care of them.

"Now, it truly is a good work done by Anthony. We need to take you to the other car. You have all your paperwork?" Peter was now standing before them with Louis.

Anthony hugged his cousin. "Peter, please watch out for Heinz. I'm not sure I will be back anytime soon. If there is any possibility to save Amelia…"

"Anthony, Amelia is married to Simon, and he will do everything he can, though his hands are somewhat tied. Since they think his family is in Switzerland, he can't admit that Amelia is his wife."

Anthony stopped before he entered the car. "Do you know how many are in his family?"

"He has a daughter and one son. His daughter is the first born. Her name is Hanna. Anthony, you need to understand that Hanna was born right after Amelia came back that summer. She was visiting you and the rest of the family. She immediately married Simon; it was all very quick."

They drove mostly in silence, each in their own thoughts. Gregory and Nicholas both needed to hook up with their counterparts in Germany. Both brothers were concerned about the Von Rahmel family; Gregory especially about Katarina because he knew Frederick Spitz was responsible for a priest from Anthony's church being taken to Berlin Gestapo headquarters on Prinz Albrechtstrasse. Many taken there did not return. Those who did tell of dungeons and torture.

Gregory decided at the last minute to go back with them. He

enjoyed seeing the payback with Allied bombers hitting Germany, but at the same time, he had grown to love the Von Rahmel family and wanted to protect them. The Gestapo burnt his city in Ukraine on the border with Russia, they killed his parents, raped his sister, then shot her as he and Nicholas were returning home. They saw it all unfold and could do nothing. Their town was burning, but he swore there would be no Gestapo standing when the war ended. They managed to move his aunt and uncle to Palestine. They hooked up with resistance fighters in Poland and Germany, where they found Anthony, who was able to deliver papers to so many. Peter had trained them well during those months in England.

Anthony was putting pieces together of the timeline and he knew deep inside that Amelia's firstborn was his child.

The train ride was short, and Edwin had a car waiting for them in Germany. In the distance, they saw the fires and the sound of Allied bombers.

It was a long drive but uneventful. They didn't make any stops as they arrived back in Berlin at Anthony's church. When they got there, the sirens sounded. Moments later, they felt the concussion of the incendiaries of the antiaircraft batteries chasing the bombers. They knew there would be an Allied bomber they would have to hide and rescue. The three of them went to the secret room and safely stashed all the documents, ration cards, and baptismal records they would need to move people out of Berlin.

Anthony told them to rest on the cots that were in the room. The food was scarce, but he managed to find some stale bread, tea, and marmalade from his mother's garden. She had also left fresh cheese for his return in the kitchen. They still had goats that they managed to milk. It was hours later, they learned the fate of Edwin's wife as

Frederick Spitz had her arrested first. The sorrow now began for the Von Rahmel family.

Chapter 8

1940-1945

Weeks passed, and Heinz's parents were overjoyed to learn he had married. The war was increasingly difficult. For Anthony, the worry was always etched around his eyes. Anthony's father saw that there was more than the war weighing on his son's heart. He found Anthony in constant prayer outside of his normal prayer and Mass time. They suffered through the Allied bombings, and they moved Allied pilots to safety. They hid and moved Jews to keep them from being arrested. It was not many, but a life was a life saved. They hadn't heard any information about those in France for weeks now.

Anthony lived in worry for his friends. Katarina performed and became more involved with Frederick Spitz. It was one of those nights that Anthony came to dinner. They were sitting at the table, and Katarina just blurted out, "Mother, do you recall a family, or do you still do business with a family called the Bushreals? We met a man named Simon Gerard. He told us the Bushreals and his wife Amelia knew us?"

Lisa Von Rahmel coughed, nearly spitting out her water.

"Katarina, we still have contracts with them, but the war has sort of put this all under the table. You were just a baby when we signed a contract with them. Why in the world would you be asking?"

"I was just curious. Simon's wife looks like the girl in the albums that are in a trunk in the attic. I saw her and Simon in pictures in France." Katarina looked at Anthony. "Anthony, you looked so happy. You were in many of them with this beautiful girl. You both are so young. On the back of the picture was the name Amelia, same as Simon's wife."

Jona and Lisa both saw the stricken look on Anthony's face. There were no words needed, but they knew the debt of sorrow that entered their son's eyes. It was the same look he had when he went back to the seminary after saying goodbye to Amelia.

Katarina observed the looks between Anthony and her parents and decided not to push the subject or ask any more questions. It was clear there was a lot of hurt on Anthony's face—a type of hurt she had never seen before. Besides, they were angry with her as she told them that Frederick Spitz wanted to marry her. They were still trying to explain why it was not a good idea.

After dinner, her parents and Anthony went into the library. The space was no longer filled to the brim with books since the book burning in Berlin. Katarina watched through the open doors as she cleared the dishes. She watched Anthony nodding in agreement, and suddenly, he brought his hands to his face to wipe the tears. *My God,* she thought. What did she say to open such a feeling of despair? Her mother went over to the desk and pulled open a photo album. She watched him move several pages and saw their mother point.

Anthony's face went pale. Amelia and her parents had come to visit Anthony's parents in Munich three years later. Amelia was with Simon, holding the baby. The baby's eyes looking back at him in the picture were his eyes. There was a younger boy also. He looked like Simon.

Katarina could not hear the whole conversation as she walked to the door to hear. She knew it was serious.

"Anthony, what happened that summer? Sit and tell us. Maybe we can help," his mother said.

Anthony sighed. "I think this picture makes it clear what happened. She must have married Simon as soon as she got back to Paris. I really don't want to go down that path."

"Anthony, we can figure all of this out after this war ends. We promise we will help in any way possible."

Anthony shook his head. "I just needed to find Amelia and her daughter. I promised her. I just pray she and Simon both stay alive."

Later that night, Katarina went into the library and pulled the picture album out. She saw a picture of herself when she was just a baby. Anthony was fifteen when she was born. And there they were: pictures of Anthony holding a young woman in a tight embrace. Both had lovely, tanned bodies. Amelia looked so happy and beautiful. Anthony looked even happier. Then Katarina turned a few pages and saw pictures of Amelia and Simon several years later. She recognized Simon immediately—even in later pictures, he had not changed much since she met him in France. They held a beautiful little girl and a little boy in a carriage. It was the eyes and the cheekbones that made the siblings look so different from each other. It was as if she were looking at Anthony. She took in a deep breath. *It couldn't be*, she said to herself. He had been in seminary at that time. He had been a priest for as long as she could remember. He was the brother who loved her the most and always protected her. *It couldn't be*, she thought again. He would never step over the line. He was perfect, and the church was his first love. But looking at this little girl, the similarities were shocking. She looked so much like Anthony in the face.

Katarina thought that if she got back to Paris after the war, maybe she could talk to Amelia—if, by some miracle, Amelia survived. Simon said she was in Switzerland. The house and grounds made it clear that Amelia had made a good life with Simon, and how he spoke about Amelia proved he was devoted to her and she was the love of his life. *It's a mystery*, Katarina thought. Simon's Amelia was Anthony's Amelia, or was she mistaken? She had to put it out of her mind. Anthony would never go against his feelings for his church.

A few months later, Katarina married Frederick Spitz against her family's objections. But he abused her so badly that she left after only a few months. Only Anthony knew she was pregnant now, so she returned to live at home. Soul-crushing sorrow filled the air as soon as Anthony walked into his parents' home. Katarina curled in a ball on the sofa, crying. Their parents were in despair as Father was trying to settle their brother Edwin down to listen and not do anything rash. Jona quickly explained that Rita had been taken. Only Katarina was home and could not stop them from taking her. They would figure something out, but Edwin was not going to waste time. He had to find his wife. Dietric, his best friend who was more like a brother, was putting his gun into his pants belt.

Edwin eventually located Rita at Ravensbruck, but as he tried to get her out, they were both electrocuted by the fence surrounding the camp. Dietric could only watch as his best friend died, clinging to his wife. Dodging bullets from the camp guards, Dietric darted to the fence and dragged Edwin's body away. He buried Edwin in the forest. Later, he would take the Von Rahmel family to the location to give him a proper burial.

Katarina

Meanwhile, the family could not convince Katarina that Frederick Spitz was not right for her. He played cat and mouse with Anthony as he would just appear at the rectory, always circling like the devil himself. Anthony could feel the evil.

The Gestapo agent had convinced Katarina that he loved her, but once they married, everything changed. He only wanted information about the Von Rahmel family and all their holdings in Italy and where Anthony was going in France. Wisely, Katarina said nothing. She told him only of her memories of a happy childhood in Italy. Each day, he became more frustrated with the lack of information until Helga told him that Edwin's wife was Jewish and had converted to Catholicism when she and Edwin married. Frederick would bide his time to have her arrested, but in the meantime, he tortured Katarina with emotional and physical abuse.

Katarina quickly realized their marriage was a sham; Frederick's love was fake, and he only married her to infiltrate her family. He wanted to know about her family's finances, their business transactions, if they moved money out of Germany (which was illegal), and if they sold land and property (also illegal). He also had heard the rumor there was a Jew among their Catholic family. The girl who married Edwin had a Catholic baptism record, but she was thought to be a Jew. Helga, in one of her drunken trysts with him, told him she had dated Edwin, but he only wanted the Jew girl. They thought they had everyone fooled but not her.

Frederick also hated Anthony from the moment they met. Anthony would feel as if the devil himself was circling when he entered the rectory for a "small chat," as Frederick called it. The

Gestapo couldn't tolerate the Catholic or Lutheran churches. Frederick knew Anthony would often leave and visit France. Katarina would sometimes go with him.

She'd tell Frederick she needed to visit her brother Heinz and say that Anthony had church issues. She always gave him limited information, but Frederick wasn't stupid, and he always felt there was more to the story. When he finally married the lovely, talented, and incredibly beautiful Katarina, he tortured her with his words and pushed her often. But he never hit her because she was performing with her ballet company for Hitler at times, and if he had hit her, others would see the bruises. She was admired for her talent and beauty, but he hated her. Everything she and her family stood for: their wealth, their prestige in German society, the airs they took with people like him. He came from a divorced family and lived with his father while his brother was taken to live with their mother.

No one would ever be good enough for the Von Rahmel's only daughter. Frederick would prove them wrong, and he would destroy the priest and his church—the church that was the enemy of Hitler. Frederick was unrelenting in his abuse of Katarina; from the first night of their marriage, he warned her not to say a word about their relationship because he had the power to have her family sent to interrogations. He said that with one conversation, he could have her entire family put in concentration camps. She didn't realize at this point that he in fact, did not have this power, but she believed him.

That is, until one night, she had the courage to leave him.

She knew enough to go because she had grown up watching her parents love and respect each other. Her brothers loved her, and what Frederick Spitz was doing was not love. She was humiliated on the nights he brought women into their homes. He would tell her to go to the other bedroom while he would take these random women in the bed they shared. He took Katarina when he wanted her but always humiliated her, forcing her to do things she didn't want to do for him. Then, she became pregnant.

As she explained later, he did not make love to her, it was rape. He wanted her to perform things she just could not do. It sickened her. He would laugh at her because she was a virgin the first night and had a lack of experience. He never made love to her, he only abused her—never a tender word or touch. Once, he even promised her to one of his drunken Gestapo card-playing friends. One night, as they were playing cards and drinking heavily, she had already gone to sleep when she heard the door swing open, and a drunken Frederick Spitz was standing there with another man. Frederick pushed him over to her and shoved the man on top of her as she begged him not to do this. He told her she would have sex with him or face the consequences of more abuse. She was lucky the man fell on the floor. He fell asleep there, and she didn't move out of fear. She prayed he would just keep sleeping. It wasn't until the next morning, when Frederick Spitz woke him, and they left the room, that she could breathe again.

Other times, Spitz made her perform to music to her total humiliation in front of men who laughed and leered at her. When she tried to stop, Frederick would walk over and slap her hard to keep dancing till he told her to stop. Sometimes, the men would grab at her, touching her inappropriately as he watched.

Every one of these men, she thought to herself, were evil. She should have had the courage to leave on their wedding night. Spitz left Katarina right after they consummated their marriage. When he returned hours later, he brought home another woman. Katarina had to listen from her bedroom as he had sex with this stranger.

She spent many nights crying for hours. She wanted to leave, but how? He mentioned once under his breath if she left, her whole family would be arrested.

Frederick would often leave and not return until the next morning. There were nights she would hear him come in late, and she'd hope he brought a woman home with him so she would be saved that night from sleeping next to this abusive, humiliating, and evil man. When he did bring home another woman, she was grateful she would be safe, but she could always hear them. She was too embarrassed to go to her parents or Anthony about her situation because she felt like she had brought it upon herself. This went on for many days and months into their marriage. It made her bitter and scared.

One night, she decided to look in his office. There was a folder he looked at almost every day, and she couldn't deny her curiosity any longer. When she went in, she saw the cabinet half open. She saw a folder with her last name on it. It was her entire family, and something took over her. Her hands moved to her growing stomach and the tiny baby inside. He'd wanted her to abort it, but she refused.

She opened the folder, and inside, she saw the note. Her blood ran cold. Frederick wanted them all dead, but those in power liked the Von Rahmel family. It all made sense now. Inside this folder was Frederick's plan to destroy her entire family. Use her, the famous ballerina beloved by Hitler, to his advantage. Destroy the priest, find his network, and dismantle it. He wrote that her other brothers, being good Germans, would be tricky. Her one brother was a top Luftwaffe pilot, the other in tanks with General Rommel. Katarina herself was held in high regard, as well as the rest of the family. Spitz wanted them gone. He felt they were the problem of the last few years in Germany with their wealth and prestige. Shattering their large family was a promise he made to himself. He refused to allow anyone to go against the German Reich, and the church was his number one enemy next to the Jews.

Hitler ordered the Von Rahmels' estate in Munich to be used by his generals. The Von Rahmels moved out of their home without objecting. They moved to Berlin, where they had two apartment buildings and their fifty-acre estate. The house was enormous, with almost a 9,000-square-foot footprint. They also owned other homes and apartment buildings. The German military took over the factories to forge equipment, but they stayed in the family. The Gestapo in Munich took wine by the case from the Von Rahmels. Before Katarina was pregnant, Hitler loved to see her perform for his military. Spitz had a hard time going against this family. He found his way in by marrying Katarina.

What had happened? She kept asking herself that question until the one night when he left and casually told her he would be with someone else that night. At that moment, something snapped inside of her, and she knew she was done. He would not come near her again or let any of his other friends bring over their whores again as they sat around discussing how to rid the world of Jews or the churches.

That night, she packed her bag. She wanted out of the marriage, which was Spitz's last expectation. As she left, she dropped a defiant note on the table: "You will never destroy this family."

She promised herself that she would always be suspicious of anyone who said they loved her. Being pregnant couldn't have come at a worse time. What would she tell this child? That her father didn't want her? Katarina didn't want him to even come near the baby after it was born. She had to protect the child.

She packed her bag that night and left. She went to the rectory and told Anthony everything while Gregory and Nicholas listened in the other room. Gregory wanted to kill Frederick Spitz for what he put her through. He and Nicholas now knew her secrets, but he would never tell her he heard everything. They saw her coming up the rectory steps at midnight with her suitcase and knew it was not going to be good news. They went into the other room but left the door slightly ajar as she cried and told Anthony of every humiliation that Spitz placed on her. Gregory and Nicholas had to fight not to leave the rectory that night to find him. But they knew, at this point, it wouldn't do any good. His time would come.

Katerina stayed that night at the rectory. Later that night, she was woken by a voice she did not recognize. She listened as the man told Anthony that Amelia was still alive but had been put in the Ravensbrück concentration camp with other French women.

This man would try to find out more information, but it would be almost impossible to have anyone escape there. Katarina waited till the stranger left, then went into the kitchen and found some old tea bags. How many times had they already been used, she thought. She also found some bread, goat cheese, and apples (quite the luxury). She boiled some water and made tea, sitting there, contemplating her life, when Anthony came in with Gregory and Nicholas. She saw Gregory's look as he stared at her long and hard. It was always difficult for him to take his eyes off her. He knew from the moment he saw her that he loved her. She quickly pulled out two more cups and used the tea bags again. The tea was becoming weaker with each use. There had been heavy bombing the night before. They hastily discussed how the part of the wall between the rectory and the Sisters of Mercy's home that they got messages through had been destroyed and they would have it fixed as quickly as possible.

It was less than a month later when climbing the steps of the apartment became too difficult. She had moved to the villa outside of the city for a few days, and Spitz found her. She hadn't seen him for months and now wished she had stayed in the city where there were more people around. After he left, it might be better to move back to the center of Berlin. She looked at him defiantly as he pushed past her. Right away, he noticed her growing belly. Spitz was furious and ordered her back to their home. He was looking out their large window, looking at the vast amount of land and stables. Grunewald, where their family home sat, was where only the wealthy lived. He thought to himself as he turned to her, maybe he should come live here.

"This place needs to be occupied by one of our officers. You and your family need to move back to the city. Or should I move in here with you and your family, and we can be one big, happy family?" He heard a thunderous voice behind him.

"You shall leave, Frederick Spitz, never to cross over our home steps again."

Jona, her father, was standing in his riding boots. He had just come back from the stables and had a horse whip in his hand. Jona knew to many in the Government that this house would not be occupied. It was a promise made to him by a friend who was a General.

"Do you hear me? If not, I will escort you myself outside."

Fredrick Spitz glared at him. "Old man, I wouldn't take such freedom speaking to me in this way. I can have you all arrested with a snap of my finger."

"You won't, Fredrick, because we know people also who could make your world very small and could make you move to the Russian Front."

Spitz turned to Katarina. "I don't care what you do, but get rid of that child, or I will." He heard the whip crack against the floor and Jona walking towards him. "I'm leaving, but you will pay, trust my words."

It seemed so quiet for months. Katarina was nearly eight months pregnant. They had moved back into their lavish apartment in Berlin, which was still standing despite the air raids. The home was closer to her doctor and nurse.

It was here that Hell came to visit. Her parents were out at the manor house, looking in on what food they had stored away that summer. They were going to make sure those who remained behind with the animals had enough food. It was now 1944. They managed to keep a few chickens, goats, and one cow. There were three Jewish families hidden in Dresden that hadn't been able to move out of Germany, and they needed enough food to stay alive. Everything was becoming increasingly dangerous for them because they were losing protection from higher-ups. It was time to go.

Lisa's sister Helena had already left for her home in Switzerland, so they had a place to stay. Anthony had arrived to escort Katarina with additional papers to get on the train to Switzerland. He knew Frederick Spitz was narrowing his sights on the family. Spitz's Nazi friends already come into the church with large knives and shovels and started to destroy the pews, though the statues remained for now.

His parents had left the manor house for the train station as Anthony promised he would get to Katarina and ensure she reached Switzerland. His mother and father departed in tears, leaving Anthony and Katarina behind. Jona had a difficult time leaving his veterinary practice and his horses, but they were left in good hands at the estate. Resistance fighters made sure there were no issues as they made their way to the train station. Anthony took Gregory and Nicholas with him to the apartment to fetch Katarina.

Jona made sure Fritz, the estate caretaker, knew what to do with the remaining food and documents from Anthony. They gave extra food to the Jewish family, and if they managed to leave the hiding place, they had a few ration cards left. Most Jews tried to escape. Some got to the Netherlands, but their freedom was short-lived. When the Nazis invaded and took over, many Jews tried to get on ships to America and England. Some managed to get into Palestine.

Fritz was always at the manor house and looked out for the property. They offered him to come along, but he wanted to stay, hoping to protect as much as he could. They were always concerned that the Nazis would try to take over the manor house, but by some miracle, it stayed untouched, leaving Fritz to plant vegetables and use the goats for milk and cheese throughout the war. Samuel, their lawyer friend, was now living at the manor house because his apartment building was in ruins from allied bombings. If anything were to happen, he was to stay and take care of everything. Their wills of who received what were drawn up, including Fritz and Dietric. Fritz and Dietric had been with the family since they were children themselves.

His parents were safely on their train, and Anthony made his way to the apartment. Once Katarina was taken care of, he would make his way to Switzerland. Nicholas and Gregory were to go with them, and then they would try to reach parts of France to continue their help. When the Gestapo entered their Berlin city apartment home, looking for her parents and asking where they were, Katarina identified herself.

Sitting in a car, a man was down the street smoking a cigarette. He had an odd smile on his face, and he thought, now it begins. I will have each one of them dead, but slowly.

Helena, Lisa and Jona reached Switzerland, but Frederick Spitz had Katarina arrested and gave orders to have the whole family shot if they were found. Anthony could do nothing as he sat in the car, watching them lead Katarina down the steps. Frederick Spitz stood outside the arrest vehicle, slapping her one more time and barking orders. Someone who had been working with Edwin changed the paperwork, so Katarina was sent to a concentration camp and not shot as the orders originally stood. Gregory, Nicholas, and Anthony barely escaped, but before they left Berlin, they placed explosives under Frederick Spitz's bed and watched that night as he laid down with a woman, and the bed exploded. Anthony did not feel guilt or remorse. He said a quick prayer for the woman who was with him but condemned Frederick Spitz to hell.

They now decided they had to rescue Katarina, and the three proceeded and plotted.

Heinz

Heinz learned of his family's troubles quickly. Dietric arrived in Lyon to tell him all communication had stopped in Berlin. Their priority now was to find Katarina, especially since she was close to giving birth.

Louis and Peter were now worried for Heinz. Would he be next? Even though it hurt him inside, he managed to be their top Luftwaffe ace fighter pilot to keep up his image. He said a prayer every time he had to take on the British, as it was his family down there. He spent part of his life in Brighton, England, with Peter. The boys all loved their visits with their cousins. Claire, Peter's wife, was amazing as she kept their home going.

The SS were watching. Heinz was able to find out if Amelia was alive and moved the news to Berlin, but the others transported with her would soon be dead. Few survived Ravensbrück under hard labor and starvation. Fritz Suhren was known to be a sadist. Amelia was placed in an inner bunker with no windows, and she lived in utter darkness. They couldn't distinguish night from day; they only knew the time by the food that was placed through a latch. One person who did manage to escape reported that those in the bunkers could hear the screams and count each strike on their back as they heard the colonel count.

Himmler found the most sadistic men he could. Dietric conveyed the horrors also from that day when Edwin and Rita died. He made his way to Lyon to meet up with Heinz and Peter. It was Dietric who had to tell Heinz of his family's fate. They knew his brother Hans was still safe in Africa with Rommel.

They had found out quickly that Frederick Spitz first had Anthony arrested weeks before he started to arrest Rita and Katarina. Dietric was the only one who knew of Anthony's arrest. Anthony only told a few people as Dietric attended to Anthony's wounds. After a few hours of being interrogated and beaten, he was released. Then came Rita, and at the end, Katarina.

Nicholas was about five-seven, a strong-looking man with broad shoulders, deep brown eyes, and curly black hair. Gregory was nearly six feet tall and slender. He had deep ocean-green eyes, his hair was not as black, his upper body tapered to a narrow waist, his jawline was square, and his nose elongated. He, too, was of a muscular build like his brother Nicholas. Nicholas reminded Anthony of a little bear, his eyes with the glint of laughter even in terrible times, whereas Gregory never smiled. But both could kill with bare hands, and killing came easy for Gregory. They had worked hard with Anthony since the day they arrived to recruit him with the help of a priest in France, which he jumped at willingly. This was at the very beginning of the war; they knew of his activities since 1934, and now here they were after years and months of terrible fear and memories. The days before Katarina was arrested, Anthony had managed to get all the papers together for his parents, Aunt Helena, and her husband to leave for Switzerland. Now, they were on a different journey, not to Switzerland or to France, but to find Katarina and some other resistance fighters.

Heinz went to Reims, France. He had limited time to visit with Peter and Louis. He, too, was afraid of being watched, so they made plans to meet at Elvie's home, where her parents now lived. It was a second home as the Nazis had taken over their chateau.

Heinz buried his head in his hands and wept over the news of Edwin's death. Peter grew up with Heinz and never saw him cry. Peter came over to where he was sitting. His voice was low and choked with emotion. He, too, was devastated by the news from Berlin, and Dietric told them every sordid detail.

"Heinz, go back to flying," Peter said. "Don't think of us or England or family. Just go and keep yourself alive. My only desire is to keep you alive and pray for Anthony and Katarina. I'm sure with

Nicholas, Gregory, and some of the stragglers of the resistance, they will catch up. They will keep them safe, and they will find Katarina."

Heinz looked up; his clear blue eyes red-rimmed, his strong jawline clenched as he grasped Peter's hand.

"Promise me, if anything happens to me, you'll get Elvie to my parents. It won't be safe for her here if the war ends. She won't be accepted since she's married to a German, regardless of her work."

Chapter 9

1944-1945 were the harshest years. The French Resistance were fighting hard. They lost many, but they all believed the end was nearing. The French police were traitors to France as Henri and Louis made sure all names were jotted down for the future.

Before his murder, Heinz managed to help Elvie escape to Spain and then on to Switzerland. She left enough information under a floorboard in her office to convict those who looted homes, and she put names and addresses in bags with jewelry, hoping they would be returned. She prayed she would be able to return on her own and watch those convicted.

By 1944, the Luftwaffe was no longer able to fight as before. Only a handful of Luftwaffe operations went to the beaches with the invasion of Normandy. Heinz, unfortunately, was told to perform strafing runs; he followed Josef Priller and his wingman Emil Lang, who scored twenty-nine victories against the Western Allies. Heinz came in second with twenty-four, making him one of the highest-scoring German aces of the campaign. Even this would not save him.

A week later while in Reims, Heinz went to the home of Louis, Henri, and Elvie. Elvie's mother had died in her sleep of heart problems, and now her father was in hiding. Heinz wanted to see what he could save in his personal belongings. The SS were waiting for Heinz, and it was clear his accomplishments didn't matter this time. They questioned him for hours on where he thought his family was in Switzerland. They asked if he knew where Elvie's brothers had disappeared. Did he know where his brother Anthony was?

Louis, Henri, and others had made their way to Reims, hoping to meet up with Heinz, whom they knew was in danger. Word had gotten to them that they needed to get Heinz to England. Heinz stayed defiant as he walked out the door; they watched them push Heinz. The Gestapo told him to stop, but he kept walking. As he turned one more time to look at the Gestapo, he looked up at the Bern, where the resistance was hiding. His eyes seemed to center on Louis. The Gestapo shot and killed Heinz with a single bullet to the head. As Heinz crumpled to the ground, his blood seeping into the yard, Louis had to hold Peter down. Peter choked back a sob as tears streamed down his face, and Louis bowed his head in prayer. His chest felt heavy, and he had to hold Peter down. His chest felt heavy. What were they going to tell Anthony?

Louis had the Gestapos' faces memorized; they would be found. Louis and Peter moved Heinz back to the church graveyard when the Gestapo cleared out. He would have a proper burial, not some shallow grave. Later, Elvie could come and visit him.

It was not until the war ended that the Von Rahmel family made their way back to Munich and Berlin. They could have stayed in Switzerland, but they wanted to go home. Their first stop was at their home in Munich, where they saw so much devastation. The vineyards that had been cultivated over three generations of grapes were burnt to the ground. Only one hundred fifty acres of their six hundred acres were still standing. The land needed a lot of care, but some vines survived.

Then, the family made their way back to Berlin. The apartment was still in one piece, and so was the house in Grunewald. They had three factories that were still somewhat operational, two in the east and one on the west side of Berlin. Elvie had her little girl in Switzerland. They were still looking for Katarina, who had also delivered a baby girl in the concentration camp. She'd managed to escape and had the baby moved to Switzerland. Katarina continued with the resistance that, in the end, was the death of Nicholas in her arms. Gregory escaped, and Anthony had been badly wounded. It took Anthony months to find Katarina in a hospital after the war ended. She'd been rescued by the British from a pile of dead bodies about to be burned. One soldier saw her hand move and pulled her out, still handcuffed to a decomposing body.

It was here that Fritz told them about Heinz. He'd received the information from a Lutheran pastor who was friends with Anthony. Anthony was in Rome, still recuperating from the wounds he sustained in Munich. By a miracle, Fritz kept the horses and goats safe, helping to feed those in need through the Berlin Airlift. The Russians tried to starve the Germans to death and freeze them.

They managed to find the canned vegetables and fruit still buried. This would have to last them a long time. They realized it was a mistake to come back; they should have stayed in Switzerland. When they considered returning to Switzerland, they could not get the correct paperwork. Lisa cried as she realized they were stuck in Hell, but better in the American sector then the Russian. The rapes of women and children were by the hundreds. The Russians were raping three-year-olds, then shooting any women they could in what would later be called the rape of Berlin. There, by pure accident, Gertrude had crossed into the Russian sector looking for Hans. She, too, fell to the Russians and would never be able to have another child. Later, in the fifties and sixties, she fell in love with Katarina's daughter Natalie, whom she treated as her own.

Elvie was fortunate she left Paris. The fate of women who collaborated with Germans, even if it was just for survival, was not good, so many who were with the resistance had to prove themselves. The French didn't realize the importance of the women who stayed with German officers to move out information. Many were found and taken out on the street, where they were stripped naked and had their hair shaved. Some were tarred and feathered, sometimes fatally. Those who collaborated with the Germans by torturing and giving up their own countrymen were hung.

Elvie, too, moved out to Switzerland, then back to Berlin with the Von Rahmel family. Dietric was good to Elvie, and they soon fell in love, and he treated her daughter as his own. She would always love Heinz, and her thoughts were with him every day. Their daughter was Heinz's spitting image, which made Elvie happy; she saw him in her every day. She and Dietric married and had a good life. Katarina's fate was sealed with memories she could not bury. She gave her and Spitz's child to her parents to raise and worked her way to America by marrying a captain in the Army. He lived in Hawaii, and she deliberately got pregnant with his son to get herself out of Berlin.

Father Julian suffered. He found his mother and sisters in June 1944 at Oradour–sur–Glane. The entire village was taken down to the ground. The men were collected and shot to death, while the women and children were herded into a church, locked inside, and set on fire. Everyone burned to death. The entire village was gone, and Father Julian swore to find those who did this and make them pay. He asked Anthony through the years to forgive him because his thoughts were still to seek those out and have justice upon them, even if it meant they would be murdered in the streets. He felt in his heart that they didn't deserve a trial, which went against any thought a priest could and should have.

Henri and Louis were caught and placed in a concentration camp filled with Americans, British, and French.

Chapter 10

1960-1969

Louis didn't want to think about the past any longer. He gestured to Katarina to go back into the living room. "It's late, Katarina. I'll sleep on the sofa. If you want, you can take my bed or go home late. We can find a taxi. I'd drive you myself, but my car's being repaired."

"It's fine. "I have no problem using your bed." It was too late for her to return to the apartment.

She decided to take off her necklace, but she dropped it as soon as she unclasped it. Digging around under the bed for it, her hand brushed a box. She pulled it out and read the label: "War Journals." She scanned through them, realizing that Louis had documented every detail, marked and written down every bit of history, and saved every document. She sat down and began to read.

Around three a.m., Louis lay awake on the sofa. He hadn't been able to drift off to sleep at all. He saw a light shining from under the bedroom door, and the occasional soft sound let him know Katarina was still awake. He got up and slipped into the room. She sat on the bed, spellbound by his war journals. When she looked up, her face paled, and she set the journals down.

As Louis sat next to her and touched her arm where her scar was, Katarina's war memories flooded back yet again, a horrifying repeat reel. The guards watching her shower and holding her baby over the fire… She wanted the nightmares to stop. She didn't want to think anymore. The nightmares were especially haunting. Sometimes, she would just sit in the darkness out of fear, curled up in a corner.

Louis sat on the bed and pulled her into his arms as she began to sob. She was crying for all of them, all the souls lost, her family and her friends, resistance fighters, Nicholas, and the Jews who were murdered for no reason other than their religion.

And, of course, Louis had watched Heinz die.

"Louis, I'm so sorry."

Louis sighed. "Katarina, it is a time we need to leave behind, though I know it's a nightmare that many of us will never wake up from. We can only pray this will never happen to the world again. People being bombed out of their homes, shot for no reason, women and children. I'm sorry you found the journals. We documented everything."

"Anthony gave us a copy of his letter to Amelia. He'd made a copy for himself not to forget her. That's how I had the letter in my journals. He knew Elvie was friends with Amelia and he had memories with Amelia and the children before he died. He and Amelia had grown close, and he spent time with her and Hanna every moment he could, especially after Simon died. He worked their books for the business till Hanna's husband knew exactly where everything stood."

He closed his eyes for a moment. The cobwebs of the past needed to be brushed away.

"Kat, I understand what you live with. Henri lives in his own hell, too. He has nightmares of when he was taken from the concentration camp and put on board the *Thielbeks*. I had managed to escape but he did not, and I listened to him many a night before he married. The Allies didn't realize the boat was full of prisoners when they began to shoot. Belowdecks of the *Thielbeks* were 2,500 inmates. As a doctor, Henri tried to keep up with the dead and the living. He was on the deck by some fortunate incident and heard the men below screaming. He saw the SS start shooting those trying to get above, so he picked up a gun and shot three SS. He jumped into the cold water as I had, but we couldn't see each other. He started to swim, still hearing the cries for help and saw German sailors start firing on those who were in the water, trying to swim to safety.

"When he got to shore, the German villagers killed as many as they could, and the locals started their culling. It was in the town of Neustadt when they later entered, and he translated for the British. I had already been returned to France. He also offered all the medical care he could. That's where he met his present wife, Sophia. He stayed until he gave detailed events about what had transpired in Neuergamme and the concentration camp as the commission of the crime listened. He told them how he managed to survive. In fact, he gave such detailed information, those taking the statements were horrified. A year later, he returned to Paris.

"He testified against those he could and watched two be hanged. We went through our own hell. He respects you, and he has a deep admiration for Anthony."

Louis shook his head. "You will never convince Henri to set foot in Germany or even speak to a German. It has taken him a great deal of time to speak with Elvie. Having a new family has helped him. We still think he drinks too much, but I'm not here to judge him. Just as no one can judge Gregory as he hunts down Nazis. He tries to make sense of what he has seen, losing his parents, brother and sister. It haunts him, too. He suffers over losing Nicholas and not being able to save you."

Katarina lowered her head. It was a whisper, his face now inches from hers, and he could feel her breath on his face. "Did you know Nicholas died in my arms? I can't recall a lot, but I can see faces still. Some are burnt into my memory, and I wish them a cruel death. Do you know how hard it is to be a prisoner of your memories? You can't be free. The rumors you heard of these places are nothing compared to having lived it yourself. Everyone underestimates horror. You lived through it yourself. How do you cope?"

Louis took a deep breath and moved back to look in her eyes, swimming in pain. Eyes filled with what she remembered. It was the same look in his own eyes and the eyes of his brother.

"Let's have brandy. You look as pale as a ghost." They went into the living room, and he poured them each a large amount. He raised his glass. "Here is to those we did catch, like Helmut Knochen. Eventually, we will find most of them."

"Louis, what about Amelia? Do you think she would meet with me?"

Louis looked down at his almost empty glass and spoke in almost a whisper.

"I went to see her once right after Simon died in 1960. She has also become good friends with Father Julian and Father Damien. She doesn't leave their estate very often. You didn't see her, but she was at Anthony's funeral with Hanna. She was in the back of the church and stood between the trees when they placed the dirt on the coffin. She just stood and watched for a long time. When everyone left, she fell on his grave in deep sorrow. Her daughter tried to comfort her, but I could tell there was a question in Hanna's eyes: why her mother was grieving so deeply."

Katarina placed her brandy down as she leaned forward. "Hanna doesn't know?"

Louis shook his head. "It was kept from her. She became a doctor and is married with three children. Her husband is a doctor as well. Hanna is stunning. She looks just like Anthony."

"Don't you think she should know she has family?"

Louis took a deep breath. "It's not our business. She has a good life. She loved Simon as her father. From the pictures I've seen, I believe your parents knew. They'd visited them a few times when Simon was living. They never spoke a word of suspicion, but I think they knew."

Katarina was horrified. "Louis, my parents need to know her. It would bring them great happiness. How could Amelia keep this from all of us?"

Louis put up his finger. "I wouldn't go there. It's a little hypocritical, given *your* history and children, don't you think?"

Her mouth gaped, and she sank back in her chair as she realized he knew everything about her. She downed the full glass of brandy. She didn't have an answer to his truth.

"Do you think I could meet her just as a friend?"

"I'm sure you and Elvie would be a welcome guest to Amelia. She receives so few, but she is fond of Elvie, and she remembers you as well."

Katarina stood and moved over to the sofa he was sitting on. She thought for a moment as she looked at him. "On another subject, did Gregory ever say why he never came back for me?"

Louis took her hands in his. "One night, Gregory told me about a woman he loved and would always love." He looked into Katrinas' eyes as he continued, knowing Katarina's tendency to run the moment anyone got close to her. It was a strange sort of loneliness left by the war.

"Katarina, Gregory's heart was shattered over you." Louis couldn't understand why Katarina stayed married to her present husband. Everyone in her life loved her, but she decided not to believe them. "That was his story to me on many nights. I know it's you he spoke of all the time."

She sat for a long time and did not speak as she finished another large brandy. Louis watched her eyes slowly close as she fell back on the sofa in a deep sleep. It was her way of coping, it seemed. He carried her to his bed and let her sleep. Looking down at her, he knew why Gregory carried her in his soul. He gently changed her into one of his shirts to sleep in.

She awoke to the smell of coffee and was wearing one of his shirts that fell above her knees. Her hair was a tangled mess. She walked into the kitchen, her eyebrows raised. He was fully dressed and looked wide awake—the exact opposite of her aching head and slight hangover.

He was pouring her coffee and had fresh rolls. He must have gone to the bakery.

"I hope you slept well," He said.

"By the looks of the sofa, it must have been a rough night," She answered.

"I've slept in worse places." He pulled out a chair and couldn't help noticing her long, tan legs that he remembered from last night as he slipped her dress off. He tried to be a gentleman, but as he placed his shirt on her, he could see she was just lovely.

Something stirred in him as she slowly sipped the coffee and buttered her roll. She was exquisite. When he placed her in the bed last night, he'd suddenly ached to be with her. He knew it would be his worst mistake. She had grown even lovelier than when she was a young girl now. He would reach for her and put her to bed if he had his way.

He knew every inch of her past, being with the French DGSE (Direction Generale De La Securite Exterieure), he knew of all her activities, and he also knew that Hans had already approached her to go into East Berlin one more time. That time was coming soon, and he knew he needed to say something to her about it. She needed to stay out of the whole affair. Let them send a real agent to play the part, not her.

Louis felt it would be her death sentence. Gregory wouldn't be there to save her; he was too busy in Jerusalem with the Mossad, putting out fires in South America.

Katarina suddenly snapped her fingers in front of his face. "Where are you?"

He shook his head. "It's time we got you dressed and back to your own apartment. Your brother already rang me up this morning, asking if I was with you." When he stood, his blazer moved to the side, and she saw his MAC50.

She took a few bites and finished her coffee, clearing her head. It was time to get dressed. She stopped at the kitchen door, stood on her toes, and brushed Louis slightly across the lips, letting them linger for a moment. He pulled her in, his desire obvious, when suddenly there was a persistent knocking at the door. Gently, he pushed her away and told her to get dressed. He closed his bedroom door behind him, took a deep breath and opened the front door as the knocking continued.

His co-worker and former lover, Sabina, stood on the other side. Folder in hand, she let herself in and strode down the hallway. She knew her way as she had spent many nights there. She walked into the kitchen and instantly noticed the table was set for two.

"Louis, we've have been calling. Your phone isn't working, and I see why now."

"Sabina, it's not what you think."

Her eyes were filled with fury. "It didn't take you long. How long have we been broken up? Three months? Did you pick her off the street?"

Louis grabbed her wrist, and the folder fell out of her hands. When he spoke, his voice was ice.

"You broke it off, Sabina. You said you didn't want to mix work with a relationship. You still wanted to live and travel, and I was too old for you. Don't you recall? Your choice, not mine."

Her breathing was fast, and now he followed her eyes as they stared directly at Katarina. Katarina was looking at this petite blond with big brown eyes, her face like a little China doll. Sabina wore no makeup, but her lips were a deep garnet red anyway. Her cheeks flushed from running up the steps, but the rest was extremely pale.

Katarina had her hair pulled back in a slight bun and was wearing just a smidge of pink lipstick. She was in the same blue skirt and pale green sweater from yesterday. It looked extremely conservative to anyone who saw her. She had yet to put her shoes on, and the fact she walked out of the bedroom sparked more rage in Sabina.

She looked at Katarina and back at Louis. "Well Louis, glad to see you've found someone your own age. I can see now that I was too young for you."

Those words hit Katarina like a slap across the face. She was insulted but also felt so much older than this young girl standing in front of her. She hated being older.

Sabina picked up the folder from the floor and handed it to Louis. She turned and left the apartment, slamming the door behind her.

"I'm sorry, Louis, I didn't realize."

"I'm not. It was over a while ago. I tried to get her back, but there are just too many obstacles between us."

Katarina walked over to him and put her arms around his neck.

"We could start again where we left off. I can help you forget her." She placed her lips on his again, letting him feel her tongue enter his mouth. She let him pull her closer as he rubbed his hands up and down her back. The phone rang, and he stopped.

"I think it's time you head home. We can leave together."

She watched him leave the room, and he truly was a very handsome man. He was thin in frame, around 5'9, but muscular, especially in his arms. His dusty-brown hair was longer than most men's, and it touched the collar of his shirt. He had striking, dark-blue eyes like Elvie, and elongated nose, thin lips, and high cheekbones.

He drove her back to the apartment, but he took her hand before she climbed out of the car.

"Katarina, when Peter and Hans come to you, tell them you are not a trained operative and have done your share out of East Berlin. Don't do it this time, Katarina. I'm afraid the outcome could be your undoing."

She cocked her head. "You know what they're going to ask, don't you?"

"I do. That's why I know you need to say no."

"Louis, I'm sure it won't be all that difficult. Times have changed, even in East Berlin."

He grabbed her shoulders and shook her. "Don't let them do this! It's too dangerous this time." He let her go, looking down as she was surprised by the outburst.

"Nothing has changed over there, and you need to be scared. You have ex-Nazis, an ex-brother-in-law, which we still have not confirmed. Is he dead? The Russians have a cold war going on with all of us. Your own husband in America has special clearance. Think of him. If you're caught over there, it could destroy him and his entire Navy life. We don't know how it will go even with Peter, Hans, and I."

He suddenly noticed the fear in her eyes. "I'm sorry, I had no right." He wanted to pull her close.

"Louis, I promise to listen to what they have to say and won't make any hasty decisions."

Before she got out of the car, he said, "Have dinner with me tonight. I'll come for you at seven."

She nodded and got out of the car. He watched her push open the large front door to the apartment complex and disappear. Looking up, he saw Peter and Hans on the balcony. He got out of the car and shouted, "We will talk later. Don't forget you're in France, and don't forget who I work for."

Elvie opened the door before Katarina could put the key into the lock and pulled her close.

"I was so worried about you. You didn't call to let us know where you were. Don't do that again."

"Elvie, I thought you saw me walk out with Louis."

"Yes, but he didn't answer his phone, so we didn't know. Kat, it's none of my business, but it's dangerous for you to take up with Louis. He has had his heartbroken; he is in dangerous places. I'm speaking as his sister. Be very careful the footsteps you take with him."

Katarina had never had Elvie speak with such harshness in her voice.

"Let me take a bath and change, then I'll be out. I learned a lot last night, starting with Anthony and parts of the war I didn't know." Katarina took Elvie's hand, "I'm so sorry. I never realized all that was going on outside of the world I was living in."

Elvie squeezed Katarina's hand. "I don't think you had a choice. You were just trying to survive like the rest of us."

Katarina sat in a bubble bath, thinking of all the choices they had made. It seemed the roads everyone took were tragic. Could any of them find happiness?

The housekeeper had laid out fresh linens as she dressed in black slacks and a purple cotton sweater. The steam made tendrils around her face as she pulled her hair back.

She joined Elvie in the kitchen, where fresh croissants were laid out, along with hot coffee. She could hear Hans and Peter in the other room having a heated discussion.

"Elvie, your brother has written in detail in journals about the life all of us led. I'm sorry I never talked about Heinz."

Elvie took her hand. "Kat, there was no point. He was the love of my life, and I was blessed. When I moved to Germany from Switzerland with your parents, I initially felt like an outsider. But your parents took me in. I had a child to raise, my beautiful girl. I never thought Dietric and I would marry. He realizes it is not the same as it was with Heinz, but we love each other.

"When I came back to France to find my brothers, it was especially difficult for Henri. He won't forgive the Germans. Anthony told him when I was coming back to Paris, so he found me first. When he knocked on my door, it was a miracle. We were close as children and even closer as we grew into adulthood. Then, of course, I met Louis by chance. I'd heard he'd sought me out in Berlin, and when I came back to Paris and went to his apartment, he wasn't there. We were constantly missing each other."

Kat reached over and patted Elvie's hand. "I find that so sad because we all had a hand in what happened. Plus, by reading the journals and from what Louis tells me, Henri had become very close to Anthony."

Elvie smiled. "Kat, you, of all people, know how Anthony won the hearts of anyone he ever came in contact with."

They heard Hans and Peter leave the apartment without saying goodbye. Elvie let out a sigh. "Let's go out and spend the day just being girls. I have two tickets to a fashion show."

Katarina's lip curled. "Not Chanel, I hope, after what she did in the war. Now, she still lives the good life."

"No, it's for Dior. Afterward, we can have dinner at Café De Flore. It's not that far from the show."

"I'm sorry about dinner. I made plans with Louis, but we can have a nice lunch."

They had a wonderful day, and both came back with bags of new clothing. They were like two giddy girls as they came in laughing, throwing the bags on the beds as they began pulling out the items. They bought dresses and sweaters. It seemed somewhat lavish, but it was a day they needed. Katarina decided to have dinner with Elvie after all. She called and apologized to Louis but felt it was better not to see him. She worried where it would go and that it might be unfair to him.

Elvie promised she would also arrange a meeting with Amelia when she returned to France.

Hans left Katarina a note in the kitchen to meet him at the train station back to Berlin the next day.

The next day, they were on their way back to Berlin. Hans was silent as Katarina joined him in the assigned cabin, and in a few moments, Peter joined them also. Kat looked at both, and she spoke before they could utter a word.

"Whatever you two want me to do, I'm not up to it anymore." She put her hand up as Peter began to speak. "I think you forget the last experience I had in East Berlin and almost died. And we still don't know if Gregory was able to kill Frederick Spitz's brother."

Peter sat across from Kat and took her hands in his. "It would be different this time. You would be with one of us at all times."

"It's astonishing to me that you would consider going back into the east sector, Peter."

"Kat, we desperately need to find out what the Soviets are doing in the East in terms of weapons. We heard there were missiles moved into East Germany, but none of the spy planes have been able to see anything."

Kat looked at Hans. "Do you know if there is any validity to this story?"

"Yes, Soviet GRU officer Pyotr Popor works as a double spy for the CIA. He has assured us of the clandestine work going on."

Peter spoke next. "One last time."

"I don't think I can. It's as if no one ever wants to rescue me from my insanity when I do this."

"Kat, we have other female operatives, but they just don't have your charm or looks. And the lie we tell can't be denied because you are a dancer," Peter said. "There is one man who is reclusive to us. He's a spymaster. They call him the man without a face or past. No one has been able to photograph him. We know he's with the Russians. He knows too many faces already, except yours. We're sure of it."

Peter clutched her hand tighter. "Kat, I will be by your side. We all will have diplomatic immunity under Sweden. We will leave Yugoslavia in the guise of being a magazine writer and editor who wants to know about the real side of socialism and living outside of the Western World. We will do one interview in Yugoslavia, then under the pretext, go and interview in the east. East Berlin especially.

"They love to throw around how great it is. Yugoslavia plays it close to the vest with the East and West. Tito's win allows him not to let the Soviets take control of his country, but he is still a socialist, communist, or whatever his flavor is that day. He has agreements with East and West Germany for trade, culture, and other areas. Most in his country speak German. East Germany is trying very hard to keep Yugoslavia in good relations with good stabilization between the two countries, but they know Tito also plays it with the West, especially West Germany. We've set up a meeting with Tito for an interview, which he has consented to."

She looked at both men and gave a long sigh. "What else, Peter?"

"We'll arrive in Yugoslavia at the same time Walter Ulbricht arrives in Belgrade. He's the chairman of the state council of the German Democratic Republic, and he'll meet with Josip Bruz-Tito. We'll convince Walter Ulbricht we'd like to come to East Berlin to interview him and others as it has been arranged to have lunch with him while there. We'll tell him it's by Tito's request. We will play upon the fact that as far back as 1955, Yugoslavia had solid cultural and economic relations with West Germany and the East. We'll convince their PR people that we'd like to write an article on why communism and socialism are good for the world. With this pretense, we'll get back into East Berlin and make our way to where we believe the Soviets have built a compound and have missiles aimed at the West. We have it on good authority the papers are already in the works for us to meet with Ulbricht—he loves to brag about the culture in East Berlin and how well they are doing. We'll first interview Tito as our front from Sweden, then move on to Ulbricht. Tito loves to give Western powers interviews. He's already agreed.

It's now all in the timing. We need the invitation to East Berlin. We are sure that when you talk to him and charm him, he will agree."

Hans leaned over as Kat closed her eyes.

"We will not leave your side. Our visit has already been finalized, and we have all the paperwork in place to show we're from Sweden. We know Tito finds Ulbricht in East Berlin an odious fool, so we'll have easy access. We will leave the east side of Berlin when we're finished and drive to West Berlin, where the British and the French are waiting."

"The only issue or topic we don't discuss is the Yugoslav friendliness with Egypt's Nazzar if it comes up," Peter said, looking at them to see if they understood.

"Trust me, Ulbricht will love the fact that Yugoslavia's interested in letting us write articles for them. They've arranged for us to meet with the culture minister who is expecting us from East Berlin."

"We'll go through Yugoslavia to reach East Berlin. Once Ulbricht signs the okay, we leave Yugoslavia and enter the East. Then we cross back to the West when we're finished. They'll all think we're also doing an article on West Germany's relationships with Yugoslavia and East Berlin." Katarina looked at Peter, who seemed so confident that it was all going to work out as he explained everything that was to take place.

"Louis is working on his side from France. France has an interest in their embassy in Belgrade. The Swedes' embassies are on board."

Katarina let out a long sigh. "Why do you need me? Louis asked me not to go. What does he know that you're not telling me?"

"We promise it's all in play. Once we're back in East Berlin, you'll meet with the culture minister to speak of the future of the ballet companies, especially in the Soviet Union. You'll ask questions about their cultural events. That'll give us the cover we need to get to the Soviet compound."

She shook her head. "I just don't know. Louis told me the Stasi and KGB have everything on record from when the tunnels were built. KGB chief Vladimir Semichastny and the MFS Ministry of State Security of the GDR will be all around us. What if they recognize us? Frederick's brother is KGB. Isn't he the one who found the last tunnel in the French sector? He found the cellar and almost caught the last East German refugees who escaped. I was told it might be him. That's why I think he is still alive."

Peter was still holding her hand, looking straight into her eyes as he spoke.

"Katarina, we know what we can talk about and what we're not able to do to the ideological political antagonism. We know how to speak with glowing writers' opinions of the East compared to the West European Economic Community. We will make it sound as if we are just glowing with how we are going to represent them, talking about socialism and why East Germany will be a powerhouse."

Hans saw the worried look in her eyes. "We will make our way into East Berlin. We will have an escort from the Stasi and the Minister of Culture."

Peter finished trying to persuade her. He could see that this time, it was much more difficult to have her on board. "We have someone on the inside already," He said, his voice low.

She looked straight at Peter with an intensity he hadn't seen in a long time. "You promise me that we will get out of there without any complications this time?"

"We have people who will get us out, I promise."

"When does all this take place?"

"In about a week or two."

She turned to look at Hans. "Why are you doing this? What's it in for you?"

"I'm just trying to protect what we fought so hard for. I don't want a nuclear weapon aimed at us or anyone. I trained in England with Peter years ago. Once they asked for you to be involved, I knew I couldn't let you go over it alone. I promised Anthony I'd look out for you."

Chapter 11

1960-1969

Katarina stared hard at Peter and Hans.

"This is the last time. Do you hear me?" She closed her eyes and thought of Gregory. He wouldn't be there to save them this time if anything went wrong.

How was it possible to miss someone this much? It was such a physical longing. She missed him with every street she walked. Her memories closed in on her at night as she tried to sleep, but sleep never came until she finished a bottle of wine on her own.

It was a long train ride, and they all slept the rest of the way till they arrived in Berlin, where they were met by a limo. As they drove down to Ku Dam to have dinner, where they stayed a long time, discussing what they would do. The three of them were not in the right frame of mind to go home.

They had coffee quickly at Café Kranz. Peter had to meet with the British, so he would stay in the city center and come to the house in the morning.

They pulled into their home's driveway and saw their father coming out of the stables. He rushed over to embrace them as they climbed out of the limo.

Jona slapped Hans's back. "Son, it is so good to see you. I thought Paris was going to keep you. Have you two eaten? Cook will pull some sandwiches out." He took Katarina's hand; she could feel his hands were calloused but warm. They walked back to the house hand in hand. Inside, family pictures were all over the library, with a large portrait of Anthony now hanging on one wall. Katarina looked at Hans, and they both thought about how much they missed him. His death was their own death in many ways. They longed for his reassurance, guidance, and the soft way he brought scripture into their lives, using it as a needed lesson.

Katarina took her father's arm. "Father we had dinner, but always could eat homemade sweets." She smiled at her father, whom she loved dearly.

They gathered in the kitchen, where the cook had tea, bread with cold cuts, lots of cheese, and cookies.

As Kat and Hans walked into the kitchen with their father, they heard the cook scolding Natalie and Alexandra, telling them to take off their riding boots because they were tracking dirt all over the floor.

Alex was a stunning woman now, and Natalie was growing into her teenage years. They quickly acknowledged everyone as they sat next to each other and loaded their plates. Hans walked over and kissed each girl as Lisa and Gertrude came into the house with baskets full of apples.

Alexandra turned to her uncle as she asked if Elvie and Sarah were doing well in Paris.

"Both of you must visit. The summer months are coming to an end, and I think a nice fall visit would do you both well," Hans answered.

"Will they stay in a nice hotel or the apartment?" Katarina asked with sarcasm.

Gertrude glared at Katarina, daring her to start a confrontation. "In our apartment that belongs to the family."

"Grandmother, I think I will take a bath and finish writing my father a letter." Natalie looked over to Katarina. "If you're interested, Mother, I placed his letters on your nightstand."

Katarina just stared at her daughter, who looked at her with full contempt streaming from her large amber eyes.

"I have mine from Philip, Father, and Aunt Lydia if you would like to read them."

"No, Natalie, you keep your letters. I have no interest in reading their babble."

Natalie left the room after saying good night to all of them, and Kat leaned on the table.

"Why is she not in boarding school?" She asked Jona and Lisa.

Jonas's voice went deep and serious. "Because it's summer vacation, and I want her here. After your fiasco last Christmas, telling us you were going to pick her up and then leaving her in school over Christmas, we decided to change boarding schools and have her closer. So, she is now in Berlin, not Munich."

Katarina sucked in her breath. "That's not fair! It was a mix-up. I truly believed she could take the train on her own. She goes everywhere across Europe with her friends and Alexandra."

Her mother lifted her hand. "Kat, it's already done. She will simply be here in Berlin. Now, if you would like to stay here in Berlin and start to raise her, then I believe you will have more say. But for now, she is under our supervision."

Her father spoke again, his voice angry. "Katarina, you went to Greece that Christmas. You didn't even spend it with us. We all went to Italy to the villa and waited for you."

Kat went to speak up, but Hans stopped her.

"Father, it was months ago. Let's just move on."

Gertrude looked at him, her eyes boring into him. "You would like that, wouldn't you? Just forgive all her sins. You two are the same. She's a slut, and you have affairs we all know about."

Kat was seething as she stood. "It's obvious you have your thoughts on this, and I'm tired. I will retire now. Do not ever call me a slut again." She went upstairs in a fury and slammed the door to Natalie's room. To her surprise, Alex had slipped from the kitchen and was now with Natalie. They sat on the bed, laughing. She never saw Alex leave the table.

"Mother, can we help you with something?" Alex asked. She knew it infuriated Kat to be called "Mother." Alex stood, walked to the door, and ushered her mother out of the room by the elbow. "Mother, shall I call Grandfather?"

"Alex, don't call me Mother; you have Helena to call Mother."

"Ah yes, my grandmother you gave me to. I wonder who is raising your child you gave up in Hawaii? I hope that child finds you and asks you in person why you took my brother Douglas from us and then have a sibling out there, never to be found by Natalie's father. You do know how to leave children behind. We're like crumbs on a path to be swept away, are we not?"

Natalie stood and came to the door. "My father would love to know what you did with his child."

Katarina tried to push Alex out of the way to cross over to Natalie.

"Not tonight, Mother," Alex said. "You will not leave bruises on her now or ever."

Katarina backed out of the room and slammed the door. She was shaking outside in the hall. *How dare they*, she thought. They knew too much. It had to be Gertrude who told them everything. She went into her bathroom to take a long bath.

Back in the bedroom, large tears were now wetting Natalie's eyes. As Alexandria went and put her arms around her, she lifted her chin to look at her.

"Natalie, remember, she does not ever hurt you. If she does, you go immediately to Aunt Gertrude, Lisa, or Jona. Aunt Gertrude loves you so much. She is saddened she could not adopt you; your father loves you, too, and wouldn't allow it. How lucky to be loved by so many." Natalie nodded.

After her bath, Katarina decided to go back into the garden. She drew a long breath, inhaling the crisp air, and she pulled her sweater closer to her body. She heard a sound and turned quickly. It was Gertrude walking into the cottage house. The other noise of footsteps came beside her. She was startled, but it was only Peter.

"I thought you were going to stay in town," She said.

"I needed to give Hans some new information we just received."

"We'll be leaving sooner than you think." She said it as a statement, not a question.

"I think so, Katarina. Within a few days. We just have to have all the paperwork in order."

He kissed her goodnight, and Katarina stood looking at the stars, wondering if Gregory was looking at the same stars. She briefly thought of John. He was a dear man who tried to save her and give her a good life, but he just didn't understand. Gregory knew hell. He knew what the war did to people. This was the difference.

After sleeping late the next morning, Katarina took a luxurious bath, then slipped on a gray, short-sleeved sweater and black riding pants and boots. She pulled her hair back and swiped pink lipstick on her pale lips. She passed the kitchen and had some coffee and a roll with butter and her mother's homemade marmalade.

She went to the barn and saw two horses were gone. Most likely, the girls were already out. Hans was just pulling the cinch on his horse, and Peter was lifting his saddle. "Can both of you wait for me?" Both turned when they heard her voice.

She went into the stalls, pulling out one of her favorite horses. "I can catch up. Do you know which direction you're going?"

"We can wait. We'll just go out and warm them up a little," Hans said.

"Do you know where Father is? His horse is gone."

"He went with the girls. Both of them were in competition for the weekend in Vienna," Hans said.

Hans and Peter moved their horses out of the stall as Katarina brushed the mare down and put on a dressage saddle. She put on the hackamore and avoided the bit today. She caught up with the men. They were just enjoying the day, no worries, no asking about any work.

When they returned to the barn, Hans handed both horses to

their help and told Katarina they would be back in two days and to be ready to go.

Two days went by. By the third day, Katarina heard Lisa and Gertrude in the library speaking excitedly on the phone. Gertrude congratulated both girls on their first-place wins and said she looked forward to placing the ribbons next to the others. Katarina continued walking up the stairs and decided she would go through the letters John had written her.

In the letters, he was no longer threatening divorce. Instead, he wrote that he was looking forward to his retirement and to when Natalie would be coming home. She crumpled up the letters and walked downstairs, throwing the papers in the burning fireplace.

She stood watching them burn, a faded love, she thought, like the ashes. She loved John, but not the way a wife should love a husband. Her heart was always with Gregory. John was a good man, but he still had not forgiven her for giving up his child without his knowledge. When he found out, something died between them that could not be salvaged. This time, her crying for forgiveness and using her sexuality did not work, so she took Natalie and left within the week while he was on another flying mission. She left their home in California and their pets all behind. She knew it would take John time to forgive her, but she knew he would eventually. Already, his tone was changing in the letters.

The front door slammed as Peter and Hans came into the library. She noticed paperwork strewn over the large mahogany table for the first time.

"You boys have been busy. Why didn't you let me know? I might have been able to help." She saw Peter looking at the large picture of

Anthony encircled by a gold frame atop Father's desk. The picture next to it was him and Anthony fishing in Scotland.

In a whisper, Katarina said, "You miss him."

He turned away from the picture and sat in the Queen Anne chair, Anthony's favorite. He had brought it with him from the rectory in Germany. Peter's eyes darkened in sorrow.

Hans broke the moment. "Kat, remember the two pups Anthony had in Paris? Peter managed to move them to England. They're having a grand time at the estate. Clair and the children are smitten."

Peter smiled. He leaned his head back in the chair and closed his eyes. He could still see Anthony on their last fishing trip. Just the two of them sitting on the banks in Portugal, the long, lazy days in the cafes, and just walking and talking. They spoke of the past and the future. Anthony spoke often of Amelia and how proud he was of Hanna. Peter opened his eyes and looked at Hans.

"My children are grown now, and it seems none of them are moving out. Two built homes on the land. Those six children are my best achievement. My boy Anthony seems to have a little of your brother Anthony in him. He's not going to be a Catholic priest but an Episcopalian. Anthony had enough influence over him growing up, he just wanted to emulate him."

He stood and walked over to the bar and drank a bourbon from the decanter. He poured two more and handed them to Katarina and Hans. Katarina had removed her shoes and let her feet dig into the soft Persian rug.

Peter went back to the desk and handed a large envelope to Katarina. Inside, a picture of her that she said was not the best. The paperwork stated she was a visitor from the Yugoslavian delegation that Sweden had arranged. They were asked to do a story on how communism and socialism worked for them and how it was affecting the arts, music, and book writing. They wanted to see the cultural development in the East, especially in sports, music and theater. First, they had to travel to a Yugoslavian city.

Peter was assigned as the minister of culture from Sweden. They had their informers and contacts in the East ready to help. The small group of Yugoslavians in East Berlin assumed they would be arriving from Belgrade and would be expecting them, but they had to change at the last minute to go back through West Germany. Their flights and trains were ready for tomorrow.

Katarina's brow was scrunched. "Peter, what about the help? Are you sure they'll be there, now that we've changed to not leaving Belgrade until after we meet with Ulbricht? And do I speak German or Swedish?"

"It's all Swedish, but they won't question your German accent since most Yugos speak German anyway. We are going to enter from the west side of Yugoslavia. After we interview him, we move on to the East Berlin Culture Center."

A week later, after accomplishing what they wanted in Yugoslavia, they stood at the border, ready to enter East Berlin again with help from Yugoslavian and Swedish paperwork. A chill ran down Katarina's back as she gave the East Berlin police her paperwork. She wore a dark blue suit and a plain white shirt with lace around the color. Her hair was pulled back, and she wore tortoiseshell glasses with clear lenses. She looked the Stasi in the face, never diverting her gaze.

The three of them passed through without difficulty. Katarina had to take deep breaths, standing on the East side as a sudden fear engulfed her. What if they didn't get back? She tried to calm herself, remembering what Peter told her about having help if anything went wrong.

A limousine was waiting for them. The driver shook hands with Peter as they exchanged a few words before climbing into the sedan. Louis was inside the limo waiting for them.

Peter saw the shocked look on Katarina's face. She thought he would meet them later.

"Glad you made it, Louis." Peter shook his hand. "No issue crossing?"

"None whatsoever."

"Well, let's find those weapons we've heard about. These weapons that not even the spy planes can detect."

Louis looked at Katarina. Even though she was trying her best to look like a demure reporter, one couldn't mistake her beauty, regardless of how hard she tried. However, her face was drained of all color. Louis leaned over. "Are you all right?"

She nodded. "Memories just entered my mind. I think you might have been right; I shouldn't have come."

Sitting at Pariser Platz directly opposite the Brandenburg Gate, the Hotel Adlon had seen better days. Most of it was still in shambles from the war. There were a limited number of rooms, and most likely, all had listening devices. They would communicate on paper only while in the room. There, they whispered so they could leave the room together to meet Herr Bauer.

In the room, Katarina pulled the curtain back. The bottom of the curtain was tattered and worn and looked like it was still part of the war. The fog was coming in and made the city look eerie. Was it her imagination, or was someone looking up into her window? She snapped the curtain shut. She changed into black slacks, boots, and a cream-colored cable sweater. She went out and knocked on Louis's door. As he opened the door, he saw she looked stressed and quickly pulled her in. She leaned over to whisper in his ear.

"Louis, I saw someone peering in the window in my room. I'm not staying in that room by myself. You have two beds. I'm moving my things into here."

He motioned with his finger to be still as he whispered in her ear. "We can talk about it later when we come back from dinner." He pointed to a picture and to his ear, indicating he had found the listening device.

Herr Bauer was waiting for them and motioned for them to follow him. "We have a table waiting for us at one of our better restaurants. It's good German traditional food called Max and Moritz."

They were reluctant at first to follow him. Every move they made was cautious. They'd been told someone would approach them but had only been given a brief description. Herr Bauer gave Peter the correct code word, which eased the tension. He turned to Katarina to shake her hand and whispered, "Smile. Laugh a little. You all must go with me as if you're happy. For God's sake, you already look as if they caught you. The desk people are already studying us."

Katarina smiled and gestured to Peter, and whispered they all needed to leave. They appeared a bit uncomfortable by not following him out as he announced loud enough for the desk people to hear where dinner was. He was a round but muscular man with gray hair, a double chin, and a spark in his green eyes.

Herr Bauer led them to waiting cars as he walked ahead with Peter, who was in deep discussions with Hans. Louis put Katarina in the middle of their group. No one was on the streets, and very few streetlamps were illuminated. Around the corner, some of the buildings still had rubble from the bombings, making it appear they had made little effort to start to rebuild.

Herr Bauer spoke to both drivers as they all got into the small cars and were whisked to the restaurant.

It was a typical old German restaurant. The floor looked a hundred years old. At the bar, they were seated at a long table. Katarina thought the waitress looked depressed, and she gave the girl a slight smile. The menu was of old German food, and the beer was weak and seemed watered down.

They made small talk while they all kept an eye on every person who entered and left. Herr Bauer slid an envelope over to Peter.

"Inside are papers that might be useful if you're questioned about why you are there. It's special permission from Captain Sergio Kondrasheir. I'll meet you tomorrow morning and be your designated driver. You must follow my instructions and lead. The area might shock you. It's a depressing area. Most homes haven't been rebuilt. It's as if the world stopped in 1945.

Peter cleared his throat. "How long have you been here as one of us?"

Bauer smiled, his eyes becoming small slits as he leaned forward. "We are many, as you know, but it's been hard for me to stay here this long. We have our special forces living here. They speak fluent German and are ready to jump if the Cold War starts and the Russians invade Berlin. They'll be ready to sabotage as many bridges and rail tracks as they can, but we haven't moved them to find what we think are ballistic missiles. Some have moved and found jobs near the Russians but haven't had success getting work on the Russian base. The Russians keep it pretty tight with few Germans. We think they've removed the missiles, but we have to be sure. We have to find out if they're aiming at the major cities of Europe."

Peter shifted nervously in his seat. "Why do you feel this is happening?" He glanced around. They were just two tables from two police Stasi, but thankfully, they hadn't looked at them.

Herr Bauer leaned forward again in a whisper. "A while back, lots of material was crossing over from Poland on lots of Russian trucks. We believe they built an entire village. We weren't able to get into the compound until you all came up with this plan. There's a colonel on the compound, and from what we understand, he loves to show off the Russian accomplishments. Miss Katarina, be careful. He is married but likes to take advantage of young women."

She gave a small laugh. "Thank you, Herr Bauer, but I'm not that young anymore. I'm sure he will find much younger women than me to flirt with."

That night, Katarina would not sleep in her room. When they returned to the hotel, she went into Hans's room.

The next morning, after a meager breakfast, Herr Bauer was outside waiting next to a large vehicle they could all fit into. He told them to keep their indemnification papers close by. The ride seemed to last forever into the middle of East Berlin. They saw a large, barbed-wire fence and guards as they approached the compound.

Peter let out a low whistle. "What in the world is this?"

"I hope we will all find out during this little visit," Herr Bauer said. "Our guide will ask for your papers. Don't write anything down; just observe. Watch every place we stop and observe. You have the cameras that can be used, from Katarina's lipstick and the writing pen. Write when they tell you or ask permission to quote them and then write, take pictures."

At their first building, a small man in stature, about five-five, looked like he hadn't seen the sun in years. His hair was sparse, so he tried to comb it forward to make it look like he had more. He was extremely thin and looked as if he had just come out of his lair. His general's uniform hung on him as he waited at the front door with two aides. He introduced himself as General Pollivsky. He kissed Katarina's hand and lingered too long for her liking. She wiped it off on the side of her skirt, hoping he didn't notice.

Generals aides ushered them into the building as they glanced at the outside before entering.

"Bauer, did you see?" Peter asked.

"I saw the military vehicles, the same we heard about in 1959. There was a slow-moving Soviet military vehicle led by GAZ-69A-type trucks from the Juterbog -Damm airfield. We now know where they were going."

They were led into a charming room with chairs and sofas in soft shades of grey. The general gestured to Katarina to take the chair next to him. He cleared his throat as the aides slipped to the back of the room, and a servant came into the room with trays of coffee and cookies.

"So, this special little group was invited here. I see no culture for you to see, but maybe we can lighten your minds of how great the Soviet Union is and how we take great care on this side of the world. You might want to tell the Yugoslavian defense minister that we have it all under control and can care for Germany, Poland, Hungry, Belarus, and anything in between. I will appease my Swedish comrades and give them a tour. Do not write anything down, my command."

He reached over and patted Katarina's hand. "I can show this lovely lady our entertainment area with movies, and we also have wonderful swimming pools."

"How many live here, General?" She asked with a smile.

"How many?" He repeated her question and kept patting her hand. "I would say we have about fifteen thousand."

General Pollivsky stood and asked his aides to call the individual cars. All of them would meet back at the entrance hall, where they entered once the tour was over.

"Gentlemen, all of you will go with Captain Dimitri here, and I will escort Frau Hanna," the general said. For a moment Katarina forgot her fake name for a moment and was confused about what was happening.

He helped her into the car, and she could feel his breath on her neck and his bony hands on her back as she got into the back seat. He was so close to her in this small back seat, but she couldn't get any closer to the door. He was sitting right next to her and put his hand on her knee and patted it the same way he had patted her hand. They'd driven for about ten minutes when she saw large platforms.

The general turned to her. "This is a country of such poisonous roots of evil from Hitler. The Germans should feel lucky we are here."

She swallowed hard. "You are lucky to be here."

"Yes, the soldiers here earn hard currency salaries, far more bountiful than what they would earn in rubles in their mother country. We find Brandenburg a nice area of Germany, actually. We venture into the town of Vogelburg often."

They passed an obelisk of Lenin and a school adorned with murals of flying swans, sailboats, and Red Army tanks in action. At the end of the base, Katarina saw it again: concrete bunkers containing missiles for warheads. She saw a short track and a clearing where there were weapons ready to launch. She pulled out her lipstick and took her time reapplying so she could snap as many pictures as possible while the general talked to the driver. The trees in this area were so thick she couldn't see the sky. No wonder the spy planes couldn't see this.

They arrived at the general's office, and as they entered, Katarina saw a map on the wall that read, "targets up to 1,200km 750 miles." It was written in German with Russian underneath that said, "England only 1,000km the word was Shyster."

The general saw her looking at the board. "Ahh, we have this board, and we only dream of nuclear missile capability against NATO targets. Nikita Khrushchev says it would only take nine with England." He picked up some papers, and the aide gave him a folder that she saw had "Vogelsburg and Fuerstenburg base" written on the front.

She tried to figure out if the missiles were still there or withdrawn. Surely, the general wouldn't have her in this room if they were still aimed at NATO countries. Is he that stupid, she thought?

"Maybe you and the others should spend the night. I have very good accommodations." General Pollivsky moved her into the other room, where there was a large mahogany desk with a large picture of Lenin behind it and a large sofa and several chairs and tables. He showed her to the sofa and sat next to her. She was in the corner of the sofa and couldn't move away. She wished she had worn slacks and not a skirt and blouse.

She tried diverting the conversation. "General, this looks like a small city. You must be proud to oversee something of such magnitude. It's hard to find good men in Sweden, except for my one special gentleman friend, who I hope to marry soon."

"I was told you have your family here with you." He moved the ribbon holding her hair back, and he pulled it forward as he grazed her chest. "I must agree that we do have a large base here, one of the largest in the Soviet Union. It's the twenty-fifth tank division between us and the West."

He leaned over the table in front of them and hit it so hard with his fist that Katarina jumped. "We must never show weakness again and let the Germans come at us. We control them. They are ours!"

The general's face was turning red with anger, and Katarina decided it was time to change the subject. "General, do you have an idea where the others are so we can join them?" He moved a strand of hair from her neck as he moved back onto the sofa and sat next to her.

"You must let me kiss off the lipstick you put on." His mouth was suddenly on hers, and his hand higher on her leg. She didn't know how he would react but quickly stopped his hand.

"Now, General, show respect. Besides, your wife's picture is staring at us."

She gently moved his hand from her thigh and closed her eyes, praying he would stop. He suddenly pulled away, giving her a half-hearted apology, then put his hand back on her knee and once again pulled her to him and smothered her mouth. She felt if she stopped him again, he would want something further. This was harmless enough, she reasoned. She even let him put his hand on her upper chest, hoping to avoid any further complications. He'd unbuttoned her blouse enough to put his hand on her bare skin. His lips came to her exposed skin, and he followed to the top of her slip. He seemed satisfied to just slobber all over her. Her blood was rushing through her arteries, and her heart was pounding in her chest, but she couldn't show her body was about to vibrate with fear.

Meanwhile, Peter, Louis, and Herr Bauer were also shown the small town built within a town. A young Russian colonel was more than willing to show off the accomplishments of the Soviet Union. They saw Katarina and the general head in a different direction of the dense forest as they separated.

Then they heard a gunshot. The colonel turned to the group and showed them where most soldiers ate and watched movies. He had an evil smile and was tall and lanky, with eyes as cold as ice. He gestured for them to continue walking.

"Not to worry, gentlemen, we take care of our own. If we think they're traitors and they aren't shot, we send them to a prison here in East Germany run by the Soviet Police."

The secret police, more likely, Peter immediately thought. He moved over to Herr Bauer. "Do you know where the prison is?"

"Yes, it's brutal. Thousands of political prisoners cross their doors for little infractions. It's called Hohenschonhausen. Some have escaped and reported that it can be worse at times than Hitler's concentration camps. They put people in cells and fill them up with freezing water. Many must have their legs amputated after standing in the freezing water. The KGB tortures them to death, and if they live, they wish they had died."

He was now moving them into a small store of all Soviet products. Next to the shop was a school, and he showed them a map of a small concert hall where the cultural center was. He guided them to the area, and they walked outside.

"We have our own Bolshoi theater and ballet. We do not allow local Germans in here. The garrison is for the Soviets only. I must say, we were surprised when we were told of your visit to see our cultural center and schools and write about it. This compound's not exactly a secret, but we have never allowed anyone to write a story."

He looked directly at Louis, who spoke up. "You must look at our notes before we leave. I'm sure you will correct whatever is needed." The colonel's eyebrows shot up at the sarcasm, and the others shot Louis daggers. Each of them inflected a different accent to sound as if they were trying to speak German.

They moved to another building where officers were eating. Inside were tables with crisp white tablecloths and Wedgewood china. The group was shown to their tables. The food was lavish, considering how the rest of East Berlin was eating. Hans cleared his throat as they sat and ordered.

"Colonel, can you ring up the general and have him and our other reporter join us?"

The colonel looked at Hans with a wicked smile, his pale blue eyes colder than before, his lips drawn into a fake smile. "The general will bring her when he is finished with her."

The men snapped their gazes onto him. Bauer and Peter were the only ones with weapons. Bauer had a Walther .38 caliber pistol in the cuff of his pants, but it was useless at this point. Peter had hidden his Minox miniature camera in a side seam of his trousers at the belt line. He'd gotten enough pictures that they could leave, but where was Katarina?

They ate without a word as the colonel watched them while others glanced over from their tables. The men grew uncomfortable. They knew at any point the Russians could send them to prison or shoot them for no reason, even if it meant a national incident. The Russians would have an excuse.

In the meantime, Katarina felt it was becoming harder to reject the general's advances as he was still slobbering all over her. She felt like a dog was licking her as one of his hands was still on her knee, working his way up her pushed-up skirt. She grew anxious and moved the general's hand away several times, but like a dog with a bone, he insisted on thrusting his tongue into her mouth as he moved his hand to the buttons on her shirt. She eased his hand away, but then his hands reached for parts she wished he would not. He quickly ran his hands up and down her chest and pushed her skirt up as far as he could.

He stopped and looked at her. "I would advise you to sit still." He ran his thin tongue over his bloodless lips. "I can keep you here as long as I want. As for your travel companions… Their fate is up to you." His eyes were cold, and she realized that denying him could bring consequences for her and the others. She leaned her back on the sofa and closed her eyes. He moved his lips down her neck, pulling her head back with a harsh tug.

"I wouldn't keep pushing my hand away. You just sit still and let me see the lipstick."

Her heart was now pounding, and she felt her temples pulsating as she leaned over to her purse and pulled it out. He opened the lipstick and followed her lips with it. He replaced the cap, and she put it back in her purse. And yet again, his mouth was back on hers as he pushed her further into the sofa. She felt like she was suffocating. But he could keep them all here if she doesn't follow his instructions. She had pictures; the West needed them. The lipstick was safe. She didn't know how much time had passed, but it seemed he was relentless; she was managing him, but it was becoming harder. Her clothing was in disarray.

Then suddenly, he stood and went to pour brandy for each of them.

"Drink this." He handed her the brandy. She took a few sips as he sat close to her again, his hand brushing her leg and his thin, ugly finger tracing up and down her chest.

He wouldn't take his eyes off her. He circled his fingers around her face and seemed satisfied. He once again reached his long, skinny fingers over her exposed skin and kissed her chest, his fingers reaching for her legs. She kept her eyes closed, but he demanded she open them and look at him as he kissed her again and again. His cold hands stopped as there was suddenly a knock at the door. He bellowed to wait.

He told her to sit up and put herself in order. She was on the verge of tears as the knock sounded again.

He looked over at her and sneered. "We'll finish later." A chill ran up Katarina's spine. She was determined he'd die before he came near her again. He called for the person at the door to enter.

"General, your afternoon coffee."

A man who stooped like the weight of the world was on his back brought in two cups and placed them on the table. "There is also your daily medication. Your wife insisted you not forget."

"Fine, just set it down."

Katarina saw something familiar in the hunched-over man, but the blond hair made her rethink knowing him. Plus, he had that buckle in his back, thick horned glasses, and crooked teeth. The general swallowed the pills and took some coffee.

"I won't be needing you any further. The young lady and I have a business to finish."

At that moment, Katarina saw the servant's eyes look directly at her and realized who it was. Her gaze snapped back to General Pollivsky, who was suddenly sweating profusely, his hand at his throat.

"I need to sit. Help me to the chair," he ordered the servant.

The general sat, and his head fell to one side, saliva drooling out of his mouth. Katarina looked at him. Minutes ago, he barely had any color, but now he looked another shade whiter. She was pulled up from the sofa with a vice grip.

"Katarina, how do you get yourself into these messes? For God's sake, let's move it. But first, help me move him to the sofa and put the blanket on him."

She couldn't believe her eyes. It was Gregory wearing a wig and something on his back to make him look as if he had a deformity.

"This is the last time I'm rescuing any of you. I could swear all of you are either stupid or asking to be killed." He saw the tears in her eyes and stopped to pull her into his arms, kissing the top of her head.

"How are we going to get past those in the office?" Katarina asked, her voice trembling. They were struggling to get the general on the sofa. "Is he dead?"

"No, but he will be sleeping for the next twenty-four hours, and when he wakes up, it will be like he dreamt all of it."

There was a rawness in Gregory's voice as he told her to take off the general's shoes. They covered him with a blanket and placed a pillow under his head, making it look as if he wanted to fall asleep on the sofa.

Gregory grabbed Katarina's hand and pulled her out of the room into the office area. Fortunately, the staff had left. He moved her to the car outside the same way they came into the complex. Once again, when he looked at her, emotions swelled in his chest, his soul captured by this deep feeling he didn't want to surface.

He drove. He knew exactly where he was going and came to a stop in front of a building.

"You wait here," He said and went inside.

He saw his comrades at the table. The colonel had left. This was one good omen, Gregory thought. He motioned for one of the aides to the colonel, and they spoke a few words.

Louis saw him first and wondered why this older man looked so familiar.

The aid walked over to the table. "You are all requested to join the general back at his office. Please follow this man to the car."

They moved out in silence, looking over their shoulders. The colonel had excused himself, saying he needed to attend to some unfinished business and would be back for them in an hour.

The car now felt cramped with one more person in it.

Gregory told them to listen and not say a word as he drove up to the gates. Katarina turned and looked at them.

"It's Gregory. The general was put to sleep for a few hours."

Louis noticed her eyes were filled with fear. "What happened, Katarina?"

"I don't want to talk about it." She lowered her eyes and shuddered as she wiped tears that were forming.

Gregory was showing the papers to the guards, speaking with them as they peered into the vehicle multiple times. Finally, Gregory returned slowly to the car and got behind the wheel again.

"Say nothing. Just wave as we pass through. You're a bunch of fools. This is the most dangerous place to be. You could have all been shot if they even got a whiff of who you were."

They drove through the open gate.

Louis spoke up first, "Gregory, I'm sure the colonel will sound the alarm."

"They'll have to find him first. I called and said he was bleeding out in the bottom of a water well that he stumbled into drunk. I think we have time. I heard him asking for a phone call to Belgrade as I was at the service center getting the general's coffee. He was talking to one of his aides, saying that he wanted to tell the general that he should be the one with that lovely Swedish blonde. He was angry she was being wasted on that slobbering old fool." Gregory chuckled mirthlessly. "The aide is also at the bottom of the well. They're both dead. Somehow, the colonel became suspicious, and I cut the line before his call to Belgrade went through. When he came out of the room, I told him his aide became sick and was outside at the large well." The general's wife speaks openly when she is bedded and satisfied.

"How did you convince the guard just now?" Peter asked.

"I had signed stationary from the general to let us out. They know me. I've been keeping the general's wife happy as a servant for some time. I was doing just fine until you all showed up. Turns out she likes younger men, and he likes younger women. These poor young female soldiers are at the whims of the general at any time. I had free access to everything as long as the general's wife was bedded and satisfied. She told me the night before of this traveling group of reporters. I just had this gut feeling this was not good."

Hans coughed. "Are you serious? She didn't realize the wig? And what about the hump on your back?"

Gregory shrugged. "She never wanted the lights on, and I was only there to satisfy her."

"Why are you here?" Louis asked. He was nervously looking behind them to see if they were being followed. It was dark now.

"The same reason all of you are: to see about their nuclear capabilities. From what I could tell, the general pulled the missiles out."

"How did you get into the compound? We were told no Germans were allowed," Hans said.

"I'm not German, I'm Polish. We had our connections as we

knew they were looking for an aide to the general's wife. She came into town and interviewed me in a café. She asked me point blank if I could satisfy a woman and keep it a secret. I looked at her and reached under the table. Ten minutes later, she said yes."

Katarina was silent as a small fury grew inside of her. What would Gregory's sweet wife think?

"We could have avoided all of this if the Israelis had let us in on what you were doing and shared what we were trying to find out." There was a sharp edge in Peter's voice.

Louis was fuming now. He thought France and Israel had come to an understanding when it came to sharing information.

Gregory accelerated. He looked back in the rearview mirror. "I don't think any of you really care how the Russians were working with Egypt. Your motives are different from ours." He saw flashing lights and told them to take out his weapons under the seat. But it turned out to be unnecessary as they passed them at a high speed, and everyone loudly sighed in relief. Gregory removed his wig.

"Did you get what you needed?" Gregory asked.

Katarina recalled the lipstick and fumbled in her purse. The memory of the general made her shudder. Gregory saw the look on her face as she peered at the compact and handed it back to Peter.

She turned to Gregory. "By getting us out, did you leave anything behind?"

"No, everything is nice in my humpback, and I managed to get a lot of information back to my home country."

He said "home country" with a defiant voice.

Herr Bauer spoke up for the first time. "I think we need to get these folks back to West Berlin as soon as possible. I need to cross later; I have some loose ends to tie up. We recruited a few Nazis here in the east. I need to see what they are doing."

Gregory laughed. "Tell them, Herr Bauer, that you're helping the CIA. You were special forces, but now you're CIA. I think they need to know."

Peter turned to Gregory. "I knew. We're on top of things in London, Gregory."

They were all now shifting nervously, anxious to get out of East Berlin.

"How long have you been here, Gregory?" Louis asked.

"Almost six weeks." Gregory turned to Louis, shaking his head. "Did you all get what you came for?"

Katarina spoke up as she looked directly at Gregory. "I took pictures of what might be launch pads and walls of maps if they wanted to invade."

Louis was watching Gregory and Katarina's interaction. They looked like they were in anguish as they peered into each other's eyes.

Gregory pulled in front of a single house and told everyone to go inside. He had this house with two other operatives. He switched clothing and pulled out papers from a floorboard. They left when he was ready, but not before he grabbed Katarina by the arms and shook her slightly.

"Why do you do this? Do you want to die?"

She looked at him. "I might."

He now turned to all of them. "I believe all of you know how close you came to being caught, and you're still not out of the woods. You still must go from the East to the West. Hans, here is the map you need to follow."

Peter and the others nodded as they piled into the car while Herr Bauer stayed behind with Gregory.

Gregory looked at Katarina one more time. "Tell me, are you all right after what happened back there with the general? I fear I arrived too late."

She stroked his cheek with her fingers and held them there for a second as she looked at him. "Not to worry, he didn't get that far. I think I would have killed him if he had tried. That won't ever happen to me again, trust me." She let her fingers trace his cheek to his chin as he took her hand and held it for a few minutes.

"Take care, Katarina." His words sounded so final.

Bauer and Gregory needed to send them on their way now. There was a tremble in Katarina's voice as she took his hand. "Gregory don't stay." He turned away from her and talked to Peter.

"If we need to discuss a new issue, I will be in contact."

Gregory watched Katarina and the others climb into the limo. He didn't want to talk to Katarina. He didn't want to rescue her again, yet here he was. She was heartbroken as he turned away from her.

He watched the car pull away and absorbed the unexpected situation again. *Amateurs,* he thought but knew better not ever to question Peter and Louis. He turned to join Herr Bauer, then shook his head to clear his mind. He had a pain in his chest, just like he always did after he saw her.

They drove with some preplanned detours so they could avoid

detection. They changed cars at a farmhouse where another vehicle was waiting for them. They didn't see anyone, but the keys were in the car. The car had diplomatic plates and flags of East Germany. They crossed at Friedrickstrasse/Checkpoint Charlie. It was always a chance. The guards were qualified, and specially trained forces were used exclusively to inspect all cars, people, and paperwork. It was up to them if you were pulled aside for more questioning or interrogated. The Germans had been given visiting rights in negotiations in 1963 for Christmas between the East and West, but only a limited number of people for Christmas in 1964 were allowed in. They pulled into the West, and it was the first time they all let out a long, collective breath.

Each went their separate ways to their contacts. There was no mention of murder or the disappearance of any Russians. And even if there were, they wouldn't admit it. It was rumored the colonel had defected, a cover-up on the Russians' part. They didn't explain his or the aide's death in communication that they heard in chatter.

Hans and Katarina were not feeling up to going back to the estate, so they stayed in Berlin City for a week before returning home. Peter called and left a message saying he would be coming out to the house.

Hans and Katarina took an early ride with the horses. Dew covered the ground, and a late chill filled the air. The snapping wind made her cheeks rosy. As they handed the horses back to the stable help, Hans stopped as he saw three figures walking up to the house.

Immediately recognizing Gregory, Katarina sucked in a breath. Her heart swelled, and she ached to run into Gregory's arms. Instead, she and Hans walked quickly to greet Peter, Gregory, and Louis.

They were ushered into the library. Cook had just brought coffee and cookies. She looked at them all with disapproval, knowing they had been up to something they shouldn't have, especially with Gregory being there. She didn't recognize this new one they called Louis. She went back to the kitchen and added more cups, pastries, and cookies. She set it all down with a slight bang and looked at them, shaking her head as she walked back out.

They slowly went over the details. It was Peter who cleared his throat. He handed Katarina a picture and asked if she knew the man in it.

Gregory looked at her. He knew this face so intimately, along with every emotion. Tears came to her eyes, and she couldn't hold them in as she sat down in the large Queen Anne chair.

"How? Where?" She asked, looking at Gregory and Peter, her voice a whisper. The photo struck terror in her heart. Peter took the picture out of her lap, and her hands clenched as she looked at it.

Peter took the chair opposite her. Gregory dared not go to her and comfort her. He knew he would not let her out of his arms if he did.

Hans went to the window and looked down at the garden of flowers that were planted in front of the house. It was fall, and the roses had started to crumble. Autumn colors were developing in the trees and flowers. Why was he thinking of flowers? Because this was something he didn't want to hear, he knew. Anthony was the one who helped her with the demons that stalked her, especially at night. He could calm her. Hans just didn't have it in him like Anthony. Anthony always had a biblical saying to ease her pain. Hans listened to Peter but didn't want to see Katarina's tears.

"Katarina, this man lives under the name of Eric Stuchart, once known as Alfred Manheim. We know what he did to you in the prison."

Her body was starting to tremble, and her hands shook. She lowered her head. They could see the tears rolling down her face. Gregory now sat with Peter opposite her and took her hand. He had to. He couldn't let her face the memory alone.

She looked up into those green eyes. Gray strands were streaming through his black hair. He let out a long sigh.

"Katarina, just tell us we got the right man."

"You did. He tortured us all, called us rabbits to be experimented on, and locked us in a dark cell for days. We only heard the cries of the other women and the whip hitting their backs. We tried to figure out the time by when they would shove food through an opening in the door. Sometimes, it looked dark; sometimes, it was light. I hope you found him, and I hope you kill him. Those are my nightmares—those memories tear through my nights, ripping me to shreds. I must rise, and then I try to sleep, but once the memory surfaces in nightmares, I can't go back to sleep. I pace, I drink."

He looked into the sodden eyes that now stared at him, a look of pleading.

Gregory leaned back in the chair. "We know he was in Moscow, and we know where he lives now. "

She snatched her hand away. "You had him in your sights and did nothing."

"We just received this other picture." Peter raised his hand to silence everyone. "Look at this picture closer. Do you not see Anthony? He was watching you both when you were bringing people back from East Berlin through the tunnels. We know he was in contact with Spitz's brother at some point. That's how he found you in the factory building. Stuchart was planning on killing you both, but Spitz's brother found you first that day."

Katarina shuddered. Twin brothers, both evil. She thought her own husband wanted her dead with the baby not yet born, and now she knew his brother was trying to kill her out of revenge for the war.

Gregory touched her knee. "I need confirmation. Stuchart leaves Moscow and travels to Munich and Spain frequently. He's also responsible for one hundred Jewish children—some as young as three years old—being pushed into a grave and buried alive. I will bring him to justice, I promise you. We just wanted to make sure because he's aged and has had so many assumed names. I knew you'd know him. You told me once everyone is etched in your memory."

Louis watched in interest as Gregory never took his eyes off Katarina and thought how she was still not out of his blood.

Katarina shuddered, looking at the three other pictures. She would never forget the four Gestapo men who arrested her and shoved her down the steps when she was eight months pregnant. They had paperwork saying she neglected her duties as a watchman, and she'd been accused of spying against Hitler. She looked at the Gestapo as if they were insane. They couldn't come up with a real charge, so they invented one.

She vividly recalled how hard they pushed her down the stairs. When she arrived at the prison, they had her kneel, sometimes kicking her to the floor as they questioned her about where her brother, the priest and her parents went since they couldn't find them. She hadn't known Anthony managed to move their parents to

Switzerland but didn't get back in time to save her. As she was escorted out of the prison to be shot, she knew someone had changed the paperwork at the last minute to send her to a concentration camp. Any camp, it said, just put her on a train.

She watched in horror as they took five men and one child, put them against the wall, and shot them. Blood seeped into the cracks of the sidewalk. She recalled the sudden strike at her back, then he was in front of her and pulled her hair. It was her husband, Frederick Spitz. He told the SS to make sure the baby was cut out of her womb and thrown away like trash, just like its mother, a traitor to Germany. She spat in his face, and he punched her in the face and back. Only later did she learn Gregory, Anthony and Nicholas made his fate.

As she was being led away, it was a young SS man who had gone to school with Edwin who helped her into a wagon destined for the train. He stared at her, and she knew he was the one who'd changed her paperwork and saved her life. He took her hand as he handed the paperwork over and told her to be brave and that help would come.

Now, her face was ashen as she let the pictures flutter to the floor, and she rocked back and forth in the chair. Everyone else was talking, but they seemed so far away she couldn't understand them. Her mind could only see the baby being born, Alexandra, the torture, how they wanted to kill the baby, Nicholas and Gregory helping in the escape... Hans spoke her name several times, and then Gregory took her by the shoulders and shook her.

She looked startled as she looked at all of them.

Louis looked at Peter as he thought about what they did to her.

Katarina looked around the room at everyone. She had gone so far away again in her thoughts, and sometimes, she feared she would just stay in those horrible moments, relive the nightmare over and over and never come back.

"Promise me you will find him and do what you did with the other one in Paris. Let him be found floating down some river, cut into pieces."

"I will find him," Gregory promised. Louis pushed another picture across the table. Her hand held it for a long time as her eyes bore into the face that was now directly in front of her, the man's cold eyes staring back at her.

Without even asking, Gregory knew the answer; he knew her face so intimately as she sat rooted, staring at the picture. She pushed it back to Louis.

"That's Stuchart's right-hand man. Alfred Krug, I think his name is. I sometimes can't recall all the names, but he is not any better than the rest."

Gregory reached for her hand, the first time in a long time he'd shown her any tenderness. He was always trying to forget what they meant to each other.

"Katarina, it all takes time. I'm afraid twenty years from now, I'll still be searching for evil." He turned to the rest of them. "First, we must stay on the good side of German Domestic Intelligence. So far, they haven't questioned my tactics. They know that when I move some of these criminals back to Israel, some don't make it. "

Peter smirked, "Yes, we know. We were right behind you in Amsterdam, but you went to one terrorist who was plotting against the Western governments. We saw the explosion on the canal boat. We found out it was you just by the description."

Gregory's response was icy. "I guess I need to disguise myself so I won't be so identifiable. Those I don't bring to justice are on their way to hell, regardless, after I'm done."

Louis was now looking at another set of pictures. He shuddered. "Where did you get these?" His voice was low.

"Herr Bauer got them for us," replied Peter.

Louis looked up. "Did you see these?" Katarina reached for them, but Louis shook his head and pulled the pictures towards himself. "It's something you don't need to see. The ruthless KGB is no different than Hitler's followers. Katarina, these are too disturbing. Don't look at them."

Louis had a point. Why look at the sorrow inflicted on others? She had seen enough in her lifetime. The fact she couldn't bear the smell of meat on a grill when she moved to the States and she couldn't sleep without seeing ghosts filter her mind every night, forced to drink herself to sleep. She jumped every time she heard a car backfire.

Louis looked at the pictures of the torture victims from East Germany. Their enhanced techniques were brutal: electrical clamps, blow torches, and instruments to pull out individual nails, like they did to so many French Resistance fighters. He put the photos down; he didn't want to look at the eyes of the victims, filled with pain and begging to die. He saw so much of the same look under the occupation in France and in the prison camp.

"Did Herr Bauer get over?" Louis asked Peter, who nodded.

"He immediately went to the American Embassy in Berlin. He had his own information from being placed for a year in the East."

Gregory walked over to the table, gathered the pictures, and placed them back into a folder. He didn't need them; his memory never forgot a face or voice. Once he looked at a place, number, address, or street, it stayed in his memory forever.

"I must leave, and I wish you boys safer endeavors," He said.

Katarina stood in a panic, walked over to him, and took his arm. "You can't leave. I need to talk to you."

She was standing so close he could smell her skin and hair. His eyes locked onto hers. There she stood again, he thought, fragile and pale with the same vivacity. His blood still churned when he looked at her beautiful face. He kept a picture of her in a safety deposit box and wept when he looked at it. It was like heavy rain, the tears of loss. Permanent tears, the kind that settles into your soul, tears of time gone still. He wore her in his heart, he tasted her in his dreams, a memory that could not be forgotten. It was as if the sun had left them both.

He removed her hand from his arm, and despair flashed in her eyes.

"I have to go." He turned and walked out of the house. She watched him out of the window. He stood for a moment at the bottom of the step, and she ran after him. Hans tried to stop her, and she shoved him aside. Swinging the front door open with a loud bang, ran after him as he was walking down the pathway. He stopped but didn't turn around as she caught up to him, and she grabbed him to turn to face her.

Tears rolled down her face. He was the only one that brought her to tears. "Please talk to me," she said. "Don't just leave as if I were a stranger. Please, I'm begging you. Is there nothing left in you for me? Nothing?" She clung to him, wanting his strength as he placed his arms around her. For a moment, she felt his love.

He grabbed her by the waist and pulled her into his arms, tightening his grip as he laid his cheek on hers.

"Katarina," He murmured. "You will always be part of me. Nothing in this world will ever add up to what I feel for you. But I just can't feel whole with you. I gave all I could, and you pulled all you could out of me, and now I feel empty." He could feel her heart against his chest. She reached up and kissed him. He didn't pull away immediately. There was this sudden flash in his green eyes as he pushed her away but held onto her arms.

"I can't, Katarina. You made your life decision. You left Benjamin, and you left me. You left anyone who loved you. I loved you more than my own life. I'm done. Understand me, I'm done rescuing you. I'm done trying to understand you. Every time I think I understand you, you become a different person. The only thing I understand is what you lived through. You are so haunted that you won't let anyone in, not even me. You say you love me, but you won't act upon it. Instead, you disappear, you move on. You're always running, Katarina. I can't live like this when you're here one minute and then gone the next. Benjamin needs a loving home. He has a mother who loves him, and she loves me with her whole heart. Unfortunately, it's something you are not capable of. At one time, you did love me, I know you did, but you ran away again."

There was fury and hardness in her eyes as she absorbed his words and backed away.

"How dare you. I have always loved you; you just wouldn't accept the fact that I needed time. I couldn't just divorce John. I had to work it out."

Gregory suddenly laughed. "Katarina, you never had any intention of working it out with John. He is the safest person right now in your life because he just accepts and ignores any part of you that is troubled. He thinks just like me, like Francis and any other man since me. I see the look on Louis's face as he looks at you. You have snared him into a web, but he will get lost. He isn't like the rest of us; he knows when to back out because he sees what you have put us through. I'm done."

He knew he had to speak harshly with her. Otherwise, he would cave.

"You have touched my pain so many times. You have articulated the essence of my pain and loss while I have had the privilege of living through life and death with you. I looked for solace so many times. I could no longer bear the pain of losing you. Katarina, my suffering touched every aspect of my life for a long time, starting with the death of my parents and brother then my friends. I had longed for you to come to me, to love me, but knowing you and your history, I knew what your disappearing meant because you vanished like a ghost so many times. You left all of us. There is a brokenness in you that cannot be healed. You sit on the fragility of life and are unable to reach joy. I have heard you cry so deeply it's as if serrated glass edges surround your heart. I can't begin to imagine how it must be to feel so much pain constantly. You cannot be whole. I have heard your footsteps as they marched over my heart to abandon me and anyone else who loves you. You are the most beautiful piece of crystal that is broken. No one judges you, but you must seal those cracks to be whole again."

She reached up with her hand, but he caught it first and slightly shoved her away and kept walking away from her. If she had seen his face at this moment, she would have seen the anguish in his expression and his will to stop and not run back to her and tell her to forgive him for everything he had just said. He knew he had to keep walking. He was furious with himself. Why did he have to come back to this house with all the sordid secrets and all the love he recalled he had for her?

He loved his wife. She didn't have any demons, she wasn't haunted. Alise loved Benjamin as her own, and she was pregnant with their first child, he longed to return home because she had made a home for them. He made promises to his new home, Israel and made promises to those who needed him to find people who had harmed them. He had always promised Katarina he would find those who tortured her. He would not break the promise.

At the top of the walk, Louis stood, watching. He had thought about leaving, but just as he was getting into the car, he saw the slight push away and the clenched hands on Katarina as she placed her head against the tree she was standing next to.

He walked down and saw her crying, her chest heaving, and she felt a hand on her shoulder.

"Kat, come back to the house." He put her into his arms and helped her into the house. The tears were flowing. There was silence as she did not speak, but he knew what she was feeling. He had felt many of the emotions she was going through at various times during his life.

Chapter 12

Gregory arrived in Munich. He checked into the old hotel that was almost destroyed by Allied bombings in 1944-45. The Bayerischer Hof was built in the footsteps of King Ludwig when they began to rebuild this elegant old hotel in 1945. To his amazement, the hall of mirrors stood in its glory and had withstood the bombings. He stood in his room, looking out the window. Munich is nestled at the base of the German Alps, where evil started. Munich was steeped in so much history and beauty, but he could never see the beauty and history. He could only see what it did to his people. It was here that they started with hate towards the Jews and worse.

The next few days, he watched.

Gregory was careful to a fault. He had to watch and observe. He would wait. He took a break to replenish his growling stomach. Sitting at a local bar, he ordered dumplings with schnitzel and looked at the buildings across the street on Neuhauser Strasse. He thought he could hear the glockenspiel in the tower of the Old City and realized it was just a local church.

As always, he took different routes, always looking over his shoulder. He would stop to pick up a newspaper, walk a few blocks, and throw it in the trash. He would stop and make phone calls from phone booths to random numbers as he looked around to see if he was being followed.

This was his private mission, not authorized by the Mossad. He knew they would applaud when he brought another Nazi to justice. He decided this had to be done and would deal with his supervisor—his friend with the details—later. He was using his own money on this one.

He walked these streets and only saw ghosts and reminders.

Germany was as it was. The last time he was in Munich was when the Nazis shot his brother Nicholas. He and Anthony escaped. He thought back and recalled Anthony managing to slide from under the imprisonments of priests, nuns, professors, and German nationals who had been detained for political reasons. It was after the Reichspogromnacht of Kristallnacht when thirty thousand male Jewish citizens were deported to concentration camps, ten thousand of them to Dachau. Eventually, 160,000 prisoners passed through the camp, thirty-two thousand of whom were executed.

Hitler dishonored a Concordat signed with the Vatican and permitted persecution of the Catholic church, and the Pope stood and did nothing. Hitler wanted to de-Christianize Germany and kill all those who were of Jewish descent. The people stood by the priests, but the thousands arrested nuns and others on trumped-up charges. Pope Pius XI issued his own encyclical denouncing the pagan ideology of Nazism, but it did little good.

How many in this bar right now helped arrest many of the Jews and priests, Gregory thought. Herr Gruen—one of many names he used—took up the full frame of the door when he walked in and waved to everyone as he sucked on his Turkish cigar, sitting two tables away from Gregory. The restaurant ordered dinner for the captain as they greeted him; he had the same meal every night. Gregory noticed his expensive tailored suit. His coat was black cashmere, and he wore a blue cashmere blazer, white shirt, and blue ascot. His trousers were tailored for his long, lanky body. He wore expensive cufflinks of gold with a diamond in the middle. His skin was dull, and his nose looked like a long beak while his eyes were an icy blue. They knew him well as they showed him to the same table where he had been seated for the last four nights. He even nodded towards Gregory. But Gregory just stared into those empty blue eyes that didn't have a soul.

Gregory watched the captain order schnitzel with red cabbage and a glass of wine. The servers brought him German apple pie with cream, which he ate every night when he was in town. They treated him like royalty, ushering him to his favorite table and giving him wine or beer before he requested a drink. They knew him well in that sense but knew nothing of his past.

Gregory paid for his one cup of coffee and a chocolate torte with raspberry filling, then left, walking slowly to where the captain lived. He groaned as he opened the heavy door. It was dark, and the air smelled musty in the hall. A woman holding hands with a child passed him. She seemed more interested in her conversation with the child than noticing him. He waited. He would soon be here if the captain kept to his nightly schedule. Gregory stood at the entrance to the stairway that led to the captain's apartment. His hope was that no one else would come out of the other three apartments on the floor. He wondered if he should throw a hood over the captain's head or just thrust the gun to his back. He decided he wanted his face to be the last one the captain ever saw.

Gregory was ready when the captain arrived right on time. He jammed the gun in the captain's back and ordered him to walk up the steps to his apartment. The captain was reluctant until Gregory thumped the back of his head with the butt of the gun. Gregory ordered him to unlock his door and smiled to see the captain's hands shaking and fumbling to find the right key. Gregory shoved the butt of the Luger into the captain's head even harder. The door slammed open as Gregory shoved him into the dark entryway. The living room light was on as he pushed him down the hallway, forcing the captain to sit, then tying his hands and feet to the chair he had bought earlier for this purpose. The captain looked into Gregory's cold eyes that held no mercy.

"I don't know who you are," He said. He babbled that he didn't know what Gregory wanted, but he had a substantial amount of cash, and Gregory was making a big mistake. Gregory shoved a wadded-up rag into the captain's mouth to shut him up and prevent him from screaming.

Gregory looked around the apartment. Herr Bauer had given Gregory the information and pictures of the captain's apartment, and Gregory didn't question how Bauer got them. Not only did this man run some of the camps, but he also worked for the Stasi, torturing his victims. The KGB taught him some even more horrific crimes to add to those he had committed in the prisons.

Gregory walked into the bedroom as the captain kept his eyes on him from the chair he was tied to in the living room. The captain's eyes were furious, like they could shoot fire, and a drool trickled from the corner of his mouth. As Gregory walked, he felt uneven floorboards beneath his feet. He looked back at the captain and saw the contempt that was in his eyes only moments ago had been replaced with fear. Gregory lifted the carpet and spotted loose floorboards. He lifted them and found a box. He opened it, and his blood ran cold as he saw the pictures.

They were photos of tortured souls from back in the concentration camps to present-day East Berlin. This sick man kept the pictures like they were trophies. There was a journal of names, dates of victims, the artwork and jewelry that was stolen. One photo showed twenty dead bodies at the concentration camp, each shot in the head. The captain stood front and center, holding a gun and smiling. He had pictures of the experiments done on women as he once again stood among them, smiling while they were naked.

Gregory knew this man well. He found the information about where he lived before he left East Berlin. He moved back to the West and made a name for himself as a good businessman.

Gregory found the East German girl who knew the captain well through her fiancé, Kurt, who gave them vital information. The girl was sweet in an unassuming way, with a heart-shaped face, full lips, and innocent blue eyes. Bauer and Gregory approached her as she entered an apartment. She immediately started to cry as they came up behind her and pushed her into the apartment. They convinced her not to be afraid. Her entire focus was on her diamond ring. Her fiancé had worked for the captain. After a lot of convincing, she sobbed and told how the captain threatened that if she said a word to anyone, she'd be arrested.

In between sobs, she told Bauer and Gregory her name was Astrid. Gregory took her by the shoulders, shaking her.

"Astrid, did Kurt tell you anything of significance? Anything that seemed strange to you?" Her red-rimmed eyes grew to the size of saucers.

"Yes, it's rolled up in the flower container." Bauer and Gregory looked at each other. It was too easy, they both thought.

"Listen, Astrid," Gregory said, "Herr Bauer is going to help you get out of East Berlin. I'm sure your relatives in the West will gladly take you in. He will provide you with the right documents to be free." She nodded, but her eyes were confused.

"You know Kurt won't be back. You know the horror stories of the prisons. You must trust us. The captain made sure he disappeared once he found out who Kurt really was."Gregory told her with gentleness

Bauer was now concerned. "Did the Stasi look in your apartment?"

Astrid nodded. "They turned over every piece of my furniture, tore my carpets apart, shredded my mattress. They were going to arrest me. I took off my diamond before they noticed I was engaged and told them we had just started to date. I knew they'd question me about my ring and take it."

Gregory gave her a smile. "You were smart."

"It was a miracle they believed me."

Bauer left the room and found what looked like a vine inside a plant. Kurt was smart, too, making it look like part of the plant. Bauer rolled his eyes, whistled, and shoved his hair out of his eyes.

"Good Lord, look at this, Gregory. Names of informants living in the West and working in different consulates. Kurt had tracked the captain down. It was personal for him; the captain murdered his entire family in the war. The captain stole first edition books, handed down for generations, a statue from the Vatican dated back to the twelfth century that had been given to his father as a gift." Bauer could see the fury on Gregory's face as he was giving him the details. Kurt watched all this from the attic and saw the captain and the SS drag his parents and sisters and shoot them on the street, kicking their bodies to the curb, then returning to ransack their home.

Kurt changed his name from Kurt Stein to a more traditional German name so he wouldn't bring any attention to himself. Gregory now came over to see what Bauer was telling him, written in a diary format. After the war, he worked with the Stasi government in record-keeping. It was then he found the captain, the noted Gestapo interrogator. The fool was so proud of his torture that he kept photos and documents of everything. Gregory fumbled through more pages, seeing document upon document that Kurt had kept hidden.

They read how Kurt followed him for months. By following him, Kurt realized he was meeting individuals who were giving him papers. Kurt followed him and watched him cross over to the West. It took Kurt a year, but he managed to track down more informers, one of whom worked in the American mission in Berlin. Kurt's fate was sealed when he was caught, but Gregory would find justice for him. The man in front of him should be taken back to Israel, but this was personal, Gregory thought. His people were picked to be put in concentration camps, and his parents, his sister, and his brother were all murdered.

Gregory looked at the captain, Herr Gruen, as he called himself now. Gregory had found an envelope of different passports with different names and pictures as he walked back to the living room with the pictures in his hand. He held them up. Slowly, the color drained from the captain's face, but his eyes showed no remorse.

Gregory held up his finger. "I'm going to give you a little bit of payback for these pictures. I have devoted my life to bringing people like you down. I have tracked down a dozen security guards from camps and those in authority. I have found many of you through our wartime claims and inquiries. My logical part says I should give you over to the German authorities, but my heart says differently."

Gregory slowly paced the living room, stopping to look at the art on the walls and the crystal vases, wondering whom the items rightfully belonged to.

Lightning flashed from dark clouds in the distance, and Gregory closed the curtains. An old friend in Austria who'd kept files on every deported person and every vacated apartment told him that this apartment used to belong to a Jewish family who never returned from the concentration camp. Gregory knew that, for the first time, the captain felt the fear endured by those whose eyes he looked into at the last moment. Fear along with sorrow, heartbreak, knowing they would never again see those they loved, parents, children, grandchildren. The last thing they saw was pure evil.

This evil man before him made it his mission to annihilate the Jews and anyone who didn't go along with Hitler. Gregory could get the German police to come and take him back to Israel, but he promised Katarina that the captain would not walk on this earth again. Loving her was a burden. He loved his wife, but Katarina was always only a short memory away. He suddenly recalled when his trembling hand caressed her cheek so softly. There were still times, even knowing he had Alise to return to, that a strange feeling of loneliness would take over him. He felt at times isolated from the world. He had no memories to look at, pictures of, pieces of clothing from his parents, his sister and brother, nothing to look at and remember. A fury would reach into his soul for those who caused this pain. Yes, revenge was good. His memories are also filled with the images of horror and death of those he loved. He once had someone sketch his family from his memory. He kept the drawing in his living room, a framed remembrance of happier times.

He walked over to the captain, took out his knife, and sliced his ear off. The captain thrashed and tried to scream through his gag. Gregory pulled the captain's head back and showed him another picture of an East German whom he had tortured.

The vein in the captain's temple was now throbbing. He was stamping his feet and tipping the chair over. Gregory picked him up, and the captain saw the murder in Gregory's eyes.

"Let me tell you, captain, about your mistress who took us to your little hideaway cabin. You furnished it elegantly, I must say. But we know it was blood-tainted money. She had no issue giving up your cabin where we found the information we needed on double spies; she showed us where you hid your documents. Who would think of hiding them in some old firewood outside? She watched you place items there and then knew you had an apartment in Munich. I admit it took me a while to find it, but I did. I'm sure your wife will be happy to know you are gone, as a nice long letter was sent to her in Russia."

For the next hour, Gregory gave him a cruel ending. It started as many had, taking his fingernails, heating East German coins over the fire, and burning them into the captain's palms. He slowly took the other ear, then the man's nose. He took a shot at the captain's kneecaps with a silencer.

At last, it was time. Gregory tied a plastic bag over the captain's head. The murderer did not deserve a quick death.

"I want you to feel what it was like to gasp for air like the millions you placed into gas chambers," He said. He watched as the captain struggled to breathe. When life finally left him, Gregory left the apartment, closing the door behind him.

Gregory stepped out into the cold rain, pulling his coat close to his neck as he walked slowly back to the hotel. It would be a while before anyone found the body. He went back to the hotel and packed his bag; he had killed many since he went back to Israel and worked with the Mossad. It never bothered him. The only time his conscience bothered him was in his dreams when a child was involved in a mission. Killing a child was the one thing he would not do, even when one child leveled a gun at him. The child had grabbed the gun from his grandfather's desk as Gregory was tying the old man up to take him back to Israel to stand trial. The child's shot missed, and Gregory grabbed him and shoved him into a closet for his mother to find later. Those memories and his past with Katarina kept his sleep in turmoil. The death of his sister and parents would wake him in a cold sweat.

He booked a flight to Iran, where his supervisor was sending him next. He was supposed to try to find a missing shipment of weapons. This stop in Munich was to last just a few days so he could complete his unfinished business. Fortunately, his boss understood when he went off the grid for a few days. It was always personal, but he was considered one of their best agents.

Gregory arrived in Iran the next day and looked around his hotel room, checking under the bed and in the curtains and bathroom to ensure the room wasn't bugged. He lay down on the bed and fell into a deep sleep. His dreams are always intertwined with Katarina. Her face always appeared in his dreams. He could feel her kisses and the softness of her skin. He always woke disturbed; he didn't want to dream of her. When he was back in Israel, he would look at his son, who had her eyes, a shade of green mixed with violet, and her cheekbones, but his smile and his dark hair and olive skin were him, his brother, his sister, the memory of them all in him. He felt guilty after the dreams, especially when Alise would look at him with all her kindness and love. The hurdle of any connection with Kat was almost done, especially since Kat would let Alise adopt his son. She promised to sign the paperwork. Benjamin knew nothing of Katarina. In his mind, Alise was his mother. In time, they would tell him of Katarina. It almost made him laugh because Kat had no reluctance in telling him to go find these people and kill them. Alise would be horrified to hear those words.

Alise brought laughter and truth into their marriage; he never doubted her love. She brought a feeling of freedom and peace to his soul.

Alise didn't want to know about his world. She'd be horrified, but she knew he had demons he wrestled with. He had people from the war whom he wanted to be brought to justice. She didn't question him when he left for weeks at a time. But she told him honestly that she wished the memory of Kat would leave him. He tried but felt he could never relinquish Kat from his mind.

Alise was always filled with kindness and never a harsh word. She always looked at the glass half full. She was a ray of sunshine in his world, and now they would have a child. She was getting close, and he promised he would be there for the birth.

There was a knock on the door, and he drew his weapon and cautiously walked to the door. He looked through the peephole and gasped in surprise. He yanked the door open.

"Good God, what are you doing here?" He asked as he pulled his friend Ayda in.

She plopped herself on the sofa, her black hair pulled back and her crystal blue eyes sparkling at him with mischief. She had on tight black pants, a gray sweater, and black boots. The outfit showcased her every curve. She and Gregory went back a long time and had their moments. Working together before Alise, they would end up in bed, just lust, no feelings. She was one of the best female agents because she didn't have a single qualm about using her looks and body to get information. She entrapped many men. She also never felt regret over who she killed. In many ways, she and Gregory were of the same mindset.

She pulled a bottle of wine from her bag, handed it to him, and told him to pour them each a glass. He walked over to the small table and found two glasses. He stood there looking at her. She was like a cat purring.

She patted the sofa and told him to sit next to her. Gregory inhaled slowly as he sat down, and she ran her fingers down his arm. "I've been told to work with you to find the lost weapons that were going to our homeland." She stood up, finished her wine, walked over to the bed and took off her boots. He went over and pulled her back up.

"I'm sure they gave you your own room."

She stared straight into his green eyes and slipped her arms around his neck.

"Contrary, we are supposed to be married on a business trip for herbs. Your new name and passport are in my bag." She pressed her lips to his. "It's been a long time," She whispered in his ear.

He tried to pull back, but she held him close.

"Remember Amsterdam?" She let go, but not before she kissed

him hard. She had been with many men for a purpose, but she and Gregory had a raw passion. She thought she loved him in a small way, but her focus was always on the job, and he was part of it sometimes. She now began undressing in front of him she told him to look into her bag to find his new identification as she went to take a bath. She strode into the bathroom naked.

He lay down on the bed and heard the bath running. As Ayda filled the tub, she sang an old Jewish song his grandmother sang to him and his siblings as a child. He closed his eyes. She had a lovely voice. He often wondered what kept her up at night when he lay next to her. His was death. What haunted *her* dreams? She would never tell him. When he asked, she'd change the subject.

There was silence until he felt water drop on his face. She stood over him with a towel draped around her. Her wet hair hung on her shoulders, and the red towel starkly contrasted her alabaster skin. His eyes traveled the length of her. She hadn't changed since their last time in Amsterdam.

She knew how to arouse and entice; she was good and didn't have a problem making love to someone and slitting his throat after she got what she wanted. She was as ruthless as any male agent. He tried to forget the woman he had slept with to get information; he reminded himself he was playing a part.

He closed his eyes. "I need to sleep." She lay next to him, and he rolled away from her. She pulled him back and pressed her mouth to his, her towel now gone. Her tongue slipped easily into his mouth.

"Play the part, Gregory. You never know who might be listening," She said as she pulled him closer. He could feel the heat of her body as her hands began to explore his. She climbed on top of him and straddled him.

He briefly touched her intimately before he pulled her head down to his face as he whispered, "Not this time. I have all I need at home."

She took his hand to touch her, but he did not move. She rolled off him. She lay on her side, her head propped up by her elbow, her eyes penetrating his.

"So be it, but remember who you are. There will be another time when you will have to play the part. If not with me, then with the enemy." She pulled the comforter over herself.

He lay back. He owed her no explanation. Every time they were in this situation, they used each other and made love many times. Even those times when he undressed her, he was searching for Katarina. Her name rolled off his tongue too easily when they were together.

He went to bed with the enemy and felt no guilt as he sought information that was needed. Ayda did the same. There was no conscience he could see on her part. That's why she was the best. But inside of him, he felt guilty for using a woman to find out what he needed. But again, he reminded himself that was the way the game was played. He could not tell Alise; it would rupture their marriage. She never asked what he was doing or where he was going. She knew it was for his country. His only mission was to protect his homeland, Israel. The Jews still had too many enemies.

With Alise, it was a need, a deep passion, a love he had not imagined he could have. But with Ayda in the past, it was filled with lust and no passion, purely to forget Katarina.

Ayda allowed him to forget for a while. Not this time. He loved Alise; he didn't need to forget Katarina this time.

But during the night, as he suddenly wrapped his arms around the woman next to him, he felt her body and said the name "Katarina" repeatedly as he now responded to her. She gave him what he needed because it was always the same name she heard.

They didn't speak of it the next morning. They got themselves out of the hotel and onto business. They had to find the weapons.

Chapter 13

Katarina was once again heartbroken over Gregory leaving. How could he just leave as she paced all night? Should she have gotten a divorce from John? What was keeping her from going with this man she loved?

Peter and Louis were having coffee. Her parents offered for them to stay the night. Haans was not there. He had to check on the factory.

They saw the dark circles under her eyes and could tell she had been crying. She poured herself a cup of coffee and took a pastry. Peter spoke first.

"Katarina, I'm leaving for England, and Louis is going back to Paris. What are your plans?"

She stared into the coffee cup. She hadn't bothered to dress and sat there in her bathrobe, her long legs showing. She made no effort to pull her robe shut.

"Well! I think I need to go back with Louis to Paris and tie up some loose ends. I promised Gregory I would finish some paperwork for our son."

They heard the laughter as Gertrude and Natalie walked into the room, not realizing others were there. Those deep brown eyes circled with amber and green, and those long lashes looked at Katerina.

"Hello, Katerina."

"You will address me as your mother."

Gertrude stepped forward. "Then act like a mother." Katarina's hatred for Gertrude was obvious; it seemed never to go away.

"You have my daughter for a few more months before she returns to the States," Katarina said. "Don't think I don't know you approached John to adopt Natalie. How stupid do you think he is? He does love his daughter." She turned to Natalie. "Yes, you will be going back. He is retiring in a few months and wants you back." She said it with such venom that Peter spoke up.

"Natalie, I think it will be wonderful for you to return to the States. I'm sure you still have fond memories of your father. I know he and your brother write to you all the time."

Kat turned on Peter. "He is not her brother. John took him off his brother, who was just sixteen, an illegitimate child."

Peter approached Katarina, standing face-to-face with her as she stood from the table. He had never been unkind to her and loved her as much as her brothers did, but there was a limit for him.

"You need to stop, Katarina. You're not exactly mother material. I don't think you have a lot of room to speak of someone's sins." His voice had turned as cold as Katarina's.

He saw her hand turn into a fist; her eyes filled with rage.

"You are my family. You turn on me after everything I have done for you."

Peter turned his back to her and looked out the large window onto the rose garden. "It has nothing to do with family, Katarina. It has to do with what's right. You must learn to be kind. This is your child. We have six boys and would have loved to have had a child like Natalie." His voice was low; he wanted her to understand. Anthony was no longer there to tell her, and Hans treated her like a fragile doll and made excuses for her behaviour.

Katarina turned to Louis. "I'm returning to Paris with you, and I will take a short trip after to our home in Italy. You can join me if you want." She turned on her heel and left. Gertrude and Peter shook their heads. Gertrude pulled Natalie into a hug.

"Natalie, I will make sure I go with you when you return to the States, and Uncle Hans and I will buy a home, as we talked about, in Florida so you can visit us when we go there. How does that sound?"

Natalie looked up at Gertrude and hugged her tighter. "I love you, Aunt Gertrude; I don't ever want to leave you."

"It's all going to be all right, my child, I promise." The front door opened, and Natalie heard Alexandra calling out to their grandmother or anyone in the house.

Natalie ran to the door. She loved it when her sister came. It meant love, friendship, and stories. Their time now was even more precious.

Peter and Louis waited for Hans and finished their reports and thoughts. Kat came in, poured herself a brandy and flopped into the Queen Anne chair. She took off her shoes and dug her feet into the soft Persian rug. She waited until they were finished when she announced she made reservations for the midnight train that Louis was taking back from Berlin to Paris. She gave Louis a big smile as if a few hours ago, the confrontation with Peter had never happened. She rose and told Hans she would join their parents in Italy. She had just spoken with them upstairs, and they informed her they would be briefly visiting the villa to check on the progress of the wines.

She walked over to Peter and gave him a quick kiss on the cheek. "Forgive me, Peter."

He let out a sigh. "You are always forgiven."

She and Louis made their way back to Paris and slept in separate compartments but had a quick dinner together. He tried to understand her, but he kept remembering the look in Gregory's eyes, the haunting she inflicted upon him. He felt drawn to her but wouldn't act on it. When they arrived in Paris the next morning, they went their separate ways at the train station. She wanted him to say he wanted to see her again, but he just left.

She spent the next two days enjoying her time with Elvie. Dietric arrived on the third day, but they didn't see him much during the day because he was handling the business part of their wine investments in France. They had dinner with Christinia. She had remarried and was still saddened that Hans would not leave Gertrude despite them having a child together. But she found new happiness, and the new man loved her son. Hans still paid support, and they were always included in all vacations and holidays if they wanted to. Now that she was pregnant again with her new husband, Christinia felt it was better to break the bond with the Von Rahmel family. She still had a deep affection for Katarina and Elvie; it was a friendship she kept. Katarina lavished Christinia with gifts for the new baby. She saw her nephew, who had grown. A slight shiver went down her spine when she saw him. He looked more like Anthony when he was a child than Hans. It made her sad when they parted. Christinia was going back to Avignon, where she lived now with her husband. Hans saw his son once a month, and they had a good relationship. Even Gertrude was good to the boy; he had no blame for the affair, and he was her son's half-brother. It was a good arrangement as long as Gertrude never saw Christinia.

Two weeks passed before Louis showed up at the door and invited his sister and Katarina to dinner. Elvie was meeting her daughter, so that left him with Katarina. He waited until she finished dressing since it was a last-minute invitation. Her dress was skintight black silk cotton with a wide red belt that hugged her small waist, red heels, no stockings, and her hair pulled up to show off her neck with the v-neck shape of the dress. The dress showed off her body's every asset.

They went to Le Grand Vefour, the first grand restaurant in Paris on 17 Rue de Beaujolais. For two hundred years, the eighteenth-century art decorating Le Grand Vefour had been the finest gourmet rendezvous of the Parisian political, artistic, and literary society.

Louis had arranged a private table in a small cubicle in the restaurant for three, but it was just the two of them. Every head turned as they walked through the restaurant.

For the first half hour, they hardly spoke as they studied the menu and ordered wine with the Gazpacho de tomates, green zebra, crispy carabinero prawn and Rumsteak jus aux anchois et capres, thin artichokes mash, and timut pepper foam. To end the evening, they ordered rice pudding, soft caramel and blackberry. Louis almost laughed, thinking that someone so thin could eat and drink as much as she ordered.

She noticed him staring intently at her, and she cocked her head. "What?"

"How long are you going to stay in Paris?"

"How long would you like me to stay?"

He hesitated to answer, leaning over the table while his eyes intensely stared into hers. "Stay so I can learn more about you." He knew she was not going back to the States. His sister told him.

"Louis, I'm supposed to take Natalie back to the States."

She slowly swallowed her wine as she looked at him. "When the time comes for Natalie to enter high school, I will take her back. It will be an easy transition. She speaks four languages fluently. She has her godmother in California and grandparents and aunts. I'm not concerned for her. I plan to take her and leave. This summer she'll be in Brighton, England, with Peter and Clair. Alex will spend some time with her in England. The two of them are thick as thieves, and it will be good for her to be away from Gertrude. That woman has too much influence over both girls. The nuns in boarding school have taken Natalie under their wing, as if she was one of them."

She was now pouring herself some more wine and looked at him. "Let's talk about us." She took his hand and ran her fingers over his.

It was still early when they stepped outside of the restaurant. She placed her hand in his. "So where to now? It's early."

"I moved to a new apartment. Elvie and Sarah helped me decorate, adding a touch of softness for this bachelor. Would you like to see?"

At that moment he wished he had not been so forward to invite her.

"I would love to see it. How far?"

"It's actually a few blocks from you in the Seventh Arrondissement. I can see the Eiffel Tower from my living room. I needed to be close to the ministries. I had thought about the seven

Trocadero in the Sixteenth, but Henri convinced me I would be bored since it attracts many families."

He hailed a taxi to drive them. She noticed a definite change when they walked into the apartment: softer colours, even if they were in muted beiges the chairs. The large sofa was leather but soft as butter, and the two bedrooms had soft blue quilts with grey sheets and dark blue accent pillows. The dining room seated six, and the kitchen was small but usable, while the bathroom was larger than most Parisians' apartments in white and grey, with large, soft, cotton towels in blue.

She twirled in the living room. "Louis, this is lovely." She walked over to the curtains and opened them to a large balcony. The moon was just appearing through the clouds as she saw the lit-up Eiffel Tower.

He was standing behind her, his hands circling her waist, and he smelled her hair as it hung down her back in a large black bow. His voice was low, and a little hoarseness seeped in. His lips were almost on her cheek.

"Katarina, I know you went to the East to help Hans, but please say no next time. The risk could have been death."

She turned her body and faced him. He took in her eyes, her full lips, and he closed his eyes for a moment.

"Louis, where do you want this evening to end?"

He backed away from her, walked over to the small bar, and poured each a glass of wine. She took off her shoes and walked over, taking the wine he offered and sitting on the sofa. He stood looking at her. She was so perfect he'd want all of her, but he'd end up like Gregory, and he wasn't going to do this to himself.

She saw the hunger in his eyes. "Come over, silly. I won't bite, I promise."

He sat next to her, leaving a small distance between them. She made the first move as she leaned over and skimmed her lips across his. "Thank you for a lovely evening, but I don't want it to end."

She leaned back on the sofa, pulled her long legs up, and placed them over his lap as she leaned back. She felt his hands on her legs. They sat there for a few minutes, slowly sipping the wine.

She swung her legs back to the floor as she inched over to him and turned her back to him.

"Unbutton my dress?" He slowly unbuttoned each one to her waist. He moved the dress off her shoulders as he kissed the back of her neck and back. She moved his hands to the front so he could feel her. He stood up and lifted her into his arms. He carried her to the bedroom, where he slowly took off her clothing, and she took off his. He explored every inch of her. He was caught, he thought, like every other man who was with her. They lay in each other's arms for a long time, not saying a word.

Morning broke, and she slipped into the kitchen and made breakfast. He awoke to the smell of coffee. He got out of bed and stood in the doorway for a few minutes, watching her. He wanted to take her back into the bedroom but needed to get to work. They still had information to go over from being in East Germany. He thought of Gregory, who loved this woman but knew she was not going to change. He looked at her, the blonde tousled hair, the long legs under the shirt. She would also break his heart, but he wanted to give it a chance. Maybe this time would be different for them.

She turned to see him staring. "Regrets Louis?" She asked.

"None. I see you enjoy wearing my shirt again."

"Well, you need to stop putting me into compromising positions." She gave him a smile. She had a glow that was refreshing to see on her. "Please take a seat and eat. I'll go put clothes on to go home."

She disappeared, and he looked at the sun coming into the kitchen, birds landing on the windowsill, chirping without a care in the world. He suddenly wished he was free.

He drove her back to the apartment in his Mercedes. She kissed him goodbye on the cheek and said she hoped to hear from him soon. She looked at him a moment longer, taking in his gaze. He hadn't shaved. He had such perfect features, she thought. Those deep blue eyes that you could melt into. For a man, he had long fringed lashes, his body lean and muscular. She shuddered for a moment. Gregory did, too. Except Louis had kinder eyes, Gregory had become hard, almost void of emotion, or was that for just her? Her thoughts made it to John, who truly was just waiting for her to come back.

"Katarina, I'll call. We'll continue and see where this goes, agreed?" She nodded, and he got out of the car to let her out. Suddenly, a woman was calling to him, waving, and his hand froze on the door.

It was Sabina. Long blonde hair and thin as a rail. Kat got out of the car on her own. The young woman looked at Louis and then at Katarina and held her hand out.

"Hello, I'm Sabina. We met once before at his apartment." The look in this woman's eyes was not friendly,

"Old friends, I see," replied Katarina.

"More than old friends. We were engaged. Did he fail to tell you?"

Sabina looked at Louis. Katarina recognized the look; Sabina was still in love with him.

With a furrowed brow, he took her hand and led her a few feet away, and they spoke for a few minutes. He held her by the shoulders and kissed her forehead.

Katarina stood there. Sabina was young. The realization of her own age struck her as she looked at this young woman. This was the first time she felt awkward. She never considered any woman competition. She watched the serious conversation. Sabina nodded and walked away as Louris returned to Katarina. He was shaken, she could tell. He cleared his throat.

"I'll explain later. It should be of no concern to you. It was her choice to break off the engagement. She couldn't handle my work."

"Do you still love her?"

Louis sighed. "In many ways, yes, but it's over. Let's just focus on seeing each other tonight."

She looked back as he drove off. She slowly went up the stairs and slipped into her bedroom. She didn't want to face Elvie. Louis was her brother. If Katarina was lucky, Elvie wouldn't realize she hadn't come home last night.

She ran her bath with lots of bubbles. Sabina shook her, and she didn't understand why. She was a beautiful woman, but she kept thinking how young Sabina was. This girl was young enough to give Louis children. Katarina shook her head and ducked under the water, knowing she was crying. She called out when she heard Elvie's voice in the hallway.

"Katarina, I hope we didn't wake you when we left so early."

Katarina let out a sigh of relief. Elvie didn't realize she hadn't come home last night.

"I just slept in late. I'll be out shortly. Think about going to one of the museums or art galleries, then to a nice café for lunch, if you would like."

Elvie poked her head in the door and looked at Kat's red-rimmed eyes. "Are you ok? You look like you've been crying."

"I'm fine. Soap got in my eyes; I'll get dressed for our adventure this afternoon."

"That sounds delightful. Kat, when you come out, tell me about your dinner last night with Louis. I hope it wasn't too uncomfortable."

"I'm sorry to say I had to decline at the last minute, but he didn't exactly give us much time, just showing up like that. What was he thinking?"

Katarina wore black pants, ankle boots, and a soft green cotton sweater. She placed pearls around her neck to class it up and wore her mother's diamond emerald earrings, which Lisa had given her the first time she left Germany for Hawaii.

There was an envelope addressed to Katarina on the hall table. It was from Louis, asking her to meet him at seven at a café on a small street behind Notre Dame for dinner.

Katarina was distracted all afternoon as she and Elvie walked, then sat at the Luxemburg Garde and park. Elvie was always easy to talk to. She never judged or asked questions. Katarina was nervous, afraid that Louis was going to tell her it was a mistake to be together. She even questioned herself. Why couldn't she be without someone?

That evening, Louis was waiting outside the café, wearing a leather jacket, black trousers, and a grey sweater. He looked rugged as she saw women turning to look at him. He looked up with a smile and embraced her as if he hadn't seen her for days. He put his arm around her shoulder as he kissed her.

"Are you hungry?"

She smiled. "I'm always hungry. What's in the bag you're holding?"

He handed it to her, and she laughed as she looked inside.

"I think you need a nightgown if you are going to stay over."

Her heart leapt; she had thought this meeting was going to be a goodbye. She buried her face in his jacket. "Thank you."

They ordered a light dinner, and he broached the subject first.

"What happened this morning was unforeseen. I was surprised to see her; it's been months. I loved her deeply. I wanted to marry her."

"Louis," she took his hand across the table, "you do know my history. You know I'm still married. That was my issue with Gregory."

"I know. I'm just going to take each day with you. If you want to run like you have from all the men in your life, you need to let me know. That's all I ask."

"You can deal with who I am?"

"I'm hoping you might see us differently in time, but I'm going to take a chance. I want to be with you. I understand that any pain will be self-chosen. If I'm hurt, it's my choice. I've learned that dreams are shattered all the time. My only answer, my defeat, will be trying to love you, and you give nothing in return."

Weeks passed. Keeping the relationship from Evie was easy for now—she'd gone to Italy with Dietric. But it would be difficult when she returned.

Louis and Kat never talked about the future; the relationship was restless on Kat's part. She knew each week he wanted more from her. He was going down the same path as Gregory. Once again, a man wanted more than she could give. Their love was deep and passionate, and they were happy in so many ways. But he grew distant when she told him she didn't want to move in with him; she wanted their relationship to stay as it was. They both liked when she'd stay with him for a few days, but she didn't want to move in permanently.

He realized it wasn't working, that she always had an excuse to pull away, just like she had with Gregory. He loved her, but Katarina could never say it back to him. Sometimes, he wondered if she could love only Gregory. Would she be with Gregory if she could? It was becoming increasingly difficult for him to try to hold on to Katarina. When he asked her again to move in with him, and she said no, something in him changed. The last night together, he knew he couldn't see her again. He wanted to marry, but she did not.

Two weeks passed, and he didn't call. He told her he had to leave town, and when he returned, he left her a brief message saying that his week was filled and he would call when he had time. It was the first time in weeks that she hadn't been with him. Her anxiety rose. She hoped it was because he was just busy with work. He'd always made a point to call her in the morning to say have a good day, but there'd been nothing since he returned. She felt in her gut that this wasn't good and decided to go to him.

Her stomach dropped as soon as she rounded the corner of his apartment and saw him standing in the doorway.

He was holding Sabina, who was smiling up at him. His eyes caught Katarina's as she turned and walked away. He didn't come after her as she had hoped, and she went home, tears streaming down her face.

Later that night, he came to her. She had been drinking heavily and crying.

"Why Louis? How long have you been seeing her?"

His heart ached for her. "Kat, I told you it would be my own punishment to decide to love you. It's been a long time since someone told me they loved me and wanted to try again and make it work. Those words never escaped your lips. You and I have been together for three months, and not once have you hinted you loved or deeply cared for me. I told you repeatedly that I would take care of you, I love you. The love-making was not the only thing I wanted to have in common."

He began to pace the room, then stopped in front of her, pulling her up from the chair. His face was in despair. He didn't want to hurt her. He had tried, but she was always evasive about the future. He needed more and took the blame for trying again with Sabina. When he'd told Katarina he was gone, he'd actually taken Sabina away for a long weekend. They talked everything out, and Sabina said she wanted to marry him. She came to him asking for another chance. He explained this to Katarina in the gentlest way he could. Her eyes became cold, and she pushed him away and told him to leave. She never wanted to see him again.

His feelings with Sabina were different. It was what love was supposed to be, not the struggle he had with Katarina. Sabina loved him, and he still loved her, though not the same way he loved Katarina. Katarina was an obsession.

"Tell me now, Kat, that you want this to work," He said. "Tell me you have feelings for me. Tell me." She winced from his strong hold on her arms, but she said nothing.

Her silence came as no surprise, and when she did speak, her voice was cold.

"Louis, you told me no strings, day by day. That's all we promised each other."

"Kat, you can't give anyone what they want, regardless of how much you are loved. You live with your ghosts, and I'm done." His face was clouded with sadness. He walked out of the room, and she heard the door slam.

She sat there, her breathing laboured. He said goodbye just like Gregory, like Francis, but not like John, who always wanted her back, regardless of the circumstances.

Elvie was suddenly in front of her.

"I just saw Louis. Kat, I know you've been seeing him. I really thought he could change your world, but it's better this way. I love you as a sister, but he's my brother, and I want him to be happy. I knew it would end this way."

Elvie sat next to her, taking Kat's cold hand and removing the glass of brandy. She had nearly finished the bottle even before Louis showed up.

"Kat, Sabina will make him happy. You won't. I'm sorry if that sounds harsh, but he wants to be married."

"No, he wants someone younger who wants children."

"That's not true. He loved you." Elvie was becoming angry because she knew Louis loved Katarina. She saw it in his eyes.

"Kat, you run the minute anyone gets close. Louis, Gregory, your current husband. They all want to give you the world, but you reject love. I know the only one who could talk to you was Anthony, but even he was at his wit's end trying to fix your demons."

"No, I reject your conclusion." Her voice slurred from drinking. "Louis left me because he wanted someone younger."

"That's not true, Katarina. I'm sorry, but Sabina came to me and asked if she should approach Louis and talk to him. She was still in love with him but didn't want to come between you two. I knew this would end, so I encouraged her to seek out Louis at work. I want my brother to be happy. I want him to have joy and smile again. Do you understand me at all?"

Kat stood and staggered to the door. "You are right. He needs to be happy. I did care for him deeply, but it always ends this way."

"Let me help you to the bedroom."

She shrugged off Elvie's hand to help herself stay steady. "I'm fine. I will always be okay. I can survive anything." She staggered down the hall to her room and slammed the door.

Elvie sat wondering what she could do to help her, but answers didn't come because everyone had already tried to help her in the past. She called Hans. He would be able to help her like Anthony used to.

Elvie looked in on Katarina the next morning. A bottle of wine sat next to the bed. Elvie sat next to her on the bed as Kat cried. Elvie pushed the wet, tear-stained hair from Katarina's face.

"Elvie, I'm alone again. Why do I do this to myself?"

Elvie didn't see Katarina cry very often, and tears like this never flowed. She pushed Katarina's hair back again.

"You're not alone. You never will be. I'm here, your brother, your parents; we will always stand by you and help you."

"Anthony loved me, Elvie. He never judged." Katarina suddenly sat straight up in the bed and hugged her pillow. "Elvie, go to Lyon with me. I need to see Anthony's daughter. I need to see a part of him." Her eyes were pleading. "You're friends with Amelia, are you not?"

"Yes, but we never talk about Anthony."

"Please call her and tell her we want to visit."

"I will call and check with her, but you must not mention Anthony to Hanna unless she speaks of him first. I'm not even sure if she will be there when we can go. If Amelia wants to talk about Anthony and Hanna, let her bring up the subject. Amelia and Hanna know of you. Amelia has seen you once in Paris, and Anthony spoke of you to them when they would visit him."

"Visit him? I didn't realize. Then please, let's go."

Katarina felt relieved. She was hoping to see a part of Anthony. She'd been kept out of that secret for so long. After seeing Amelia, she'd stop in Israel to drop off the adoption papers for Benjamin.

It took two days before Amelia got back to Elvie. There was some reluctance since Hanna was visiting at the time, but in the end, she agreed. Katarina and Elvie arrived by train in Lyon. Amelia sent a driver to meet them, and Katarina saw the colour drain from Elvie's face.

"What's wrong?"

Elvie gave a weak smile. "It's been a while since I've been here, and it always brings back sad memories."

"I'm sorry, I should have realized. You spent a great deal of time here with Heinz."

Elvie swallowed hard to hold back tears. "It's not as bad as when I passed the church where we were married in Paris. That's when I cry." She paused and swallowed again. "I think of Heinz every day. I see so much of him in Sarah. Her eyes are his; her hair is the same as his, the cheekbones, her height. Her stubbornness and, at the same time, a heart of gold. She is all him."

Katarina squeezed her hand, and they climbed into the waiting car.

It took about forty minutes to get to the chateau. It looked the same as in the war, except now the beautiful gardens were taken care of, roses were in bloom, and trees were everywhere. They came to the front of the house with its large steps. Three large German Shepherds came barking, and a woman ran behind and yelled for them to come. She had a simple, long-sleeved dark-green dress with white cuffed sleeves and a Peter Pan collar. Her dark, grey-streaked hair was pulled back, and she was leaning on a cane.

"So happy to see you, Elvie. It's been a while." She turned to Katarina, who immediately saw the same eyes described in the journals and Anthony's letters that Louis had copied: corn-blue, deep in color, were kind eyes. She wore no makeup, but her skin glowed with sun-glistened cheeks.

Amelia looked long and hard at Katarina. "Come in, both of you. I have coffee and pastries waiting."

She walked slowly behind them, stopping to catch her breath. She didn't want Katarina to see her eyes filling with tears. Amelia guided them into the sunroom filled with plants and an easel with a picture of a little boy that wasn't finished yet. The table was set, and the housekeeper came in with a pot of coffee.

Katarina looked around. She'd sat in this room so long ago, holding a baby they needed to rescue. The room was now painted a fresh peach colour, the furniture was new, and a few antiques were scattered around the room. The hallway they entered was also different. Lots of paintings and tables along the wall filled with flowers. Katarina's breath caught. There was a picture of Anthony between Amelia and a young woman, who was looking up at Anthony adoringly.

The room was bathed in sunshine, large windows overlooked the picturesque lawn, and there were plants everywhere. Amelia noticed Katarina looking at the nearly finished picture.

"That's my grandchild. I'm painting. My daughter has three children, two boys and a girl."

Katarina swallowed hard. *Anthony's grandchildren,* she thought. Her parents' great-grandchildren.

Katarina did not speak as Amelia and Elvie made small talk. Amelia moved strands of silver from her face that had fallen. She leaned forward and offered Kat a pastry.

"So, Katarina, what really brings you here? I only know you from a long-ago memory. I saw you as a little one in Italy while I was on vacation, and then, once after the war, you visited Paris. I, too, was visiting Paris, showing Hanna the sights, and I wanted her to meet a dear priest friend of mine, your brother."

Katarina swallowed hard. "I didn't realize Anthony had met Hanna."

Amelia smiled. "Let's cut to the real reason you're here, which I don't blame you for. Yes, he met her several times. He performed her wedding in the church and baptized all her children. Hanna was very fond of him and loved him in many ways. They wrote to each other weekly. She was heartbroken by his death. We both came to the funeral and sat in the back of the church." Amelia's smile fell. "I'd never seen my daughter cry so much."

Katarina was going to say something when she heard a voice.

"Mother, I heard a car. Did your visitors arrive?"

"Come child, meet them."

"Mother, I have riding boots on. I know how you feel about the dirt."

"Come in, Hanna."

Kat's heart dropped. Hanna was a mirror image of Anthony.

The young woman came and kissed her mother's cheek.

"Where are Claude and the children?" Amelia asked.

"Still at the barn, fussing over the new foal."

Amelia introduced Katarina. Hanna already knew Elvie.

Hanna shook hands but couldn't stop staring. "You look so familiar."

"This is Anthony's sister," Amelia said.

Hanna's eyes grew wide. "Mother, why didn't you tell me his sister was visiting? I thought only Elvie and Sarah were coming."

"You were out of town at the doctor's conference."

Hanna noticed Amelia shifting in her chair; her eyes filled with pain, and she sighed. "Mother, I wish you would take it easy and see a different doctor who specializes in hips."

"You are my doctor, and you tell me the same thing: stop gardening, stop walking so much. Sweet girl, Elvie called, and we just made these arrangements two days ago."

Hanna was still staring at Katarina. Hanna was tall and lean like Anthony, nearly his height of six feet. She had charcoal black hair with vivid blue eyes like Anthony, the same cheekbones, and when she smiled at Katarina, she lit up the room with Anthony's smile.

Amelia rang the bell for the maid. "Liza, please bring another plate, saucer, and cup for my Hanna here."

Liza looked at Katarina. She, too, recalled her being here as a young girl. Liza had been a housekeeper in this home before the war when Simon lived there with his parents.

Amelia rose. "I need to change chairs. My hip is bothering me a great deal today."

Hanna jumped up. "Mother, I told you not to work so hard in the garden today." Hanna made her mother comfortable with pillows behind her back and a footstool. Amelia's dress slipped up, revealing a constellation of scars and burn marks on her legs. Amelia quickly pushed the dress down.

Hanna sat opposite Katarina. "Katarina, I'm so happy you have come to visit. Father Anthony spoke of you often."

Katarina swallowed hard again. "Did you have many conversations with him?"

There was a light in Hanna's eyes and a broad smile. "Oh yes, he was wonderful. My father and mother adored him. I would also visit him in Paris. We'd meet for lunch or dinner. He loved my children, and we would send him pictures."

A veil of sadness entered Amelia's eyes as Katarina looked over to her, and Elvie shifted uneasily in her seat.

Hanna looked at her mother and smiled weakly. She saw a glitter of a tear on her cheek that she wiped quickly. What would bring tears so quickly, Katarina thought. She saw her mother weep uncontrollably for days after her father died and even more when Anthony died. There were days she would not come out of her room. They'd hear the weeping outside the door, her asking why, why? Here now again, the tears.

"My mother becomes very saddened when we speak of Father Anthony," Hanna said. "I'm so sorry if I have just chatted on and on about him. I'm sure you have suffered a great loss."

She rose and poured them all more coffee. Her hands were so long and graceful. They seemed to be all she'd inherited from Amelia. She sat back down with a look of concern, staring at her mother, who had briefly closed her eyes.

Hannah's voice was quiet when she spoke again. "My brother Max also loved your brother. Anthony got him into the university in Paris, where they became very close. My brother and I are only fourteen months apart, but very different, as my father always says. Max looks just like my father, and his children all look like my mother and father. We must figure out sometime how all three of my children have blonde hair and my eyes. My husband has brown hair like me. Did you know my father?"

Elvie coughed as her coffee went down the wrong side of her throat. It was Amelia who spoke up. "Yes, Hanna, they know Simon. We discussed the past and the war."

"Mother, I'm sorry." Hanna and the others looked at Amelia's saddened face.

Laughter rang out from down the hall, and three children, two teenage boys and a young girl burst into the room. The boys looked nothing like Anthony except for the eyes, but the little girl looked just like Anthony.

They were polite as they shook hands and introduced themselves. The oldest boy was named Anthony, then there was Claude, named after their father, and the girl was named Bernadette. Their father came up behind them. He was a striking, tall man who shared Hannah's height. His eyes were a deep grey blue.

The girl ran to her grandmother and sat on the floor beside her, never taking her eyes off her grandmother's company.

Katarina cleared her throat, and she spoke in almost a whisper. "You named one of your sons after my brother?"

"Oh yes. When we thought about naming our first-born Simon, my father insisted it should be Anthony. But His middle name is Simon. Anthony was thrilled, especially when he was able to baptize him as well as the other two here."

For a strange reason, Katarina felt annoyed. "I'm sorry we never met during your visits to Paris. I'm just surprised he never mentioned any of you."

Elvie and Amelia noticed the change in Katarina's demeanour as they looked at each other.

"I'm sorry also. He did mention you many times. He told me you were part of his heart."

Katarina had to swallow hard as she felt the trickle of tears in her eyes.

Little Bernadette suddenly spoke up. "Mother, Father Anthony said we were all part of his heart, don't you remember? He met us in Val d'Isere and told me I was part of his heart. Remember, he gave Grandmother a large envelope when we left, and you told Grandma that he looked sad."

Amelia was now looking uncomfortable. "Bernadette, you don't forget anything, child."

Katarina's voice took a tinge of coldness as she looked at Hanna. She turned and spoke while looking directly at Amelia.

"He was a good man. We all loved him, and we miss him. My days have not been the same without him. He was my guide in life since the day I was born."

Hanna never took her eyes off Katarina, which was unnerving now since she felt she was looking into Anthony's eyes. Except Anthony never had the coldness she was seeing now in this woman whom Anthony spoke with such love about. She didn't fit his description.

Amelia finally spoke up. "He left Hanna and the children part of his estate in his will. He must have known he was sick because we received the contents of the will shortly after his death. Your brother Hans and a lawyer, his friend Christinia, wrote up the wills here in

Paris. Anthony mentioned his family was well taken care of. Your daughters Natalie and Alexandra were also mentioned, as you know. I'm sure you read the will."

Katarina stammered. "I have not. Hans just deposited the money that was left to me into my account. I assumed the estate that Anthony had was part of the family business. I always thought that as a priest, he couldn't own anything."

Hanna looked at her mother, then back at Katarina. "Katarina, if you wish to see the will or wish to have what was left in the vineyards, I will gladly oblige. My husband and my family are not in need of anything. In all honesty, it was a shock to us. There's a letter to be given to me upon my mother's death. That was the only item we didn't see."

Claude stepped forward. He could see a slight tension building in Amelia's eyes. "Come, children, we need to do some cleaning in the stalls before the sun sets, and we have to bring the horses in."

Bernadette came and stood in front of Katarina. "You are very beautiful, just like Father Anthony described you. He made me laugh all the time. He always told us such silly jokes. My grandfather Simon loved it when he could join us for vacations. They would go off and fish, and sometimes someone named Peter would join them."

This made Katarina smile. "Thank you. Yes, he was tall, was he not? I must admit I never recall him telling many jokes."

"Oh yes, he was always so funny with us and always told us how much he loved us. He introduced us once to his parents. We went to Italy once with grandmother, where he also joined us with his mom and dad."

Hanna stood and looked at her mother, who looked anxious and tired. This was so different from when just Elvie came to visit. Mother was clearly uncomfortable with Katarina. Anthony never once tried to introduce them, even when Katarina was visiting Paris. He always said she was busy. She always knew there had been well-kept secrets between her mother and Anthony, and she never wanted to ask. It was uncomfortable enough to know of the torture her mother suffered in the prison camp. She did know her spirits were always uplifted when she was around Anthony, then sadness came when they said goodbye. When Simon died, Anthony stayed with them for weeks, giving Amelia comfort. When he left, she cried as much as she did when he died.

"Mother, I'm going to join them. Katarina, it was nice meeting you. Elvie, please come more often with Sarah and Alexandra. We love seeing them. Sarah, I heard, is smitten with a young doctor. My brother's son Thomas is in the same medical school, and they see each other often, her at the Sorbonne and him in medical school. It keeps them busy."

She left, and Amelia turned to Katarina. Katarina saw for the first time the heart with sapphires and diamonds around her neck that slipped out. Amelia brought her hand to her neck.

"Anthony gave this to me many years ago. I kept it hidden from the Nazis. It was always safe. Now, it will be passed on to Hanna."

Katarina nodded. She'd seen pictures of her mother wearing that necklace.

"Katarina, there are two letters. One, he wrote to me when I returned to France when I was eighteen. I read it often. The other one I haven't opened. I just can't. The lawyers gave it to me…"

Katarina went to ask a question, but Amelia spoke first.

"Yes, we loved each other, and I think that is all you need to know. You can come to your own conclusions but do not interfere with my daughter and her memories. Anthony was an important part of our life, especially after Simon died. It was difficult for my children, and he helped them through the grief, so I would appreciate it if you kept your thoughts to yourself. I think you know the answer, but my daughter does not know, and she never will if it is up to me."

Katarina sighed. "Don't you think my parents and brother should know?"

"Know what, Katarina? There is nothing for you or them to know. But I trust they do know. Why else would he leave so much to Hanna? Hans told me he knew the whole story weeks before Anthony died as if Anthony knew he had to tell someone. I suspect your parents know. They, too, received a letter for their eyes only. When they first met Hanna, I knew they knew instantly but said nothing."

"Please, Amelia," Katarina said, "Hanna is a duplicate of Anthony. Let my parents get to know her better."

Amelia moved the conversation away; she didn't want to answer any more questions. Her heart was heavy every time Anthony was spoken about.

"I think I need to rest now," She said. "It really was lovely to meet you again. I know you've had a difficult life. Anthony shared the significant sorrow that was in both of our hearts after what we both went through. I'm sure you saw the burns and scars on my legs. The SS were not kind to me, just as they were not kind to you. So, Katarina, my heart is with you on this issue, and I deeply admire what you did, but my children and grandchildren are off-limits. There is nothing to discuss about them."

The room took on a noticeable chill. Amelia stood and took her cane and rang the bell for her housekeeper. "If you will excuse me, I'm very tired. I do hope you both visit again. Katarina, you know the truth, but it's of no consequence to you."

Katarina's voice was low. "I know, Amelia. I found a journal."

Amelia raised an eyebrow. "Katarina, I also know that your son in Hawaii thinks you died in an accident. We all have our secrets. Anthony told me how you left the child behind, just like you left behind the son you had with Gregory. I loved Simon, and we never discussed Hanna. He never believed she was premature. He knew in his heart that she looked like Anthony, but he never asked. We had a wonderful marriage and were deeply in love. Anthony respected my wishes. We never spoke of that summer but once before he died when he read the letters to me that he wrote every month but never mailed. I read them every night till I fall asleep. They were filled with his life, his sorrows, his love for me that never left. I can take that to my grave, just as he took to his grave knowing that his daughter was grown and beautiful and smart."

Amelia stood tall and regal, her sorrow etched on her face, and she rang the bell again in agitation.

She turned and looked in the distance outside the window. "I will go to my grave with regrets of not sharing his daughter with him. The feeling was so deep when I first saw him standing at my door after the war, he only wanted to know how I was doing. Later, when we met in Paris, I told him the truth about Hanna. He would see himself in her right away as she came bouncing into the room the day he came to visit. I saw his eyes fill with tears, and I know it touched his heart. He looked at me as if his own heart was going to break. The anguish on his face was unbearable to look at. But within years, it was a love with all of us. I know Simon knew, seeing them together. He was the one who requested that Anthony be more involved in the children's lives. "

Her voice sounded as if it was fading as she swallowed hard.

"I do not resent your knowing, but my daughter shall never know. She has grown up with love, and she is happy. She loved her friendship with Anthony, and they were very close. I think that it was good that Anthony found out. He, too, felt it was better not to open that can of worms. I think you would also want to keep your brother's wishes. Understand that when I saw Anthony in jail and screamed out to him to find our daughter, I truly thought I was going to die, and Simon would also be caught and killed. I don't believe I would have said anything otherwise. Why bring back a time I couldn't recapture? It hurts. I cry when I think of him, all he missed by not knowing her. I wish you well, Katarina, but I think it's best you do not visit again."

Katarina gasped. Why would Amelia be so cold toward her?

The housekeeper appeared at the door and helped steady Amelia, who did not look back as she left the room. Katarina walked over to the large bay window and looked to see Hanna walking out of the barn. She glanced up and caught Katarina's eyes. She stood and looked at her but only with a question on her face as she walked away and out of sight. Katarina only saw Anthony with the same back and posture as she walked away. It was as if Anthony's ghost was walking beside her.

Katarina and Elvie did not speak a word on their way back to the hotel they had registered at. It was on an old cobble street and had been there since the 18th century. The rooms were small but quaint and had luxury comforters and pillows. They were exhausted and didn't want to take the train home this late. They went to a small restaurant with traditional French food and good wine.

"Elvie, you've been quiet since we left Amelia's."

Elvie leaned back in the chair and looked around the room. "I came here with Heinz after we were married. We felt safe that there weren't any SS around. But it looks very different now. We share so many memories in this town."

Katarina poured her second glass of wine. "Yes, Anthony spent a great deal of time in this part of France, even after the war. I wonder now was it because of Amelia that he wanted a church in France?"

Elvie broke off another piece of the French bread, buttering it slowly.

"I think it was part of his reason, but he also loved France." She leaned forward as she looked directly into Katarina's eyes. "Promise me you won't make trouble for Amelia. I'm sure this secret weighed her heavily, especially when Anthony found out. If there is one thing I do know, he loved her, but he loved God more. She accepted this. She had a good life with Simon. She's the one who lives with torture. At Ravensbrück, they placed her in a cell without any lights. And just like you, they whipped and beat her repeatedly. She didn't see daylight for six months except through a sliver in the door when they shoved stale bread and water through. You have lived through the same. You both live with the memories. She doesn't need any added worry at this point in her life."

Katarina suddenly felt a deep sympathy for Amelia. "I won't say anything. But I wonder what the letters to Hanna say. Do you think he tells her the truth?"

Elvie shook her head. "I don't think he would tell Hanna. He'd respect Amelia's wishes of her never knowing."

"Well, I hope Amelia has the blessing to live a long life. I just feel Hanna knows how she could look so much like a complete stranger."

They walked back in silence to the hotel. Elvie slept restlessly, praying that if the truth came out, Hanna would be okay with it.

Finally, she spoke, her voice soft.

"Anthony came to me and asked if I would call Amelia to see if she was open to seeing him after the war. Amelia came to Paris, then he was invited to her home. I will never forget how both immediately began to hold each other as Amelia sobbed. I hated to be witness to such love and sorrow but also regret on both sides. He met again at Amelia's home. It was Simon's idea. Simon and Amelia invited him to Switzerland to meet Hanna at the university. When the time came, Anthony declined but later returned and sat at a café and watched her with her friends. He never interrupted her. Once or twice, she would acknowledge him as she caught sight of him."

Elvie sighed deeply before continuing.

"A year later, Amelia introduced Anthony to Hanna as a priest friend she knew from the war. It seemed like the two immediately recognized each other. It made perfect sense to Hanna. She knew the history of her mother and France. She'd been told the stories of priests helping, and it was no surprise. Amelia and Simon were also friends with Father Julian so that Hanna wouldn't suspect anything. But no two people could be so similar and not be related. That was Amelia's fear. Simon was very good about the situation. He married

Amelia, not knowing she was pregnant, but he never asked when Hanna was supposedly born a month early. She never lied to Simon, and he loved her and never asked, but it was apparent the minute Anthony and Hanna stood next to each other. Simon and Amelia had a good marriage, and they loved each other, not like Anthony and Amelia, but it was love. Her having Simon's baby just made them closer. Amelia told me Anthony lingers in her soul every day of her life."

Elvie stopped as tears ran down her face. To love and lose someone weighed deeply on her thoughts. She now thought of her love for Heinz. She would never love anyone as she did him, so she knew what Amelia felt. She saw Heinz every day in their daughter. It was a blessing, but it also brought a deep-rooted sadness.

"Katarina, Amelia is sick. She has congestive heart failure and has a year to live at most. But her heart is free. She saw Anthony a week before he died and told him she was sick. She asked him to go to Hanna when she died, but only to comfort her as a friend and priest. He gave her his word and said he would remain close to all of them after she was gone. The sorrow is that Anthony left us first, and the secret died with him, as it will with Amelia. I doubt he would have written and told Hanna in his letter who he was. When he died, Amelia locked herself in her room for days. Hanna convinced her to go to the funeral. I watched them both as they sobbed in the church. I think Hanna knows, Katarina. Let her figure it out. Maybe in time, she might come to Hans. In Anthony's will, he told Hanna if she ever had any questions about what he left her, she should go to Hans. Anthony told Hans because he wanted Hans to know why everything he had was left to someone Hans only knew in conversation and later in business."

Elvie saw Katarina's hands clench. Her mouth was set with anger.

"So, Hans knew but wouldn't tell anyone?"

"Anthony told him not to. He didn't want to keep Amelia's secret but knew with clear and peculiar acuity he accepted not saying anything to anyone. It was a burden he carried alone. Our lives are so entwined, some of us with this unrelenting misfortune. Our memories serve us well."

Katarina shook her head. "I knew Anthony was troubled when I saw him. It's disconcerting that he wouldn't tell me. I recall how upset he became when I saw pictures in an album. My parents were always talking to him in whispers about the pictures."

"Katarina, you know Anthony was a burden bearer. He had been with all of us through our dark times. He was a priest foremost; I can still hear him saying to Peter and me: 'The Lord is close to the brokenhearted and saves those who are crushed in spirit. Psalm 34:18.' Remember?"

The night was long for Katarina as she kept going over it in her mind. She kept thinking how everyone knew something but her.

She and Elvie spent most of their return journey to Paris the next day in silence. Only once, when they were passing a church in the countryside, did Elvie speak.

"I loved Heinz. He was my light in the darkness of France. He wanted a large family and he so loved life, like your brother Edwin. To die at the hands of evil like he did just didn't make sense to me. I would pray he was in some POW camp and would return to us. I only had my child to hold onto. Louis took me to where they first buried him before they moved him back to Berlin after the war. I don't think I will ever love anyone as I loved Heinz. I was honest with

Dietric when I told him my memory stays with Heinz. In the end, Dietric and I are good together. It's a good marriage; he has been such a good father. I couldn't have gotten anyone better."

She sighed as she went back to looking out the window as Kat watched the tears fall. Kat didn't have friends, and Elvie was the only one who had stood by her and been there at every turn. She took Elvie's hand to let her know she was there for her.

The rest of the train ride was met in silence. They arrived back in Paris, and Katarina did not mention the day before. Instead, they made small talk.

Elvie parted ways at the train station. She wanted to visit her daughter and would see Katarina back at the apartment later.

Katarina walked for a long time, feeling more than ever that her life was in the trenches and as impenetrable as a river fog, so thick you couldn't see the bank. There was a gloom that felt like it was smothering her. She stopped as she looked up at Anthony's church. She had walked a great distance and was suddenly there, and she slowly walked up the steps and stepped inside.

She heard his last words to her in the church.

"Katarina, find the Holy Spirit. Find your peace."

She sat there for a long time and recalled Gregory sitting next to her, reminding her of all that Anthony did. She felt a breeze upon her and looked over to see Louis sidling up to her.

"I just spoke with Elvie. I wanted to check on you."

"How did you know I was here?"

"Elvie thought you might come here, so I decided to drive by. I spotted you as you entered."

They sat in silence, Louis looking up at the cross. Katarina didn't look at Louis as she spoke again.

"Do you know the story about the SS and Anthony in this church? Gregory told me in bits and pieces one time, but I don't know the whole story."

Louis nodded. "I was part of it, especially after you recognized the officer on your first visit to France after the war. We put a large net to find those that the officer gave up. He thought it would save his life. I walked out of the flower shop. You had already left before whatever was to be done to him. I didn't want any part."

"Louis, I never followed up on it. I just wanted him dead, and I was obliged when they found him in the Seine River, but it's what happened a few years later that almost killed Anthony's spirit. He was never the same. Do you know the whole story?"

"I do. It was a difficult time for Anthony, but he persevered. There were times he acted like any one of us and not a priest. But he always came back to his church obligation when it came to forgiveness—which is more than most of us can say."

Louis bent his head back and looked at the ceiling of the church. Cherubs painted on clouds in pastel colours. Ironic, he thought, that they were all smiling. He sighed.

"All right," He said. "This is the story of a past he never told you. It was when Anthony had his Parish for about two years here in Paris after the war; you knew he wanted to be back in Paris, so in 1958, the opportunity opened to him."

"Anthony had just finished listening to confessions one day when one of the parishioners came to the rectory door. Anthony knew of many Germans who came and confessed. The church's previous had given papers with name changes and helped them get to South America or Austria right after the war. Some stayed and some worked with the Americans and us as double spies."

"This man showed up years later as he befriended Anthony as being a member of Anthony's church. He knew his time would come to the surface, as we all were seeking out the names that were given to us years before by the Nazi we killed. He showed up in disguise as a priest just to get through the streets and into the church. His name was Erik Hoffman, but he changed it to Hugo Moulin."

"Did he have children?" Katarina asked.

"He had a German son but left them behind when he knew he needed to escape. He knew he'd be caught going back to Germany. He knew people were looking for the Nazis and Gestapo, so that it would be only a matter of time. He was responsible for having resistance fighters tortured and shot. I came into the intelligence office and had been following Hugo in a different situation. At one point, he'd been working with us and the CIA and had a lot of information we and the Americans still needed, so I was following him. He'd given us some bogus information, and I wanted to know where he was going. When I saw him dressed like a priest and headed towards Anthony's church, I knew he was on the run. We're still not sure who tipped him off, but we'll find the person who did. I wanted to stop him before he reached the church, but I couldn't catch up with him. He entered the church and asked Anthony to hide him. The church couldn't refuse to hide or help anyone asking for help. He wanted Anthony to protect him until he got the CIA on board to take him to the States. Anthony was perplexed at first. He was obligated to help him, but why the disguise? What was the man guilty of? So Anthony began to question him."

Louis shifted in the pew. He didn't want to continue, but Katarina needed to know.

"I caught up with him as I entered the rectory right behind him. He told Anthony he needed protection and to make a phone call. He recognized me immediately as I entered the room. I'd seen him in pictures and knew of his work with the CIA. He and I had even seen each other once, so he knew right away I was with French Intelligence. I immediately knew there was no way he was going to leave with me. He didn't trust me and told Anthony that the church was obligated to protect him. I could see Anthony was confused; he only knew Hugo as one of his parishioners. Just then, Father Julian burst into the rectory and confronted Hugo. He and Father Damien had been listening to the conversation in the outer office. Julian recognized him immediately, fell upon him, and beat him with fierce blows. Anthony pulled him off, and Father Julian started screaming about how this man was in the town where they locked the church and burnt women and children, including Julian's sister and mother. Hugo then had the men shot, including Julian's father."

"I'd never seen Father Julian in such a rage. He tried to attack Hugo again."

Louis took a deep breath and leaned his head back with closed eyes as he recalled that day.

"We held Father Julian back. I don't think I'll ever forget the look on his face. There was no forgiveness, only a desire for revenge. He told Anthony that Anthony didn't call the police. He'd exact his own justice on Hugo."

Louis stopped talking, and he and Katarina sat for a moment in reflective silence, each with their own memory. Katarina shifted uneasily in her pew.

"What happened to him?"

"Someone knocked on the door, and we all stood in silence as Dietric called out to Anthony that they wanted him to join them for dinner, meaning Gregory and Peter. They didn't yet know I was there." Louis rubbed his eyes, still reluctant to continue, but Katarina needed to know.

"Dietric entered and noticed Hugo's bloody nose. Hugo was still dressed like a priest, so Dietric was confused. We all just stood there in silence for a few moments. Finally, Gregory approached Hugo. He was surprised to see the commotion and blood on the floor. I stepped between Gregory and Hugo to keep Gregory from doing anything. This was Anthony's call. Would he cover for this man or seek justice for those who perished by Hugo's orders? Anthony took a key out of his desk, asked Dietric to escort Hugo to the third floor, and locked him in the room. He also handed him a change of clothing as he rummaged through the donation box he was going to deliver to a men's shelter.

"Hugo was brazen enough to complain that he couldn't wear used clothing. I thought Julian was going to explode when he said that. Dietric didn't ask for explanations, only moved the man out. Anthony soon explained the situation. He didn't know what to do. The confessions he'd heard from Hugo over the years were just about the mundane things in life; Hugo had never admitted to being a war criminal.

"Anthony went upstairs to speak with Hugo, and Father Damien followed him. Then we heard a gunshot. We didn't know Hugo had a concealed weapon under his priest's cassocks, and he fired it the instant Anthony opened the door. The bullet grazed Anthony and hit Father Damien in the stomach."

"Gregory and Dietric ran upstairs to find Damien on the floor with Anthony kneeling over him, trying to stop the bleeding while Hugo held the gun at Anthony's head. Gregory rammed into Hugo, who fired another shot, which splintered the casing around the window. Anthony helped Damien up off the floor the best he could as Gregory and Dietric dragged Hugo downstairs."

"Still pressing a towel to Damien's wound and ignoring his own, Anthony glared at Hugo and said, 'You and the likes of you are all spawned from the devil. You will spend eternity in Hell.' He stared at Hugo with a look I'd never seen in his eyes, as if he, too, wanted to kill Hugo. He pulled back the fist on his good arm and punched Hugo so hard in the face that we heard Hugo's nose crack and blood spurted out."

"We couldn't wait any longer to get help for Father Damien. We needed to get him to a safe house and call a doctor; the local hospital would ask too many questions. Anthony got right in Hugo's face and said, 'I cannot help you. You must pay for your sins. The church has allowed too many of you to escape. My friends here will take you to a police station.'"

Louis looked over at Katarina. So beautiful, he thought, but so unattainable. Sunlight was streaming through the stained-glass window as orbs of colours danced in the dust that floated down.

"Did they take him to jail as Anthony requested?" Katarina asked.

Louis gave a slight laugh. "No. Anthony asked how many lives he'd destroyed; how many did he know went to concentration camps and then to ovens. Anthony was screaming at this point. We'd never seen him so furious."

Louis reflected for a moment. He could still see the scene in his mind.

"Hugo's eyes were cold. A smile crossed his lips like a maniac, his face blazing with the personification of evil. But his breath smelled of fear, and he turned into what he was: an SS man whose true side came to the surface when he ranted, stomped his feet, and screamed obscenities at us. He said, 'I sent hundreds to prisons and enjoyed each one I sent away. I sent the deplorables to the gas chambers, or I had them shot, I made sure the children were killed so as not to continue their genes.'"

"Anthony made a fist again and punched him right in the jaw again. Then he blessed himself and looked up and said a prayer. The betrayal was so hard for him. Hugo had been part of Anthony's church for years and even invited Anthony once for dinner. The worst was when we discovered Hugo was the one who tortured and sent Amelia to a concentration camp. We found out later that the CIA knew of Hugo's crimes all along. There were a lot of Germans who got away by befriending the CIA or MI6."

He cleared his throat and tried to explain what happened next.

"I was going to take him to headquarters, but Gregory stepped in front of me. He insisted it would be a waste of time to have hearings and let judges make the decisions. They asked me to go back to Hugo's apartment and see if I could find any evidence of his involvement to bring to prosecutors. Then they might consider handing him over."

Katarina touched Louise's arm with her cool fingers. He continued in a hushed tone.

"I knew it was not a good idea to leave him in Gregory's hands. I saw the fury in his eyes and knew he was already working with Mossad. He joined a small unit whose sole mission includes assassinations and sabotage of those who mean Israel harm. But I didn't care about the outcome that would befall this man. I saw my wife. I saw Henri's wife and child. I saw Heinz. When we cleaned out Hugo's apartment later, it was filled with stolen art, jewellery, books, and rugs. It was filled with the blood of the lost."

"Anthony had a hard time accepting he had let evil come into his church and didn't see it. He told me he felt the evil swirl around your first husband, Frederick, and it was noticeable. He didn't see it with Schwinn. Hugo's fate was sealed when Gregory and Peter moved him out of the church. I'd hoped to stay out of it—I knew it was my place to arrest him, but I could only see what I went through."

A luminous, inquisitive smile crossed Katarina's face. "Then what happened?" She asked.

"Gregory and Peter and the others moved Hugo. Dietric moved Anthony and Damien to a safe house. Before Anthony left, he turned to me and said, 'Louis, do not kill Hugo. Killing is not what we want. Vengeance belongs to the Lord. If you kill him, I don't want to be told.'"

"Gregory had a hood over Hugo's head as his hands were tied, and we all decided to see this to the end. We took Hugo to an abandoned warehouse where the church stored boxes of clothing to go to the needy. It was a good distance out of Paris, and Dietric caught up to us there. Dietric had his gun in his hand, and the moment we undid Hugo's hands to retie him to the chair, he grabbed the weapon from Dietric and charged into another room, blasting at us. The room was full of boxes, old bikes, and steel cabinets holding more boxes. Gregory had managed to get a shot off, and we just followed the blood."

"We heard the boom of the weapon again, and a bullet just missed Dietric. Based on the number of shots fired, we realised that Hugo had a second weapon hidden under his priest's outfit. We hadn't thought to check him; stupidity on our part. There was madness in the firing of weapons, bullets smashing through the boxes. Gregory climbed up on some big, sturdy boxes and saw Hugo getting ready to fire again. Hugo spotted Gregory, dropped to one knee, and fired at him, his face a mask of hate. Hugo smiled when he caught Gregory's arm with a bullet. Gregory shot him in the chest, and the others watched Hugo stumble toward them. Hugo reached for Father Julian's cassock hem, and Father Julian backed away, turned, and left. Gregory fired three more shots, which was the end of evil—of this one. There were many more left to catch."

"Several hours later, we returned to the rectory. Anthony had tried to bandage Dietric and Gregory's wounds, but they needed more than a few bandages. The same doctor we trusted with Father Damien was now attending the two of them. He was a Jewish doctor whom Father Damien had kept hidden till he joined the resistance, wanting to help in any way possible."

"Gregory had taken two shots—one to the arm and one to his side. They weren't severe, but he needed the bullets removed and the wounds stitched up. The doctor looked at Gregory's scars, shook his head, and mumbled, 'too many.' Gregory stayed there for a week.

"Anthony didn't ask what happened to Hugo. A week later, the news spoke of Hugo being found dead in a garbage bin in an alleyway. The police were now all over his apartment. Gregory left silently a week later, Dietric returned to Berlin, and we went on as if nothing happened."

Louis leaned back his head closed his eyes as he spoke.

"We never spoke of it again, any of us. Anthony bore a thousand scars for us. He lit the light and the path of love and forgiveness. He felt everyone could redeem themselves if they asked God and the Holy Spirit to enter their life. I started going back to church regularly after really seeing the goodness in Anthony but also the man who could give a good punch." Louis chuckled. "I came to his church where I could feel the Holy Spirit because Anthony ensured it would surround us all. He took the most hardened students at the university who didn't have any belief, and they suddenly were sitting in the back of his church. He touched and changed everyone."

Louis lowered his head to his chin and swallowed hard.

"I would come to Anthony to confess. When I thought it wasn't working, he would always tell me that he himself had sinned. He said he killed SS men to save twenty children and that he loved a woman and still felt close to her. He was special, Katarina, but he died thinking he could not bring you peace. We became close. We had dinner once a week and played cards and drank wine. He always had this amazing twinkle in his eyes that warmed anyone who came across him. After mass, everyone wanted to just talk to him and be near him."

Louis turned to her.

"I believe Anthony was right; he told me once over dinner he couldn't help you because you were fractured and wouldn't let anyone in. Here, you sit like a lonely soul. You're lost, Katarina. Watching you is like watching a glass fall and break into a thousand pieces, and I pray you find happiness and love in the years to come."

She grabbed his hand.

"You could have given us a chance. You know there comes an illness with memories that you want to forget. The events of the years shaped my life into what it is now. You know I loved Gregory, and I was learning to love you."

"No, you won't divorce, and you won't let Gregory out of your system. I, too, need peace; I do not need drama. Sabina is stable. She knows what she wants, and she wants me. You didn't."

Tears now ran down Katarina's face as Louis stood and kissed the top of her head. "Find peace."

She murmured, "It seems Gregory has the same speech."

He left her sitting in the pew, and she made no effort to leave as he walked down the steps of the church and saw the limo. Louis recognised him from pictures as the man got out and walked by him. He was an impressive physical statue, his suit expertly tailored, and his eyes looking straight ahead. His walk was smooth and confident, his hair black with greying on the sides. He made a statement as he climbed out of the limo and past him. What was *he* doing here, Louis thought. Hawaii was a long way from Paris. Louis hesitated. He considered going back inside the church but decided against it. Most likely, Francis Lee still felt he could change Katarina. Louis stood there for a moment, wondering what Katarina would have become if not for the war.

***

Francis Lee stood before the church doors and hesitated momentarily when he saw Louis watching him. Then he quickly entered. Francis saw Katarina with her hands in front of her face, weeping, her shoulders shaking. He took a deep breath. It was pure coincidence that he saw her at the same time Louis did. Louis simply made it up the stairs faster. Francis's investigators had shown Katarina with Louis, so Francis knew who he was immediately.

Francis knew every one of Katarina's movements through the years. He had been in Berlin, saw the Von Rahmel family, and gave them pictures of their grandson. They welcomed him into their home with open hearts. They told him Katarina was in Paris at the apartment. He took a chance as he made his way to Paris, unsure why he was making his way to see her. He was happily married to Maria, with whom he had a little girl. Douglas was a wonderful child and grew up to be an upstanding young man. He never asked about his mother. He took it at face value when Francis said she'd died in an accident.

Francis was a millionaire three times over. He wanted for nothing, but there remained this need to see Katarina. He was tormented with thoughts of her. There was no answer at the apartment in Paris, but when his limo turned to go around the block, he spotted her walking toward the church. He waited in the limo, thinking of how her children had grown, including their son, who didn't even know she was alive. He was astonished by Alexandra's beauty and Natalie's sweetness.

He often wondered about the first child Katarina had with John and gave up for adoption. Sometimes, he felt guilty for arranging the adoption. He always wondered why Katarina didn't tell John the truth, and maybe he would have told them where their child was adopted, in the end, the child had a better life being adopted. He sought the best, with money and prestige, so the child would go through life not wanting anything. If he had told Katarina, maybe she could have gone and got the child, but she didn't even bother to ask what happened to Johns and her child. All she cared about was getting the divorce and leaving their son. He knew John and her child were in good hands with loving parents, and someday, the child might find out when he is told he was adopted. Hawaii had sealed adoptions. It was impossible for John to find the child.

Francis couldn't leave Europe and not catch a glance of her. When he did business in Berlin, he would catch glimpses of her but never approached her until today. He saw her walk a few blocks from the church. He followed her in the limo and saw her as Louis followed her into the church. He waited until Louis left, then slipped into the building. He didn't expect to find Katarina weeping. She so seldom cried. He touched her shoulder, and she jumped when she looked up. Clearly, she was expecting Louis to have come back.

Her hands began to shake as he offered her his hands. She stood, straightened her back, and wiped the tears off her face. Her long lashes were wet, making those violet eyes stand out even more.

"What are you doing here, Francis?"

He didn't know what to say as he looked at her tear-stained face. His voice was calm and quiet as he helped her out of the pew.

"I was here on business. I first went to Berlin, and your parents told me you were here, so I thought I'd take a chance."

She gave him a slight smile, and he brushed the wisp of hair that had fallen in front of her face.

"Francis, nothing you do is by chance." Her eyes were desperate as he moved her to the church door. There was a raw, sick feeling inside her. It was as if someone had pulled a plug, and her energy was sapped. She silently walked down the steps of the church with him, looking at him in the light, thinking how he had aged well.

"I'm at the Ritz. Come have dinner with me." He kissed her cheek where the tears had just lain. He brought her hand to his lips; his tenderness brought a strange ache. They had fought so many battles, each so cruel to each other.

"I'll go with you, but only dinner."

"Only dinner," He answered.

Chapter 14

Katarina returned to the apartment the next evening, and Francis left to go back to the States. She walked into the apartment, hoping not to have any questions. She had stayed with him, and they both left their past behind for a few hours.

She had just walked into her bedroom when the doorbell rang, and she heard Dietric and Elvie shout with glee. Katarina quickly changed as she tried to decipher the voices. When she entered the living room, a young man introduced himself to Hans.

"I'm Edward Renaldi." Before he could say another word, Sarah lifted her hand for her mother and Dietric. The brilliant diamond on her finger had to be two carats, and emeralds surrounded it.

"We're getting married, Mother," Sarah squealed.

Edward was beaming. He had dark black hair, combed back and a little long in the back. He had deepest grey eyes, a strong jawline, a square chin with a dimple, and was about an inch shorter than Sarah, who was tall like Heinz.

"Sit, both of you," Elvie ordered. She rang the bell for the maid to bring in coffee, and saw Katarina and motioned for her to join them. Sarah gave all of them big hugs. She glanced briefly at Katarina but didn't approach her with any hugs. She almost ignored Katarina as she made introductions, giving Katarina only the briefest acknowledgement.

"Sarah, when are you two thinking of getting married?" Katarina asked.

Before Sarah could answer, Edward spoke up.

"I'm in my medical residency at the hospital. I have a few more months left, and it would be good for Sarah to continue with her studies. After I finish, I plan to open my own doctor's office. I'll be taking over my father's practice. Please don't worry. Sarah will become a brilliant chef here in Paris. I have no intentions of interfering with her goals in life."

Hans left the room and came back with a bottle of their best Champagne. "Time to celebrate!" He said.

Alexandra came in before Hans could pop the cork, followed by her own fiancé of just a week. He was a tall, blonde man with broad shoulders, a big smile, high cheekbones, and messy hair that looked like it hadn't been combed that day. He wore a blue sweater that brought out his crystal-clear blue eyes. He was from Sweden and was finishing veterinary school in Berlin while Alex was in her last year of law school. Alex and Sarah ran into each other's arms; they were sisters at heart.

Everyone was laughing and talking at once as Alex showed off her diamond, which she had received the previous week. There was no hiding the expense of either ring. Alex was surrounded by rubies. The drinks were poured, and a toast was given. Alex noticed her mother had slipped onto the balcony.

Alex walked out to her mother. "Kat, come in and meet Stephan. He is a wonderful man."

"Did you tell him about me?" Katarina's voice was cold.

"I have not. He only knows Lisa as my mother, but in time, I will share your story."

Kat smirked at Alex. "Why not tell him? Afraid to let him know who and what your father was?"

"No, Kat, I'm not worried." Alex turned to leave, and Kat grabbed her arm.

"It won't last, Alex. You and Natalie will never be able to hold onto men, just like I haven't. You both can mark my words, and men will leave you."

Alex narrowed her eyes. "They leave you because your heart is so black. Now let go of me and try to be civil if you know how."

Hans saw Alex walk back into the room, her face stressed, so he went to her side. "Don't let her upset you, Alex."

Katarina came into the room, and before Alex could stop her, she strode up to Stephan.

"Hello, I'm Alex's mother." She took his hand, and Sarah saw the stricken look on Alex's face. She hurried over, took Stephan by the arm, and pulled him away. Then she returned to Kat and spoke, her voice a hiss.

"You are the most tormented, hateful person."

Alexandra stood frozen in shock. Stephan walked over to her and took her in his arms as he whispered in her ear, "I know, Alex. Lisa told me from the very beginning. I knew you were just waiting. Not to worry, dear girl. I love you. There is nothing Katarina can say that will affect our relationship. She is inconsequential."

Sarah walked over to Alex. "Stop trying to get Kat's approval. She sucks the air out of life, and she lives in her own darkness. You are happy. We both are in a wonderful time in our life. Let her be. Where she has no heart, you make up for it with so much love to give."

Alex looked at her mother who was now leaving the room. She hadn't said goodbye to anyone. Hans followed Katarina into the bedroom as she was taking down a suitcase.

"Where are you going, Kat?"

"I have to deliver adoption papers to Gregory."

"You can mail them." A breeze was coming through the window, which made her shiver. The sky turned dark, and pellets of rain began to come down, matching her mood.

"I do. I'm not going through this chaos again. If they are lost in the mail, then it starts all over again. Besides, he might not even be there."

Hans shook his head in sadness. "When you're finished, come back to Berlin. There are a few letters from John. We need to discuss Natalie."

She ignored him as he left the room. Her flight wasn't until tomorrow morning, so she decided to go downstairs to the café to be alone.

Kat was restless as she watched the morning sun come through the window and made her way to the airport without saying goodbye to anyone. Hours later, she arrived at the consolation in Tel Aviv, she was staying at the Sheraton on the beach and north side of Independence Park.

Everything looked so new, she thought, as the waiting car took her to the hotel. It had changed from just a few years ago. In the Rothchild neighbourhood, she passed King George Street to the west, and she saw private villas popping up. She could walk from the beach area to Gregory's home on Rothchild Blvd. Tomorrow, though, she thought. The flight was long, and she was tired. She could deliver the documents tomorrow.

It was unusual to see a woman travelling on her own, and she was admired just walking through the lobby. She went to a café and sat and ate alone. There were times she felt she could just cry. She didn't want to be alone.

The next morning, she took a long bath. She wore a long, dark cotton skirt that touched her ankles, a light blue sweater set, and white sandals. Her hair was pulled up into a ponytail away from her face, which brought out her cheekbones and those eyes that everyone noticed.

She had the cab drop her off a few blocks before Gregory's home and asked the driver to return in an hour. She paid the driver in advance to make sure he returned to the address she gave him. She took her time walking to Gregory's, admiring the quaint but beautiful houses along the way. She arrived at Gregory's home and found Alise in the front yard. Katarina stood there, not knowing what to say. Alise was pregnant and looked like she could have the baby at any time. A sudden, surprising surge of rage coursed through Katarina. Gregory had told her about the baby, but seeing Alise with her own eyes cut deep. She was ready to walk away and let them squirm for the adoption papers when she saw Alise clutch her stomach and drop to her knees. Benjamin was holding her hand. He had grown. He was a beautiful three-year-old and had his father's eyes but her blond hair. Anyone would think his blond hair was from

Alise, but Katarina knew the truth. Alise looked terrified and looked up and saw Katarina standing at the end of their walkway.

Katarina spoke in a low tone. "I'm here only to bring you the adoption papers."

"My water broke. Please help me into the house." Her voice was small and weak.

"You'll be fine. Let's get you in the house. Do you have a doctor we can call?"

Alise suddenly let out a scream. "I think it's too late for a doctor."

Benjamin started to cry.

"Come, Benjamin," Katarina said, "Help me with your mom."

The child started to cry harder. His little chubby hands were now patting his mother's hand, and his big green eyes looked at Katarina.

"Alise, can you walk to the house? I have to hold on to the child."

"I think so." They limped back to the house and walked into the living room with its large bay windows. Alise pointed to the bedroom.

Katarina hesitated. She didn't want to enter Alise and Gregory's room, the room where they created this baby. Her heart sank as she followed Alise into the bedroom. It had a large, four-poster bed with a light green comforter and matching sheets. The room was of oak hardwood with a large oriental rug on the floor.

Katarina went into the attached bathroom and brought out towels and a large comforter she saw on a Queen Anne chair for Alise to lie on. Within minutes, Alise let out another cry, telling Katarina the baby was coming.

Katarina removed Alise's skirt and underwear and helped her into a position for birth. She told her to take long, slow breaths and propped her head up with pillows.

She saw Benjamin standing at the door. *He can't stay here*, thought Katarina.

"Alise, does Benjamin have his own room to play in?"

"Yes, down the hall."

Katarina took Benjamin in her arms and lifted him up. "Benjamin, can you play in your room for a while?"

He nodded, and Kat placed him in a dark blue room full of fire engines and car toys with a large drawing board against the wall. He had a nice twin bed that sat under a ceiling painted with constellations and stars. She sat him down in front of his fire engines and walked back to Alise's room.

Alise was so pale and vulnerable looking. Why was she alone this late in her pregnancy?

"Alise, where is Gregory's aunt?"

"She went shopping, and Gregory had to leave for a few hours for work." Before Alise could say another word, she cried out.

Katarina propped Alise's head up higher and raised her legs. She decided neither an ambulance nor the doctor would get there in time.

"Alise, I'll help you deliver the baby. I've done this several times myself, so I know what to do. Let's do this together. Trust me. I will help you."

Alise nodded. For the next forty minutes, Alise and Katarina worked together to deliver her baby.

The baby girl came out screaming. Kat took her in her arms and wrapped her quickly in a bath towel. Alise was reaching for her and crying for joy. Suddenly, there was a roar from the door. Katarina whirled around to see Gregory, his eyes glowing with anger and contempt; she'd never seen him direct at her. A wave of anger in his voice she had never heard before. Alise spoke up immediately.

"Gregory, Katarina helped me deliver the baby. There was no one else here. She was an angel to be here at the right time. She saved me and took care of Benjamin. He's in his room."

Gregory hurried over to Alise, who brushed her wet hair from her face as Gregory leaned down to kiss his new baby girl gently.

"Alise, she is as beautiful as you are."

Katarina backed away and went out the door. She left the adoption papers on the hallway table. The cab was already waiting, and she was grateful he had come a bit early. She took in a deep, long breath of fresh air. Her heart was aching. She couldn't bear to see them a moment longer. She just wanted to get back to her hotel so she could clean up and catch her flight back to Italy tomorrow. She needed to be back in the hills and see the olive groves and smell the flowers, she needed to breathe again.

Later that night, she decided to sit on the beach. The crisp air smelled of salt. She pulled her sweater closer; her hair was blown in every direction.

She sensed Gregory was behind her before he could speak. He sat next to her, and they listened to the waves crashing onto the beach.

"I'm sorry, Kat. Alise explained."

Katarina stared straight ahead and laced her voice with sarcasm. "What, did you think I was going to hurt her?"

"I found the adoption papers. You could have mailed them."

Her throat was tight. She was choking, trying not to cry, but couldn't help it, and tears rolled down her cheeks. "I came because there was this little bit of hope you would leave her and come to me."

He bowed his head, his voice stifled, his suffering chiselled deep on his face. He was struggling not to hold her, to comfort her as he always had. "Kat, you made the decision to leave. It was your choice. I wanted a future with a woman who loves me and our son. Alise treats him as if she gave birth to him. He doesn't even realize who you are. He's known only Alise as his mother."

Katarina turned to him. "No, it was your choice. We could have gone on as is. Was it because she was young?"

Gregory shook his head. " I did fall in love. I loved you and I still carry you in my soul, but as long as you were staying married, there was no future for us. Please never question how much I loved you. You were always enough for me, but you couldn't give me your heart. I didn't leave you because I didn't love you."

"Gregory, John is safe. You disappear. You are like a lone wolf, taking on missions to find everyone who your government wants to find. You yourself have your own demons. I've seen you cross the line both morally and legally when you see fit. I didn't know if I wanted that world. I don't know what world I want. I just knew I wanted to keep you in my life. You're the only one who knows everything about me. You saw my open heart, you saw what I went through, you knew every inch of me, you just couldn't understand me."

"Yes, you're right. My job *is* dangerous, but we had three chances to make a future together: when you divorced Francis, the first time you left Berlin with him, or when you came back. I knew I couldn't truly have you, so I came back to Israel. I had to bring justice. We vowed we would never again let another Hitler try to destroy us as a people. I will hunt those who hurt us until my last breath. You knew this. You worked alongside me. You did the same in Berlin as you entered those tunnels for the Germans who needed out. You helped families escape during the war. I only know how to kill by stealth and surprise or bring them back to Israel. If they don't want to stand trial here in Israel, they must be dealt with so they will never walk on this earth again. One less evil soul. They all need to return to hell."

He got up, dusted the sand off his trousers, and started to pace.

"Do you have any idea how many nights I lay in bed with the phone inches from my ear, hoping to hear from you or scared to death you were in trouble? Or that Peter and your brother put you up to one of their missions that you have no business being part of? Kat, at the end of all of this, I have the best part of you in Benjamin."

He stopped and rubbed his hand over her back. He let out a long sigh and took in a deep breath as he looked down at her.

"Katarina, you are one of the bravest women I know. I wear you every day in my soul. I have tasted you in my dreams. You are a yesterday, a memory now out of reach. I recall your sweet, gentle beauty when I first met you. I miss you as if the moon would not rise or the sunset set failed to appear. But I've also started my new life, and it is good for me. Everyone you touch ends up hurting. Everyone tries to save you. I can't anymore. You have to save yourself."

His face was set in a furrowed scowl as he looked at the water washing ashore. The stars were brilliant as he looked up at the darkened sky. He let out a sad sigh. She rose and stood next to him.

"Kat, I met Anthony once in Rome. It was pure coincidence that we crossed each other at Saint Peter's. I was there for a conference on how many Nazis the Vatican and the churches had given safe passage to. We had coffee in a little pastry shop he was determined to introduce me to since he had been going there for years. They make all the cakes on the premises. It sits on a side street where the tourists don't go, and he desperately wanted to share this place with me. It was a safe place for him." A smile crossed Gregory's lips as he recalled.

"He was called to the Vatican to be reprimanded for his part in Berlin with the wall. He sat back and just closed his eyes as he reminded me to appreciate life, to smell the coffee, the sweet smells of the bakery, to just look around that there was goodness in the world. During our conversation that morning, he asked me to pursue anyone who might cause you harm. He was very clear on his blessing to me. He looked in the direction of an old church, whose cracks and foundation crumbling, sat across from the cafe. He smiled as he said, 'That is where the Holy Spirit is, not at the Vatican with all its glory of paintings and jewels. That is not what rules the Holy Spirit. It's the old churches with the people who take their prayers and ask the Holy Spirit to help them."

"It caused your brother physical pain to say what he said next, that it was time I released you in my soul. He told me to find happiness that you could not give me. I watched him walk away that morning, a proud man but filled with anguish at the same time. He gave peace to me. He knew I would find those who came in your tortured dreams. I would find those who murdered Heinz and those who placed Rita in the camp. There were others who signed those papers. I promised him I would find them and give them justice in my way. He didn't want them killed but rather taken to court. I didn't tell him that sometimes that couldn't happen."

A slight tremor went through as she still saw how they pulled Rita off the sofa, kicking her down the stairs outside. Katarina could only watch from the window as they beat Rita. Katarina inhaled the salt air, at a loss for words.

"I hadn't realized he'd spoken so openly with you," She said. "He seemed not to share a lot with me at the end."

Gregory placed his hand on her shoulder. "He never wanted you to worry about my world or his fears. He sat with me in England as MI6 informed me they had caught the man who ordered my village and my family to be killed. He said he was there to visit Peter in Brighton, but he was always a terrible liar. He *was* visiting Peter, but he also came to support me. While the man who murdered my family locked eyes with me while he testified that he was innocent, Anthony pulled me back into my seat when I rose up to rush the man and kill him with my bare hands."

Gregory lowered his head in deep thought before he could speak again.

"This man was also charged with the 1942 incident at the Vel d'Hir roundup where over eight hundred arrest squads broke into homes of Jews. Almost thirteen thousand people vanished, more than four thousand of them children, their future just gone. Then, in my mind, I saw when they arrested you while you were eight months pregnant, and I stood by and could do nothing. It stays with me to this day, so I hunt the murderers. I hunt those who wish Israel harm as they are springing up, especially with the Palestinians. I go after looted items taken from homes." His fist was not clenched, his jaw was set tightly.

Katarina placed her hand on his arm. He still was looking straight into the blackness of the sea. The sky was clear, and the stars looked like thousands of diamonds.

"Kat, you understand better than anyone in my world. Alise never saw the horror. She is almost innocent in life. She doesn't ask me where I'm going; she just knows I'm working for the Israeli government. You have never been safe to any man. Alise only knows one man—me. She wouldn't even begin to understand what you have seen or done for preservation."

She removed her hand, sat back down on the sand, and brought her knees to her chest, placing her head on her knees. He silently sat now next to her; he could feel the warmth from her body, the smell of her skin. The breeze was blowing her hair into soft curls. He took in a deep breath of the air of the land he loved. It was sweet as he looked straight out into the darkness before he turned to look at her pale face again.

They sat for a long time until he pulled her close and placed both arms around her, giving her his silent strength. His body's warmth seeped into her. His strength was always soothing. Her self-esteem was low at this point, and she felt her emotions were raw. He held her as she buried her face in his chest. He felt her shoulders shudder as he felt her tears on his shirt.

"Come, you need to go back to the hotel. I'll walk you back."

He helped her up as she wiped the sand off her clothing and walked back barefoot till they reached the street area. The two of them walked in silence. He was a stunning figure to see walking down the street. He carried his body with authority, but she noticed his eyes were always looking for an enemy who might surprise him.

He walked her to her room, took her in his arms, and kissed the top of her head.

"Kat, you will always be in my blood." Once again, a tightness rose in his chest. He placed the key in the door and opened it for her. She pulled him in.

"Don't go, Gregory. Please."

It was like a thousand punches to the gut. He exhaled as he moved her away from his embrace. She pulled him back.

Her lips found his, and he responded in kind as they moved towards the bed. He was just holding her, his head swimming. He kissed her mouth tenderly, wanting all of her. He kissed deeply and long. It was familiar as always to him. Then he suddenly stopped.

"What's wrong?" She said as he pulled away from her.

"You have the power to destroy me. You're like my breath that can keep me from breathing. I can't stop loving you, but it's no longer a path I can go down. I'm sorry." He backed away from Kat. "I love Alise. I made vows to her. I'm sorry. I see the best part of you in Benjamin. He will grow up to be an outstanding person with Alise raising him. We now have a daughter to love, and I'm grateful you were there for Alise. The kindness you have in you came out for a brief time. I'm sorry, but I have to leave. This will be the last time. My life, my future can't be with you. My thoughts can't be with you. I have to erase you."

She began to sob as she tried to pull him towards the bed. "Please don't do this."

He turned from her and stopped for a moment before he reached the door.

"Be happy, Katarina, that you will always be part of me. We have a history that no other has. You are in my blood, and I pray the sun will dance in your smile again. I miss you sometimes like the sun would miss the moon. But it's over. The path has ended with me."

He opened the door and left. He could hear her sobbing behind the closed door, and he leaned his head against the door and closed his eyes. The one thing he'd never wanted to do was hurt her, and now he'd done it.

He walked for hours in the dark night and suddenly felt tears on his face. The last time he'd cried was when Benjamin was born. Before that, when he saw his parents and sister murdered. Tears were not part of his vocabulary. He knew there was a brokenness in Katarina that no one could heal. She lived with emotional nightmares and demons she was not willing to seek help for. She was the only one who prevented her own happiness. Now, he needed to return to his newborn, his son, and Alise. Katarina would remain with him, but it was the end for him.

The next morning, Katarina woke to red, swollen eyes. After a bath, she wiped the fog from the mirror and stared at her ghostly reflection. Her eyes were heavy with sadness. She dressed in black to match her mood. The front of her dress had a ruffle that ran to the hem. She put on large sunglasses as she checked out of her room, sat, and sipped her black coffee. Then she walked out to the driver who was waiting for her.

Gregory stood across the street and watched her leave. She saw him watching her, gave him a weak smile and waved. He waved back. He watched the car drive away as she looked back, tears flowing again. He brought her tears. Every memory of him brought her tears.

He returned to his car and leaned his head against the seat. She was his weakness, he thought. He realized he couldn't keep his promise to Anthony to always watch out for her. He carried with him a note Anthony gave him.

Psalm 16:7-1

"I will praise the Lord, who counsels me; even at night, my heart instructs me. I have set the Lord always before me. Because he is at my right hand. I will not be shaken. Therefore, my heart is glad and my tongue rejoices. My body also will rest secure. Because you will not abandon me to the grave, nor will you let your Holy One see decay. You have made known to me the path of life; you will fill me with joy in your presence. With eternal pleasures at your hand."

Yes, Alise was his eternal pleasure with the grace of God.

Chapter 15

Katarina was happy in Italy when she arrived. She wanted to put everything behind her and spent days wandering the old town of Cingue Terie. She also travelled and stayed in a villa on Lake Como, invited by a gentleman she met when Hans was in town with a new client looking at the olive production and wine being bottled. It was upsetting to Hans when she left with Lucio Blanco, but she didn't care. Elvie came with Dietric and begged her not to go off with someone she didn't know. She replied that he must be okay if he can do business with Hans. She was back at the villa two weeks later, looking tired, but didn't explain what she'd done with Lucio Blanco.

Hans was worried. Katarina looked frail, and he had never seen her so unhappy. Even her tan didn't hide the circles under her eyes. She went to Greece with Lucio several times. He was rich and renowned for the women he travelled with. He was old and loved the young woman, so he paraded Katarina around the finest restaurants and casinos.

Katarina was always unhappy upon return but loved that he smothered her with attention each time he came to visit, and they left on another adventure. He had several villas all over Europe, and she even took a trip to his penthouse in New York, where she spent days shopping while he was doing business. She didn't care what people thought when they looked at her with this old man. This would be the last trip she would take with him. She was bored and decided he lacked any intimacy and only used her to show off and look good on his arm. She had to break it off, but even with the lack of intimacy, she was grateful for brief relief it all brought her from the memories that stalked her.

Several weeks later, after a long journey back to Italy on his yacht, she decided to be honest with him and wished him goodbye. She was bored with all the travel and especially hated his yacht. He couldn't understand why she was ending the relationship. He'd grown very fond of her, more so than any of the other women he'd known. He offered to let her move in with him, and she told him she didn't want to hurt his feelings, but there was nothing for her to look forward to. She sent Hans a message to meet her at the hotel in Florence. They spent a few days in Rome he completed some business. They didn't share many conversations, but he was relieved she was back.

She was sunbathing alone back at their villa—everyone else had returned to Berlin—when a shadow crossed her body. It was the voice that always lingered in her thoughts.

"We need your help."

She looked up at him and nodded yes.

1966

Natalie knew time was closing in, and she was getting ready to return to the States. She was torn. Her life was full of her grandparents and Aunt Gertrude.

She spent days with her grandfather, going on vet visits to other farms. She spent a lot of time with him with the animals in the barn. She learned so much from him and would drink up any information on how to care for horses and other pets.

She missed Alexandra, who had seldom been back at the house since she married. Natalie often went into the city with Aunt Gertrude because she didn't want to be around Katarina. Their conversations when Katarina returned to Berlin were never cordial. Katarina only berated her for her looks and her style. She did the same with Alexandra if she was there, telling them both that future husbands and boyfriends would leave them because that is what men did.

It was unpleasant that year at Christmas as they all went on a ski vacation in Courchevel, France. Natalie was excited to go, but there always was the lingering hope that her mother would not show. When they arrived, she was already at the villa. Natalie made sure she stayed close to her aunt and grandparents so she could avoid any confrontation. It was not to be avoided with Alexandra; Alex came at the last minute, leaving her fiancé in Berlin to take finals. Natalie heard the raised voices, her mother again decided not to ski but instead drink. Her words were slurred as she insulted Alexandra, but this time Alex shot back.

"You are not allowed to talk to me in this manner, I'm a grown woman. You are a wreck of a human being, and I no longer have any desire to win you over. You can insult me and Natalie about the men that are in our lives or will be, but we will be happy. You speak very frankly about our looks, considering you yourself are now old and even Gregory chose a younger woman over you. Look at yourself! You are not what you were. Who are you going to convince that you still have charm and allure? It's gone."

Alex took in a deep breath. She had never spoken to her mother with such venom, but she wanted to hurt her back, just like Katarina continuously hurt her and Natalie. She knew Katarina depended on her looks, and telling her that she was old would cut deep, even though Alex knew her mother was just as lovely as ever.

Kat pulled her arm back and slapped Alex's face. Alex shoved her mother back, and Katarina fell to the floor. Natalie walked in and saw the red hand mark on Alex's face. Her mother did not get up. Natalie rushed to her sister's side.

"Come Alex, don't stay here."

They turned, and as Natalie reached the door, Kat yanked her hair. Natalie turned and reached for her mother's hand. Kat was screaming in a blind rage. She was so drunk she could barely stand.

"You both are wicked girls." She punched Natalie on the arm before Alex came and pried her hand off Natalie's hair. Natalie backed away with Alex, and both saw the rage in their mother's eyes.

Gertrude heard Kat screaming about how she hated the girls. Then came the thunder of their grandfather's voice.

He slammed the door and told everyone but Katarina to leave the room. His raised voice threatened Katarina, which was something he had never done. They listened through the door as he said Katarina could either go to her room and sleep off her drunkenness or find a hotel in the village. He went on to tell her not to come near the girls while in any of his homes. It would be best in the morning if she would leave after she slept off her drunkenness.

Natalie disappeared upstairs, and Gertrude came into the room with a bowl of soup and tea. Natalie was rubbing her arm where a large bruise was blooming. Gertrude's heart shattered. She so wanted this child to be her own. She begged John to let her and Hans adopt her. His answer was no, and she understood letting Natalie out of her life would not be an option.

She sat next to her and held her hand. "Natalie, she will be gone tomorrow."

"What about my tomorrows, Aunt Gertrude? What about when I go back to the States? You know she will go also."

"We will figure it all out. I want you to sleep. We have a big day tomorrow. You have new skis to try out."

Katarina didn't wait till the next day. She phoned the five-star hotel that sat on a gentle slope in town. Few words were spoken, and she acted as if nothing had happened, begging her brother to take her there. Katarina packed her bags. She didn't have the energy to fight with anyone, look at her daughters, or see the disappointment on her father's face.

The lobby of the small but elegant hotel had a roaring fire. Katarina handed her luggage to the bellhop and got her key. Hans walked her in. He'd agreed to drive her and maybe talk some sense into her so once she cleared her mind, she could come back to the villa. But he recognized the look on her face. She wanted to be left alone.

"Hans, you are welcome to stay, but I'm heading down the street to have some drinks and dinner."

"No, I think you will do just fine on your own. You always do. Try to make yourself go back to Berlin. Katarina, you need help. You need to stop drinking."

"That's easy for you to say. How do I leave the past in the past? How do I stop the nightmares that visit me so often? Tell me."

"It's not good to keep dwelling on your memories. All your pain motivates your behaviour. Don't you see that's why you need help?"

Katarina felt like shouting. Her face grew pensive. He didn't understand.

"Katarina, your memories are getting in the way of you living a good life and a healthy life."

She looked at Hans, her breathing shallow. "I'm not sure where I'm heading. You think I haven't tried to forget? I cannot forget. I might stay here or go to Switzerland. I have an open invitation from a young man who doesn't think I'm 'too old,' as my daughter stated. I met him in Greece. He's been asking me for a few months to join him. Why not? Hans, you are looking at me with that worried look. Or is it distain this time? I just need to get away from all of you. I need to feel wanted by someone young who doesn't know me and wants to have a little fun."

He let out a long sigh. "Kat, you're married."

She raised her hand. "I wouldn't go there if I were you."

"Kat, that was one woman. A woman I loved, a woman I would have left my marriage for, not a parade of women as you have a parade of men. Big difference."

Caught off guard, she turned her back on him. Hans had her back like Anthony used to. He, too, was turning on her. All because of those two girls. She turned back to face him.

"Hans, it was not my fault. Both those girls are spoiled. All of you let Natalie live in this world of books and animals. You never let Natalie look at life and the harshness of it. She will be let down when she ends up out in the world. I think you all need to let her grow up."

He was shaking his head, his lips tight, his eyes now hard.

Katarina opened her mouth to respond but she had no excuse on this one.

"Hans, I love you, but it's time you got back to the house. I will be fine here. I'm always good on my own."

"Yes, you are. That's your strength. You are a survivor. I will tell you this: Natalie *has* learned the harshness of life. Every time you are around her, she learns about a mother hating her. She learns about pain as you strike out at her. She learns about mean-spirited words that no mother should ever say. She learned fear when you left her in East Berlin. She knows about life. You made sure of it. She can only escape you by going into her own world of books or being with Gertrude and me. Don't you think we know what she suffers when you visit her at school? The sisters call us because they see the bruises. We can only give her love that you've never given her or any of the children you've left behind. My suggestion for the future is don't visit her again."

He grabbed her arm tightly. "I wish you happiness. But you won't have any because of your actions."

He quickly let go of her arm. He was done with her. He left her standing in the lobby, and her face lost all colour. He'd never spoken to her with the harshness and finality of his words. She ran after him and caught up with him before entering the car.

"Please, Hans, don't do this. Forgive me. I promise I'll seek help. I have a doctor in Sweden that can help me. I'll go there. I promise I'll fight my demons. I'll change. Just don't you leave me."

He pulled her into his arms and whispered in her ear. "I love you. Get help. Come back to us as a whole person again." He got in the car and left.

She was so angry. She didn't need a doctor, she thought. They just failed to understand her. They didn't understand that each of her children reminded her of something she wanted to forget. None of them held any happy memories. She would go to Switzerland. She didn't need doctors in Sweden. Hans would forgive her. He always did.

As he drove away, Hans could only think of how to smooth things over. He'd never seen his father so angry. He promised Anthony to take care of Katarina, and he would. But at a later time, after she sought help. But would she?

Chapter 16

The following morning, Hans left the others to enjoy a day of skiing. He had rung up Katarina to see how she was doing, and he decided to go down to the village and have breakfast with her. He didn't tell the others where he was going.

She was waiting for him in a small café. She could tell the moment he entered that he had forgiven her.

She stood to embrace him. They ordered breakfast; the cafe was filled with people getting ready for the day on the slopes. The room was bright with the smell of chocolate croissants and strong coffee. They ordered soft-boiled eggs and rolls, and Hans caught the eye of a gentleman who would not stop staring at her.

"Do you know him?" He asked.

She shook her head as she sipped on her coffee and looked over. The man diverted his eyes. "I know he's German; he is reading the *Spiegel*, and someone addressed him as 'Professor.' I ran into him last night briefly in the bar."

Hans noticed the man's hands were shaking. "Katarina, sometimes I look at the Germans, and I can't help but wonder if they changed their names, their whole identity as the one did with Anthony. It's incongruous that they walk around without conscience of what some have done."

She gave him a weak smile. "We catch them. It takes time."

Hans cocked his head. "We?"

"Yes, we. It's hard not to want to find every one of them. When you've heard the screams that pierce through time, it does not leave you. Last night in the bar, he was telling someone he was writing a paper on the Holocaust to teach his students the evils of the world. As I left, I stopped and told him that no one is free of the past."

Her voice suddenly sounded almost detached. She reached for Hans's hand and gave him a smile that melted many a heart.

"Well, sweet brother, I really must go back and pack. I must leave."

"Are you going to Sweden?"

She hesitated. "Yes, after I have my visit to Switzerland."

"You're not going, are you?"

She leaned back in the softness of the chair and looked at him for a long time. "I will be back in Berlin before you know it. I always return, don't I?"

"Yes, you return when you want to feel safe. You are so damaged inside you won't find peace. Being around you is like living with earthquakes."

She didn't know how to answer. She knew she was damaged to the very core of her soul, and she couldn't climb out of her own darkness to be happy.

She glanced one more time at the old professor as they left the café. The outside air was cold but crisp, and people were dashing by with their skis, some dressed as if it was a fashion show. She placed her hat on and kissed her brother goodbye. She walked away as they parted, and he looked back at her. She seemed so alone and lost, he thought, but in many ways, she wasn't. She knew the direction she wanted to take regardless of how it ended.

Katarina walked slowly, looking in the store windows. She passed one and stared at her own reflection. Memories were like water washing over pebbles, she thought. Some got stuck in the rocks and never moved, others washed down the river. She looked a little longer. No, she was not old. The young man she'd met in Greece had pursued her for months. He was ten years younger. She would have a grand time in Switzerland.

Natalie was just putting on her boots when Hans returned to the house. She looked up at him with overwhelming trepidation. "My mother isn't coming back, is she?"

"No, child, she left."

Natalie sat back in the chair and closed her eyes.

Hans knew Natalie feared her mother. A few months back, they'd taken her to the hospital after finding her in the barn badly bruised, her lip swollen. She'd said nothing, and the doctors harshly questioned Gertrude and him. On the way home, Natalie explained that it was her fault. She'd taken out her mother's horse, and Natalie slipped and fell when her Katarina came into the stables. Then the girl stopped talking and wouldn't tell her story any further. Gertrude gathered her into her arms and held her tight as Hans looked out the window from the limo and could not speak. He suddenly asked the driver to turn around and gave him the address to Natalie's favourite ice cream parlour. There, the laughter returned as Hans made his favourite faces that Natalie so enjoyed watching while he told hilarious stories.

When they returned to the house, Katarina was packing, as usual. Gertrude charged into her room, shaking with fury.

"You love to live in your darkness. You're the queen of darkness, but you will not ever bring your darkness into this child's life. She is kind and thoughtful, and she has everything you will never possess. Leave. Get out of our lives."

Hans looked at this little girl; he could hear the raised voices, and relief flooded Natalie's eyes.

"Will she stay gone for a while, Uncle Hans?"

"I believe so, Natalie."

Katarina would come home occasionally. Otherwise, no one really knew where she was or what she was doing. Hans kept what he knew to himself. She would appear, but she would leave Natalie and Alex alone when they were near her. Conversations were as if they were two strangers to her, asking about their lives.

Alexandra finished law school and had a joyous wedding, then her first baby. Her happiness was apparent with every visit. She had Natalie over to her home many times for sleepovers. They went to visit Sarah often. She, too, was married and was a chef in one of the grand hotels in Paris. At Christmas, the entire family would gather at their home in Italy. Now, the laughter of babies filled the house as Sarah and Alex had their own.

Natalie relished her holidays. She'd write copious letters to her father, and she loved it when she received letters from her American grandmother as well as from her brother and Lydia, her godmother, who was looking forward to her returning to the States. It had all been arranged that Natalie would start her freshmen year in a Catholic private school. When Katarina decided to appear during Christmas, Natalie tried to show her the letters, but Katarina slapped them out of her hand. Some nights, the thought of leaving everything she loved weighed heavy on Natalie's mind, she would lie awake in her bed, just staring at the ceiling. Sometimes, she would sneak downstairs in the kitchen and call the dog upstairs to sleep with her. Everyone in the family and the sisters at school saw the dark circles under Natalie's eyes, and her nails chewed to the quick. It was clear that Natalie feared going back with her mother.

Finally, Katarina returned to announce the final arrangements for Natalie to return to the States. The whole family could hear Katarina and Gertrude shouting at each other in the library, Katarina's venomous voice reminding Gertrude that Natalie was her daughter and Gertrude had no say.

A week later, Sister Beatrice called Gertrude to express her concerns about Katarina taking Natalie back to the States alone.

Several weeks before the scheduled departure, Katarina appeared at Natalie's school. No one realized she'd slipped onto the premises and walked into Natalie's classroom. Sister Benedict spotted Katarina pulling Natalie out of the back door to the garden and rang the emergency bell. The sisters chased after her, but by the time they caught up, Katarina was already in the distance, walking away. Natalie sat on a bench, her head in her hands. Sister Benedict saw that Natalie's long braid, previously down to her waist, had been cut off. Natalie wouldn't say a word about what had happened between her and her mother.

Gertrude took Natalie to a hairdresser to trim the harsh edges of the cut. Alexandra joined them and tried to make Natalie feel good about her look, showing her magazine covers of young models with bangs and shoulder-length hair. Natalie still never said a word, but Gertrude knew Natalie would carry this with her.

Gertrude and Sister Beatrice, who was in communication with the sisters of the Catholic school in Pennsylvania, decided they'd travel with Natalie to the States.

Natalie came home from school for the weekend, and Gertrude took her into the sunroom as the warm spring breeze, and the smell of lilacs floated into the room. Natalie sank into her favourite Queen Anne chair, green with golden threads running through it that fit in the cheerful room where she spent many a day reading. Natalie hated shoes, and she took them off as soon as she was inside.

She sat looking at her aunt's serious face. Gertrude pushed Natalie's hair out of her eyes since she now had bangs. She was wearing her favourite pink sweater set with black slacks. She hated wearing a dress or skirt. The sun struck her eyes, and when it did, they would change to a unique colour of green trimmed in brown.

Katarina tried to undermine Alexandra's and Natalie's confidence with every visit through the years, but it didn't work because the family was always there to tell them the truth. But Natalie still struggled with the harsh criticism. She tried not to listen to her mother, and her grandparents and Aunt Gertrude always brought her back to a place of self-confidence.

Natalie didn't want to hear bad news. She told Gertrude she needed to go to her bedroom. Gertrude followed her.

Gertrude had to tell her that she was leaving them in two weeks, and when she did, tears immediately sprang. Natalie gathered a soft pillow to her stomach and sobbed into it. The room had given her so much comfort over the years, with its stuffed animals, bright pink comforters, and flowered walls. Her grandfather was getting ready to change the wallpaper to horses, as they'd discussed. Directly below the window was the rose garden, which waved in sweet scents during the spring and summer. Natalie never wanted to leave this room.

"Aunt Gertrude, I can't leave. Maybe we should tell my father I will just visit him during vacations." She was almost pleading.

"No, my child, it is time. We talked about this. Uncle Hans and I have bought a house in Florida for the winters, so you can come as much as possible, and we will visit you too. We promise."

Sobs now filled the room as her grandmother walked in and Natalie ran into her arms, not wanting to let go. Gertrude was crying with Natalie as her grandmother tried to stop the tears by reassuring her it would be okay.

The following weeks were difficult as they packed bags, placing lots of pictures in her suitcase. Natalie could not stop crying; in fact, the entire house was in a deep depression as her departure date neared. Her grandfather took her out riding almost every day. Natalie would stay behind in the barn when they finished, and he watched her kiss every horse, dog, and cat that existed in their home and barn. When they would go to wake her, she had dogs and cats on the bed with her. That typically wasn't allowed, but they let her have these moments. One morning, they found her in the stalls sleeping on the hay bale outside the door to the stall of her favourite horse, who seemed to know as he hung his head out of the stall and watched over her all night.

A week before leaving, Natalie had a long conversation on the phone with her father, who gave her a lot of encouragement and let her know she was wanted. She also spoke with her grandmother, who reassured her that everything would be okay in the United States and she would be able to come back and visit as many times as she wanted. It gave Natalie the courage to accept the circumstances of her life.

On Natalie's day of departure, Alexandra came to the house with the baby to wish her goodbye and give her a cross to wear. Her grandmother gave her rosaries that she had carried through the war. Alex smothered her with kisses and told her not to wait too long before she came back. The sorrow etched into her grandparents' and Uncle Hans's eyes was unbearable as they said goodbye to the child they so loved. Her grandfather couldn't bear to accompany her to the airport. When he said goodbye, he held her so tightly she couldn't breathe, and he had to go back into the house before the car pulled away so Natalie wouldn't see his tears. He hadn't cried since his sons died in the war. He went to his place of solace: the horse barn, where he and Natalie shared their most private conversations and laughter.

Katarina was annoyed that a nun and her sister-in-law would be travelling with them. They were on a TWA flight that would stop in Boston and then continue to Philadelphia. It looked more like a funeral as everyone, but Katarina was wearing black and acted very subdued. Katarina sat two rows ahead of the three of them, and neither of them even acknowledged each other during the flight. Natalie was in awe of the stewardesses. They all looked so perfect, like models. One came and got her and took her to the cockpit. The captain told Natalie to promise to apply with TWA when she got out of college. Natalie only giggled. What a funny thing to say, she thought.

The plan was for Sister Beatrice and Gertrude to stay for a few weeks while Natalie adjusted. The family in the States agreed but wondered why Natalie needed the women to travel with her. They soon learned why. Gertrude only spoke with Natalie's godmother, Lydia, telling her to please take care of Natalie. Lydia promised she would also speak with John's cousin, who lived across the street and who would later become a central figure in Natalie's life as she stayed in the States with her Aunt Jane.

The day was bright and sunny when they landed in Philadelphia. People lined up to greet their loved ones as they got off the plane. John rushed to them, and Katarina held back when he kissed her on the cheek. He crushed Natalie with hugs, and everyone was introduced, but Katarina stayed silent. She saw John's sister Elizabeth look at her with no love in her eyes. Katarina knew this would not be an easy stay. In her mind, it was only temporary.

"Kat, get your life together. Make it work." Those words from her father now seemed a distant dream as she looked at all of them. No, she could not make it work. She already hated the whole situation.

They were all talking at once, Gertrude and Sister Beatrice trying to understand all the fast-talking. Philip arrived late as he hurried down the hall while they waited for luggage and immediately gathered Natalie in his arms, swinging her in a circle.

John moved over to Katarina, and there was this silence between them. Elizabeth and Gertrude watched, and a shiver ran down Gertrude's back.

They gathered the luggage, and everyone marched to the waiting car services. Gertrude made sure Natalie sat with Philip and Elizabeth and not her mother.

They arrived back at the home John and his sister bought

together, which was a good middle ground between their parents' summer and winter homes. The house had three floors, and one of them was rented out. It was a great investment. Their parents still owned a home in the Delaware countryside near Greenville, dating to the seventeenth century.

Gertrude and Sister Beatrice would stay for a week or even longer if needed. Katarina was quiet but made sure she played the wife role again.

Philip, her brother, had only been on leave from the military. He was a young lieutenant and had graduated from VMI at the top of his class. John was disappointed that Philip went into the army instead of the navy, but he was proud of him. It was at times difficult for Philip, knowing that John adopted him and his own father never acknowledged him, but he knew his father was too young, at sixteen years old, to be a parent. John was his father's brother and adopted Philip at birth. Philip's mother died at childbirth, only fifteen years old, and John bear the thought of his nephew being adopted by strangers. The rest of the family all helped John with raising him.

Philip loved Natalie the day she was born, he was there in California on that day. His relationship with Katarina was nonexistent, but he loved Natalie wholeheartedly. Philip spent a few days just with Natalie, driving her to the Greenville home where her grandparents were waiting. Then, they all went to the house in Oxford, Maryland. Gertrude and Sister Beatrice joined them in Oxford and John later that week. Katarina stayed behind.

Natalie was amazed by everything. She found it so profoundly different from Europe. Her new Aunt Jane, who lived across the street, welcomed her with open arms. She had six children, and there was always laughter and chaos in the house. Natalie had never watched television, and when she first met them, they were all sitting in front of a television watching *I Dream of Jeannie*. Natalie thought that seemed senseless. At the dinner table, there was so much conversation going on at once. Her grandmother would admonish any of them if they spoke over each other. It was then Natalie realized she sounded different. She'd learned to speak English with a British accent. She felt awkward, but Sister Beatrice reassured her it was charming to hear. Sister Beatrice and Gertrude held tightly to Natalie's hand to give her reassurance. Katarina said nothing to any of them. Jane tried to draw conversation out of her, but nothing came.

Natalie was in awe of this gentle woman whom she now called Aunt Jane. Jane's husband was John's cousin. Jane had short, dark brown hair and hazel eyes. She was thin and about six feet tall. She had the warmest smile, while her husband was much more serious. He and Natalie's father were second cousins and had been close since they were young boys. His name was Jim. Over coffee that night, Aunt Jane promised Gertrude and Sister Beatrice she would take care of Natalie.

Katarina had excuses for why she couldn't join them for dinner. When John and Natalie ate at home, she would disappear into the library. John and Elizabeth couldn't help her at this point. If Katarina wanted to be alone, they'd centre their attention on Natalie. Before they left, Sister Beatrice and Aunt Gertrude explained Katarina's abuse of Natalie in detail. Jane was horrified; she couldn't imagine doing that to her own children.

Sister Beatrice and Gertrude accompanied Aunt Jane and Natalie's father to the Catholic school in the days that followed. The week prior she had to take an entrance exam, which she passed with flying colors. She met many of the sisters that day, and they welcomed her as the ones in Germany had. Natalie was excited about her new school but knew that many of her European customs—like curtsying—would seem odd to the other girls. Many changes were coming for Natalie.

The first week everyone left, she never felt so alone in her life. She sat on the front porch, tears falling, as she ached for her aunt and Sister Beatrice. She was alone at the house with Katarina, and she was frightened.

Suddenly, at the bottom of the steps, looking up, stood a beautiful girl with blonde hair down to her waist and big blue eyes.

"Hi, I'm Jeannie Sullivan," the girl said with a big smile. "I've been trying to meet you. I live right down the street. You might have seen me with all my brothers playing football out front."

"I'm Natalie," Natalie said with hesitation. She'd never dared to wear shorts and stared at this girl with blue shorts and a gingham blue shirt.

"Come take a walk with me, Natalie."

Natalie looked back toward the door. *Why not*, she thought.

Suddenly, the door swung open, and her mother stood there, her eyes glazed over from the alcohol she'd been drinking since early morning. Jeannie immediately saw the fear in Natalie's eyes and stood in front of Natalie, holding out her hand.

"Hi, I'm Jeannie Sullivan. I was just going to take a walk with Natalie and let her see the neighbourhood."

Katarina gave a wicked smile.

"Natalie, go have your walk. Stay out as long as you want." She stumbled on the porch and caught her balance. Her eyes were menacing as she looked at Natalie.

"Natalie, maybe this beautiful girl can teach you how to look better. She looks like the first child I had with your father: blonde with dark blue eyes. They keep the child hidden in Hawaii, but I know. He's what I wanted in a child, especially compared to you and Alex."

Natalie stepped back. She knew of the child in Hawaii; he was no secret in Germany. She knew everything, even the story of Gregory and Benjamin.

Katarina waved her hand for her to leave as she stumbled back into the house.

As they reached the sidewalk, Natalie turned to her new friend. "I'm sorry you had to see my mother in this state of drunkenness."

Jeannie Sullivan placed her arm around Natalie's shoulder. "Not to worry, I won't tell anyone if you don't."

They both started to laugh.

Almost every day, Jeannie would appear and take her away shopping or for ice cream. Natalie dreaded the days Jeannie wasn't there. She hated being alone in the house with her mother and tried as often as she could to spend time with Aunt Jane. Jane would teach her about clothing patterns and show her how to make garments. Natalie took in every word of advice. Jane's daughters Marybeth, Denise, and Patty treated her as if she was an adopted sister. Natalie would tease her aunt that she needed to take some cooking lessons and learn about spices. Her father worked late, so Natalie often had dinner with them, and some nights, the girls invited her to stay overnight. Natalie was eager to show Aunt Jane some of the dishes she had learned in Germany and at boarding school.

Jane took her for a uniform fitting and shoes and noticed how thin Natalie was, especially compared to Jane's own children. The child's bones sticking out. Jane observed how Natalie hated to go back into the house when her father or Elizabeth was not there. Jane had come over often with her husband to play cards and vice versa. Natalie would hover but remain quiet as a mouse. Jane hadn't yet seen Katarina act out like Gertrude and Lydia had warned her about. She had seen bruises on the child's arm, but Natalie explained that she had fallen or bumped into something. However, Jane did notice that Katarina started drinking early in the day.

Jane caught Katarina's wrath one day when Natalie was having lunch at Jane's. The girls were all talking at once. Jane's three daughters were having silly girl conversations that Natalie so enjoyed. Being with Jane's family always felt warm and loving. The front door slammed, and Katarina marched into the kitchen, looking straight at Natalie. Before Jane knew what was about to happen, Katarina pulled Natalie off the chair, slapped her across the face, and threw her on the ground. She was about to kick her when Jane stopped her. Jane's children sat in stunned silence. They'd never seen an adult inflict such brutality on a child. Jane picked Natalie off the floor, and Katarina screamed that Natalie had worn a bracelet that was hers.

"You do not have the right to take my personal belongings," Katarina screeched.

Natalie looked at the bracelet on her wrist. She'd thought Aunt Elizabeth's, not her mother's. It was a gold bracelet with a small emerald in the middle and had just been sitting on the kitchen table.

Welts bloomed on Natalie's face, and Jane stepped in front of her.

"Are you crazy, woman? Why on God's green earth would you hit your child like this?"

"Because she needs to learn right from wrong, or she won't amount to anything in this world!" There was a spittle at the corner of Katarina's mouth as she lunged again at Natalie, catching a handful of hair and yanking her away from Jane.

"Let go!" As Jane removed Katarina's clenched hand from Natalie's hair, she caught a strong whiff of alcohol on Katarina's breath.

Natalie's eyes were large and filled with dismay and shock, but she never cried out. She'd learned early on never to cry over Katarina's actions because it would send Katarina into an even worse tirade. Natalie turned and stared at her mother in defiance.

"She is staying here until John comes home," Jane said, trembling. "Now leave."

Katarina moved closer to Jane. "No, she is not. She is coming home with me."

Natalie looked at Jane with pleading eyes, but Jane just sighed. "Fine. But I will walk her over."

Jane walked Natalie to her mother's porch, and Natalie made herself comfortable in the swinging chair with Jane. Waiting outside, her hands clenched, Jane was so furious she couldn't articulate her feelings. But she'd tell John and Sister Agnes to be on the lookout for bruises or any type of depression. Natalie was so quiet, to begin with, and she never said a word against her mother.

Katarina entered the house, returned with a stack of books, and threw them at Natalie. "You stay here and read. Don't come into the house until I tell you." Natalie and Katarina looked at each other for the longest moment. Katarina glanced over and saw the fury in Jane's eyes, but she didn't care.

Jane reassured Natalie that she would look out for her till her father came home. To Jane's relief, Jeannie Sullivan was walking over from her house. She had seen Katarina pulling Natalie across the street.

Jane let out a sigh. "Jeannie, can you stay with her? I need to make a phone call."

Jeannie nodded and smiled at Natalie. Natalie's hands were shaking, and she had red marks on her face. Katarina slammed the front door open and gave Jeannie a smile as if nothing had happened.

"Jeannie, it's good to see you. Teach this girl how to look pretty and not look so pathetic." She turned and walked back into the house.

Natalie flinched at the words. There wasn't a day her mother didn't berate her, and it didn't stop until Elizabeth or her father came home. Jeannie put her arm around Natalie's small shoulders.

"Natalie, come back to my house. I think it would be better for you."

Jeannie knocked on the door and opened it slowly. Katarina was sitting on the sofa with a glass of wine. Jeannie didn't walk in; she just told Katarina that Natalie would be at her house for the rest of the day. Katarina nodded without saying a word.

Natalie didn't know what Jane said to her father, but her mother didn't speak to her for several weeks. Natalie loved the silence and again dreaded when Aunt Jane or Jeannie weren't around. When they were gone, Natalie spent much time on the porch or on long walks. Having Katarina ignore her was a relief.

Her father apologized for her mother's actions. She wished her father would divorce Katarina. He always seemed so sad. Natalie knew Katarina was trying to persuade him to move somewhere else, away from his family, job, and friends. She promised him she would change and become a better wife. At times, he believed her. Until she drank again, Natalie swore she would never drink. She hated what alcohol did to people.

The good news came when Aunt Elizabeth told her they would be going to the generational home—as everyone called the big house where the entire family gathered—for a week and then to the Chesapeake Bay to stay with her grandparents. Her American grandparents were so much like her ones in Germany: kind, considerate, and loving. School would start soon too. There were only two weeks left of summer vacation.

Natalie was overjoyed to get away. She saw her mother's clenched teeth when she was packing. She knew she would be left alone because her Aunt Elizabeth was in her own bedroom packing. It was the weekend, and her father was working. He couldn't come on the trip and was trying so hard to make his marriage work. Katarina acted like a perfect wife when she was alone with him. She was like magic with him, but Jane and Elizabeth knew better.

Katarina stood at the door with a drink in her hand, watching Natalie.

"I'm glad to see you leave," She said. "I'll have time with your father without your inference in our life. I'll convince him you need to be sent to boarding school. You really need to be away, Natalie."

Natalie just ignored her remarks. She didn't even look up at Katarina; she kept silent and packing. Then, thank goodness, she heard Aunt Elizabeth call to be ready in an hour. Her mother just turned and left her room, and Natalie let out a deep sigh of relief.

The rest of the summer was heaven as they left to visit her grandparents at both homes. Her grandparents taught her how to fish and sail. There was an abundance of dogs and cats to fawn over, and her father came on the weekends with Katarina. Katarina ignored everyone; she was almost hostile to each of them. She didn't hide the fact that she didn't want to be there.

One weekend, Philip came. Katarina called a cab and went into the small town of Easton, where she called John and told him she was staying at a hotel, enjoying the old town while he enjoyed his time with Natalie and Philip. She told him to pick her up on his way back.

Katarina's absence was a relief to Natalie and Philip. John made an excuse for her like he always did. He always told them that they didn't understand what Katarina had gone through and the memories that haunted her. He put her affairs in the back of his mind and made excuses to everyone. No one accepted the excuses, though.

The summer was coming to an end, and school was about to begin. Natalie was looking forward to the new school. She had already met with Mother Superior, who had promised Sister Beatrice that she would watch out for Natalie.

To Natalie's dismay, Aunt Elizabeth announced she had received a teaching spot at Wellesley College. Everyone knew it was something she wanted and congratulated her, but it only brought dismay and sadness to Natalie. That left Natalie with only her grandparents now.

Her grandmother was still a fifth-grade English teacher, and her grandfather, a lawyer, was quiet.

She met Phillip's real father one weekend. Her father and Phillip's two dads had a good relationship. Phillip's father had married and had other children. He'd been only sixteen when Philip was born, and the boy's mother died during the birth. John raising Phillip was the best solution.

Natalie loved the generational house. It had a large wraparound porch with a quarter-mile pathway to the house lined with ancient oak trees. Standing in the front of the house, you immediately noticed the floor-to-ceiling windows and the large porch swing. The oak door was heavy but well-maintained, and a spacious foyer led to one side of the living room as you walked in. On the other side was an all-white kitchen with a hearty wood stove and a hidden stairway that led upstairs.

The upstairs had several bedrooms decorated in different shades of muted yellows and lavenders with colourful quilts on the large, four-poster beds. The walls were soft beiges and yellows in the large front room with its light-colored oak floors and old oriental rug. The windows were as tall as the ones downstairs, with lace curtains that fluttered in the breeze.

Natalie's grandparents had converted one bedroom to a brand-new bathroom, one of the few with a shower and bathtub. The ceramics were all white. Another small room served as her grandfather's office and library and reminded her of her German grandfathers. The room had a dark mahogany desk and shelves with large windows that looked out to the front of the house. Behind the house was a barn and a large acreage. Her grandmother had an English garden that was labelled with botanical names.

Here, Natalie felt as if she was back in Germany. When school started, this is where she escaped with her father. Sometimes, her grandparents would drive and bring her to the farmhouse as they closed the house on the Chesapeake for the winter. It was at this time that her American grandmother started to write her beautiful letters. Natalie received a letter a month before the day her grandmother died. Her grandmother with her beautiful, full white hair and big blue eyes. She always complained about her weight, but her grandfather would tease her and reassure her he loved every inch of her. Her grandfather was the quiet one compared to her grandmother, who loved to talk about gardening and her love of nature when Natalie was with her. She openly hugged Natalie all the time, and her first gift to her was the pearl necklace she always wore but wanted Natalie to have for her first cotillion.

September came, and Natalie began her first year in school, but not before her Aunt Elizabeth and her grandparents had her cotillion arranged. It was the first weekend of her new school, and the young man accompanying her was the grandson of a friend of one of her grandfather's law partners. The boy was only one grade ahead of her.

Jeannie came and fixed her hair. Natalie wore a beautiful white dress with small red roses stitched in. Her sash was red, and she felt like a princess wearing a sleeveless gown with long white gloves. Her hair hung loosely around her shoulders. Everyone was at the house and took dozens of pictures. She never saw her mother. It was a mystery, though, where Katarina went during the week. She often left in a cab. Natalie didn't say anything to her father because Katarina was always back before her father came home from work. She felt awkward because this was the first time she had to make conversation with a young man. He was beyond polite and made her feel special.

On her first day of school, Natalie made her first friend. In front of her in homeroom sat Rosanne. She had black hair that went down to her waist, her skin was alabaster white, her lips were full and red, and her eyes were so dark they almost looked black. She was so beautiful, and they were instant friends.

Several weekends later, she went to visit her grandparents. Her father was so excited to take her, saying a big surprise awaited her. When she arrived, her grandparents immediately took her by the hand and led her to the barn. In a stall was a horse they had bought for her. It was an older horse, eighteen years old, but had a loving temperament and best yet, it was all hers. They had a permanent help who lived on the grounds of the rental house and would take care of Thunder, as the horse was called.

Natalie loved school, but she also looked forward to going home. There, waiting for her, was Aunt Elizabeth who brought her a kitten and a Golden Retriever puppy. Her father immediately named the kitten Sam and the dog Lacey. The puppy and kitten slept with Natalie, and in the following months, they both waited for her when she got home from school. The dog always ran into her arms the moment she arrived at the door, and the three spent hours a day together.

Katarina ignored the puppy, and the cat hissed at her at every opportunity. She was not cruel to them, but one day, when Natalie came home, the puppy, now five months old, was nowhere to be found. Natalie and her father looked everywhere while Katarina just glared at Natalie and said she should have taken better care of the dog, and it was her fault it was missing. Natalie cried for a month; she knew her mother had to have taken Lacey away. She still vividly recalled how, in a fit of rage several years ago in Germany, Katarina killed Natalie's kitten. Why would this be any different? The memory was etched in Natalie's mind for the rest of her life. She prayed every night that Lacey was in a good place. She told her Aunt Jane she suspected her mother was responsible for the dog having gone missing, and she told her about the kitten. Jane was horrified. From then on, Sam stayed in Natalie's room when she went to school.

During this time, her father finally had it with Katarina when he saw her raise her hand to hit Natalie while the girl was crying over the dog. He caught Kat's hand in midair, sparking their first big argument. Katarina couldn't make any excuses. He heard the venom in her voice for the first time as she ranted about how bored she was living in this house.

"Oh, please, John, Natalie bats her eyes at you, and you give in to her wishes," Katarina went on. "She doesn't deserve to be spoiled by you or anyone."

Watching from the hallway, Natalie so wished her father would just divorce her mother and be happy—this was something she'd tell him throughout his lifetime.

John just shook his head. "What is wrong with you, Kat?"

She shrugged her shoulders, looking him straight in the eyes. "I just don't like Natalie or any of the children in my life. Oh please, don't look at me like that, as if you didn't know. Let's face it, she is just a child and should go to boarding school. We would have a much better life without her here. You have enjoyed having me back in your bed, haven't you?"

She waved her hand in the air and walked over to the bar, where she poured herself a bourbon, then turned to John and smiled.

The relationship began to change at that point. Katarina was no longer hiding her drinking from John and would drink anytime she wished. Most of the time, she passed out at night. She knew how to calm John down when he began to get angry. She'd use her sexuality on him, and he would forgive her. She gave him everything he wanted in the bedroom, and all was forgiven. Throughout his life, John truly believed Katarina did love him in her own way. He ignored all the bad parts and lived with a memory of what he felt when he first met and married her.

Natalie would disappear into the bedroom when she came home from school. There were times she would hear her mother on the phone speaking in German to someone, explaining she would be at his side soon. The words of endearment made Natalie feel ill. She knew those words should only be spoken to her father.

Natalie wrote letters to her family in Germany once a week. Her Aunt Gertrude told her she and Hans would be in Florida after Christmas. Gertrude had already talked to John, and he would have her visit during the school break.

The students had a day off in November, and Katarina was not pleased Natalie was home. She dressed in a tight grey skirt with a lavender chiffon blouse and put her hair up. She had just the right amount of makeup on when she saw Natalie staring at her as she came out of the bedroom and took her cashmere coat out of the closet. It was only 10 a.m. Where was she going? Katarina disappeared again in the bedroom. Natalie decided to tell Jane of this odd behaviour that had been going on for months. Katarina would leave in a cab in the morning and slip back home just before John returned from work.

As Natalie crossed the street to Jane's—they had made plans to bake a cake for Philip, who was coming home for the weekend—she saw Jeannie walking down the street hand-in-hand with her boyfriend. Natalie let out a sigh as she waved, wondering if she would ever have a boyfriend.

Phillip loved his sister, and he told his father that his time with her was precious. The weekend that her mother had stayed in Easton was one of their best weekends together. Natalie's pale skin turned to a nice light brown tan, which brought out her eyes against her auburn hair streaked with blond highlights. It was the first time Natalie noticed young men looking at her as they took the ferry to Saint Michael's for a lovely dinner. Since it would be a while until she saw Philip again, he hovered over her. The only time that Katarina could anger John was if she spoke ill of Philip and the love he had for his sister. Katarina always pointed out that Phillip was adopted, not related by blood. John would always give it back, reminding her that her brothers were only cousins as her own mother, Helena, had abandoned her.

Natalie looked back at the house to see if her mother was coming out or if the cab was arriving as Jane came to the door. Jane looked in time to see Kat getting into a cab. What was she doing, leaving this early, dressed as if she was going on a date? If Natalie hadn't been home, Jane would never have known. She put it in the back of her mind, but it bothered her. She shrugged it off for now but kept it in her mind. She decided not to ask any more questions. Natalie was so excited to bake her first cake for Phillip.

Natalie loved school. She was especially fond of Sister Agnes, who had taken her under her wing. Sister Agnes was always waiting for her in the morning. She walked her to class and waited for her at the end of the day. She openly gave Natalie hugs. She also knew how attached Natalie and Rosanne had become. The girls were together all the time, which pleased Sister Agnes. Natalie felt secure with Sister Agnes just like she did with sister Beatrice. Sister Agnes saw the bruises on her arms when Natalie changed clothes for gym class. She didn't confront her because she was told before the school year started that her mother handled her roughly.

Rosanne and Natalie were together all the time and always laughing. Natalie told Sister Agnes she knew Rosanne would be in her life forever. Her friend Jeannie went to public school, so they didn't see each other much since Jeannie had a boyfriend. Natalie had hoped Jane would take her to Gimbels department store, but Aunt Jane had her own children to worry about. That left Sister Agnes to take her to buy her first bra. She even had her buy some CoverGirl mascara and a little lipstick.

Natalie was adjusting and went to see Hans and Gertrude in Florida after Christmas. She told them all what had happened and how her mother would disappear for a few days, leaving her father in a panic. If it was a weekend, her grandparents would come for her most of the time. They only told Natalie to keep clear of her mother as much as she could. Natalie hated to leave at the end of the visit, but she always had a ticket waiting for her once a month to join them in Palm Beach for a weekend.

The strength of everyone's embrace gave Natalie courage and hope. She could cope with the minefields she walked through with her mother. She spent a great deal of time after school with sports, and she had her two best friends.

To her delight, her godmother, Lydia Adams, came to visit in March. She did not stay at the house; she was with her grandparents. It was the last time Natalie saw Lydia, who died of cancer the following month. She'd come to say goodbye to John but never told

Natalie her diagnosis. In her will, she left money to Natalie to receive when she turned twenty-one, along with the use of the cabin in the mountains in Santa Rosa, California, for her and her boys never to be sold unless they all agreed.

The school year was coming to an end, and Natalie was learning a lot about the woman she was becoming. She had a deep soul and a quiet strength. Within her fragility was an unbreakable part of her that smiled through any sorrow. She had depths of strength within her and no darkness.

Sister Agnes knew she had an open heart, always speaking of forgiving her mother. Natalie would spend hours talking to Sister Agnes. She didn't want school to end because she knew she wouldn't see Rosanne, but summer meant she could spend time on the Chesapeake Bay and out at the generational house. At the end of April, she had an empty period, so she sat outside the school on a bench to wait for Rosanne so they could walk home together.

That's when she saw him for the first time.

The boys' Catholic school was next to her school, and he had been watching her. He told her later that the way she moved and the innate confidence in her look was what initially attracted him. She was reading a book as he walked over to her. Her hands were long and eloquent, he thought, and she looked up at him with the brightest eyes and longest lashes he had ever seen. He had the most intense stare from his green eyes. He had the best smile, his hair was black, he had prominent cheekbones, and he was tall and thin. His was a smile you couldn't ignore. He wore the standard boy's Catholic blue blazer, white shirt, and blue slacks. He was wearing a red tie and had on a leather jacket over his blazer. He now sat next to her.

"What are you reading?" He asked.

She didn't know how to answer. She'd never had a boy sit so close to her, and she blushed, which amused him.

"My name is Lucca Molinaro. And yours?"

"I'm Natalie," She stammered. "I'm reading Thomas Harding." She showed him the cover of the book.

"Did you know you look like Natalie Wood, the actress?" He leaned over. "You're so beautiful. I guess every guy tells you that?"

"I can't recall anyone telling me." Her voice was barely a whisper. He touched her hand, and Natalie shivered."

"I'm a sophomore here, and my cousin is a senior, lucky him. His name is Frank. I also have a sister, Rose." He paused. "I actually saw you shopping in the food store I work at. You were with your father. I stock shelves there."

"I didn't realize. I'll try to say hello next time I see you." She relaxed enough to smile at him.

"Do you think it's fate we met here?"

She suddenly laughed. "No, I believe in chance."

"Ahh, I was hoping for fate." Unbeknownst to each of them, it was at this moment both their lives would be changed forever.

Natalie jumped when she heard her name called. Sister Agnes was standing outside the door to the side of the school, her eyes boring into the young man's. Before Natalie could say goodbye, he rose and walked over to a girl who was waving at him.

"Child, come inside. Look at your knees. They're red from the cold. It's only early spring."

There was a pause as Natalie watched the young man place his arm around the girl's waist. Her heart lurched.

"Natalie, come to my office next week. I want to talk further about our conversation about how you thought you might want to stay with the sisters forever. I want you to think about it over the summer."

Rosanne was walking down the pathway, waving. Rosanne was the sister Natalie wished she had lived here, comforting in so many ways.

Sister Agnes watched the girls walk off the school grounds. Whatever was said, they both stopped and were laughing hysterically. It was so good to see Natalie laugh. The child was always so serious and years ahead for her age as if her childhood had already passed. Sister Agnes felt sometimes that Natalie was forced to be a grown-up and didn't have the joys a child should enjoy at her age.

Natalie and Rosanne parted at an intersection, and Natalie walked the last few blocks home alone. The house was silent as Natalie entered. She heard her mother speaking in French over the phone, telling someone she needed time before she could come back.

Natalie went into the kitchen to fix a snack and sat at the large window, looking out at the birds. Spring was slowly approaching, and she could see yellows popping up among the spring blooms. Sam was purring around her legs.

A wave of dread washed over her. Her mother had not hit her in a long time, but as Natalie slid off the chair and turned to see her mother's eyes blazing, fear gripped her heart. Katarina screamed at her, telling her she had eavesdropped. Katarina came toward her, and Natalie pulled the chair in front of her. Her mother was not going to strike her again. Just then, the kitchen door slammed, and Aunt Jane appeared in the room.

"Do not come near her, Katarina. You will regret it."

Katarina clenched her hands and glared at Jane and Natalie with venom. The room was engulfed in silence.

Kat turned to Natalie, "Look at you. 'Plain Jane,' they should call you. The uniform fits you. I saw the paperwork from school for you to apply for the convent. You might as well. You won't amount to anything and will never marry. Who would marry you? It would be the best alternative for you."

Jane was seething. She could smell the alcohol on Katarina.

They heard a car honk and noticed now how Katarina was dressed—a tight black skirt, a pink silk blouse, high heels, and a Chanel jacket. As Katarina walked out of the kitchen, Jane grabbed Natalie's hand. Together, they slipped out the back door to Jane's car on the other side of the street.

"We're going to follow her."

Natalie's eyes widened in shock. "We can't just follow her, Aunt Jane! She'll be so mad."

"Yes, we can. Enough is enough."

The cab was just turning the corner as Jane caught a glimpse of it, hoping it hadn't gotten too far. They followed it to downtown Philadelphia and were in luck as they found a parking spot directly outside the hotel Katarina was walking into.

Jane and Natalie stood in the distance as they watched Katarina sit in the lobby. She'd taken off her coat, and as usual, the men walking by all took a second look.

A man approached her and kissed her hand, lingering for a moment. Natalie noticed he was dark and ruggedly handsome, and she realized she'd seen him before. She leaned in close to Jane.

"I know him," She whispered.

They moved in closer and heard Kat say, "Do you have any idea of how many solitary nights I wished for the phone to ring just to hear a few words from you? Hans told me you asked about me. I had no choice but to call you. I don't care if it was at your home. No one ever answers except your snippety aunt, and I had every right to ask about our son."

There was a look in her mother's eyes that Natalie had never seen before. Her mother's eyes held secrets that only she and this man knew. Natalie knew she could never tell her father what she was witnessing.

The man drew Katarina a little closer. She stood from the sofa, and he placed his hands around her waist, making sure she looked him directly in the eyes as he lifted her chin. Suddenly, Katarina kissed him, and he pulled away. He looked long and hard at her, then quickly pulled her into an embrace.

Natalie and Jane moved where they could hear his exact words.

"You won't be able to call the house. Alise wants the number changed. I can't be drawn into your world. When you called two nights ago, Alise called me upset. She knew it was you. I'm in Washington, dealing with CIA matters. I told you when I called you, it had to stop, I'm here because you asked me to come one more time. I know you're lying, saying you want to explain the adoption to Benjamin when he's older and making sure he knows about you. Kat, this is blackmail of the worst kind, and you know I don't handle blackmail."

She pushed him away, visibly seething with anger. "Then why are you here, Gregory?"

"I just want to get through to you that you can't go on this way. You can't interfere with my family. Stop calling. I will not let you hurt my wife, my son, or my two daughters."

Katarina gasped. She hadn't realized Gregory and Alise had another child after the baby she helped deliver. His hand now circled her arm with a tight squeeze.

"I get the message, Gregory, and it doesn't matter. I'm meeting someone here regardless."

Shaking his head, he let go of her arm, and she fired at him again.

"I'm meeting Francis here. Maybe it's a good time for you to leave. I think we've said enough."

He hesitated, then thought of Alise back home. Life had indeed changed, and he was not going to fall into her web.

"My fault, Katarina. I should never have asked for your help In Brazil, and I regret the week I spent with you in Italy. So many broken promises from my side—not to love you any longer or betray Alise. All we do is torment each other. What you're doing with Francis makes me wonder if you even know how to love anyone, even me. You constantly say you do, but then look at your actions. You don't think I know about the others from Greece and Switzerland? I came because I truly was worried about you, but now I realize John is not tormenting you as you told me on the phone. I expect it's the other way around. There was a time your memory could destroy my days and nights, but I leave now, seeing how deeply you need help.

We all live with memories of what happened, but you are letting your thoughts destroy you."

Natalie saw deep hurt in her mother's face that she had never seen before. The man now spoke kindly to her.

"Katarina, don't meet with Francis. It takes you to dark places in your mind."

"I have to. I need to find out information on the child he made me give up. Besides, he owes me money he never gave me after the divorce and promised when I saw him in Paris." Now, she looked at Gregory and wanted to hurt him. She smirked. "Yes, he came to Paris, where we had a good evening and morning." Gregory pulled his hand away from hers that he had taken.

Striding across the lobby was Francis Lee. Gregory stood till they were face to face. They exchanged a few words that Jane and Natalie could not catch, but from the expressions on their faces, the conversation was not pleasant.

Natalie whispered to Jane, "I know him too. My mother was married to him. My grandparents and Aunt Gertrude showed me pictures of my half-brother, who I never met. He lives in Hawaii. Don't you think it's a long way for a visit?"

Jane looked at Natalie and almost laughed. "It seems *both* men came a long way."

Gregory watched Katarina walk to the elevator with Francis and resisted the urge to call her back. He watched as Francis touched her and held her hand, and it broke Gregory to see her leave with this man who had hurt her in so many ways. Gregory watched and once again couldn't understand the misery and the haunting memories that surfaced. He had to leave before he went after her. Why was she doing this? The elevator doors closed as Francis took hold of her hand and looked back at Gregory, his upper lip curling smugly.

Gregory shook his head, deep sorrow etched around his eyes, as he looked up and walked straight for Jane and Natalie.

"Miss Natalie, you didn't hide very well. Not to worry, your mother didn't see you." He shook hands with Jane, introducing himself. Jane saw the most spectacular green eyes set in a lightly lined face. Greogry was tanned, grey was around his temples, and his handshake was firm. He wore a black leather jacket with a white shirt and jeans with boots.

"Take care of this little girl. Her mother has never been kind to her or any of her children." He looked straight into Natalie's eyes and gave her a soft smile. "Natalie, I hope as you get older, you will meet your brother Benjamin when we tell him about you. I also hope neither one of you tries to be a spy. You're not very good at it. Have a good life. Don't let your mother's words or actions ever make you doubt who you are. If you do this, I promise your life will be good and filled with happiness."

Natalie nodded, knowing she would carry this meeting with her for the rest of her life.

Gregory disappeared out the hotel door while Natalie and Jane looked back to the elevator, thinking Katarina might change her mind.

They went back to their car and were silent for a while. Not knowing what to say, Jane saw it was obvious Natalie was aware of her mother's indiscretions. It didn't seem to shock her as much as it shocked Jane. Suddenly, Natalie started to laugh, and Jane looked over at her.

"What's funny?"

"Well, Nancy Drew, we're not exactly Sherlock Holmes. No prize for us." They both started to laugh, then fell silent again. "Jane, don't tell my father. I think he suspects it since they no longer sleep in the same bedroom. I just wish she would leave. She keeps telling someone on the phone that it wasn't the right time, but soon. I suspect she'll go back to Europe. I think it would be the best."

Jane looked at Natalie. "You're too young to know about issues like this. Has your mother always been this way?"

Natalie let out a long sigh, "As long as I have known her."

"We'll keep this between us, and if my kids ask where we've been, I'll tell them I had to drive you back to school for a project." Natalie nodded in agreement. "I'm sorry you had to see all of this, Natalie."

Natalie shrugged. "I've seen this before. It's nothing new, but I promise, I will never ever be anything like my mother as long as I live."

They remained silent the rest of the way home. Jane was furious that Katarina would be involved in such behaviour. She was also very upset she had to keep this secret from John and from her own husband. Meanwhile, Natalie was deep in thought. How much hurt could her Father take? Why was he trying to convince himself that Katarina loved him? Natalie felt angry and sad for her father. She only wanted the best for him and vowed to always care for him.

"Natalie, your grandparents are coming for you this weekend, are they not?"

"Yes. Dad's working all weekend, and I certainly don't want to be home with Kat."

Natalie was quiet again, chewing her bottom lip, almost afraid to ask the next question. "Jane, am I too young to be interested in someone? There's a boy who approached me at school. He's extremely handsome, but he has a girlfriend. I saw her right away, but this part of me was interested. However, I've also been speaking with Sister Agnes about joining the convent."

Jane almost hit the brakes.

"Natalie, you must wait until after your junior year to determine if you want to join the convent. You're much too young to make such a serious decision. As for a young man, it's all right to be curious, but you know as well as I do that your father won't let you date. The cotillion almost did him in, knowing you would be with that nice young man."

"All right, I'll give it all serious thought." She got lost in her own head again as they got closer to home.

"Natalie, I have to ask, do you ever call your mother 'Mother,' or is it always 'Kat'?"

"I've never been around her enough to want to call her 'Mother,' and she certainly doesn't treat me like her child, so I see no reason to call her by that name."

Jane sucked in her breath. She couldn't imagine her children not calling her "Mom." Natalie acted much too old for her age. She seemed to analyze things straight out and accept facts for what they were. As she pulled up to the house, she invited Natalie to have dinner with them.

"Thank you for asking, but I think I'll just have a sandwich."

Jane watched her walk into her house, wondering how she would manage not to tell her father what she saw.

Katarina arrived within minutes of John coming home. Natalie looked at her, noticing that her hair was no longer up, her lipstick was gone, and she looked dishevelled. She looked at her mother long and hard as she watched Kat take off her shoes and throw her jacket on the sofa. Minutes later, they heard the car pull up, and Katarina disappeared into the bathroom. Natalie heard the water running in the tub.

When John came inside, he greeted Natalie with a big hug and asked where Kat was. She whispered to him that she was taking a bath. He told Natalie to go and pack a bag because they were going to go open the Chesapeake house for the summer. This brought a great deal of joy to Natalie, and she looked back to see her father enter the bathroom without knocking as he usually did. The words were muffled, but she didn't care to hear the argument. She was happy to leave with her father, especially when she heard Kat scream at him to get out.

Whenever Kat argued with John, Natalie always made a point to hug him and tell him that she loved him and would always take care of him. She spoke those words to him for the rest of his life.

Chapter 17

Going into her sophomore year was glorious for Natalie. She spent her summer with her grandparents on Chesapeake Bay and made visits to the house in Delaware. She safely kept all the letters Aunt Gertrude and Sister Agnes sent her over the summer in a shoe box.

The Sister's last letter was about how she was looking forward to seeing her at the beginning of the school year. She always sent a passage in her letters. This time, the passage was:

"And I pray that you, being rooted and established in love, may have power, together with all the saints, to grasp how wide and long and high and deep is the love of Christ, and to know this love that surpasses knowledge, that you may be filled to the measure of all the fullness of God." Ephesians 3:17-19.

Throughout her life, Natalie constantly reminded herself that Christ was present and standing next to her all the time with his angels. She told her grandmother that he never left her or forsook her. Her grandmother began to cry and took Natalie's hand.

"You have such a deep belief, Natalie. Where does it come from in someone so young?"

Natalie remembered thinking she had always felt that angels were always hovering around her.

The summer ended much too soon, and she returned to

Philadelphia. She had a quick visit with Thunder before Aunt Elizabeth needed to return. The college school year was soon to begin.

When they returned home, Natalie saw her father's car parked outside. It was strange for him to be home so early in the day, and she hoped he wasn't ill. She walked inside, calling for him. The house was dark as she and Aunt Elizabeth entered the living room, where they found him and Aunt Jane sitting with the drapes drawn. Jane was holding a letter in her hand.

Elizabeth spoke. "John, what has happened?" She looked at her brother's swollen red eyes.

Jane turned to Natalie. "Natalie, let's walk across the street. You can join us for dinner."

Natalie shook her head, her eyes never leaving her father. "She left, didn't she? Left you a letter of goodbye!"

He nodded. Relief coursed through Natalie, even though her heart broke for her father. She turned to Jane.

"I need to stay with him. I need to look after him for the rest of his life, Jane."

Elizabeth and Jane left Natalie and her father alone. Later that evening, Natalie walked out back and spotted a smouldering barrel. Inside were a stack of letters that had been burnt, along with dozens of pictures that were still melting away. She managed to salvage some. Katarina tried to burn away all existence of her life, her children, and her past. There was one letter from Germany where her signature was on the bottom. Kat still wanted those who tortured her caught and put on trial, promising she would bear witness to their crimes. Natalie pulled out pictures of Douglas and herself on the beaches of Hawaii.

There were pictures of Alexandra as a baby. Katarina had wanted to destroy every part of her children's lives and leave them with nothing.

Her father still had news articles from Katarina's time dancing, her arrest records, and pictures of her as a baby. Even though Kat tried, she couldn't destroy everything. Natalie found a small slip of a birth certificate for the baby born in Hawaii whom Kat had given up—John's child, whom he searched for. Natalie could only think this would be good for her father. She saw how her mother manipulated him when he confronted her about drinking. She would clutch at him, asking him not to leave her or divorce her. He knew she drank to numb her emotions and promised her he would always make sure she was taken care of. Natalie now hoped her father could move on.

Natalie salvaged what she could and placed it in a box next to her journals. She looked at the last entry about her mother in her journal that she had been writing for years as she tucked all the burnt pages and pictures inside. She looked at her last entry.

"I will never forgive you for my memory of every slap, every punch, the pain of each strike, the blood running from my nose and the bruises you placed on my body. I will not forgive you but pray for you as Sister Agnes told me to. It did not matter how many times you told me I would not amount to anything, that I wasn't pretty like you, or that I wouldn't ever marry, or that Philip was not all my blood because father adopted him. None of it matters because you do not matter to me."

Natalie looked at the date of her writing—April, just before summer vacation. Her mother overheard her speaking with Jeannie on the porch about meeting a young man outside of school. When she came back into the house, her mother, a drink in her hand, pushed her against the wall. She thumped a finger into her chest and called her and said every ugly thing she could think of. This time, when her mother went to strike her, Natalie grasped Katarina's hand and twisted it, telling her never to touch her again. Natalie pushed her away.

Her sophomore year began with peace. With her mother gone, she felt a weight lifted from her shoulders. She tried to make her father happy by making him go to the movies or visiting her grandparents in Delaware. She was always there for him. She welcomed Rosanne with a large hug on their first day of school. Once again, they'd be in the same class to start the day, but their other classes were different. She was so happy to see Rosanne as they caught up on their summer activities. Sister Agnes was waiting for both girls at their lockers and embraced them. Natalie and Rosanne were slightly embarrassed in front of the other girls, and Rosanne wiggled free from the hug.

"You know she hugged me because I was standing next to you," Rosanne said. "I think I'll stand a few feet away next time."

Rosanne and Natalie had their futures lined out. They would go to college, move away—but not too far—and start careers. Boyfriends or husbands were not part of the picture.

Each day, around the same time that she and Rosanne arrived at the foot of the hill to school, a boy pulled up in a green car, and a girl climbed out and headed for the nearby public high school. Then, the boy would continue into the parking lot of the boys' Catholic school. The girl was a pretty redhead with a deep shade of red. Natalie could see she had large blue eyes, and she wore miniskirts. Natalie would laugh as she looked at the strict uniform she was wearing. She couldn't imagine going to public school, where you wore everyday clothing. Natalie would smile at the girl but never talked.

When Natalie told Sister Agnes what had happened with her mother, relief crossed the sister's expression. But Sister Agnes also became more persistent, making sure Natalie would come to lunch or breakfast with her if Rosanne was not around. Sister Agnes knew Natalie was concentrating her life on taking care of her father and, in doing so, was leaving her childhood behind. Sister Agnes spoke with her grandparents and Aunt Jane, hoping she could get out more and have more fun as a young girl.

In November, Philip came home for a week-long leave before being shipped off to Vietnam. It was the first time Natalie was permitted to attend the boys' Catholic school teen dance. Jane helped her dress in a slim black skirt with a lilac cashmere sweater and black shoes with black stockings. Her hair had grown down to her waist again, and Jane pulled it back with a large, lilac headband. She used makeup sparingly but accented her amber eyes and added pink lipstick without any foundation or blush.

Philip escorted her, and she looked at him as girls surrounded them. He was wearing a brown suede jacket, blue striped shirt, and black pants. His longer hair had been cut very short, and when she hugged him, she could smell English Leather. His eyes held a twinkle, especially when he looked over at Natalie. She talked with Tommy Thompson, who escorted her to the cotillion. Tommy was a nice boy, and Philip watched the laughter emerge from Natalie easily.

The last dance of the evening was to Jimmy Ruffin's "What Becomes of a Broken Heart." It was Phillip's dance with her. Natalie closed her eyes and inhaled the scent of English Leather as she felt the suede jacket at her fingertips. He asked her if she had a good time. She was ecstatic to have this dance with her brother. She knew Father was worried about Phillip being sent to Vietnam. He wore the same sorrow etched on his face as when her mother left.

Natalie looked over the room in its entirety several times to see if she could spot Lucca. She recognised the young man who always dropped the girl from public school. He was here with someone else, and they shared long, lingering kisses. Natalie wondered what happened to the other pretty girl. Lucca had approached her several times at school and asked how she was. He stammered several times, talking to her, which amused Natalie since she was the shy one, but in the end, there was always some other girl from her school tucking him away. Once, he was standing at the end of the path in an embrace with one of the girls from the public school. Natalie smiled to herself that day, thinking he did get around, but then he had the charm and looks to get away with it.

After the dance, Natalie stayed home for two days because she wanted to spend as much time as she could with her father and Philip. There were many tears when Philip left, and she was glad when her father agreed to spend Christmas in Florida with her and Aunt Gertrude and Uncle Hans. It was good for her father to relax and sit on the beach. Uncle Hans was honest and said they hadn't seen Katarina. She didn't come to Germany when she returned to Europe, heading instead for Paris and Italy. They'd heard she'd been to the Greek Isles as well. They knew she was living well off her trust fund.

January and February were cold, and it seemed like it was always snowing. It was always a rush into school to get out of the cold. Natalie still saw the same girl exiting the green car, sometimes with a lingering kiss and long hugs.

Her father and Aunt Jane were meddling after she made acquaintances with a young man named Jimmy, who had graduated from high school two years earlier. Yes, he was older, but they just spoke casually. After a few long conversations with Aunt Jane, he was permitted to spend time with Natalie. She'd laugh because he also played the fourth hand in cards with her father, Jane, and her husband. Jimmy was pleasant to talk to. He was broad-shouldered and had a little paunch developing, even though he was so young. His hair was curly, his eyes bright blue, and he stood about 5'8".

They would talk at great length. He had a great sense of humour, but he would also talk of someone else he had deep feelings for, though that relationship was on and off. Natalie recognized for the first time the differences between different young men. She liked talking to Jimmy, but her stomach only did flip-flops for Lucca. She often saw him stocking shelves at the grocery store, and she desperately wanted to talk to him, but there was always some girl who worked with him hovering around. He waved once to her and smiled. If only she could have a small conversation with Lucca, she thought.

One day in February was particularly cold. Natalie had just sat down in biology class, where she and Rosanne were trying to get out of dissecting a frog when her name was called over the intercom to come to the principal's office. She looked at Rosanne and shrugged.

"What did you do?" Rosanne asked.

"I don't know. I might have forgotten that I was supposed to help clean the sisters' convent."

Sister Gloria came over to Natalie and told her she should leave and take her books. Natalie walked to the principal's office with great trepidation. She'd never been in trouble at school. She walked in slowly and saw Sister Agnes and three others standing there with clenched hands. Sister Agnes had tears in her eyes as she came and embraced Natalie.

"Sit, my child."

A horrible thought struck Natalie. "Is something wrong with my father?"

The other sisters looked away. "No, Natalie, but you must go home," Sister Agnes said. "Father Jobe will drive you."

"Tell me," Natalie insisted. "I don't want to drive home with Father Jobe. I want you to come home with me, regardless of what is going on."

Sister Agnes held onto Natalie's shoulders and looked directly into her eyes. She swallowed hard. She didn't want to deliver this news—Natalie should hear it from her father—but the pleading in the child's eyes forced her hand. "Natalie, your brother Philip was killed in Vietnam."

The air seemed to leave Natalie, as she suddenly couldn't breathe and gasped for breath. Tears started rolling down her face as she placed her head on Sister Agnes's shoulder and her arms around her neck, clinging to her, asking her to tell her it was a mistake.

Her sobbing affected the rest of the sisters. They had never heard such anguish from a child of her age. The deep sorrow was immediate, and they knew it would never leave her. Sister Agnes looked into her eyes, and there was another part of Natalie that stood out. She could see this amazing and powerful strength in this girl's eyes. It could not be missed. Natalie hugged Sister Agnes as she told her it would all be okay as another sister blotted tears from Natalie's face with a handkerchief.

"Sister Agnes, our lives are in God's hands. God is sovereign,"

Natalie said. "This is not in our control. Remember what you told me when my mother left: *Proverbs 3:5-5 'Trust in the Lord with all your heart…And lean not on our own understanding in all your ways; acknowledge him, and he will make your paths straight.'*"

"I need to tell my father this. He needs to remember. This is a sorrow that I feel he might not recover from. I can only pray for grace to carry us through this."

"Yes, child, He will give you grace as He has done so many times in your life."

She would never forget the image of her father coming home on that terrible day. Jane and Father Jobe were waiting for him. They spoke in the kitchen as he held onto a chair as if his life depended upon it. At that moment, he looked lost. It was the same look he had when her mother left him and told him in a letter. He looked empty, defeated, and devoid of life.

The weeks went by, and the sadness remained. At night, Natalie would read her letters from Phillip over and over again before crying herself to sleep. She wanted her brother back so desperately. She begged some nights to God that it was a mistake and to just bring him back.

She didn't speak much to anyone in school and never smiled. She spent a great deal of time with the sisters in activities that needed to be done in school. She dropped out of sports and joined the library team. She lived among the books and spent every free period there. After school, she'd hurry home, her only focus making sure she got dinner on the table. She and her father would make small talk while they ate, and then he would withdraw to his office or bedroom. He lost a lot of weight, and suddenly, his hair was greying.

The entire family tried to bring some happiness into their lives by having them come to the farmhouse. Natalie would spend hours in the barn, but the sadness didn't leave her. She would cry into her pillow at night. No one would hear her, but her red eyes betrayed her.

Sister Agnes and Aunt Jane would take her shopping and out to dinner. She and Rosanne now had different classes except biology, and they had little time to catch up on life.

The images through the months and years played in her mind and would never leave her thoughts. She'd remember Philip dancing with her and the smell of English Leather. She'd hear the Jimmy Ruffin song and start to cry.

The summer before her junior year, the sorrow began to lift as she went to the New Jersey Shore for the first time with Rosanne and her mother. She loved Rosanne's mother, who looked just like an older version of Rosanne. Spending time with her friend left her feeling warm, and her mother welcomed her with love. Rosanne had a younger sister named Karen, who was stunning with the most amazing green eyes that looked like a cat's. Rosanne's brother was younger but a sweet boy.

Karen and the little brother always wanted to be in the middle of things. It was fun being part of their family. Rosanne's mother spoke with John to allow them to be at the beach and convinced him that Natalie could wear a bikini instead of a Burka, as they kidded him.

She and Rosanne walked the beach, giggling at the attention of young men who wanted to talk to them as lifeguards called them over. They just kept walking, not realizing they were both beautiful girls. They were so innocent in their enjoyment of life.

Natalie was able to stay overnight at Rosanne's on weekends when she wasn't visiting the farmhouse in Delaware, where she would spend hours in the barn with her horse, and they would take small rides over the fields just the two of them. Weekends with Rosanne consisted of listening to Barbara Streisand and the Rolling Stones. They would dream of having boyfriends as they listened to Motown, Little Anthony and the Imperials, and Smokey Robinson. Natalie's world of friendship never went much beyond Rosanne and Jeannie. They had one friend named Janet who entered their lives junior year. Her aspirations were so different from Rosanne and Natalie's. She wanted to marry and have lots of children. They soon learned she was very crafty and could sew and cook, and they enjoyed her light-heartedness.

The only young man who paid her attention was still Jimmy. He would disappear for weeks, returning to a young woman who always went back to someone else. The story never seemed to change. Once in a while, her father allowed them to go and have an early dinner, but the relationship remained platonic.

The November of her junior year, Natalie went to the supermarket on her own and was looking at the prices of items and deciding on something her father wanted when she heard her name called. She turned to see a familiar face smiling at her.

"Remember me? I'm Lucca."

Natalie held her breath. She could only nod, and she closed her eyes for a moment.

"I haven't seen you in here for a while," He said.

Natalie stammered as her cheeks started to turn red. "We sometimes shop at the PX on the Navy base, and I've been busy with school."

Lucca smiled. "I know. I see you with your head down, dashing into the building."

"You see me?" She asked.

"Yes, but you are so quick to get inside; plus you have this nun always hovering over you, and she gives me the evil eye when she sees me walking towards you."

Natalie laughed. "She isn't that bad."

"Oh, yes, she is." They both laughed, and then Lucca grew serious. "Natalie, do you think you might want to go out with me? We can see a movie and have something to eat."

Natalie felt her stomach flip several times and swore she could hear her heart racing. She'd never thought he would ask her out. He always had a girl on his arm. "I must ask my father. Can you call me tonight?" She couldn't contain her excitement when she walked away, the smile was broad on her face, and her eyes were lit up.

He handed her a piece of paper and pencil, where she scribbled her phone number down.

"I hope the answer is yes," He said, placing his hand on her cheek. She immediately flushed tomato red, and he smiled. "I had to touch your cheek; it looks so soft."

Natalie finished at the grocery store, ran home, dropped off the groceries on the table, and ran over to her Aunt Jane. She arrived gasping for breath.

"What's wrong, Natalie?" Jane asked from the sewing machine.

"I need to have you talk to my father. There's someone who wants to take me to a movie and afterwards to eat. You've seen him; he works at the grocery store."

"Ah yes, a very nice-looking boy." Jane had never seen such pleading in Natalie's eyes.

"You must talk to Father tonight. He's calling at eight. Please!"

"All right. I will speak with your father when he arrives home."

It took much convincing, but John agreed to allow Natalie to go on her first real date. When Lucca called, Natalie's heart fluttered with anticipation.

Natalie called Rosanne immediately after getting off the phone with Lucca. Rosanne was the only one she knew she could confide in besides Jeannie. The next morning, on her walk to school, Natalie met up with Jeannie. She had two best friends who shared her happiness for her first date.

Jeannie came over later that week and helped Natalie pick out an outfit. They settled on black pants, a yellow cashmere sweater set, and black slipper shoes. Jeannie put on eyeshadow and eyeliner on Natalie before her date. But she was in for the surprise of her life when Jeannie decided to pluck her eyebrows. They both laughed as Natalie cried in mock desperation at the pain. It made her eyes look even larger. She was also wearing a small amount of blush and pink lipstick and had pulled back her hair in a straight ponytail.

You would think she was going to a ball the way Jane and Jeannie gathered in the living room when Lucca arrived to pick her up for their date. Her father stood back and smiled.

Her hands were sweating as Lucca walked her to his car. A loud car rumbled down the street. It stopped near them, and Natalie saw

Jimmy peering at them through the window. Then he took off with the wheels spinning.

"Do you know him?" Lucca asked.

"Believe it or not, he's our mailman. He graduated from your high school two years ago. We talk sometimes, and he plays cards with my father."

She got in the seat and pulled her sweater tighter, her sweaty hands clasped in her lap.

"Do you mind if we skip the movie?" Lucca said. "I want you to meet my parents. Then we can leave for dinner at a place where I made reservations."

Natalie swallowed hard. She'd never met someone's parents except for Rosanne and Jeannie's. A small amount of insecurity started to run through her.

She stammered, "I guess it's okay if that's what you want." He gave her the biggest smile.

He lived in a lovely house in an upscale area. He held her hand as they walked the long walkway. He called out to his mother, who came out of the kitchen, wiping her flour-dusted hands on her apron. Directly behind her was a young woman with a broad smile. She had collar-length black hair and dark brown eyes like her mother's. They both stood about 5'4. Lucca pulled his sister to the front.

"This is my sister, Rose, my mother, Carmen, and my dad should be around somewhere."

His mother immediately ordered them to sit. The living room was spacious, with two sets of sofas and comfortable chairs. One sofa had plastic over it. The hardwood floor was dark and covered with brightly colored rugs. The large windows were adorned with light green draperies.

The smell of freshly baked goods permeated the room. Lucca's mother rushed out of the room and brought in tea and cookies. Lucca excused himself for a moment, and Rose sat opposite Natalie and immediately took her hand.

"So, you are the young woman my brother has been talking about nonstop. You know he says he's going to marry you."

Natalie started to laugh. "I think I better finish high school and college first."

"No, he has it all planned. Both of you will live here while you finish college."

Natalie stopped laughing. "You're serious…"

"Very serious," Rose replied.

Lucca returned with his older cousin Frank and their father. Lucca was smiling like a Cheshire cat as they all sat around and talked.

Lucca's father, Lorenzo, was very engaged with conversation but also very quiet as he listened. He wanted to know all about all the fishing and sailing that Natalie had done, while Rose wanted to know about Europe. She and her husband had been on their honeymoon but didn't make it to Germany. Lucca's father watched her intensely, saying very few words. Finally, Lucca looked at his watch.

"We must leave. I made dinner reservations."

His mother clasped her hands. "Lucca, stay. I made lasagna, your favourite."

Rose looked at Natalie. "Can you skip your first dinner out and stay here?"

Natalie looked at Lucca.

"Do you mind?" He said. "My mother is from the old country, and she knows how to cook."

Natalie brightened. "I love homemade food! My family has a home in Italy where we spent holidays, and our cook was wonderful."

Lorenzo clapped his knee. "Then it's settled. You'll stay and have dinner with us."

Rose took Natalie to the dining room to keep her company while she set the table.

"I'm glad you stayed. I don't get home much, and I was anxious to meet you. My brother has been talking nonstop about you. He never calls me on the phone, but this past month, he's been asking me nonstop how to ask you out. He's smitten. My husband is gone for a business meeting this weekend, so I thought this was the perfect weekend to visit. How delightful you are here with us so I can get to know you."

Natalie took the fork and knives and followed Rose, placing the plates and glasses down. Natalie had only felt this immediate liking for Rosanne and Jeannie, but Rose immediately took her. She marvelled at how beautiful she was. Her speech was so articulate, and her smile filled the entire room with warmth.

Lucca's parents entered the room with plates and rolls, enough dishes of lasagna to feed an army and a big bowl of salad. She hadn't seen so much food prepared since she left Germany with her. Her American grandparents made dinner eloquent but simple. Here, it was abundant. When it was time for dessert, Lucca's mother brought out three separate dishes. The whole time, everyone was engaged in conversation on different subjects. Natalie just sat and listened.

Lucca looked at the time. It was nearly 10:00 p.m., and he'd promised to have her home by eleven. The drive would take thirty minutes. "We have to leave in half an hour or so," He said.

Natalie looked at his mother. "Let me help clean the dishes."

"No, no, go have some private time. We've manipulated your date night as it is. Your first date, and here you are with all of us."

"It was delightful," Natalie responded as she stood from the table.

Lucca ushered her into the living room, as Rose and Frank followed.

"So, do you feel overwhelmed yet?" Rose asked with a smile.

"Not really. I'm used to the family dynamics on both my mother's and father's side."

Lucca went to find the coat she'd grabbed from home at the last minute. She was now glad she did, since it had gotten so cold outside as spring had not yet arrived. She went to use the bathroom, and her heart stopped as she heard Lucca's mother's comment from the kitchen.

"Lorenzo, she does not have a mother. She only lives with her father. I wonder how is that good?"

Lorenzo replied gently. "I find her delightful. She obviously has had a good upbringing. How many young women has he dated that know three languages, have gone to boarding school, and have an ambition to attend college? So far, he's gone out with some shallow young girls. I like her a lot, and I want her around my son. Rose has already said she feels delighted he is dating her."

"I don't know, Lorenzo. I just feel it would be better if she came from a home with a mother and father."

"Well, I must disagree with you. I think she will be very good for Lucca."

Natalie silently left the hallway. She wished them all a good night, wishing herself that she hadn't heard Carmen's comments and reservations about something that was far outside Natalie's control.

Natalie sat so quietly on the car ride home that Lucca noticed.

"Is there something wrong, Natalie?"

She turned to look at him, her heart leaping as she looked at his handsome profile.

"Does it bother you that I only have my dad and my grandparents? Your mom is a little worried. I overheard her telling your dad."

Lucca turned and smiled, but his brow was furrowed. "No. I'm dating you, not my parents."

"So does this mean we'll see each other again?"

He reached over and took her hand. "You're the only one I want to see."

They reached her house, which was dark except for the porch light. On Friday nights, her dad, Jane, and her husband went to the corner bar for drinks, dinner, and a little dancing. Dad was always alone. Why wouldn't he divorce Kat? He should be with someone who loves him.

Natalie sighed as she looked at the dark house.

Lucca moved her hair back off her shoulders. "What are you

thinking? Having second thoughts about dating me?"

"Oh goodness no. I was just thinking random thoughts."

"Let me walk you to the door." He turned and brushed her lips slightly with his, feeling a desperate, aching need to be with Natalie. "I'm sorry," He said.

She smiled. "No need to apologize."

He came around to her side of the car and opened the door. He took her hand and stopped, leaning toward her and kissing her softly on the lips. This was the first time she had ever been kissed. His lips were soft, and she wanted to kiss him longer, but he pulled away.

"I'll call you tomorrow morning, and we can plan the day."

"Two days in a row?" She asked jokingly.

"Yes, two days, and every day after that. Tomorrow, I'll take you out to dinner. Ask your dad." He started back to the car but then returned to her quickly. "Natalie, I love you," He said. And just like that, he hastened away.

He did call the next day, and Natalie and her father had a long conversation. He agreed to let her go out again. He knew Natalie was much more mature than other girls her age; she knew right from wrong.

Thus started a grand adventure.

Her junior year was ending, and Aunt Jane made her first prom dress. They designed it themselves: light green chiffon with see-through arms and pearls at the cuffs and around the waist and neckline. She went to Lucca's senior prom as well in a dark-blue chiffon dress. Rose gave her a beautiful white silk shawl she had purchased for her at the first prom.

Natalie was disappointed when Rosanne told her she was not going. She so wanted her best friend to be with her that evening.

Life had not changed for Natalie. True, she was dating, but Lucca also worked on weekends. While they shared some weeknights together, it always related to homework and stolen kisses. They would sit in his bedroom, his mom never far away, making sure she always knew what they were doing. In between her checking in, he would sneak in for the kisses he wanted, but it never went any further. They spoke frequently of their future, both finishing college and getting married.

Natalie shared her experiences with her inner circle of friends, Aunt Jane and Sister Agnes. Sister Agnes knew she would not follow the steps of being a nun, but she wanted to ensure she had her to talk to.

Lucca graduated and went to Villanova, which changed their time together since Natalie was entering her senior year of high school. He was eager to show her the campus where he was in college the first fall. When he sat on a bench, drew her close and kissed her long and hard, her eyes stayed on his.

"I want you to hear these words, Natalie," He said. She drew in a deep breath as he said, "I love you, Natalie."

She trembled hearing the words, and her mother's voice came to her mind. She could hear Kat saying, "No one will ever love you and want to marry you."

Lucca kissed her again with a deep passion. She threw her arms around his neck as she shook her mother's words from her mind.

"I love you too!"

His eyes were dark and intense as he looked at her. The tenderness she felt for him brought an ache she had never experienced, and she wondered why. This memory stayed with her from that moment. What future was ahead of them, she thought.

Meanwhile, Natalie was enjoying her senior year. She'd been accepted into college with Rosanne. It had been a while since she had seen the red car pull up to school and drop off the girl. This time, when the girl emerged from the car, she was crying. Natalie didn't know how to approach her, so she walked over and simply smiled.

"I'm Natalie. I've seen you being dropped off here, and I know you walk to the public school."

The girl had large blue eyes with lots of mascara that was now running down her face. She had shoulder-length red hair, and she was petite.

"I'm Ruth. I always see you standing here."

"Yes, I am waiting for my friend Rosanne."

Ruth kept wiping her tears as Natalie handed her a Kleenex. "You have mascara on your cheeks. Let me help you." Natalie gently wiped the streaks off her face. "Will you be okay?"

"I think I'll skip classes and go home."

Natalie realized that the idea of skipping classes had never entered her mind in all these years. She then laughed to herself. She could never have skipped with Sister Agnes always hovering over her.

"Maybe we can meet some place later," She said.

"That would be nice. I just broke up with Donald. He dates me and another girl from my school. He just found out I was seeing another boy named Arthur. I told him it wasn't fair for him to expect me only to date him, when he's not only seeing me."

Natalie didn't know what to say. She would never think of seeing someone besides Lucca.

"I must buy some items at Gimbels at three o'clock. My boyfriend will drop me off, but I can meet you at the Woolworth counter for a shake."

"That sounds good. I would love to."

Natalie saw Rosanne coming up the hill, and she waved, quickly introducing her to Ruth. Ruth and Rosanne didn't smile at each other. Ruth bid them a quick goodbye and headed in the opposite direction, truly not heading to school.

"Why the frown, Rosanne?" Natalie asked as they walked themselves up the hill to school.

Rosanne stopped and peered at Natalie with a serious look on her face. "A shiver ran down my spine when you introduced us. I think there's something you should worry about. I immediately felt like you should not trust her."

Natalie looked at the intensity on Rosanne's face. "I'll walk cautiously. I promise."

That afternoon, Lucca dropped her off and was meeting his cousin Frank at a bookstore.

She saw Ruth approaching her at the Gimbels door on time.

"I have to buy a dress," Natalie told her. "My boyfriend has a dinner dance at Villanova University."

"Oh, let me help. I love to look at dresses."

While going through a dozen dresses, Natalie finally picked a silver satin sleeveless dress with a short matching jacket trimmed with various stones. The dress had an empire waist and a scooped neck. It was the most mature dress she had ever bought on her own. She only had a little help from Ruth, who she decided had a lovely taste in clothing. Ruth purchased a very short dress and white boots to match. They left Gimbels for Woolworth's.

Ruth chatted about her love for Arthur and Donald, but Arthur was older and was working as a plumber, and Donald was a senior like them. Natalie almost choked on her milkshake as Ruth nonchalantly described her sexual relationship with both boys.

Ruth looked at the surprised look on Natalie's face. "Don't you have relations with your boyfriend? What is his name?"

"No, we promised to wait until marriage. His name is Lucca." They were quiet for a moment, and then Natalie had to ask. "When you decide to marry, what are you going to tell your husband about being, you know…"

Ruth looked at her seriously. "I guess I will have to lie, but I just know Arthur will come around. He promised he'll divorce his wife."

Natalie once again was stunned. "He's married?"

Ruth narrowed her eyes. "Why? Would it bother you?"

"I just wouldn't be with a married man. It's a sin against God and everything I have been taught."

Ruth shrugged her shoulders in a gesture of indifference.

"I don't plan to marry until I'm out of college," Natalie said.

"You're going to college?"

"Aren't you?"

"No, I just study office work and shorthand. I want to be a great, powerful secretary."

"Ruth, I think that is wonderful. I took typing classes, also. I know I'll need them in college. Lucca makes me type his papers now."

"It sounds like you both are on the same path."

"We are! We both know what we want and understand it won't be easy. His sister thought maybe we should marry during his senior year of college."

"That's amazing how you both have so many plans. What do you want to be?"

"I want to be a writer and write novels, but next summer, I have an internship at the UN to be a translator for two weeks. I'll take the train to New York." Natalie glanced at her watch. "Oh shoot. I'm late. I'm sure Lucca is waiting in front of Gimbels for me." She scribbled on a napkin and gave Ruth her phone number and address. "Call me if you need to talk again."

Natalie ran down the street and saw Lucca pacing outside the car.

"Where have you been?" He was slightly annoyed.

"I'm sorry. I told you about the girl outside of school. I tried to help her with some issues."

"Natalie, you don't have to help everyone that comes to you. I've noticed a lot of people who ask for your help."

She shrugged. Sister Agnes told her the same thing.

She felt like a princess at the dance the following week. At the end of the night, in the car of all places, in front of her home, he pulled a small box out of his pocket. He seemed suddenly shy as he handed it to her.

He must have bought her the earrings that she admired when they were both looking in the window of a jewellery store.

She sucked in a large gulp of air when she saw the ring. It had a sapphire in the middle surrounded by diamonds. She started to cry. Lucca wiped away her tears with his fingertips, but she shed even more tears.

"Are you crying out of sadness or joy?" He asked.

She took out the ring for him to place on her hand.

"I know we said we wouldn't get married until we both finished college, so I wanted you to have something to remind you that I'm serious." He kissed her once, then several more times; the kisses were tender as he pulled her body into his, and he felt the rhythm of her heart next to his. His hand went to her waist. He wanted to be more intimate, but they'd promised each other. He whispered in her ear how hard it was not to have more of her.

She pulled slightly away. "I'm sorry."

"Natalie, don't be sorry. We have so much time ahead of us."

She took his face in her hands and kissed him tenderly. "Thank you, Lucca. This ring must have cost you a fortune."

He walked her to the house but decided not to come in.

"Natalie, I worked overtime for the ring. You'll hear from Rose tomorrow. She and my mother searched every inch of my bedroom until they found it. They'd found the receipt in my jacket pocket when Mom took it to the cleaners, and then the search was on, as my sister said. When I came home, she was standing there with this broad smile, but my mother not so much. My father was also overjoyed.

You know how much he loves you. My sister is crazy about you, and so is Frank."

Natalie didn't know how to describe her joy. Every doubt and insecurity that came into her mind from her mother was gone.

The next day at school, Ruth was waiting for her.

"I don't have a first period, but I need to make up a test. I thought I'd catch up with you since I haven't heard from you in a week." There was an edge to Ruth's voice.

Natalie saw Rosanne in the distance and waved. Ruth frowned when she saw Rosanne, then she looked at Natalie's hand. "That is some ring. I don't recall you wearing it."

Natalie smiled. "I just got it over the weekend from Lucca. We were at his university dance."

Ruth stared at the ring. "You're so lucky. I wish I could have someone nice in my life. Arthur and Donald don't put me first."

Rosanne waited at a distance. There was something unnerving about Ruth. Why couldn't Natalie see it? Ruth just kept looking at the ring, not with joy but with envy. Ruth's jealousy was apparent to Rosanne, but Natalie just never saw anyone in a bad light. Rosanne rolled her eyes. She didn't want to wait any longer. She approached Natalie and Ruth.

"Don't let me disturb the conversation," She said. "I'm going to the library since it's a free period." Rosanne couldn't keep the edge out of her voice as she directly looked at Ruth. Then she turned and started to walk up the hill to school.

Ruth chimed in, "Play hooky with me, Natalie. We can go to the drugstore and look at the new makeup."

Natalie shook her head. "I'm sorry. I have to catch up with Rosanne. We agreed to study chemistry together. I'm having a hard time with it."

"Natalie, you are always so serious about school."

Natalie simply smiled as she said goodbye. Ruth's smile drained away as she watched Natalie walk up the path to school.

Natalie caught up with Rosanne. "What is wrong with you?" She demanded.

Rosanne stopped and looked Natalie straight in the eyes. "I do not trust that girl. Watch your back because the knife is coming."

Natalie hesitated to follow her. Rosanne was never so blunt. But she slipped her arm through Rosanne's. "You are my best friend in the world. I don't have a lot of friends, and I don't want a lot of friends. I promise I will heed your advice. So, let's start talking about where we're going to stay during senior week. When we graduate, I think we should rent a house for a week. I've saved enough money from babysitting."

Sister Agnes was waiting at the library door as usual, "Where have you two girls been? You're both late."

"It's a free period," Natalie answered.

"Let me see the ring you called me about."

Natalie held out her hand, and Rosanne and Sister Agnes goggled at the size.

"That looks more like an engagement ring than a friendship or going-steady ring," Sister puffed at her.

"Sister, it's just a going steady ring. Marriage is years away."

"Well, both of you go to the far corner and study. Natalie, you have to bring up your chemistry grade."

Natalie rolled her eyes as she and Rosanne found a quiet corner. Natalie waited a moment, then cleared her throat.

"Rosanne, you really don't like Ruth, do you?"

Rosanne let out a long sigh. "I just don't trust her. There's something about the way she looks at you. It's almost like envy."

"That's silly. She's a pretty girl and seems to have her mind made up about life."

"She might say that, but why is she crying over two boys, one who's twice her age? There's something wrong." Rosanne slammed her textbook open.

"On to more pleasant subjects," Natalie said. "Are you still going to come with me to this party Lucca invited us to? He says he has a friend named Kevin who's seen you and wants to meet you."

Rosanne sat back in the comfy old chair. "I'll go because you asked me."

Natalie looked out of the library window. The rain had stopped, and the sky was now indigo and cerise with green and yellow streaks on the horizon. Natalie smiled to herself. Life was beautiful.

The following week, Rosanne was in deep conversation about the party and how well things went with Kevin. She was excited for her first date with him. Natalie wasn't going to be able to see Lucca this weekend; it was a heavy time for him in school and he needed to study.

She took a babysitting job on that Saturday and was home by dinner time. She noticed Ruth's car outside her house. Strange, she thought, since they hadn't talked to or seen each other in weeks.

She walked into the house, calling for her father, who responded he was in the kitchen. She found him sitting at the table with Ruth, who was in tears. There was money on the table.

"What's wrong?" Natalie asked.

"Ruth here needed some fatherly advice."

"Are you okay?" Natalie asked, pulling up another chair. Why had Ruth come to her father? She had parents.

Ruth took Natalie's hand. "I'm so upset. I need to see a doctor. I think I'm pregnant."

Natalie pulled her hand away and looked at her dad.

"Your father was kind enough to lend me the money to see a doctor since I had nowhere else to go."

Natalie got up without looking at her and put the teapot on. "I guess you have to wait till Monday."

"I know. The wait is horrible."

"Natalie turned and looked at the blotches on Ruth's face from crying. How could anyone still look so pretty when they were crying so hard?

"Have a cup of tea, Ruth. You can stay the night. Just call your parents to let them know where you are."

"Thank you. I'd love to stay here. It's always so welcoming."

Natalie thought that was a strange thing to say since the girl had only been there twice.

Late that night in bed, Natalie had to ask. "Do you know if

Donald would be okay if he found out you were pregnant?"

She lay there in the darkness. Ruth was silent for a long time, and then she sighed.

"I don't know. I just found out he has no intention of leaving his wife, even though he told me repeatedly that he would. And in all truth, it could be Arthur's."

Natalie sat straight up in bed. "You had sex with two people? You're only a senior in high school."

"I know, I know. I made a mistake. It won't happen again."

"Have you just this one time?"

"No, several times with Donald."

"I'm truly sorry you're going through this, Ruth."

Ruth left Sunday night, and Natalie was annoyed with her father. He hadn't once told Ruth that doing this was wrong. Dad would have put her in a tower for thirty years if it had been her.

That Wednesday night, someone pounded at their door. Dad opened it to find a man standing there with his fist clenched. The stranger's face was bright red, and his blue eyes looked as if they were bulging out of their sockets. He started to walk into the house, but John stopped him.

"Excuse me, who are you?"

Aunt Elizabeth now appeared from the study, where she'd been grading papers, one of the few times she was home over a week from school.

"I want to know where my daughter Ruth is. She told us she was staying here over the weekend but didn't come home or go to school.

She seems to have a lot of weekends here."

John's eyebrows shot up. "First, your daughter was here one weekend, and this was her first time here for an overnight. Secondly, she is not here now. I would suggest you take more control over your daughter and figure out what she is doing with her life."

Natalie stood behind her father. She could see the amount of rage in this man. Why would Ruth tell her dad she had stayed with them on a weekday as well as the weekend?

Aunt Elizabeth cleared her throat. "Sir, I believe this is a matter between you and your daughter. Do not come into our home with the temperament of a bull."

The angry man deflated. "I'm sorry, we're just worried about her. This isn't her first time skipping school for a few days."

"I'm truly sorry, Mr. Hensen. If she calls here or shows up, I will make sure she knows you are looking for her, and I will insist she return home." As Aunt Elizabeth slowly shut the door, she turned to Natalie.

"Stay away from this girl. She's bad news."

"I'm sorry."

"Why are you sorry? You didn't do anything wrong," her father replied.

That night, Natalie didn't sleep well. She worried about Ruth. She called Rosanne and told her the sordid details, but Rosanne had no sympathy for Ruth. Just the fact she wouldn't know whose baby was inside her made Rosanne sick.

A week later, Ruth caught up with Natalie at school with a big smile on her face.

"Walk with me, Natalie."

Natalie remained still. Today was one of the rare occasions when Lucca could pick her up, and she didn't want to be missing when he arrived.

"Your father came looking for you," She said. "What happened?"

Ruth grinned. "Not to worry. I told him I was on a class trip, and the school failed to tell him. But listen, the good news is, I'm not pregnant, and I'll pay your dad back as soon as I can."

Natalie just looked at her, searching for the right thing to say. "I'm very happy for you, but my advice is not to engage in these activities."

Ruth cocked her head. "You really are a good girl, aren't you? You never once thought about it with your boyfriend?"

Natalie opened and closed her mouth before she could speak. "Actually, no, we haven't. We're waiting."

"Well, I'm happy for you. I would hate to see anyone else go through this scare. I agree. I think it's time I just look for someone who respects me and wants a relationship. Do you want to get a milkshake?"

Natalie shook her head. "Lucca's meeting me here today for a ride home."

"Do you want me to wait with you? I'd love to meet him. You're so secretive about him."

Natalie's eyes locked onto Ruth's, and the other girl gave her a long, steady stare. Goosebumps popped up on Natalie's arms, and she had a sudden ache in her stomach, like when her mother would walk into the room.

"I'll be all right waiting by myself. You can meet him another time." She was relieved when Ruth said goodbye and walked away.

The weeks went by. School was coming to an end, and Rosanne and Natalie were excited to attend the same college, Saint Joseph in Philadelphia. They were able to stay at home, and Natalie and Lucca would be able to stay together. She truly did not want to go to college out of state, though she had several offers. Penn State, Northwestern, LSU, and Yale had all accepted her, but she decided on a smaller school to stay at home.

Ruth and Natalie still met up once in a while. Ruth found a great secretarial job that paid money. They never talked about the episode months back.

Rosanne and Natalie found a little house in Sea Isle City, where eight girls went in on a place to rent for senior week after graduation.

It was an exciting time in their lives. Sister Agnes held Natalie tight and cried a lot. She was so sad to lose her. She told Natalie a piece of her heart would be lost since she was no longer able to see her every day. Natalie promised she would call her every week, but it was still hard for Sister Agnes to let go. Natalie was the child she never had. She came to understand the strong feelings that Sister Beatrice and Natalie's aunt Gertrude had for her.

Aunt Gertrude sent Natalie a ticket to fly to Berlin after graduation. She missed Jeannie, who was not there for this special time in her life. Jeannie married her true love, Frankie, who joined the Marines.

Before Natalie left for Berlin, Lucca's parents held a little party for her. Natalie was anxious to see Rose. Next to Rosanne, Rose was her true friend.

As they walked to Lucca's car to head to his house, a car pulled up that she didn't recognize right away. It was Arthur and Ruth. Ruth jumped out of the car, running over to give her a hug.

"I'm so happy for you, my dear friend, for graduating and going on to college."

Natalie felt cold suddenly, despite Ruth's warm embrace.

Ruth turned to Lucca. "You must be the famous boyfriend." She looked at him deeply and long. Then Arthur called her, and she said she had to go. Ruth hugged Natalie again and whispered in her ear, "I think Arthur is finally over his other girlfriend. We've been together for two weeks now, nonstop."

"I'm happy for you, Ruth." Natalie saw Ruth stop and give Lucca another long stare before scampering back to Arthur.

Lucca stared at the car as it left. "So, that's the famous Ruth you've talked about. I see she has a boyfriend?"

"Yes, she does." This horrible feeling came to the pit of Natalie's stomach again.

When they stepped inside Lucca's house, his family greeted her with balloons and cake. His father gave her a pearl pinky ring from all of them. The day was glorious, sitting and relaxing while discussing their future. It was hard to say goodbye to Lucca. She wouldn't see him again for a month—she, Rosanne, and the other girls had their week in New Jersey, followed by Natalie's three weeks in Berlin. She promised to call Lucca every night.

Rosanne and Natalie spent their days at the beach laughing as lifeguards tried to get them over to their stand. But the girls were not interested. Coming off the beach one day, to Natalie's big surprise, standing right in front of her, was Jimmy and a beautiful blonde. She had the largest blue eyes Natalie had ever seen. She was tall and shapely and could have been on a magazine cover. She wore the tiniest bikini Natalie had ever seen, but it looked good on her.

Jimmy said hello and turned toward the blonde. "Natalie, this is Patricia."

Patricia immediately began to chatter away happily to Natalie, but her face turned serious when Jimmy interrupted her. "Patricia here dates Arthur off and on. You know, Arthur, who's dating Ruth?"

"I have heard about him. I met him once," Natalie replied.

Patricia leaned in, her voice nearly a whisper. "You need to be very careful around Ruth. She worked very hard to break up my relationship with Arthur. She lies and manipulates. I'm just giving you a warning in case you're involved with anyone. She pretended to be my friend."

"I'm so sorry she did this," Natalie stammered. There was this sick feeling again in her stomach, like a warning.

"Well, I'm lucky. Jimmy knew who she was for a long time, but I didn't believe him. I'm at a good place. Jim and I are dating."

"Yes, I recall him talking about you a lot." She smiled at them both. "We must go. The other girls have plans and most likely are wondering where we are. Have a good time for the rest of your stay."

Natalie and Rosanne were rushing down the street when Rosanne noticed the worried look on Natalie's face. She stopped in mid-stride and took Natalie's arm.

"Natalie, don't worry. They don't know Lucca. He loves you. He lets the whole world know. Don't take Patricia's words seriously. I don't see Ruth coming between you and Lucca. I don't like her, but that's just me. You're always so kind to people."

A weak smile crossed Natalie's face. They almost ran the rest of the way, immediately took showers, and dressed. The girls all piled into cars and found dinner. They passed the nightclubs with blasting music but knew they wouldn't even attempt to try to get in. A few girls managed to get fake IDs and made their way to the beach clubs, but Natalie and Rosanne returned to the beach house and sat there watching the stars. They let the smell of the salt air fill their nostrils. Natalie decided to walk to the corner to use the pay phone. She needed to hear Lucca's voice to be reassured. She called Collect, and luckily, he was home like he usually was on the weekend.

"Natalie, are you okay?" there was a moment of silence, he wanted her to come home but was awkward in asking her. It was her Senior week; how to tell her he just wanted her to come back.

"I am. I just missed you and wanted to hear your voice."

"If you want, I can come down with Kevin for the day. I know he'd love to see Rosanne. You can decide if you also want to come home, just a suggestion."

"That would be nice. I'll tell Rosanne. I think I might want to come home. I miss you."

The following week after returning from the beach was a whirlwind. Natalie had to pack to leave for Europe. She would be gone for a month. They would be in Germany, Paris, and Italy. She hesitated about leaving for so long, but both her dad and Lucca convinced her to go since, with college starting, it would be a while before she would have this much time again. Lucca was supportive of her visit overseas and promised to be waiting for her when she came back as he wanted to discuss their future.

With lots of goodbye tears, she boarded a Pan Am flight. She slept most of the flight and felt rested when they arrived at Berlin Airport.

Everyone was waiting for her with flowers: grandmother, sister Alexandra and her baby girl, even Sister Beatrice. Gertrude couldn't wait as she ran to embrace Natalie. It had been a long four years.

They arrived at the manor house, and Uncle Hans was on the step with her grandfather. She had never seen her grandfather cry as he, too, held her in his arms.

Nothing much had changed at the house. The walls had been painted, and the dining room had new curtains and a new rug, otherwise it was all like she remembered. She could smell the pastries from the kitchen as the cook came out. She seemed to have gotten rounder and there was lots of flour mixed into her now-gray hair. Natalie hugged her and ended up with flour all over her navy-blue pants suit.

They brought her luggage to her old, familiar room. Nothing had changed there, either, except there was new bedding. Her pictures on the wall were still there, and the one she painted was still hanging.

She undressed in a lovely cotton pink blouse and jeans. She wanted to go out to the stables as soon as she could. In the closet were her riding boots that still fit perfectly. As she came down the stairs, her grandfather was just leaving and caught sight of her.

"Natalie, I'm just going to check on Star. She's about to have a foal. You came at the right time. I hope we both have the chance to witness the birth. We're keeping her stalled so she won't give birth out in the pasture."

Nothing had changed in the stalls either. She and Grandfather caught up with every detail of the last four years as they walked through the stables and outside grounds.

"Grandfather, you keep looking at me as if I have two heads."

Her grandfather seldom showed emotion, but he gathered her in his arms and hugged her. Then he put his hands on her shoulders and looked her in the eyes.

"No child, I'm just admiring how grown you are. You went from all sweetness to this beautiful young woman who has accomplished so much. Gertrude told us all about your young man. She was upset at the beginning because she felt you were too young. I told her we have all raised you right, and your mind and heart will always be what you listen to."

"Thank you, Grandfather. My American grandfather told me the same thing. I just want to make all of you proud, including my father. I so wish he would divorce my mother and find a woman who will love him."

"Yes, that seems to be a problem for him." Her grandfather bowed his head. "I also think it would be best if he divorced Katarina, but I don't think he will for some reason. Gertrude feels he leans too much into being Catholic, till death do us part."

Natalie sighed as she patted the neck of the horse, leaning out of its stall. She walked out to the pasture with her grandfather, and there was Prince. He lifted his head from eating, stood, and looked at Natalie, his ears moving forward. The moment she called him, he trotted over. He hadn't forgotten her. Natalie laid her head on his neck and looped her arms around his neck. He just stood there for a moment and then started to rub his head against her, at last lifting his head and showing all his teeth in a smile.

"Oh, Grandfather, he remembers me!" It brought tears to her eyes. He had reached the good age of thirty and was still going strong. She and her Grandfather rode over the property for hours, and Natalie noticed a for sale sign during that ride.

"Grandfather, are you selling the place?"

"Not all of it. It is becoming harder as your grandmother, and I become older. Hans isn't here that much as he stays in the apartment in the city. My help is as old as I am. You remember we all stuck together through the war. Just like me, they need to retire. Younger people are not interested in devoting time to horses, even when we set up lessons. We're keeping thirty acres out of the one-fifty. Very few people in Germany actually own property, so we sell it to families who want to build out here in the fresh air. They'll most likely put homes or apartment buildings on the land. Natalie, it's a good thing. Look how long we've been out here today, and we haven't even covered all the land. Most of it is forest, so we don't use much more than we are riding now."

They rode in silence that afternoon, enjoying their time together.

Natalie had been there a week when she tried to phone Lucca. She tried his dorm and home number, but he was not there and still had not responded to her letter.

They were getting ready to leave for Paris when the telegram arrived.

"Natalie, I miss you. Natalie, I love you with all my heart. I'll be here waiting for you.

Lucca."

Natalie's eyes filled with tears, and she felt her worries vanish.

Gertrude and Natalie left Berlin to spend a week in Paris at the apartment. Natalie felt at ease since the telegram from Lucca.

Elvie was anxious to see Natalie. Sarah had a meal planned at her newly opened restaurant. It was going well for the first year. Sarah remained close to Alexandra, but marriages and children left them seeing each other only a few times a year. However, they spent time on the phone weekly.

Elvie had Gertrude and Natalie picked up by private car at the airport. They hadn't taken much luggage. Natalie had suggested they take the bus and subway, but Elvie wouldn't hear of it.

They arrived in front of the apartment building where Elvie was waving from the balcony. When they reached the third floor, Gertrude was a bit out of breath. Elvie had the door open for them to come in.

There were greetings of hugs, and Elvie ushered them into the living room. The housekeeper moved their suitcases into the bedrooms. Natalie looked around; a few things had changed since the last time she was here with her grandparents. There were new curtains, and the paint on the wall was a creamy buff colour, different from the grey that had been there before.

The entire living room had new furniture, except for the two Queen Anne chairs and end tables. The deep Chinese blue and green rugs still took up much of the living room. The living room had two sitting areas of sofas and chairs. The fireplace was filled with unlit wood, the balcony door was open, and the air from outside was flowing in. Car and bus noises and people talking floated up to the balcony.

The housekeeper brought in coffee and cakes. Elvie asked Natalie a hundred questions about her last four years and was saying how happy she was to see her when they heard a door slam.

Elvie looked at Gertrude, "Don't get mad, but I couldn't tell her to leave. Katarina showed up five days ago. She isn't well."

Before she could say another word, Katarina walked into the room. She was deathly white, her hair looked drab, and there were dark circles under her eyes. She walked with a cane, and her leg was bandaged with blood seeping through. Katarina gave Natalie and Gertrude an icy stare but otherwise didn't acknowledge them. She just turned and went to her bedroom.

Natalie wanted to say something to her mother, but there were no words. They were preparing to leave for dinner when she saw her mother on the sofa with her leg propped up.

"Katarina, are you all right?" Natalie's voice was almost a whisper.

Katarina picked up the bottle of wine next to her chair.

"Do you need something for the pain?"

"Natalie, wine does the trick for all that ails me."

Natalie suddenly felt so sorry for Katarina that her eyes went glassy with tears.

"You still won't call me Mother, will you? I actually prefer not being called Mother."

Katarina opened her eyes and looked at Natalie. She observed how the girl had grown so much since the last time she saw her. A beautiful woman stood before her, nothing like the meek little girl she left. Then, she never thought Natalie to be meek or weak. Natalie would never understand what an unbalanced life felt like or having overwhelming emotions. Katarina always seemed to be paying for sins she couldn't recall. How lucky Natalie was to have a free mind.

"Natalie, you surprise me. You have changed into a lovely woman." Natalie's eyes widened at the comment, and Katarina saw the empathy in them.

"What did you do to your leg?" Natalie asked. "It looks like a terrible injury."

Her mother took a deep breath and started to cough, and a journal fell to the floor. Natalie looked down at it, curious, but then Elvie called that they needed to leave for dinner.

Natalie gave her mother one last look. Katarina's eyes were closed again.

"Mother, I will only say one thing. Dad didn't just grieve when you left. He shattered. And for that, I will never forgive you." Katarina never responded.

Sarah's restaurant was on Rue du Four, a few streets off Boulevard Saint Germain and not far from the famous Café de Flore. Her achievement received the Michelin three-star. Her place was considered exceptional cuisine. Her aim was to be a five-star restaurant, and considering this was only her third year in business, she was pleased.

Natalie was in awe. Posh crystal filled the dining room, and thousands of suspended crystals hung from the ceiling. White tablecloths and green chairs filled the room which was painted a light green and was filled with tropical plants.

They were ushered into a private room where they were served authentic French dishes. Their speciality was scallops from the

Somme Bay, duck foie gras, and grilled suckling lamb. The quality of ingredients was exceptional, and there was a list of forty-six wines to choose from. Natalie had a concasse of raw oysters, green and blue lobsters, the best caviar with smoked sabayon, and duck breast that was aged with spices.

Sarah made sure all her ingredients came from a province she knew. From the cheese marketers to livestock breeders to fisherman. In soups, her speciality was the creamy celeriac gratin or a leek potato soup in the summer. This time of year was tomato gazpacho with a minted cucumber salad. She had a small garden outside the kitchen where she grew her own vegetables and herbs during the summer. Her best seller was truffle and artichoke soup. Desserts were too many to mention. Natalie noticed the spiced bread with a slice of mango jelly and the chocolate mousse piled high with madeleines and assorted mignardises.

Sarah focused on no cruelty to animals with the goal of being more in tune with nature.

Natalie couldn't even try the duck, just the thought made her ill. But the Carpaccio of line-caught sea bass with chestnuts and an onion gratin that oozed with the liquified onion was more to her liking. She had the medallions of lobster in a Jerusalem artichoke with tapioca. She was now happy she dressed in such a nice outfit. Those who were entering were all dressed in suits and very nice dresses. She had a light blue shift dress with a white ruffle running down the middle and lace around the sleeves. On her feet were simple blue ballerina slippers.

The evening was long before they said goodbye and went home.

When they returned to the apartment, a light was on in the hallway and one was coming from her mother's room. They all said goodnight as each retreated into their own room. Natalie couldn't sleep and went into the living room. On the floor was the closed journal. Her mother's light was off now in her bedroom.

Natalie curled up on the sofa and opened her mother's journal. Inside, pages of different dates, including the day she left Philadelphia. She wrote things about how she was looking forward to being out from being under John's thumb. Looking forward to him leaving so she could breathe again. Reading these words had Natalie close to tears. The pages she had written were filled with a deep affection for Gregory. Natalie skipped to the last pages. The top said "The Past."

Natalie began to read about what her mother had been up to these past four years.

The Past

I hope this will be my last entry ever about working with Gregory and Peter. I'm tired and do not want to be involved with any more of Peter and Gregory's trips. This was the last one for me. I'm going to try not to regret the past and the mistakes of my imperfect life. Peter and Louis came to Italy and persuaded me to work with them one more time. It took some convincing, but finally, it was my desire to see Gregory, who hadn't contacted or responded to me in over nine months, that got me to agree. I was hoping to see him and restore our relationship.

I managed once again to make my way back to safety. People were asking too many questions in Berlin, so I ventured to Paris, where I sit alone and drink my misery in order to forget. I still think I'm crazy for letting them talk me into this, but I needed it somehow. A man named Nathan Gaineshad been on Peter's radar for years. Nathan was a double agent who killed several MI6 agents, and Louis wanted him for a bombing in France. Gregory has always wanted him for crimes against humanity and has gone to Brazil to search for him. Nathan was as guilty because he worked for Bremerhaven, who was responsible for the killing of Jews and robbing them of their treasures at their homes.

Then the gunshots. The bullet of a .38 had splintered the wood and lodged into my ankle and leg. The bastard Nathan said he didn't have a choice. There were already two dead bodies on the floor—Nathan's guards, it was a kill shot to the heads of his bodyguards. Nathan was protecting Herr Bremerhaven all these years. Nathan was cornered in the apartment, there was an urgency in his voice as he told me to move to the other room. He knew he had to get out of the apartment building, but it was looking less like he could.

Natalie continued reading. What had her mother gotten herself into?

Katarina's Entry

Katarina started with a plan Peter and Louis had laid out. First, she made the acquaintance of Gerhardt Oberstein, who was Bremahaven's personal accountant and lawyer from Switzerland. He'd been sent to Vienna to close a business deal with an art buyer, and he'd be in contact with Nathan.

Gregory, Louis, and Peter had been searching for Bremahaven and Nathan for two years now, and they were relieved to finally be on the cusp of capturing them both. Each man had their own reasons why, but they could make no mistakes to have Nathan slip away now. He'd slipped through MI6's fingers more than once, so they had to ensure he suspected nothing.

They'd discovered that Nathan was a double spy for a long time, betraying MI6 as he worked with the East Berlin intelligence. Many operatives had died thanks to him. The last place they thought they had caught up with both was in Brazil. Nathan worked for Leo Bremarhaven, who'd stolen five hundred pieces of art from Paris, some of which were taken from Jewish homes. Bremarhaven also took Jews' took jewellery and money, looting their homes after sending them to concentration camps. They had pictures of him cutting off fingers to retrieve rings he wanted from the dead and living.

Bremahaven deposited the money into Swiss banks during the war, and Nathan, as an MI6 agent, was to establish a working relationship with Bremahaven and notify MI6 of his whereabouts and what Swiss bank he was visiting. But the money was too good to pass up, and Nathan began working for Bremahaven instead. At first, MI6 thought they were receiving good intel, but they grew suspicious after they barely missed Bremahaven one too many times at locations Nathan had given them. Then Nathan disappeared off the radar for years. They had thought they had caught him a few times, but he was always one step ahead of MI6.

Now, Nathan worked for Bremahaven as the go-between for anyone who was to meet with Bremahaven. Once Katarina established a relationship with Oberstein, she could ply him for information regarding Nathan's whereabouts. That would lead them to Bremarhaven as well. Going to the police wasn't an option. Bremarhaven had a lot of influence, and they didn't know which of the police he had in his pocket.

Peter had an inside contact at the bank Oberstein was using for the business deal and was able to find out which hotel Oberstein was staying at. They paid the desk clerk at the hotel to alert them when Oberstein checked in so Katarina could "happen" to run into him. Now, she waited and watched him check-in. He gave the bellhop instructions to take his bags up because he was going out. Katarina smiled. This was the perfect opportunity.

Katarina gathered up the books she'd brought and deliberately walked smack into Oberstein on his way out. Oberstein apologized over and over and asked if she was all right. Katarina smiled sweetly as he helped her gather up her books. This was the moment. She told him he could buy her a cup of coffee to make up for nearly running her over. Oberstein and Katarina met for the next three days, Katarina waiting for him to talk openly with her.

Over drinks on the third night, he explained he had to meet an important client in Vienna. His tongue was loose from a few drinks, and he had no issue telling her where the meeting with Nathan would be. Katarina kept feeding him drinks as she poured hers into a plant. She let him kiss her right there in the bar to keep things going. He was a slight man with steely grey eyes and a balding hairline. His face looked pinched, and he had thin lips, but he was not to be underestimated because he, too, had been linked to doing assassinations for Bremahaven.

He tried to impress Katarina with how important he was to Bremahaven and all the money that went through him. He made himself sound as if he was the lead. Nathan never handled the money, he said. Nathan only brought in the clients, and Oberstein took the money to the bank. The deal they were working on right now was their largest ever for a painting, so it was necessary for Oberstein to take the check back to Switzerland personally. He himself had never met Nathan, but he told Katarina what he'd been told Nathan would be wearing, as well as the rose in Nathan's lapel that would be Oberstein's signal to approach him. He was very drunk at this point, and as Katarina walked him to the elevator, he invited her up. She declined but promised she'd go up with him tomorrow after dinner.

The next night, they met again to make sure nothing changed and to get the date of the meeting with Nathan. Oberstein hinted that it would not be long. During dinner, Katarina slowly unbuttoned the top of her blouse to show some cleavage. Oberstein took the bait, and after dinner, he wobbled slightly to his room as he held his arm around her waist and fumbled for the key to let them inside.

He quickly embraced her as they entered the room, his hands running down her back. Before she could refuse his advances, he had his tongue down her throat. His hands fumbled with the buttons on her blouse, and she tried to pull his hands away. As planned, she'd slipped a piece of paper in the door lock so Peter and Louis could get in, but she hadn't expected Oberstein to move so quickly. She'd thought they could sit and talk a while to give Louis and Peter time to burst in, but Oberstein was not going to wait. He wasn't taking no for an answer as Katarina sat in a chair. He pulled her off the chair— he was stronger than she had expected—and pushed her onto the bed. She tried to shove him off, telling him they needed to take it slow, but he suddenly had a knife at her throat. He must have had it hidden under the bed.

"No more games," He sneered. He was no longer this placid little lawyer, and she froze as he smirked at her.

Suddenly, he flew off her, and Katarina saw Peter there, slugging Oberstein in the jaw and knocking him to the ground. Peter and Louis shoved him into the chair and held a gun on him. Oberstein's eyes slanted with pure hate as he looked at Katarina, and it took little convincing for him to give the answers they wanted. They told him they would put him in a safe house until everything was over. Before they led him out of the room, he turned to Katarina and asked her if she was happy with her role in all of this. She just smiled, then shuddered as they led him out of the room. That was too close.

She rebuttoned her blouse and headed back to her hotel when Gregory suddenly appeared in the room. He grabbed her by the arm and led her out. He pulled her in his arms at the elevators and kissed the top of her head. No words were spoken as he led her out of the hotel to a waiting cab. On the ride back to her hotel, a sigh left her. Gregory was here. She was safe.

Nathan was to meet Oberstein at Café Landtmann in Universitätsring. It was the oldest café in Vienna, dating back to 1873 and specialized in coffee, fresh cakes, and pastries. It was easy for Katarina to stand out because of her looks and the expensive dresses she wore. They knew Nathan liked women—it was one of his failures, as sometimes he would almost get caught because he was involved with a woman in different countries.

The first morning at the café, there was no sign of Nathan. Katarina ate the Apfelstrudel with cream, consuming each bite slowly. Several men approached her, but she told them she was waiting for her husband, and they beat it. She wanted to establish herself at the café, so her presence there didn't seem unusual if Nathan started asking questions. Katarina came again for two more days, and finally, on the fourth day, she spotted him.

He had the red rose pinned to the lapel of his black cashmere blazer, just as Oberstein had said. He sat at a table opposite Katarina, and she moved her chair once he sat so he could see her entire profile. He glanced around as he took his seat and ordered coffee and breakfast. He was watching the door and sneaking looks at Katarina, noticing her long legs under a skirt that sat above her knees. He worked his way up till his gaze was met by those brilliant eyes. Katarina looked straight at him. She gave him a smile and returned to her magazine and coffee.

Because Bremahaven liked to keep his secrets, Nathan had never met Oberstein, so Nathan didn't know that the man he was meeting was an agent posing as him. Peter and Louis's agent was well briefed on the conversation he was to have with Nathan, and the men watched from a nearby van. They saw Katarina open her newspaper, and as soon as Nathan went inside, their agent entered as well and went to Nathan's table. They spoke a few words as he apologized for not being in the café on time, saying he hadn't received Nathan's message at the hotel till late that evening. Their agent sat down with Nathan and pulled some paperwork out of Oberstein's actual briefcase. Nathan looked at the documents intently. The agent and Nathan spoke for thirty minutes, Nathan continuously looking over at Katarina all the while.

Nathan gave the fake Oberstein some notes and a piece of paper which had the price for the painting that Herr Klein was to buy and the check to put in Bremahaven's account immediately. Nathan briefly described when and where Herr Klein was going to be arriving and staying, which was a sigh of relief to Peter and Louis because it was the same hotel that Katarina was in now; they wouldn't have to move her. Now that they knew Klein's arrival details, they could intercept him like they had the real Oberstein and replace him with another of their agents. Meanwhile, Nathan would retrieve the painting from Bremahaven's home and place it in his office. He would let Oberstein know by messages in his box to receive the check at a meeting and place.

The placed agent left, but Katarina kept up her charade. They still needed to find out where Bremahaven and Nathan's office were, and she hoped her look would invite him to approach her. Sure enough, he sauntered over to her table and introduced himself as Nathan Gibbs. She invited him to sit, and they conversed casually for over an hour. He asked her many personal questions—he was a cautious man—but Katarina had her story down pat. She said she was from Italy and recently divorced. By the end of breakfast, he asked her to join him for dinner in downtown Vienna. She played coy, pretending she didn't want to join a stranger she didn't know. He said she could take a cab to meet him at a restaurant in town if that would make her feel safer. He spoke German with an accent, and he did not speak Italian. Katarina was careful to use her Italian accent in speaking. He told her where to meet him and kissed her hand before he left. She watched him leave and noticed he was slight of build—about 5'11—with sandy brown hair and non-descript blue eyes. His shoulders were broad, and his hands looked as if he had done hard work. He was a handsome man in his own way. Via the brooch she wore, the men in the van could hear everything.

Gregory, Louis and Peter had been searching for Bremahaven and Nathan for over a year now. They felt this was the end for both to finally capture him and Bremahaven. Each had their own agenda, they could make no mistakes to have him slip away, but they had to make sure he suspected nothing. Nathan worked for Bremahaven, a Nazi with war crimes. Katarina would find out all the information they needed. Nathan never changed his first name, only the last, but MI6 always found him, but he always slipped away. He was a traitor to MI6.

Nathan was found to be a double spy for a great length of time; due to his actions, many operatives died, and he betrayed MI 6 as he worked with the East Berlin intelligence. They had been pursuing him and his employer Bremahaven, for two years, the last place they thought they had caught up with both was in Brazil. Nathan worked for Leo Bremahaven, after the war when Nathan was MI6, he was to find out as much information about this man as possible as they knew Bremahaven was involved in war crimes and suspected he was an arms dealer and he was going back and forth to East Berlin, the information always came back scarce, MI6 started to suspect Nathan, Nathan and Bremahaven had ventured into East Berlin to many times. Bremahaven stole five hundred pieces of Art from Paris. Some of the art was taken from Jewish homes, he also took jewellery and money. He looted their homes after sending them to concentration camps. They had pictures of him cutting off fingers and retrieving rings he wanted from the dead and living. He tortured people, two homes were from Jewish families he owned, those were empty they could not find the third home where he was now living.

Their first dinner went without a flaw. He told her he wanted to see more of her if she was willing and, during dinner, continuously touched her arm or shoulder and, at times, her knee. She knew she had him, so she didn't remove his hand. They continued to meet, and she always made sure that her dinner outfits left him wanting more of her. She allowed him to kiss her goodnight, and he would sit in the hotel lobby in a quiet corner as they had a drink at the end of the evening. They were out of view, and he became more familiar with her by slight touching as she led him on. Nathan ushered her all over Vienna, acting like the perfect gentleman, taking her to museums and on walks in the park. They did this every night for a week, and Katarina felt he wanted more every time they saw each other, and it was harder for her to say no to him. She let him have a little more each time in terms of kissing and touching her in intimate areas as she played along. Louis, Peter, and Gregory never let her out of sight. Sometimes, Gregory would look away, not wanting to see any more. They could hear Nathan suggest they go back to her room, but she always rebuked the advances, and Gregory would let out a long sigh of relief. He knew she could pull this off, but he also didn't want her to go any further than the small gestures from this man.

At the end of each night, they would meet in her room, which was next to theirs. They knew they were close now. They had someone in place following Herr Klein from Heidelberg, and they had surveillance and listening devices to know what he was doing and when he was going to arrive in Vienna. They could have taken him in Heidelberg but wanted to wait till he got to Vienna, and they would let them know of his arrival.

This time in her room, Katarina's heart leapt as she saw Gregory standing in the corner against the wall. She hadn't seen him since Oberstein's. He'd disappeared for several days, gathering his own information, and now, at last, he was here. He just stared at her, never saying a word. She wanted to run into his arms but saw a look in his eye she had seen before and knew not to approach him. He was watching Nathan and her, and it sparked a fury in him again.

Peter was now pacing in the hotel room. They'd worried that Nathan would figure it all out, but so far so good. Katarina knew how to play the part, but they didn't want her to compromise. Once Nathan insisted they be more intimate, they had to figure out how to get her out of the situation. Peter was more worried that Gregory would just kill him if Nathan insisted on going to bed with her. They were so close now to getting a war criminal and traitor and someone who killed in Paris. Katarina hoped the next dinner, she would find out more. They sat way into the evening, trying to figure out what their next move should be without putting Katarina in jeopardy.

Louis and Gregory were never far from where Katarina and Nathan went—Nathan was not as cautious as he should be. Peter stayed away, usually in the vans where they were constantly taking pictures and listening to the conversation. Katarina always wore a bugged piece of jewellery so they could hear her and Nathan. Peter played it safe, not knowing if Nathan would recognize him from years past. That night, Louis and Gregory followed Katarina and Nathan with a great deal of caution.

Nathan and Katarina left the outskirts of Vienna and went to a small, intimate restaurant. Louis and Gregory had a table in the back that was more hidden, but they could still see them. They didn't trust Nathan not to harm Katarina—he'd murdered women as easily as men, and this restaurant was on the outskirts of the city. It would be too dangerous for her if she tried to get away. Nathan had no control over himself once dinner was over and they were back in the car. He slid the car seat back on her. Gregory was ready to jump to her defence as he saw Nathan's face go down next to Katarina. Louis held him back, and they let it play out as Katarina let Nathan become more intimate with her.

She accomplished what she wanted over dinner. Nathan had told her that his business dealings were with Bremahaven, and he'd even given her the location of the house. He also said he was to meet Herr Klein in the same hotel where she was staying, and he gave her the date of Klein's arrival. He apologized that he might not be able to see her as much once Herr Klein arrived.

As always, Gregory ached for Katarina. She was still in his blood, coursing through his veins like shards of glass when he saw her. It killed him to know what Nathan was doing, to know he was touching her, kissing her in deep passion as she played along. It was difficult for Louis also to know Gregory's feelings for Katarina and his own past with her. He's never told Gregory about his and Katarina's affair, but Gregory knew they had been together for a brief time. Now Gregory and Louis were watching her every move as she was with Nathan.

Gregory thinks of the past.

As Gregory watched Katarina, his thoughts went back to their angry words at their last parting. It was wrong to visit her in Philadelphia because he felt baited back into her life of drama. He refused to read her messages at first, but once he came to Washington, he took them out and read them. She begged him to change his mind; she loved him. She called his house several times, upsetting his wife, who wanted Katarina out of their life. He sat and read the message to please meet him in Philadelphia. She gave him a time and place. He reached her and would be there before returning to Israel.

Their meeting didn't go as planned. That day, he felt she deliberately tried to hurt him. They had a heated twenty-minute conversation, then Francis Lee arrived and left with her. Gregory's soul felt crushed. What was the point of meeting her, he thought. Had she wanted him to ask her to take her back to Europe or elsewhere? He'd never find out.

Back to the Present

Now, Gregory watched Katarina at the table using every bit of charm she had, and in the car, he knew she would be able to convince any man to do anything with just a whisper in his ear. Gregory kept his feelings in check because he really wanted this Nazi Bremahaven, and Peter wanted Nathan. Nathan was responsible for three MI6 agents being killed years ago, and Bremahaven had murdered three hundred children as young as three months old with single gunshots to the head. They had a picture of him standing over the graves.

This was a world others did not understand. There were no second chances to bring Nazis to justice. If they couldn't bring them to justice, they killed them.

They also realized they could get Katarina killed. There were days when Gregory could not help being terrified for her. He didn't feel so assured of her safety as the others, who kept saying she could hold her own.

Fortunately, Nathan did not suspect her. She wore the best clothing designer clothing, silks and dresses that hugged her body when they went to dinner, and diamonds and pearls on her neck and arms. She commanded attention and was elegant and sophisticated. She walked and spoke like the upper class. Nathan noticed immediately that she was different. He also noticed how other men noticed her the second she walked into a room. His one thought was that he would have her.

He pulled the car seat back up. Katarina's hair had fallen from its updo, and they saw her buttoning her blouse as Nathan now slowly moved away from the restaurant back to the hotel.

Back at the hotel, Nathan and Katarina made themselves comfortable for a nightcap in their usual place in the lounge's far corner. Nathan suddenly laughed out loud, catching the attention of Gregory and Louis, who sat not far away.

"Did we meet at the Hotel de Carillon in Paris?" Katarina asked.

"Way too rich and sophisticated for me, but yes. I frequently stay in Paris to get away. I go almost every five months. I would have noticed if I had seen you."

Louis's eyebrows lifted. He'd known Nathan was in Paris but never got close to him. The man was as elusive as a cat hiding. There had been two car explosions, and French and Israeli agents working for Louis had been killed. He was there prior to the bombing of two diplomats from Brazil. The agents had been targeted, and they'd suspected Nathan was in France. Now they knew for sure. She stared steadily at Nathan without flinching.

"It's ultra-luxurious. Obviously, you have stayed there, Katarina."

She just smiled and answered, "Rich husbands."

The next morning, the invitation came to the café to have dinner. She had hoped they had heard their conversation in the van, but if not, she had to get back to the hotel somehow and tell Gregory and Louis where she was going. She strode out of the Café and hailed a cab as Nathan kissed her on the cheek and told her he would be back for her in two hours. He had some business to finish before then.

They were running out of time to get Nathan with Bremahaven. Herr Klein was supposed to arrive in two days, so the clock was ticking. They needed to learn the exact time Klein was arriving so they could put an agent in Klein's place as they had done with Oberstein. They finally were getting closer when Nathan invited Katarina to take a ride to Bremahaven's estate. He had to pick up a painting for Herr Klein. It was the slip of his tongue that he mentioned the name of the man coming from Germany to buy the painting. It would be an easy trip, and from there, he would take her back to his apartment with the attached office to place the painting in a vault for safekeeping. Bremahaven was going to let Nathan know if he wanted Klein to visit him at the estate.

Katarina rushed into the lobby, leaving a note at the desk for Peter. She knew they never let her out of sight but wanted to ensure. She dashed upstairs, changed into a more comfortable outfit of slacks and sweater and rushed back downstairs. She was speaking with the desk clerk to make sure the message was delivered when she saw Louis coming into the lobby with Nathan right behind him. Her heart was now beating fast. Louis immediately saw her talking to the clerk, and she saw Nathan take a seat. Her hands were shaking as Louis came and stood next to her. She turned to Nathan, waved and walked over slowly, knowing the clerk was giving Louis the message, looking a little confused. Regardless, Louis followed them as he walked across the street to his Mercedes and watched Katarina and Nathan pull out into the street as they followed.

Gregory and Peter were already in the van. They hadn't heard the whole conversation in the café because of the interference of dishes and servers asking questions, but they knew something was up as Katarina hailed the cab right back to the hotel. They followed slowly, stopping just outside the hotel when Katarina spoke into the brooch and told them to wait. She was going to change quickly and leave Louis a message because Nathan was coming for her. Katarina came out of the hotel with Nathan, and Louis stayed back before leaving and entering the van, which they were now following.

Nathan and Katarina were travelling to an estate outside of Vienna. The estate was encircled by a menacing six-foot wall. It looked like a small castle. As Nathan drove up to the gates, two guards asked for identification even though they knew Nathan. This worried all of them as they followed and watched, and they studied the large wall with cameras and looked at the two guards, who meant business against anyone who was not supposed to be there.

They now knew the location of Bremahaven. They had concerns about Katarina entering an area where they could not reach her because they knew Nathan's personality could change on a dime. They'd seen his brutality when he turned against MI6. He'd put bullets into two MI6 agents whom he'd known for years and pushed the car over the side of a cliff, making sure they were dead. He knew how to torture. Nathan was a dangerous man and now worked for an even more dangerous one. And he'd pursue anyone Bremahaven felt was a possible threat.

Nathan continuously slipped out of their fingers. When he was in Amsterdam, he'd sensed he was being watched and ordered one of the East German Stasi to stay in the room that he had occupied. Nathan told the East German to order room service under his name and that he would return in three days. Nathan watched from a comfortable spot when the MI6 with Peter descended upon the hotel. They all wore hoods, so Nathan could not identify Peter. When MI6 broke down the door, the East German began to fire upon them. They in turn killed him, realizing they'd been fooled and had killed the wrong man. Nathan quietly made his way back to Vienna.

Gregory, Louis, and Peter moved on to Vienna and decided to use Katarina. She'd have to play her part starting with Oberstein. Gregory took the Oberstein had pulled on Katarina and sliced off his ear as he screamed into a muffled cloth.

"I promise I will let you go, but if you do not answer, the next part that goes is the man parts. Then your tongue so you will never speak again."

The lawyer's face went pale as he nodded. They removed the gag, the knife pointed at his man's parts.

With a raspy voice, Oberstein told them that Nathan was on his way back to Vienna from Brazil. Nathan had an apartment in town with his office attached. The lawyer knew most of the books and logs were kept in the Vienna office where Nathan lived most of the time. Oberstein was to meet with Nathan at the cafe and later with Mr. Klein at Nathan's office about two art pieces. Oberstein told Louis and Gregory that Nathan most likely had to bring the paintings from Bremahaven's estate. The lawyer truly didn't know where Nathan lived. They always met at a café or hotel but never in his office or at the estate. One more reason Peter, Gregory, and Louis needed Katarina.

The Present: Natalie

Natalie felt sick; she didn't know if she wanted to read any further, but there was a part of her that realized her mother was a brave woman and did things that could not be explained. Why would she continue in this line of work? It seemed as if she had a death wish.

Natalie thought of her poor father. He loved Katarina and looked past all her wrongs. Natalie begged her father to get a divorce to move on with his life and find happiness. Aunt Gertrude told Natalie the trouble Katarina would get into. Of course, Natalie would never forget her visit to East Berlin as a child when her mother left her with strangers, only to have the Stazi come to the house and arrest the couple as she hid. Natalie had to hide across the street in the playground. She waited for hours until her mother and Gregory appeared. This put fear in Natalie for many years.

Natalie decided to keep reading the journal. Her mother kept everything a secret and would often burn anything from her past. She was certainly careless, leaving this to be read, and Natalie might never have another chance to learn about her mother. She decided to take it to her bedroom to finish reading, then return it in the early morning hours. She hoped Katarina would not come looking for the journal. She silently left the living room and headed to her bedroom to read the next page.

The Past

It had been a long week till the invitation, till Nathan felt comfortable enough to have Katarina go with him.

She invited him to escort her upstairs for her to change for dinner. She left the door to the bathroom ajar for him to watch as she changed. While he took a seat, she slowly changed. He walked into the bathroom—a move she hadn't anticipated. He wanted to undress her again, as she had already pulled the silk blouse over her head. She rebuffed the idea to him as she moved out of his embrace. He roughly pulled her back and whispered in her ear that maybe they shouldn't leave so soon."

"Nathan, I promise you, it will be better later when we have time to enjoy each other. I promise it will be worth the wait."

He pulled her into his arms again, his hands touching her. She pretended to enjoy the touches and kissed him long and hard as his hands continued running over her body. He nodded in agreement, but he now wanted her more than ever. What was it about her? He had many women. He slept with many on the first date, but she wouldn't. Looking at her now, yes, he would come back to the hotel with her to finish this little adventure. He looked at the watch on his arm,

"You're right, Katarina. I want this to be right and all night, not done hastily with you. Time is short now." He let her go as she started to walk out of the bathroom. "Katarina, we will do this again." He thought the shiver that ran through her was of pleasure, but it was nothing but distaste and fear. He did not return that night with her. He had an urgent call and matters to take care of but would meet her the next day for breakfast.

At breakfast, he did not convey the urgent message he had to take care of, only said for her to be ready in two hours.

Gregory and Peter waited outside till Nathan had pulled the car around for Katarina in front of the hotel. As they slowly pulled away from the curb, the others followed safely behind them till they came to the estate. Louis was now a block away as they slowly went by the entrance to the estate. Bremahaven villa was in the Vienna Woods and sat at the city's outskirts, fifty kilometres from Vienna's city center. It was known for its wine gardens, vineyards, and picturesque villages. The home chateau was near the historic forest, which, at one time, was the hunting ground of Viennese royalty.

Once Nathan was ushered through the gates and pulled up in front of the house, he walked Katarina into the library from a long hallway. The walls were covered with art. In the middle of the hallway was a large cherry table with a big Asian vase filled with fresh flowers. On each side were the stairways to the second floor. Hundreds of books lined the walls, and deep Persian carpets of blue and white covered the oak floors. The house was silent. Nathan opened a vault behind the books and retrieved an oil painting on canvas. Katarina looked around, taking in everything so she could tell Peter and the others. Bremahaven was nowhere to be seen.

"Do you know this painter?" He asked her as he held the painting up for her to see. She acted as if she knew nothing about art.

"I'm more into the museums in Paris and Italy and just look at art. I have no real interest."

His eyes seemed glazed over as he looked at the painting.

"This is a Hendrik Cornelisz van Vliet. It was done around 1670. He was known to turn his attention to almost exclusively painting the genre of church interiors, but this is a special field of flowers with the church in the background."

"Is it a family heirloom?"

"You could say that."

Katarina knew it was stolen art. "Are there many more pieces that you keep hidden?" Katarina asked.

He smiled at her. "We have them on the walls all through the house, and a few are in the vault. "

"I guess you better put it back before the owner comes in." Katarina was beginning to feel nervous.

"No, I'm taking it back to our business. We have a buyer and are waiting to hear from him. We'd rather he not come here at this moment. We want him to meet me at the Vienna office, where I also have my apartment. We have a lawyer waiting in Vienna at a hotel who needs to move the money once the painting is sold. I only stay here at the estate on occasion. Bremahaven likes his privacy."

Nathan went into another closet, brought out paper and rolled up the painting. It was not a large painting, maybe 11 by 15, and he gently rolled it.

"I guess I better get you back to the hotel. I'd hoped Herr Klein would have met us. I'm not sure what's taking him so long."

"Let's take the painting to the office first," Katarina urged. She needed to know where the office's exact location. She needed the logbooks and bank statements. She also needed to know how many security guards he had, how many rooms, and the exact location of the safe. She had a camera in the large button on her black jacket. She left by accident the lipstick holder in her purse. It was a 4.5mm pistol capable of firing a single .177-calibre round. She'd had it with her in East Berlin, and they named it the Kiss of Death. How stupid, she thought, to have forgotten it in her haste.

He looked at her. "It's not that far from your hotel, but yes, we will go there first. The office is in District 1—the Innere Stadt, near St. Stephen's Cathedral and the Hofburg Palace. It's really an apartment and office. Let me show you the rest of the house before we go back to the city. This house once belonged to a Jewish banker. He never came back from the war, so Bremahaven bought it."

Katarina shuddered as she thought the house was most likely stolen and the banker and his family dead in a concentration camp. Nathan took her hand. Their last stop was the bedroom. Katarina quickly moved the conversation back to the painting.

"We really need to go, Nathan; I know he is your employer, but this place leaves me feeling uneasy."

They moved through the house quickly as Nathan picked up the painting from the office and proceeded to the car. There was no one else to be seen, but for the second time, Katarina heard someone screaming. She couldn't place where it was coming from, but it sounded like a cry for help.

As they reached the car and she was about to get in, a tall gentleman with swallow skin, bushy eyebrows, and thinning grey hair grabbed her elbow. She let out a cry in surprise.

"Nathan, such a lovely woman, and you did not wait to introduce me to her? Come back in and have some wine."

Nathan frowned. "Herr Bremahaven, you know I have to get the painting back to the office. Herr Klein will be arriving soon. I also must try Oberstein again to let him know the transaction will soon be complete."

Herr Bremahaven lifted his eyebrows, and a stern look entered his lifeless light-blue eyes. His thin face looked nearly transparent as Katarina stared at him.

"No, you will come back into the house."

Nathan reluctantly followed him as he whispered to Katarina, "If you weren't so beautiful, he would not have cared to invite you in. I have brought other women, and he never asked me to stay with one of them."

Katarina shrugged her shoulders.

"So come, young lady." He rubbed his thin, skinny hands over her back. He rang for the housekeeper to bring wine as they entered a sunroom.

"So, what should I call you?" Bremahaven asked, his eyes boring into her.

"I'm Greta Napoli." She always used an alias.

The old man began to speak Italian, and Katarina answered him without a flaw. Her Italian was perfect, and his was broken. He leaned back in his chair, clasping his hands on his lap. His eyes were like ice.

"Nathan, I'm going to show this young lady my gallery. You wait here."

Katarina looked at Nathan, confused. Nathan came over to her as Bremahaven walked out to the hallway.

"Do as he says. It's the only way we both will be able to leave at the same time."

She swallowed hard. "Why can't we just leave?"

"He might not open the gates. Just play along."

She shuddered as she saw him waiting for Bremahaven with his head tilted, and he held out his skinny, cold hand to her.

She smiled sweetly as he took her hand. Katarina looked back at Nathan, who sat down for a moment and then called back to her that he needed some air and would be outside in the car.

Bremahaven flashed a wicked smile back to Nathan, and for the first time, Katarina saw the worry in Nathan's eyes.

"We won't be long, Nathan." Bremahaven's hands were ice cold as he folded Katarina's hand into his.

"Are you married, Greta?"

"No, I'm divorced."

"Good."

He led her through the house, showing her his art hanging on the walls. Stolen, she thought. Next, he led her into his other office, where he moved her to a chaise lounge.

"You know, Greta, you look familiar. When I was a young soldier with Hitler, I watched a performance by a ballerina. You look very much like her."

Katarina's mouth went dry.

"I have two left feet, Herr Bremahaven."

"Well, let's see how badly you dance." He walked over to a record player and put some music on, then returned to her and pulled her out of the chaise and into his arms to dance. He had one hand on her waist and the other skimming her buttocks as he pulled her in tighter.

"I really can't dance." She deliberately stepped on his foot. She had heels on and saw him wince. She backed away, but this time, he pulled her in a little closer. He heard a cry as well as Katarina. It was faint in the distance, but his face turned into a darkness that she thought came from hell itself.

"Excuse me, but I must attend some unfinished business. Go back to Nathan." He held her hand and studied her face again. "I still say you look like her. I never forget faces. No one has eyes like yours. I'll ask Nathan to bring you back."

Katarina wondered if he remembered the faces of all the people he'd murdered.

"I promise, I was born and raised in Italy." A shiver ran down Katarina's back.

Bremahaven guided her now back to the hallway, his skeletal fingers rubbing her back as they walked. Katarina glanced at his face, and it was clear he was furious about something. Then there was that faint cry again. It sounded as if someone was saying "help" in Polish.

She heard Nathan's voice in her head. "Do as he says, or you won't leave."

Bremahaven guided her outside where Nathan was sitting in the car, his head back and eyes closed. Katarina knocked on the window and he jumped, his hand snapping to his side, where he had his Glock. He got out and helped her into the car.

"I'm sorry, Greta." He noticed her hands had a slight tremor.

"What did you mean when you said some didn't leave here?"

He quickly pulled the car out of the driveway and sped through the gates that opened for them. She saw the van with "Plumbing" written on the side in the distance.

"He has women brought to him. Some have not been heard from again. Most are prostitutes, so no one is looking for them. Others come from across the border, stay a while, and return."

A shiver ran down her back. She went pale and felt sick at the thought of women being killed. She leaned her head back against the car seat.

"Are you all right?" Nathan asked. "It has upset you."

She gave a weak smile. "I'm upset to think of what has happened to these women. Also, I'm just a little under the weather." She shrugged. "Italy is much warmer than Vienna. I should have worn a jacket."

As he drove, Katarina noticed he looked in his rear mirror several times, and frown lines appeared on his forehead. He relaxed when the van turned off a side street. Once they arrived back at his apartment complex, he ushered her in past the guards. It was only a three-story building, so she quickly said the address, hoping Peter, Louis, and Gregory would pick up the conversation.

As they arrived, Nathan placed the painting in a vault. They hadn't spoken much on the ride back after the conversation about the women. He called from his office phone and asked if Herr Klein had arrived at the Hotel Regina. They told him no.

She looked at the writing on the door: "Import, Export Business."

Thank God, Katarina thought, that his office was close to her hotel. She wished now she was at a cosy bar and restaurant because a chill came over her as Nathan pulled out an envelope. She could see a photo of bodies in a ditch, all wearing the yellow star. She wanted to throw up, as two children were lying on top of three adults, with two Nazis standing over the grave. One was Bremahaven. He was younger, but it was unmistakably him. Nathan quickly shoved the picture back into the envelope and placed it back into the vault.

Nathan apologized again for taking his time as he locked up the painting, escorted her out of the complex to the car and drove her to the hotel. He walked inside with her and asked if Herr Klein had arrived. This time, there was a message at the desk.

Herr Klein had phoned to say he would arrive around ten p.m. It was now seven p.m. Katarina saw Louis and Gregory sitting at the bar. They had slipped in ahead of them.

Nathan bid her goodnight and wished they could continue from the afternoon, but he had to return to the office. He said he would ring her room tomorrow to make up for not taking her to dinner. Before he left, he asked the front desk to leave Herr Klein an envelope Nathan handed them. The envelope held his and Bremahaven's phone numbers, along with the amount to be paid for the painting.

Louis and Gregory were on high alert, waiting for her. They had followed her to Nathan's from Brehmahaven's and watched his apartment building from down the street, but they took no action. It was now up to them to find Herr Klein to play this out.

Katarina waited until Nathan was out of the building to march over to the bar. With tears in her eyes, she explained to them what transpired. She went into detail about Bremahaven's lurid activities. Katarina only wanted to take a shower to get Bremahaven's touch off her, but first, she wanted to eat and have a drink.

They had the plan ready to set in motion. They'd get Herr Klein out of the way by representing themselves as Nathan. When he arrived, they wouldn't let him into the hotel. They would tell him Bremahaven had changed his mind to just listen to Nathan for instructions.

Gregory knew Herr Klein was indeed an art collector. He had galleries in Munich and Heidelberg, as well as questionable ties to the Nazi Party. He was in Amsterdam and Paris during the deportation of Jews, but they could never prove anything. He joined the Nazi party and went up in the ranks. They knew he was involved in the logistics of moving troops as well as trains to concentration camps. His hands were dirty. Somehow someone got him into the art business, and they traced it to several Nazis who all owed him favours. Gregory and Louis wanted to find out from Herr Klein the names of those Nazis and their current locations. Gregory had already settled on taking Klein and Bremahaven back to Israel. He didn't care about Nathan; that man was Louis and Peter's problem.

"I'm hungry. I need something to eat first." Katarina gazed out across the lobby. It looked empty. She left the bar and walked over to the restaurant, and Gregory and Louis followed. Peter had been out all day, setting up communications to England on Nathan, and now joined them.

She drank too much at dinner, and afterwards, Louis and Gregory helped her to her room. Gregory stayed in her room till she finished her bath. She emerged wearing the fluffy white bathrobe and climbed into bed. He leaned over over her, pulling up the comforter to her chin. He pushed the hair off her face and couldn't stop himself from leaning over and pressing a soft kiss to her cheek, telling her to sleep soundly. He felt no guilt, but it pricked at his soul to have her here and involved again. He tried to drive back his feelings to the shadow of his mind. They left her to sleep and would see her in the morning. They kept their adjoining room door open.

Gregory and Louis both called on secure lines to find out about Herr Klein.

"We can prove where he moved trains and take out three at one time," Gregory voiced his thoughts.

"He is not on the instructions," Louis answered.

"Well, he's on mine. Klein will be delivered with Bremahaven," Gregory answered.

They both settled on the beds and lay quietly for a few moments until Gregory spoke.

"Louis, as of this moment, Klein is part of the story. We'll ask him some easy questions. He should recall what he did during the war and how he got into the art business. We have a safe house here where we can take him. My agents are already awaiting their next move."

Louis looked at Gregory. "Let's find out all the information before you take them all back to Israel or kill them."

"I won't kill him. I want to see him hang or rot in a dungeon." A small muscle twitched in his cheek as he thought of the harm these two men had brought now and before the war.

"Gregory, do you want to talk about the ice in the room in regard to Katarina?"

"Not really. I know you two were together for a while. I really don't want to know the details. I do understand why, no hard feelings, except you understand where I have come from all this time." Gregory closed his eyes and shut off the light.

The next morning, they ordered room service. Gregory ached when he looked at Katarina as she joined them for breakfast. Her hair was tousled, and she wore no makeup, making her look vulnerable. She was much thinner, and her eyes looked dull, not bright as they used to be, but they still drew you in. He loved Alise and his children with all his heart, but Katarina was part of him. It was as if their blood mixed as one.

Gregory was looking at her pale face. "Kat, did Bremahaven yesterday—" Kat put up her hand to stop him.

"No, he did not. He was just an old man, but when you do bring him down, check for buried bodies. Local police should get in on it. I truly think he has murdered women that went to his home. It's in his DNA to murder."

She froze when the phone rang. She rose and went back into her room. "Hello?"

"It's Nathan. I want to make up the dinner we missed."

"You might miss your client if we're out."

"It's fine. He sent a message that he had been delayed and would be in contact. He's coming in from Heidelberg. He was supposed to have been here yesterday, so now it's still this evening. What time shall I see you?" Gregory was pointing fingers for time.

"Nathan, I have some shopping to do first. How about we meet around six? Will that leave you enough time?"

Gregory had his ear on the phone with Kat.

"Well, I was hoping we could make it an overnight date and not worry about time. After I meet with Klein, you can come to my apartment." There was silence for a few moments. "Katarina. Are you still there?"

"Yes, I was just a little surprised you still wanted to come up after meeting with Klein, but I, too, think you should stay overnight here in my room."

Nathan hesitated. "Okay, after I leave you at the hotel after dinner, I'll try to catch up with Herr Klein. Fortunately, he's staying at your hotel. I left a message at the desk telling him I'd meet him in the lobby and take him over to the office. I'll escort Herr Klein back, and then I'll come to your room."

Katarina sat on the edge of the bed. "Now what?" She whispered to Gregory as her hand covered the phone. Gregory nodded.

"I'll see you around six," She said, and Nathan hung up.

Louis was pacing. "When Herr Klein arrives at the hotel, we will have people meeting him outside to escort him away as we put our plan into action."

Gregory got up and poured some more coffee; Katarina was sitting on the edge of her bed with a faraway look in her eyes.

"We have an operative at the safe house," Gregory said. "He's our oldest man—a fellow named Jurgen—and mostly works on surveillance. He'll fit the picture perfectly. He's already been informed who he's supposed to be and knows the history. He'll meet Nathan after we intercept Klein. Jurgen will take the place of Klein.

He's a little younger than Klein, but if we put glass on him and a little gray in his hair, he should pass."

Katarina got up to dress. "Both of you should know that Nathan carries a Glock inside his coat on his left."

Gregory nodded.

"How are you going to move Klein?" Katarina asked.

"Easy. We'll meet him outside before he enters the hotel. Tell him that it was late and Bremahaven needed to move the picture right away. He'll come with us voluntarily. His driver is also his bodyguard, so we'll have to take care of him too."

Louis arched his eyebrows. "Gregory, you make it sound so easy, but nothing is ever that easy with you."

"It's going to work. Jurgen pretended to be someone else before. He's adept at this."

Katarina sighed. "I'm going to dress now. I need to shop for a very nice dress."

Louis caught her arm and handed her a vial. "Before you take Nathan up to the room, pour this into his drink. He'll sleep straight through the night."

Katarina let a long, relieved sigh. "Thank God. I was trying to figure out how to avoid actually going through with it."

Louis looked at her. "We wouldn't let that happen. I think Gregory would kill him first."

Katarina went shopping and found a slinky, dark blue silk dress with a plunging neckline. She had to keep Nathan interested until they met up with Klein.

Louis and Gregory never judged her or anyone who did their job well. Gregory had worked with enough Israeli operatives and women who knew that they had sometimes used their bodies to trap someone, but it made his blood boil to think of men touching Katarina. He and others would do anything to find those involved with the final solution. Katarina did it well, if not better, than a trained agent. Sometimes, he felt she enjoyed the challenge, that she liked using her sexuality. She'd learned it in the concentration camp and prison to stay alive, and she'd used it ever since. The image of his mother and father being led away while his sister was raped and murdered and Nicholas lay dying next to Katarina never left his thoughts, and he knew it didn't leave Katarina's either. This work they were doing now was her revenge on those who participated in the horrors of the war.

Klein and Bremahaven were both mass murderers. Even though Klein didn't work in the camps, he was still indirectly responsible by orchestrating where the Jews were, having them arrested, and telling them what trains would be moving where. He was just as involved as anyone else.

Klein and Bremahaven stole the riches from those they sent to the camps. And still, after almost thirty years, Klein was still stealing and buying looted art and was in contact with Bremahaven.

Nathan was waiting in the lobby for Katarina. He, along with every other man she passed, looked twice. Gregory and Louis looked from the back of the lobby. Yes, she was stunning.

Nathan didn't want ever to bring her back Bremahaven's estate but Bremahaven told Nathan to bring her at the first opportunity. The old man liked younger women. Nathan knew the women were tortured and raped. He'd heard the cries and knew Bremahaven buried or burnt them behind the house. Old habits die hard. Nathan thought of the old man's involvement in the war and would not put Katarina in that position. He couldn't place his finger on it, but she stirred an emotion in him of actually caring for a woman, which he had never done. Nathan wanted her to be his and his alone for a long time. Bremahaven always tried to find Jewish girls if he could. Nathan knew Bremahaven was evil, but he was paid well and didn't care what Bremahaven did in the past or the present as long as he made millions off the old man.

Nathan wanted to be with Katarina and had hoped it would be back at the apartment. But the hotel room would work. First, he had to meet Herr Klein before Bremahaven came unglued. Bremahaven hated delays.

Jurgen dressed in a nice suit, like Klein's clothing, but they made him look older than he was. They gave him grey hair and used contact lenses to turn his eyes from brown to grey. Jurgen was their oldest operative in Vienna, mostly taking pictures and putting listening devices into places. He'd had worked with Gregory before and respected his reputation. Gregory was known as one of the best. When Gregory wanted to retire, Mossad offered him more money and pleaded with him not to go, or so the rumour went. They promised to send him out into the field less, and he agreed, but now Gregory was back.

Everyone waited in the van except for Jurgen and Peter. They were at the entrance area where the vehicles pulled up. They knew the vehicle Klein was driving, so they knew it was him as soon as he pulled up.

His driver came around and opened the door. His driver had a Glock in the back of his pants. Peter came from the back, pointed his own in the driver's back and removed the man's weapon. They hadn't anticipated the driver to be so very large. He stood at six foot three and had to be two hundred and fifty pounds of solid muscle. They had to shove the weapon a little harder to get the message across. Then, they moved to Klein. Here, too, they placed a weapon at his back and told him to move across the street. They ordered one of the operatives in the van to move Klein's car. To be safe, they plunged a needle into the guard's neck with a serum to knock him out.

They shoved both men into the van, and immediate outrage came from Herr Klein. They placed hoods over their heads and tied their hands and feet tightly. Jurgen and Rivlin moved quickly to the car; Rivlin would drive. They moved the car around the corner and waited for Nathan to return. It wasn't more than thirty minutes before they saw Nathan's Porsche. He led Katarina into the lobby and returned to wait outside for the arriving car, looking at his watch every ten minutes. It was ten p.m. when Jurgen pulled up with his hat pulled low over his eyes.

The bellboy who was part of the team came down. "May I help you?"

"Yes, I'm Herr Klein. I need to check-in. Please take my luggage immediately to my room."

Nathan approached the car. "Herr Klein."

Jurgen turned to face Nathan. "Yes, and who are you?"

"I'm Nathan. I've been waiting for you."

"Oh yes, you were supposed to meet me, I thought, tomorrow?"

Nathan nodded. "We changed plans. Bremahaven wants this done sooner."

Nathan saw the irritation on Herr Klein's face. He thought that Herr Klein should be older but supposed the photos he'd seen hadn't been accurate.

Jurgen was playing the part well.

Nathan cleared his throat. "I can drive you to the apartment now so we can close this transaction. Unfortunately, I haven't been able to reach Oberstein. Herr Bremahaven would also like to meet with you tomorrow and show you other items you might be interested in."

"I'm only interested in one. I will have to see if I care to stay around tomorrow."

"Herr Klein, I promise it will be early and worth your time."

Herr Klein let out a long sigh, pushed his hair back as he took off his hat, and stared at Nathan long and hard. Gregory and Louis watched from across the street, hoping Jurgen wouldn't slip up and tip off Nathan.

"Herr Klein, Herr Bremahaven is very discreet. He knows you would like to meet young ladies. In fact, he has picked one out for you personally."

Jurgen wanted to spit in his face, but he kept his expression neutral. "It's been a long drive, so let's get this over with at your office and I'll think about tomorrow. I would like to sleep in a little."

Gregory and Louis had confiscated Klein's briefcase before they let him get into their van. They looked at the contents before Jurgen met with Nathan. In it was a check for five million dollars for the painting, paid to the business, not personally to Bremahaven. It's how he did all his business. He'd move the money later to the banks in Zurich.

"My driver and I will follow you to the business, and then you can go on your way. I would like to return to the hotel as soon as possible."

They had taken the real Herr Klein and his bodyguard back to the safe house by now, given them sedatives, and locked them in a room naked. They would be moved back to Israel to stand trial for their crimes.

Nathan led Klein/Jurgen to the office, but not before he slipped back into the hotel. While Herr Klein registered at the desk and ordered his suitcase be brought upstairs, Nathan told Katarina he would be back to wait at the bar area as she had suggested for a nightcap. The transaction would not take long.

The rooms that led to the apartment were closed. Nathan walked over to the safe and took out the wrapped painting. Jurgen unwrapped it, took out the glasses they found in the briefcase and pretended to look over the signature and paint. Nathan was pacing.

He handed Nathan the check. "All is good. Tell Bremahaven to call me in the morning to arrange a time."

Nathan placed the check into the vault, walked over to the window, moved the curtains, and looked outside onto the darkened street. He felt uneasy and couldn't figure out why. Herr Klein looked different from how Bremahaven described him. He shrugged his shoulders. He'd done what he was told. The money was in the safe, and the painting was delivered. Where was that ass, Oberstein, he thought. The check had to go back to Zurich, and he could not be reached.

"Nathan, call me in the morning," Jurgen said. Then he walked downstairs to his waiting car and driver.

Jurgen knew he was going to say yes in the morning. They needed to get into Bremahaven's compound. From what Katarina told them, they had several guards at the front gate more than the ones they observed when they first checked out the premises. Gregory would take care of the rest.

Nathan followed Klein in the car back to the hotel and watched Herr Klein go to the desk with the bodyguard. He was given a key, and Nathan noticed Katarina sitting in the lobby.

He watched Klein disappear in the elevator, then approached Katarina. She had changed into black leggings, a solid green cable sweater, and ballerina slippers.

"I'm glad you waited, Katarina."

"I thought we would have our drink first."

The vial was in her sweater pocket; she had already loosened the top. It would take effect in about twenty minutes, and she could move him to her room. He'd never remember tonight.

He ordered German Schnapps, and she ordered red wine. She placed her arms around his neck and leaned in slowly to kiss him. He placed both his hands on her hips as he kissed her back. His hand traveled up under the long sweater and rested below her bra line. His fingers moved back and forth till they were under, and he felt what he wanted to.

Before she'd wrapped her arms around Nathan's neck, Katarina had slipped the drug-filled vial out of her pocket. She hated having his hands under her sweater—even though they were in a dark corner of the bar, this was still a public place—but she had to be believable, so she kissed him with as much passion as she could muster. Her one hand unclasped the vial and tipped the substance into his drink. Then she leaned back, moved his hand from under her sweater, and took her drink.

"Let's drink to a wonderful evening upstairs." She knew he would drink quickly so they could get to her room. He finished in one swoop, almost dragged her off the chair, and walked her to the elevator. He held onto her waist as they walked back to her room. The drug wasn't working as quickly as Louis had told her, and she grew uneasy.

The minute they entered her room, Nathan pulled her sweater over her head, unclasped her bra, and pushed her onto the bed. He rubbed his hand over her and down, feeling her womanhood. Katarina closed her eyes, hoping the drug would work quicker. She didn't want this to go any further. Suddenly, he pulled his hands away and rubbed his eyes.

"What's wrong, Nathan?" Katarina asked, a wave of relief washing over her as she saw his eyes starting to close.

"I'm not sure. I feel sleepy. Here, come lie next to me for a minute." He fell hard on top of her as he pulled her close. And just like that, he closed his eyes and began a deep snore. She got up and quickly pulled her sweater back on.

Gregory, Louis and Peter returned to the hotel room and waited till Katarina knocked on the adjacent room door. She didn't care to let them know she had been almost undressed. They came into the room and helped remove all Nathan's clothing. She had to stay in the room with him. Gregory and Louis stayed awake almost all night, worried the drug would wear off sooner, putting Katarina in a bad situation. If so, she'd have to follow through; they still needed Nathan.

When Nathan woke in the morning, hopefully, he'd think he and Katarina had a good time. Gregory and Louis still needed to get into Nathan and Bremahaven's offices. Nathan's safe might contain documents that would incriminate Bremahaven. They'd hit Nathan's office first, then Bremahaven's. Jurgen would wait till Nathan called and told him he was ready to visit Bremahaven

Nathan slept until morning and woke groggy. Katarina hoped he would want to go to the office immediately so he could call Herr Klein or call from her phone. She stood at the edge of the bed, leaned over, and kissed him quickly, making sure her robe was tied snugly. He tried to have her come back to bed. She made an excuse that she had to meet a dear friend in town for breakfast.

"You were a great lover last night, but I really must get dressed."

He watched her move into the bathroom and called out, "Come back to bed. It's still early."

She smiled back at him. "I really must get ready. We made love several times last night, and I'm a bit worn out." She stood there, and he took in every inch of her.

Something was wrong, but he couldn't recall. He looked at the nightstand and saw an empty brandy bottle. He called out to her, "Did we finish the bottle of brandy?"

"Yes, we did, Nathan."

He suddenly panicked. He was naked, and his weapon was in his jacket. He got up, feeling a major headache. He walked over to a pile of clothing and breathed a sigh of relief to discover the weapon was still in his jacket. He must have taken everything off. He walked into the bathroom, where she was wearing only a bathrobe, which she now pulled tight.

"Where did you get these scars?" He asked, rubbing his hand over her back and moving the robe from her shoulders.

Katarina shook her head. "When I was young, I came off a horse, and my foot got caught in the stirrup. I was dragged over rocks and hills and caught my arms on a jagged rock that sliced it right open."

It sounded reasonable to him. He took the towel and gently wiped some water from her neck as he kissed it. He reached from behind and held the parts of her body that were intimate. He rubbed her shoulders and unfastened the tie on the robe, exposing all of her. He was pulling her to the floor when the voice came through the door.

"Room service!"

Katarina immediately pulled the robe around her, got up quickly, and walked into the bedroom.

Nathan was disappointed he still didn't recall the night before.

He dried off after a quick shower and came into the room. Katarina was dressed in last night's clothing. He recalled removing her sweater, and that was all. He just needed coffee; his head was pounding. She gave him two aspirin after he complained. He picked up his phone and called Herr Klein.

"Nathan, I have decided to join you," Jurgen said. "Tell Herr Bremahaven I will come to his place."

Nathan then placed a call to Bremahaven, who demanded he bring Katarina with him and Klein.

"I'll try, but she is just a friend. I'm not sure if she would be interested."

Nathan called Klein back to set up a time, and Jurgen said, "I need to also return to your office. It seems I left my glasses on the table. They were a gift, and I need to retrieve them. I'll meet you at six."

"I can bring them."

"I'm not sure of the exact spot, so I will meet you there, and we can then proceed in one car."

Nathan was going to object, but he heard the tone change in Klein's voice, and Bremahaven would blame him if he didn't come. A lot of money was at stake, and Nathan was expecting to receive a hefty sum. He'd have to try Oberstein again, that fool.

Bremahaven most likely had prostitutes at the house. Klein most likely had participated in the perversion they both had. He looked at Katarina and knew she wouldn't come along. He saw how upset she was being around Bremahaven.

"Katarina, I have to return to the office. If you don't mind, our client Herr Klein would like to visit Bremahaven. They have business to go over. I'd like you to come with me."

She stammered, "I'm not sure I want to see that old man again. I hate to disappoint my old friend by not showing up. I know he is your boss, but he is creepy. I heard whimpering coming from the other room."

Nathan knew Bremahaven had taken a young woman down there. He never asked what he did, nor did he want to know.

"I promise I won't let him near you."

She agreed with a sweet smile. "All right. What time?"

"I'll be back for you at four. I hope to find that fool Klein's glasses so we don't have to hunt around for them when he arrives."

Nathan went back to the office to see if the glasses were, in fact, there.

Gregory, Peter, and two others had been in Nathan's office during the night, which is why they'd needed him to be with Katarina. They went through business files and took bank ledgers with them. They would have to wait for Nathan to open the vault.

Nathan looked around the room. Something was off. He'd been an MI6 agent too long not to notice. Finally, he realized it looked as if the file cabinet had been moved. He quickly checked the files in the top drawer, and everything seemed fine, so he didn't bother checking the other. Old man Klein must be wrong about the glasses, he thought as he looked around.

He went into his apartment. Nothing looked touched, but he got this uneasy feeling that someone had been in there. He sat at his desk, wondering what to do with Katarina. He really didn't want to take her to Bremahaven's chateau. She'd be leaving Vienna soon, and he wanted her to himself. He had plans with Katarina in his mind, especially since he couldn't recall any love-making from the night before. It didn't make sense to him that a bottle of brandy would knock him out. He'd drunk a bottle before.

He felt as if he had taken drugs. But no, she couldn't have, he thought. Why would she? He was the one who approached her at the café. She paid him no mind till he went to talk to her. He sat at his desk, waiting for the phone call he needed. Finally, he went back to the hotel, ready to ring her room, when he spotted her.

She was caught by surprise when suddenly he was standing behind her by the concierge desk.

"Did you forget something?" She asked. "I thought we made

plans for later."

"Change of plans," Nathan said. "Klein will come on his own, while you and I go back to the apartment earlier."

Gregory, who silently followed her, saw the look on her face. He stood next to her, pretending to pick up touring information, as Nathan walked over to the phone to call Klein one more time.

Katarina whispered to him, "He wants me to go over sooner. He's calling Jurgen to ask him to come by at seven, and then he will take him over to Bremahaven. He'll tell Jurgen to meet him there."

Gregory told her to leave. "I'll call Jurgen and tell him seven is too late, which means you won't be in there that long with him."

Katarina rolled her eyes. "Just long enough for him to take me. I barely stopped him this morning. I don't want to have any compromising situation with him. I understand the mission, but I just can't do this."

"Katarina, I promise we will get you out in time." Gregory didn't want her in the position either, but they had little choice, and she'd agreed to all of this, as much as he hated it. It wasn't like when he worked other missions and used women or pretended to be married to agents in the field, and they played the part. These were the secrets he kept from Alise, and this was the part he didn't want Katarina to play. It had never gotten this far, but this time, it was different. Katarina couldn't control Nathan as easily as she had the others.

They called Jurgen, who answered after one ring.

"Call Nathan back," Gregory said. "Tell him you want to be over there earlier, and don't let him tell you no. We can't leave Katarina with him that long. He's still in the building, so page him."

Nathan heard the page to pick up the phone. Nathan agreed to let Jurgen come over an hour earlier. It shouldn't take that long with Katarina.

Jurgen called Peter's room and told him the changed time. "He said he'd drive to Bremahaven, but first, he wanted to show me another item that Bremahaven thought I might be interested in. He said he couldn't find my glasses, so I told him I'd look for them."

They went about their business and made their plans one more time before Nathan came for Katarina. They followed them, three to four cars behind. Nathan was a well-trained agent, and he would pick up being followed. They knew where he was going, so they turned corners and went down other streets, crisscrossing with other vehicles.

Katarina felt uneasy. Nathan wasn't himself. He was quiet. He had his hand on her knee, pushing her skirt higher till his hand rested where he wanted. When she went to push it away, he turned to her. "I wouldn't push my hand away. You told me last night what a great lover I was, so leave it there."

Gregory, Louis, and two others waited outside the apartment. They'd arrived before Nathan and had their headphones on in the van, listening in through the devices they'd planted in three rooms the night before.

Something was off, Katarina thought. There was a coldness in Nathan's eyes that she hadn't seen before, and he was gripping her arm as he pulled her out of the car and toward the apartment building. When Nathan and Katarina entered the building, Gregory and the others moved the van opposite where Nathan parked. Fortunately, the two guards weren't at the building's front door this time, and Gregory figured they must be upstairs in front of the office.

Katarina walked up the stairs slowly. Nathan was behind her, and she could feel his eyes laser-focused on her.

He cautiously opened the door, ushered her in, and pointed to a chair in his living room where he ordered her to sit.

"I'll be back in a moment. I have a few things I need to bring out of the vault for Herr Klein."

She sat there wondering what he was going to show Herr Klein. He was not gone that long.

He sauntered into the room, came up behind her, placed his hands on her shoulder, and moved down the front of her. She immediately stiffened. She thought, where were Gregory and the rest of them? She hoped they were listening and waiting. Nathan's hands were rough as he moved them back and forth on her shoulders, digging deeply into her shoulders until she winced in pain. He bent over, his teeth bared.

"Did it feel this good last night?"

He came around front. "I asked you a question. Answer me." He leaned forward and harshly kissed her, pulling her off the chair. He grabbed her hand and pushed her down the hall to the bedroom. She pulled back when they reached the door, but he pulled harder and brought her into the room, then roughly shoved her on the bed.

He had all his weight on top of her, pinning her arms down. He kissed her even harder now. She felt her bottom lip bleed.

"Stop, please stop."

"Did you ask me to stop last night?" He was now pressing harder with his hands into her shoulders around her neck. "Greta, or should I call you Katarina?" His eyes were boring into hers. "You see, I made some phone calls. There had been this rumour that when bodies were found, agents killed, or those who were caught for various reasons, there was always this mysterious blonde woman whose eyes and body were unforgettable."

"You're mistaken. I have no idea who you are talking about." Her breathing was now laboured as he pressed his body harder into hers. There was no escape. She couldn't get away from the onslaught of him. She gained all the strength she could, and sudden flashbacks came across her eyes. The camp, the Colonel, the sick sneer. They were now floating in front of her. She thought this would never happen again, and for a moment, she felt limp, like she was going to shut out what was happening to her, just like she had done so many times before. But this time, something inside her stirred. At that moment, she used all her strength and kicked him in the stomach while at the same time biting hard into his face, drawing blood. The kick pushed him off her. He stood up, yanked her off the bed, and slammed her to the floor. This time, he was even stronger.

"Was it the same last night?"

"You were not even good last night."

He slapped her hard. "Get up. Your hours are numbered."

He started to shake her as he pulled her up off the floor. He pushed her into the chair, went to his desk, and withdrew a gun, which he pointed at her. He pressed the barrel at the bottom of her chin and ran it down her chest. She couldn't make it to the door. He would shoot her before she reached it, so she sat passively.

"You think this is funny." Standing there looking at her, Katarina had a defiant smirk on her face. "Is this still amusing to you?" He ran his hand down the front of her again with the gun, stopping at her heart. She closed her eyes. He dug one hand into her shoulders as he held her against the chair for a moment. Then he dug harder as his hand ran over the front of her with the gun, touching her bare skin briefly when he saw her wince. He came from behind the chair now, pulled her hair loose, leaned over, and kissed her neck.

Suddenly, he stopped, thinking he heard something. He rubbed his hand over his hair and began to pace. Something was way off. He could feel it in his bones. Anytime Katarina showed up, others followed. He just had to wait for Klein. He couldn't figure out if she was afraid or not, as she just glared at him. "I think Bremahaven would love to have you, don't you think?" She didn't respond.

"Make yourself presentable. We're going to Bremahaven with Mr. Klein. He should be here anytime. I thought we had a lovely time this past hour, Katarina." He came in front of her, pulled her off the chair, and kissed her hard, his hands exploring with haste, wanting to humiliate her one more time. She just stood there and closed her eyes; he still held the gun in his hand. She didn't dare try to run; she knew he would shoot her.

"Herr Bremahaven doesn't care about you," she said with a coldness in her voice that showed no fear. It surprised him. He was the one with the gun. He pulled her to the door with one hand holding tightly to her arm. He dug in hard; he could see he was hurting her and enjoyed it. She stopped at the door before he opened it.

"He would sell you to the highest bidder," she continued. "You're a traitor. You're not going to receive the money he promised you. He doesn't like those who betray their own. It's his old Nazi way of thinking. You sold out MI6. He would never have done that in WWII, so he doesn't respect you."

There was a loud knocking on the door of his office. Nathan smiled at her, his expression dripping with evil.

"Katarina, we can continue this little charade at Bremahaven's. Shall I help you button your blouse?" He once again ran the gun down her chest. She stepped back as he let go of her arm, and he put his arm around her waist with the gun in her back. He kept it there as they walked out of the room.

"This time, you might not be seen again if it is up to Bremahaven and me. You'll disappear like so many others have at Bremhaven's. He learned his skills from the concentration camps. But first, tell me, who are you working with, and where are they?"

There was still the knocking on the door, and Nathan wondered where his guards were. They must be downstairs. Now that he knew this woman was Katarina, there might be some issues. She wouldn't be working alone, so he opened the door cautiously.

Jurgen walked in and saw the gun and thought, *Jesus, what did he do? Gregory will kill him, there is no doubt.* Katarina didn't look at herself. She looked terrified, and she shook her head at him.

"Herr Klein, it's good of you to come," Nathan said. "You are right on time. My friend and I had some catching up before you came, so the timing worked out perfectly."

Jurgen looked at Nathan hard. "Mein Herr, why the gun? I do not like guns. Do we have a problem?"

Nathan shook his head. "No, this is someone for Bremahaven, and she is an unwilling participant." He pushed Katarina forward to the middle of the room, his eyes fixated on her. "She's going with us, but first, go over to my desk and look for your glasses."

Jurgen walked over to the desk. He noticed the gun still pointed at Katarina's back. On the desk now was a necklace of emeralds and diamonds and a matching ring and earrings. There was a picture of a woman from a concentration camp and a picture of her home where the jewellery was taken. Her eyes filled with despair as she stood in front of officers, including Bremahaven, trying to cover her nakedness.

"Bremahaven thought you might like to see who it came from. He knows how much you like pictures, and he has a whole lot more to share with you at the chateau."

Nathan was staring hard at Herr Klein. "Herr Klein, you seem too young to have known about Bremahaven's indulgence in the war."

Jurgen cleared his throat, thinking quickly. "I guess my grandfather and Bremahaven did not tell you I took his place. He isn't well."

Jurgen quickly walked over to the desk to avoid any more questions. He picked up the necklace and pretended to admire it as he walked with it to the window. When he held it up to the light, that was the signal that the others needed to come in, but it would be difficult if the guards were at the front door this time.

Nathan heard the footsteps and his guards firing at someone. Jurgen reached for Nathan's gun as Nathan pointed it at Katarina, and Jurgen was certain Nathan was going to shoot her. Jurgen brought the gun down as he grabbed Nathan's wrist and fired it, hitting his own shin. They struggled as Katarina stood in terror, blood pounding through her veins. Her heart hammered in her chest, and she was now vibrating. The next bullet came right next to her leg. The wood splintered and pierced the flesh of her leg. She screamed as she looked down at the large piece of wood that was stuck in her leg. More bullets were hitting the window now, and a large lamp fell to pieces.

They heard the door opening, and in a rush, Nathan's bodyguards ran up the steps but were stopped quickly as they fell into the room with a shot in the head. Peter and Gregory were right behind them as they heard the shots.

Nathan was fighting over the gun with Jurgen as both were now on the floor. A shot rang out. Nathan had been hit in his leg and had dropped to the floor. Louis moved to Katarina. Gregory pulled Nathan up, wanting to kill him right then and there, but they needed him to get Bremahaven. The minute he looked at Katarina, he felt a rush of insanity enter him as he saw the blood seeping from her leg. He pointed the gun at Nathan, but Louis screamed at him not to shoot.

The only thing that stopped Gregory from pulling the trigger was that Katarina's leg needed attention. He told Jurgen to tie Nathan's hands for now, ran down the hall, and found towels. He ripped them to pieces as he ran back. Jurgen had stuffed a towel in Nathan's mouth and tied him to the chair, and he and Gregory pulled the two bodies fully into the room. Jurgen never got used to the blood part of the job, and he tried to look away at the brain matter now splattered across the wooden floor. They were not sure who heard the shots or might have called the police. He, too, was now looking at his wound. It wasn't too bad; Katarina had worse. Gregory pulled the splintered wood from her leg and wrapped it tightly after pouring some vodka he'd spotted on a table over it.

Louis and Gregory both now tried to stop the stem of blood from

Katarina's leg as well as Jurgen's and Nathan's. Gregory handed Jurgen the rest of the towels to place on Nathan's leg.

"What took you so long?" Katarina asked as she winced in pain.

"We didn't hear anything from you, so we waited for Jurgen to signal us to come up," Louis replied.

"Well, that didn't happen. He figured out who I was. Obviously, you didn't place listening devices in his bedroom."

Gregory was trying to help her stand. He didn't want to hear about the bedroom, knowing something awful might have happened.

She looked over at Nathan, who was glaring at Gregory and her. She realized they would not have put a bug in his bedroom. Why would they?

Nathan saw the look on Gregory's face and turned to him. "She did very well in the bedroom but wasn't as good as some."

Gregory raised his gun again, but Louis came and lowered it. "We'll deal with him later. MI6 has a nice cell waiting for him."

Katarina limped back to the bedroom, dripping on the oak floor. She needed to clean herself up. She gathered her purse and sat on the edge of the bed with her head in her hands and started to cry. She waited a few minutes and went to the bathroom to splash cold water on her face. She walked back into the office dragging her leg, and they noticed immediately she had been crying.

The vault was open, and Gregory walked into a treasure trove. The space was filled with paintings, jewelry, pictures, and documents of those who had been put on trains to their deaths. Gregory walked back into the room, moved to the window, and motioned for the others to come up.

They walked in with trepidation, having heard all the gunshots. They saw the guards lying prone on the floor, the blood seeping into the floor.

Louis looked at the other two operatives. "Move the bodies to another room. Take everything out of the vault and move it to the van. We'll sort through the stolen items later and hope we can find some living soul to whom they belong. The pictures are evidence."

They took out Nathan's gag, and the man spoke with laboured breath. "You're not Klein, and I'd suspected it from the start. You're too young." He glared at Katarina. "She was the one that got me off guard."

Gregory handed Nathan the phone. "Call Bremahaven and tell him you're running late but will be there soon with Herr Klein." Gregory held a gun at Nathan's head as Nathan spoke on the phone. They could hear Bremahaven through the phone.

"Well, don't take much more time. I already had to remove one woman because she wasn't into our kind of games. We still have three waiting down in the basement. What did Klein think of the necklace?"

Gregory pushed the gun harder into Nathan's temple. "He's looking forward to seeing what else he can purchase."

"Good. Tell him to have his chequebook ready and be prepared for some fun. Bring back that young woman. I'm sure you don't mind sharing." Bremahaven hung up.

Jurgen looked at Louis and Gregory. "How do we get in without Nathan?"

Louis turned to Nathan. "We can kill you here, or you can help us get onto the grounds and into the house. Katarina said there was an elaborate combination and code words to the guards. If you give one wrong code, you're a dead man. If you cooperate, we'll hand you back to the Brits and let them deal with you. Take your pick."

Nathan realized he was dealing with individuals as good at this game as he was. He knew that there were various ways to escape once he got to the grounds. He had enough money. What did he care about the old man? Katarina was right about one thing, though: Bremahaven didn't care about him. The realization made him angry, and he turned to Katarina.

"Katarina, you're getting old," He spat. "The allure won't last. You were even a stretch for me. I like them younger. Just remember how good it felt and how much you enjoyed each button coming open. Let it burn in your memory." Gregory put the gun to Nathan's temple again, but it was Katarina who spoke.

"Just let it be for now," She told Gregory. "We need to get into the compound. He only wishes something happened between us, but it's only his fantasy." She glared at Nathan, almost shivering at the thought of how he touched her, how she once again felt violated. There was no need for any of them to know what happened.

There was dead calm on the streets as they ushered Nathan into the driver's seat. They were able to stop the bleeding for now on both Katarina and Jurgen—fortunately, both only had flesh wounds. When they got in the car, Gregory took a hard swipe at Nathan's temple with the butt of the gun for his comment about Katarina. Nathan's eyes were starting to swell, and a trickle of blood ran down his face.

Bremahaven's guards saw nothing out of the ordinary as the

group pulled up to the gates. The car was dark, and they couldn't see Nathan's swollen eyes. They were told that there would be four of them. Jurgen sat in the back with Katarina while Gregory was up front, discreetly holding the gun at Nathan's side. Louis and Peter were in the trunk. The guards only glanced inside after Nathan gave the code words; they knew Bremahaven was anxiously awaiting Nathan's arrival. One guard pushed a button, and the gate swung open with a metallic clank.

The house and the grounds were lit up. They all felt something imperceptible, like a cold hand on their back. Two men stood at the door. They released the trunk, and Louis and Peter silently slipped out as they made their way to the door from the side of the house.

The two guards made no effort to conceal the automatics on their shoulders. They knew Nathan and had seen Katarina with him the previous day. They ushered them in as they entered the hallway. It was then that Jurgen and Gregory used the silencer and shot both guards. They quickly moved the bodies to a hallway closet. Peter and Louis followed.

"Where is he?" Gregory whispered to Nathan.

"Down this hall. It connects to a small cottage. That's where you'll find him." Gregory pushed Nathan as hard as he could with a punch to the back, the gun never leaving his back.

They slowly made their way to a cottage that was really the size of a house. They went inside and knocked on the door to the library, where they saw Bremahaven taking items from his wall safe. He turned and was startled as he saw Nathan's blood-stained shirt. Gregory looked into the soulless, pitiless blue eyes.

"Nathan, what is this?"

There was a conciliatory tone in Nathan's voice. "Your end is upon you, old man. I would suggest you go quietly. These men will take you back to Israel to stand trial with Herr Klein, who is most likely waiting for you in the next cell."

Bremahaven made no movement, his eyes becoming belligerent. He realized he was not in a good position and had to bargain with them. Everyone wanted money, and a lot of it. Footsteps echoed in the hall.

Bremahaven looked at them and trembled with fury. "Let me go, and I will give you all the money you will ever need in your lifetime."

A woman burst into the room, the French doors from the side garden slamming open, her Browning Hi-Power pistol pointing at her father. Her eyes swam with hatred. Gregory immediately grabbed Bremahaven and held the gun at his head.

"Ingred, shoot them," Bremahaven yelled. Bremahaven's eyes were wide, and spittle came from his mouth as he shouted and tried to move away from Gregory.

"I don't think so, Papa. He'll have to wait to kill you because I'm first." She stood about five foot four, with dark black hair and large blue eyes. Her skin was tanned and thin as a rail, but her eyes were filled with hate. She looked at Gregory holding the gun as she aimed her gun at her father's chest. "I just stumbled over another woman you killed. No more, do you hear?" She screamed as the gun went off right into her father's chest. He slumped next to Gregory as the crimson blood seeped into the Oriental rug. Bremahaven screamed in pain as his daughter smiled and reached to shoot again.

The old man clutched his bleeding chest with one hand and reached for her with the other. "Why?"

"Because I saw your will," Ingred said. "You left almost everything to your mistress in Zurich. Every penny, every home we have. All you left me was a painting that was ripped from someone's home. I saw the pictures of what you did and what you were. Then I found the tortured souls in the basement and more pictures, all buried in the forest. You couldn't get enough of torturing people in the concentration camps. I think you killed my mother, too."

She aimed the gun again, and Gregory held up his hand to her and spoke softly. "Don't shoot. We will give him a trial and punishment for all he did. You can rip up the will. You're his daughter, so no one will question that the homes belong to you. Just let us return the stolen items to their families, and we'll never breathe a word." Gregory moved slowly towards her. Her eyes were glistening over.

"Okay, but not for me. For my children and his grandchildren. I know now he had to have killed my mother. She just disappeared. He tried to convince me she decided she didn't want to be married to him any longer and just left."

Suddenly, Nathan was behind her. He'd moved silently away while everyone's attention was on the woman. He couldn't reach the French doors, so he had to take another way out. He hit Ingred's solar plexus, then punched her in the nose. He wrenched the gun from her hand and fired two shots as he pushed her to the ground and made for the door. The bullets just missed Louis and Gregory.

Nathan's eyesight was clouding over from the previous hit to his head, but he rushed out the door towards the river. Footsteps were catching up to him, so he turned and shot, but his bullet went wide. Gregory caught Nathan at the edge of the river, and they both fell into the water as they wrestled. Nathan was shooting under the water and hit Gregory in the arm. Crimson rose to the surface. Gregory was trying to calculate how many more rounds Nathan had. He still had amazing strength, even with his wound. After tumbling, they both came up for air, and he caught Nathan from behind and dragged him out of the water.

Still holding the gun, Nathan aimed again at Gregory and missed. Nathan fell on his back; he was bleeding from his chest. He lay at the edge of the river. Gregory pulled himself out of the water and made it to the lawn before he dropped to his knees, coughing up water. Katarina ran to him and tried to lift him off the ground.

Louis caught up with Ingred, who was making her way to Nathan on the banks of the river. Peter and Jurgen stayed behind with Bremahaven. Nathan was crawling back to the water with his gun still in his hand. He tried to get another shot off, but the gun was empty. Ingred reached him and kicked him in the ribs, then dragged him into the water. Gregory couldn't get up, and he watched Ingred using all her strength as Nathan tried to move away from the kicks. Louis stood and just watched.

Gregory sat on his knees, looking up at the stars, trying to catch his breath. He lowered himself again to the ground, and Katarina knelt beside him, holding him in her arms. His breathing was laboured, and he wished he were younger. Ingred kicked Nathan toward the water and tried to drown him, but he slowly floated into the river out of their reach. They all thought he must surely be dead. Katarina stood back and watched. *Revenge is sweet*, Katarina thought. They heard Ingred screaming at him as he floated downstream.

"You bastard! This is for all the times my father gave me to you while he watched through his peepholes. You both are perverted, evil men."

Louis walked over to her. MI6 would miss putting Nathan in a cell, he thought. They saw no movement, only a lot of blood swirling alongside him as he moved downstream.

"Is Bremahaven dead?" Gregory asked. He looked at Ingred, who peered at the river. They helped Gregory up. They all looked awful, and blood was draining out of Gregory's arm. He shivered; the night was cold as the wind picked up. The leaves were swirling around him, and he looked ghostly.

Ingrid turned and slowly walked toward them. "I'll take you to his two other safes. I know the combinations, and you'll find everything to take my father to trial, plus the pictures of the murdered woman and three that are in the basement and still alive. Gregory, I will get you some dry clothing."

They didn't speak as they made their way to the house. Jurgen had helped Bremahaven to the sofa, and Peter glared at this man, who had caused so many to suffer. Bremahaven looked at them defiantly with eyes like hot coals, showing no remorse. Jurgen had stuffed towels into his chest. He wasn't going anywhere as his breathing was laboured, and the wound was extensive, but he would live to see his day in court. Peter just looked at him with revenge in his own eyes.

Gregory and Katarina looked at Bremahaven as they made their way back to the house. They both felt the chill of ice in their veins, knowing what he had done to so many and continued even now. Katarina and Gregory found two chairs to rest on as they both leaned their heads back, looking at the ceiling painted with a beautiful mural of flowers and pasture. Gregory looked over at Katarina and saw the silent tears running down her face. He took her hand and held it tight. Her leg was now very swollen; she needed a doctor.

They went through Bremahaven's safe and desk, where he had saved his perverted memories. They removed paintings and jewellery. Bremahaven had several cars in his eight-car garage. On two of the cars, Ingred showed them the vehicles' hidden compartments her father had used to move paintings to other countries when they were sold. Katarina watched while the crew worked. There were so many more items to be moved that they'd have to make another trip. They sent what they could back to the safe house with Jurgen in a brand-new Porsche. A couple more guards rushed toward them, and Peter shot and killed them both. They moved the bodies to a garden shed for the Vienna police to sort out later.

They asked if Ingred would take them to the bank and empty out the deposit boxes. Then she could call the police and report everything her father had done and point them to the shed with the bodies. She could pretend she had just returned home to find the chaos and assumed her father had escaped from some individuals who came for him. They gave her pictures to share with the police as proof of her father's torture of girls, as well as pictures from the concentration camps and grave sites. There were so many pictures that they had enough to convict him in Israel.

They found the three girls who had been smuggled from Romania. They were taken to the train station with money and told to find a consulate. Since they were removed from a communist country, they needed protection.

Bremahaven had a private plane, and they would drive to Lienz, Austria, and board his plane to move him. Ingred was good friends with the pilots and made the arrangements to be there in two days. She told the pilots that she was now their new boss. Ingred didn't actually need her father's fortune. Her mother had been wealthy in her own right and left her everything with legal protections set up to ensure Bremahaven couldn't touch it. Bremahaven didn't know that until he killed Ingred's mother and couldn't access her millions. Ingred had made good use of the money, investing it wisely and ensuring that her children were safe in boarding schools in the United States.

"You can't be serious, Gregory," Katarina said when Gregory suggested she come with them to Lienz. "I'm done. Look at us. You're bleeding, I'm hurt, we need to see doctors. Take me to the hotel. I'm going back to Berlin. You all can clean all this up. I almost had to kill Nathan myself because all of you never thought to wonder why you didn't hear anything or what was happening. Do you have any idea how scared I was?"

She stopped herself. She didn't want them to know. She went into the other room and just sat there. Gregory followed her, taking her by the shoulders. She was shaking, and tears suddenly came to his own eyes.

"What happened? Tell me, tell me." He took a deep breath and exhaled, his heart beating fast just thinking she was hurt.

"Nothing! He just got rough with me. Go home, Gregory. Go home to your wife. This is the last time. Neither you, Peter, nor Louis will ever call on me again. I'm done."

He sat and gathered her in his arms, kissing her wet face. She cried like she had never cried before. He looked at the bruises on her wrist, and her leg was swelling even more. No, he would not call on her again. This was not a world she should be in. She could heal her soul if all of them had stayed out of her life. Maybe she could even find happiness.

He held her and didn't want to let go. He pushed the hair away from her face and held her gaze. "I will make this right for you, I promise."

"Will you love me again? Come to me when I need you."

He buried his head in her shoulder as she stroked the back of his head. He simply nodded.

They all went back to the hotel and called a doctor they had used before—one who didn't ask questions. He patched them up as much as he could and told both Katarina and Gregory to rest for a few days. The doctor shook his head, seeing all the scars on Gregory's body.

Louis promised to help Ingred. Katarina and Gregory, for two days, kept to themselves. Louis and Peter helped sort out all the boxes in the banks. To Ingred's relief, the original will was in one of the boxes, and she could tear up the second one, which hadn't yet been signed and sent to the lawyers. They kept Braverman alive in the same basement where he tortured and killed. For two days, their doctor tended his wounds, smiling at him and letting him know a Jewish doctor was fixing him up.

Herr Klein was already on his way to Israel to stand trial for his crimes, and soon Bremahaven would follow. The deposit boxes were filled with more pictures, names of those who had been deported, and jewels. The also found the original title to Bremahaven's house in Lienz, showing that it belonged to a Jewish family who might still be living. Ingred decided to try to find them and reunite them with their home. Jurgen had taken a liking to her, and she'd go and make a new life for herself and her two young children whom Nathan had fathered. They'd never find out about him. She now wondered at the last moment before he floated down the river, did he move his hand

and did his eyes open? No, it had to be her imagination. She mentioned it to Peter, and he said they hoped he was dead, but if not, Peter would find him again.

Gregory and Katarina indulged themselves for the last time with Vienna coffee, Sachertorte, and chocolate cake with apricot filling. The two went to the café one last time. They had not spoken much in the last two days while they stayed at the hotel. He looked in on her, but she didn't want to talk. She didn't want to care for him or anyone. He would sit in the chair the first two nights and just watch her sleep.

Looking at him now, she had to ask, "Gregory, why didn't you fight for me?"

The question stunned him for a moment. "Katarina, I always fought for you. We've gone over this so many times. I wanted a family, a new beginning, but you didn't."

She gave him a genuine smile. "I'm going to move on. I'm not sure what I'll be doing or where I'll be going, but you always find me."

He took her hand in the café for the last time.

"Gregory, there is nothing for me to go back to in the States. I'll stay here on the continent and find a place to find some peace. I'll most likely go back to Italy for a while. I so love the Italian villa. There are no ghosts, no bad feelings. It is a peaceful place."

They sat for a long time, lingering over their coffee. Katarina was almost in tears and felt like she was always saying goodbye to him. She reached for his hand. "Gregory, be well and take care of your family."

He swallowed hard. Once again, he didn't want to let her go. He watched her rise from the table and walk out of the café. This time, she didn't look back for that last glance. He saw her climb into the car they had sent for her from his hotel room a few hours before. She'd been ten thousand German Marks under her room door. Ingred left her a note telling her how much she appreciated her help.

Jurgen was told to take her to the airport. She made a reservation to fly to Paris and was not returning to Berlin. She left Louis, Gregory, and Peter at the hotel. Looking at Peter and Louis in the lobby in a stern voice, she reiterated her feelings again. "Do not call me to help you ever again. I'm done. Do not! I will disappear, and neither of you will ever find me."

"We won't, Kat," Peter said, "but Gregory will always find you, make no mistake."

Chapter 18

Natalie closed the journal, sat on her bed, and cried. She dried her tears, silently went back, and left the journal at the exact spot. Her mother would never know she read those pages.

Natalie could only think of one thing after reading her mother's journal. Kat altered the course of everyone's life. How could she betray Natalie's father in such a way? Why could she not love him as she did Gregory?

Later that morning, Kat must have come out because she and the journal were both gone.

Elvie wanted the whole family to come to Paris because this might be the last time they were all together as a family. They came for the week, Hans, her grandparents, Alex and the new baby. Natalie spent time walking with her grandparents to the parks. The trio sat in cafés, enjoying the end of August. They all left, leaving Natalie with Elvie and Gertrude.

Katarina was polite as Alex let her see the baby girl, who reached out to Katarina. She took the child reluctantly in her lap and seemed to enjoy herself for a little while. She spoke politely to Alex and Natalie, wishing Natalie well for her years to come in school.

Katarina wanted to leave Natalie some of her own pieces of jewellery, a necklace her mother had given her and a small diamond bracelet. While trying to find a spot for them in Natalie's suitcase, she found the telegram from Lucca. *Stupid girl*, she thought. He was going to break her heart, and she just had a feeling. She left Natalie a handwritten note in her suitcase, "Natalie, I have broken your father's heart, and I have had mine broken. Do not let this man Lucca break yours. Walk away now."

At this time, Natalie called early one Saturday morning, knowing Lucca would be home. He was excited to hear from her. They spoke and couldn't wait to see each other. But the end of the conversation made her shiver like there was ice in her stomach.

"Natalie, I must tell you the strangest thing that happened," Lucca said. "Your friend Ruth was at our home last night. She said she had car issues and felt it was safe to stop at our house. Did you tell her where I lived? I wasn't home, but my mom entertained her and told me she was a lovely person. Did you know she knew our address?"

Natalie stammered, "No, I never told her."

"Strange," He replied. They spoke a little longer before she had to hang up as she heard her aunt calling her. Natalie ended the call shaken.

"I heard you on the phone, Natalie," Her mother said when she entered the kitchen, ignoring Gertrude's looks to her to be quiet.

"Yes, I was talking to Lucca." There was sadness in Natalie's eyes.

"Natalie, just a little advice: they always leave you. There is always someone better, prettier, and who gives them what they want when you can't. Do not be surprised when you go back and everything has changed."

"That's enough, Katarina." Gertrude was furious that Kat upset Natalie. She'd seen the girl's body stiffen and her face go pale.

"Oh, please, Gertrude, be honest with her. You know as well as anyone, men leave, they cheat and have children with their mistresses."

Natalie stood up from the chair and spoke to her mother harshly. "That's enough, Katarina. Just leave us alone and go on your way. You're the last person who should be giving advice on anything."

Katarina gave Natalie a weak smile. "Natalie, in the end, you really are a good girl. I do hope you have a lifetime of happiness." She turned and walked out of the room.

They still had a week in Paris and spent their time shopping and exploring. Natalie was able to buy a jacket from Chanel House. Elvie had changed the bedroom to a very Parisian motif. All the windows were draped in the most beautiful light-blue taffeta and trimmed with thick lace. Natalie would miss this glorious bedroom. The trees outside were thick with rich green leaves, and she looked out on the canopy from her window as birds always chirped. Elvie told her how sad it was when the Germans came. It was dark even in the daytime. Life seemed dark, and her only light was Heinz, whom she wished Natalie could have met. They explored the narrow cobblestone streets and ate so many chocolate croissants that she felt she gained ten pounds. She would ask Aunt Elvie to tell her what happened during the war. They'd sit over coffee while Elvie related the tales, Natalie writing them all down in her journals.

Going home, they always passed the same homeless man with a basket with two puppies inside who looked like Lassie. She looked at both her aunts as they were coming home from Sarah's restaurant.

They couldn't stand seeing the sweet pups in that basket, so Gertrude and Elvie took both. Natalie named them and promised to give the puppies to her grandfather and uncle Hans.

When they went to Café de La Paix, located on the Place de L'Opera, Natalie would visualize and make up stories for her aunts of what it might have been like in 1862. Paris with its unmistakable smell of French bread and croissants. The smell would always stay in her memory, but her aunts would be memorialized as Natalie wrote a short story right in front of them. She told them someday she would write books about these places and about animals.

The last week was magical; she realized she didn't want to leave Europe. Maybe she could come back and study here. Then, her thoughts went to Lucca and her father. She couldn't leave them. She promised herself she would find a job after college that would bring her here several times a month. Her favourite places in order, she would tell Elvie, were Italy, France, and Germany. Elvie asked why Germany wasn't first on the list.

Natalie would always frown. "Memories there make me sad. I don't want to be in a place that makes me sad. I have my favourite memories with my grandparents, Gertrude and Hans, but the things my mother put me through bring me pain in my heart. It's difficult to see the Berlin Wall and know she left me on the other side. If it hadn't been for Gregory, I might have ended up there. She killed my kitten; the abuse, I just don't want to remember. But I promise I will be in and out of Berlin with visits. I promise."

Elvie told her, "That's running away," but she understood what Natalie was saying. It was difficult for her to go back to Lyon or pass the church Heinz and she was married in. She felt like running, too.

Natalie sat for a long time on the balcony, watching the birds and squirrels while listening to the hustle and bustle of street life. There was a part of her that couldn't shake what her mother said. Lucca's voice rang in her ears and mind, "Did you give your friend our address?" She didn't recall giving Ruth his address. Why, of all places, did she have car trouble and knock on their door?

She saw her mother before she left. As she passed the bedroom and saw her closing the suitcase, her mother was dressed in black ankle pants, beautiful gold-coloured shoes, a silk shirt with flowers, and a black jacket. Her hair was pulled back tightly. She wore no makeup, but she was beautiful regardless. Natalie knew she looked nothing like her mother. She wished she had some of Kat's beauty that people called stunning and turned every head. She heard Louis tell Elvie one night how alluring and bewitching she was to men. Katarina was older now but still pulled people in, like when she was in her twenties.

Katarina looked up and saw Natalie, who gave her a reluctant smile at the door. And for a moment, Katarina smiled at Natalie.

"Natalie, I'm sorry I'm not the mother you had hoped for, but I'm the person who can give you advice. Do not let this young man of yours tell even a small lie because he will never tell you the truth again. Trust me on this. Life moves on, we make choices, and I know you would like to see me with your father, but it won't happen. He's a wonderful man. One of the best, the most honest, the most loyal. It's just fate entering one's life. Somethings you can't change or wish away. I'm truly sorry, Natalie. Move on with your life. Don't think I will change or you will ever get the phone call where I tell you I love you. It won't happen to you or any of my children. Please don't start tearing up, it doesn't become you. I see in you a little bit of me. You're strong, and you will do well in your life."

"Katarina, where are you going?" Tears glistened on Natalie's lashes. Despite everything her mother had done, she felt this tremendous empathy for her.

"I'm not sure. It will be where no one will find me for a long time. I'll disappear as I have done many times when life and my memories become unbearable." Her mind wanted to release seeing torture and dead bodies. She didn't want to see the dead bearing down on her in her dreams. She especially wanted to escape from those who said they loved her because she ended up hurting them. It was better to leave for a time. It was what she did best, she thought.

"Natalie, I run. I leave memories behind, thoughts that can plunge me into a dark place. I just leave."

Natalie looked at her mother. She wanted to call her "Mother," but the word could not pass her mouth as she looked at Katarina, thinking how Kat could never shake her sadness. She clung so tightly to her memories that she stopped living. There was this howling emptiness that no one could help.

Gertrude and Natalie watched Katarina leave the apartment with several suitcases. She said goodbye to Elvie and told her she would eventually be back. They watched from the balcony as she limped to the taxi, the wound clearly still bothering her.

Katarina arrived in Italy, where she always found peace. She stopped for a cold soda before getting on the train from Lucca, Italy. She was lost in her memories as the landscape went by her. She had one of the hired hands greet her as they moved across the area with a cart and donkey to the villa.

When she reached their property, the sea was glittering like small stars floating on the surface. She looked up and saw the villa perched on the hill, sitting among groves of olive and lemon trees. The grapevines were heavily laden, sitting on one of the richest vineyards in the area; the cabernets would be exceptional this year. Workers were in rows as she walked up the well-tended path lined with flowers. All around the perimeter of the structure, she looked at the worn, oatmeal-coloured stone and walked into the coolness of the living room. The terracotta floor tiles were cool under her feet, and the walls had been painted to a soft yellow. The doors were open to the pool, and the flowers on the terrace were well-tended. Everyone in the family had an attachment to this property. It was a place of peace.

Katarina could smell bread coming from the kitchen. The staff knew she was coming. All the windows were open, and she walked over to the bar, poured herself a nice glass of their wine from two years ago, swirled it in her glass, and looked at the richness of the colour. She relaxed on the soft sofa and closed her eyes. She could stay lost here, no one would ever bother her again. She knew somewhere in that time Gregory would seek her out again, but she would not go with him. She thought she heard the laughter of Anthony and Amelia. She thought she could smell Gregory, his skin smelled like a light musk. She just closed her eyes. She wanted the good memories.

Natalie was troubled as she packed her suitcases to go home. She looked at the vase she picked up for Lucca's mother, handmade Limoges. She hoped she liked it. She won the heart of Lucca's father but not his mother. She wasn't sure why.

There were many tears at the airport as Gertrude promised to see her at Christmas in Florida. She hoped her father would come again so they could stay longer.

The flight seemed endless, but she loved Pan Am. Hans made sure she was sitting in first class. The stewardesses were all so attentive. Each one of them looked like they belonged on fashion magazine covers.

She knew her father would be picking her up at the airport. There was a long break in Boston with a plane change, and she slept most of the way to Philadelphia to arrive refreshed.

Her father met her at the luggage claim. He was waving to her, and he looked unwell again. When she left, he had gotten some life back in his eyes.

"Good Lord, child, you left with one suitcase, and you're coming back with three."

"Lots of clothing and gifts, Father. Bottles of real German beer in one of those suitcases."

They placed the suitcases in the trunk and pulled out of the parking lot to heavy traffic. He was pensive, and his lips set tight.

"What's wrong, Dad?"

He sighed. "Natalie, you'll be upset. We moved while you were gone. I sold the house and moved us into an apartment for a short time. It's a little crowded with the dog and cat, but it's only for a few months. I bought some acreage with a cottage on it that's being fixed up. It needs new plumbing."

"Where? Why?" She was starting to breathe hard, and she didn't understand.

"Your mother needed money. The house was too big for just the two of us, and I'll end up by myself once you finish college. You'll most likely move to wherever your job takes you. I'll take you over to see the cottage. It's very close to the old house."

"What will Lucca think, moving from a house to here? Why did you need to send her money? My God, Dad, she has enough. She lives all over Europe. Why are you always falling for her stories? She betrayed you. Why do you love her?"

He saw tears running down her face. "Natalie, don't cry."

"Why can't we move into the farmhouse in Delaware?"

"I thought of that too, but it's a long way for you to drive to school and me for work. Besides, my brother moved in with his new wife. She's got two children from her first marriage, and they have one on the way. They needed it until they found their own place."

"Natalie your Mother called, she needs money, I was thinking of moving to the house in Delaware for a while and selling were we are now."

Natalie flared with anger and was tempted to tell him where Katarina had really sustained the injury, but she didn't want to hurt him. "Well, you know she isn't opening a school here, and she can't dance regardless. She tried that once before from what Aunt Gertrude has told me. Why would you not demand she come back and open one here? I just don't understand. You're giving in to her again, making her first over me. How is that fair?" She started to cry again.

She could hear her father's dog, Dudley, barking he adopted Dudley after ther Mother left.h He greeted her with a wagging tail and sloppy kisses. Why he had a basset hound baffled her. When he brought the puppy home, he told her it was found in an empty lot, and he couldn't just leave it there. Her grandmother had given her a kitten, a Maine coon, who was sitting on the sofa.

"Did you see your Mother much?"

Natalie sighed. "Yes, and nothing in her has changed. She's still a mean, heartless person who only cares about herself."

"Did you see the wound on her leg?"

Natalie nodded. "It was a large gash, deep, swollen and red. She made sure to let me know that she only gave birth to me, and that's as far as our connection goes."

She looked at her father defiantly. She was tired of his always protecting Katarina. It seemed all men did, including Uncle Hans. God, she was so tired of it.

"I need to walk, Dudley." He looked at Natalie with a sadness she had never seen before.

She needed to call Lucca and her grandmother, who was in the house in Delaware. She always came home at the end of August. She enjoyed seeing the last of summer's bloom. Her grandfather stayed on the Eastern Shore of Maryland till October. They went back for Oyster Season in November for a week.

She called Lucca first, but he wasn't home or in his dorm. She spoke briefly with her grandmother and asked how her horse was doing. Then she called Sister Agnes and told her about her trip. She told her about her Father wanting to move them to the house in Delaware, it was so far from Lucca, she told Sister Agness. Sister Agnes could hear the desperation in her voice.

Then she told Sister Agnes every detail she'd read in her mother's journal. Sister Agnes gasped a few times during the retelling. Natalie briefly mentioned the conversation she'd had with Lucca. Sister

Agnes didn't approve of such an early commitment, and she didn't trust Ruth. She'd seen her talking outside the school with Natalie and felt there was something evil about her. She felt terrible thinking these thoughts after all—they were just young girls—but it was the look Ruth had for Natalie as she walked away. Sister Agnes had caught that look in her eyes change, and the smile she gave Natalie disappeared in exchange for a look of dislike.

When they hung up, Sister Agnes was troubled for Natalie. It had been long since she poured her heart and soul out to her. Sister Agnes held so tight on that last day of school. She could never recall crying for a child leaving school, but she didn't want her to go. Jane promised she would look out for Natalie. There again, Sister Agnes warned Jane to be aware of Ruth. There was something in this girl that frightened her.

Natalie paced all day after unpacking, waiting for Lucca. She glanced out of the window and saw his car pulling up. She ran down the steps to greet him and fell into his arms as he got out. She hugged him tightly. The rhythm of their hearts could be felt; there was a long, deep kiss, and she could feel he missed her.

"Lucca, let me take you to the house we'll be moving into. It is the cutest house. We won't be living here much longer. Thank you for helping my father move. It was a kind gesture. First, let me go upstairs and bring down the gift I got for your mother."

She ran upstairs and was down in a flash. The gift was wrapped in a beautiful box. He started to laugh. "Natalie, calm down, you're like a whirlwind. Do you need any help in the apartment?"

"No, everything is done. My father was very efficient."

He saw her look up at the apartment, but not happily.

While they drove to his home, she told him about the trip and all they had done. She kept the conversation going, but part of her wanted to ask why Ruth had car trouble in front of his home. She let the thoughts die in her mind for the time. His mother was in the kitchen, making meatballs for dinner.

"Hello, Mrs. Molinaro, it's so good to see you." She handed the box to her.

"Thank you, Natalie." She sat down on the sofa in the living room and opened the box. "This is just lovely! Thank you for thinking of me. Will you stay for dinner?" Natalie looked at Lucca and waited for him to speak.

"We'll stay, but I'm sure Natalie doesn't want to stay late after her long trip yesterday."

"Lucca, I'm fine." She gave him the brightest smile.

His father came in from work and gave Natalie a large hug. "My dear girl, you look lovely. Your trip agreed with you, I see."

Lucca led her up to the second floor to his bedroom. He closed the door and took her face in his hands.

"Natalie, why don't we marry now? We both can finish school. My father agreed that we can both live here. He adores you. I'm not sure I want to wait till we both finish college." He kissed her gently.

"Lucca, I'm not sure, we promised each other that we'd get married in your senior year. I'll be a junior by then, and it will be easier." He looked as if she had slapped him, clearly unhappy to have his suggestion so blithely dismissed.

"Natalie, are you sure we should wait?"

"Lucca, we love each other. Time will fly. What could go wrong?"

He sighed. "You're right. I guess it was missing you that had me reacting and thinking."

She smiled at him and brushed the hair from his brow. "It will be all right."

They talked about her trip the rest of the evening and how Lucca's family would eventually go to Italy once his father retired.

That night, as Natalie arrived home, Aunt Jane was in the living room, waiting. She saw Natalie and Lucca pull up. Natalie waved goodbye and saw Jane at the window. Strange, she thought. It was eight at night.

"Jane, what's wrong? Where's Dad?"

"He went down to get a drink with Scott." Jane was clenching her hands. "Sit, Natalie. I have a letter for you, but I must tell you something first. Mother Superior called. She had given me the letter last week as Sister Agnes entered the hospital."

Natalie's heart felt like it stopped. "Jane, I must go visit her right now. Can you drive me?"

Jane's eyes swam with tears. "Natalie, Sister Agnes died this morning. I was just told about an hour ago. I'm so sorry. I know how close the two of you were."

Jane handed her the letter. Natalie's hands were shaking.

Jane got up to leave. She looked back at Natalie as she was closing the door. Tears coursed down Natalie's face as she opened the sealed envelope.

My Dear Natalie,

My time is short, but my life as a servant to God was my Glory. Then you entered my life. I loved you from the moment I set eyes on you. You were the child I could not have. I want you to keep going into this world with your heart open to all the beauty you always seem to see.

Realize there are some unkind people in this world but keep moving on. Do not let them break your spirit. You have always fallen back on prayer and your deep belief in God. Keep that in your heart.

I weep as I write this, thinking of the first year when you came to school with bruises that your mother inflicted upon you, but you never said a word. I worry about you because you don't see the bad in people. You've always given everyone the benefit of the doubt.

I want you to always be brave, be kind, and, most of all, be strong. Never fear, and depend on the Lord to guide you. Shine light where you see darkness. You have the wisdom and strength to forgive the deepest offences. You have always looked past the insult that life deals out. You told me once how you always hope for those who deal with the unbearable and are in despair and bring joy to them. Let them see there is always hope. Those thoughts will guide you through life.

Remember:

"And surely I am with you always to the very end of the age."

Matthew 28:20

Natalie, recite this when your heart is troubled.

"Trust in the Lord with all your heart and lean not on your understanding. In all your ways, acknowledge him, and he will make you walk straight. Proverbs 3:5-6"

I love you, child, and I worry about leaving you. Remember you have Rosanne and your Aunt Jane, your aunts and uncle, and your friend Rose, whom I have spoken with, who you can always turn to for help and conversation.

I feel there will be difficult days for you, but you are strong, and you will continue walking in the Lord's footsteps as he guides you. I truly feel you have had angels around you to have survived what your mother did to you. You are a strong woman. Never ever let someone take your spirit from you. I want you to pay attention to a new friend in your life. I feel something around her that is evil. Remember this: do not trust her, my child. I see the way she looks at you, and it is unholy. I do not want someone ever to hurt you. I know it will come, but stay strong and move on from anyone who you feel is not a positive influence in your life.

I love you, Natalie as if you were my own child. I wish I had been given a longer life to be with you, but the Lord wants me now. Do not cry for me; I have always been at peace. My only unrest has been when you came into my life because I wanted to protect you from the world. It can be an ugly place, but in all the ugliness, you have always seen the beauty. I marvelled at your simple pleasures in life, from a bird singing in the trees or the first spring flower coming up to seeing the beauty in a snowflake. You saw life sometimes as a child, not as a young woman. You could heal a kitten and dog just by giving it love. You abound with gentleness to love people, family, animals, and nature. Stay kind in this world. I will only miss leaving you, but I'm on this fabulous journey to be in the Lord's arms.

Yours,

Sister Agnes.

Natalie wept for a long time. She sat in the chair, not feeling well, thinking it was her nerves after receiving the news. Suddenly, there was a searing pain in her side. She called Jane to ask if it was something to worry about. Jane would know since she was a nurse.

Jane said she would come over in about thirty minutes; she was worried about Natalie receiving the news about Sister Agnes. When Jane arrived and knocked several times with no answer, she found the extra hideaway key and let herself in. Natalie lay on the floor, barely conscious. Jane called an ambulance because her blood pressure was dropping, and darkness engulfed Natalie.

Natalie woke in a haze, and her father and Lucca were at the end of the bed. She was deathly white. Her appendix had ruptured, and she'd nearly died. She felt her father kiss her cheek every time she opened her eyes. Lucca was by her side reading. She woke once to see Ruth standing and talking to him, her hand on his arm, and she heard a partial conversation. She was trying to convince him to have dinner with her because Natalie was not awake. Natalie told herself she'd imagined it. The pain medication must have her mind playing tricks on her.

Rosanne and Jane were there almost every day to visit, but Lucca failed to show up in the middle of the week. He didn't call either, which was strange. She tried to reach him at his dorm, but they told her he was out. A sickening feeling entered her bones.

At the end of the week, she was released. Lucca was attentive as he came and brought her home with her father waiting.

Two weeks later, she noticed Lucca was not calling or coming by as much. She told herself he was busy getting ready for school. It was the second weekend when he came for her because his parents wanted her to have dinner with them. Dinner was unusually quiet. His father was not there, which Natalie wished he was. He would have broken the feeling as if ice had fallen on all of them. The conversation was little. After dinner, Lucca's mother took her aside.

"Natalie, I must talk to you. This is such a private conversation. It should just be between us."

They sat out on the sun porch. Natalie's hands were clenching her skirt.

"Natalie, you do look well. Lucca was very concerned the first week. You have a wonderful friend in Ruth who came by several times to see if Lucca was doing okay. She was worried about him."

Natalie almost stopped breathing. Her cheeks lost all colour, and her lips were transparent. The inside of her body started to tremble.

"Natalie, I want you to be honest." She took Natalie's hand, but Natalie pulled it back. "Ruth told me that you could not have children; that was the truth of your surgery. You know how much grandchildren mean to us, and it would be just awful not to have them. Ruth was very concerned about the fact you were not being honest with Lucca and that you rebuffed his offer of getting married right away and coming to live with us. She is such a lovely friend, Natalie, and is so concerned for you."

Natalie stood from the chair. She felt as if she could fall over. Her body trembled inside as she stood there stoically, trying to process what she was hearing. Her voice came out in almost a whisper. "She is telling you a fabricated story. She lied to you." Natalie was trying to breathe as her chest felt as if it was going to explode.

"My dear girl, Ruth is honest. She's just concerned about you telling Lucca such a lie. Where would that lead in marriage? As his mother, I have to tell him."

Natalie wanted to scream at her not to believe someone who had sex with two men. Later, she wished she had. She felt as vulnerable as when her mother would lash out at her. Rosanne and Sister Agnes were right: Ruth was trying to destroy her. How someone that young could be so evil stayed with her the rest of her life.

"Mrs. Molinaro, I really need to leave. These are such wild accusations, I can't listen to them. I'm not feeling well. Just remember she lied to you. There is no truth in what she said. I will get to the bottom of this, I promise."

"Now, Natalie, I know it's hard when you only have one parent to discuss this with. Ruth feels sorry for you because she comes from a stable home. She thought you might react like this."

"I'm not reacting, I'm just telling you the truth."

Lucca's cousin Frank came into the room, wanting to ask a question, but could feel the tension in the room. Natalie walked by him and went to find Lucca. She abruptly turned to Frank. "Ruth is a liar; heed my words."

She found Lucca in his room. Natalie stood at the door and looked him straight in the eyes. "How many times have you been out with Ruth?"

Lucca looked down at his feet, shaking his head. She didn't want to hear the next words, but they flowed out of him. "She just needed someone to talk to. Her boyfriend broke up with her and went back to his old girlfriend."

"Which boyfriend?"

He looked at her, not understanding. Natalie felt helpless, sensing now the viciousness of this woman, a woman her father helped, a woman who slept with two men, someone who pretended to be her friend.

"Just take me home."

They were silent most of the way. Natalie's voice was small when she spoke.

"Lucca, were there dates you went on or, as you said, just conversation?"

"Natalie, I'm sorry. That's all I can say. She's so different from you. She isn't shy, she knows what she wants. You just pushed me away when I talked about marriage. She wants to get married as soon as possible. She wants a boyfriend she can trust. I'm confused myself. I thought you were the only one I wanted."

She looked at him as he stared straight ahead. "So, what are you saying?"

"Natalie, I really don't know. I just think maybe we need a break."

"Lucca, we made a choice that marriage would take place after you graduated. I would live with you and your parents until I finished college, then we would find our place. I'm not sure how that equates to pushing you away. Not having sex, is that what changed your mind? She isn't who you think she is. I want you to remember that."

They pulled in front of her home, and he stood next to his car and spoke.

"Natalie, remember these words. I fell in love with you the moment I saw you when you came in shopping. I looked up and saw the girl from school who fascinated me. Your skirt swung so gracefully around your thin legs, the sweater so demure, you were so eloquent-looking. Your eyes were bright and filled with enthusiasm the first time we talked. Your carriage was filled with confidence. Then, when you smiled, I knew why heads turned. I loved every inch of you. I just need time. I promise I will think hard. I'm just confused right now."

Days went by without a call. Natalie cried until there were no more tears. Her tears were etched into her bones, her memory. She would never forget this life lesson or forgive. It was her first great sorrow. She would experience more, but these tears—her tears of loss—were so heavy, the kind that settles into your soul. For weeks, they made their memory in your skin and mind for the rest of her life. She wept all night. She missed him, but new life would go on. She prayed to have the eyes to see the best in people. She prayed her heart would forgive and her mind would learn to forget the bad. Rose, his sister, called at the end of the week. Natalie desperately missed hearing her voice and said her tears at night were her only companion.

"Natalie, I talked to your dad. We're going to come get you and bring you back to my home, and you can stay as long as you want."

Natalie agreed. She needed to get away. She'd thought she would visit her grandparents at the farmhouse, but she wouldn't have peace with her father's brother's family there. She felt betrayed—a lesson that would stay with her. The whole week it went through her mind as she tried to sleep, and sleep would not come. The question always came: Why? How could he? Then, her mother's voice would creep into her mind. "No one will love you forever. They all leave. You won't hold onto this boy. He will move on."

The words repeated in her mind. Rose came and got her as promised at the end of the week. Rose was good for Natalie and was furious with her mother and Lucca. She would never be a friend to Ruth; that was made up in her mind. She would help Natalie find closure.

They would talk for hours, taking long walks on the nearby

beach. Rose knew Natalie cried every night. She was losing a lot of weight and looked pale. She had deep circles under her eyes. It was her rock, even knowing there would be consequences taking Natalie's side and bringing her to her home to stay and recover. Rose would never trust Ruth, and with good reason. Rose was the one who guided Natalie through the difficult time of a breakup, the time of not understanding how someone could lie and manipulate. Rose spent days talking to her and telling her she would be there for her always and she could never trust Ruth or forgive her for what she had done. Rose felt the wrath later in years from Ruth, but Rose just accepted the fact that this woman was not good.

Eventually, Natalie had to go home. She'd already missed the first week of school. She'd spent so much time with Lucca it seemed surreal and then he just left and went on in life with someone else. It was hard to grasp at first. Ruth was cold, vengeful.

Months later, Natalie had the misfortune of encountering Ruth at a department store. She froze as Ruth looked at her with hate. Natalie turned to walk away, but Ruth caught up with her, so Natalie turned to face her.

"Ruth, just leave me alone. I don't want to talk to you."

An evil smile spread across Ruth's face. There was a short silence and Natalie spoke her words slowly as she asked Ruth what would possess her to even think of talking to her. Then she asked in a whispered voice, "Why, Ruth?"

Jeremiah 33:3 came to her mind while she was looking at her.

"Call to me and I will answer you and tell you great and unsearchable things you do not know."

Natalie did know evil, and it was standing in front of her. This unsearchable thing was now in front of her.

Ruth, in a high-pitched voice answered her. She looked like a coiled-up snake, Natalie thought.

"Because, Natalie, I was constantly left. You had the perfect boyfriend, while the two men I thought loved me went on to their girlfriends and left me. You had what I wanted, so I made sure I got it. It was too easy. His mother didn't like you because she wanted her son to be with a girl who came from a two-parent family. I just had to suggest you couldn't have children, and I knew it was over for you." There was a silence of hostility between the two of them.

"Ruth, I'm not sure where your hate comes from. You must sit in the darkness where no light shines. Nothing good comes out of what you did." Natalie looked at her with a steady gaze. She only saw hate in Ruth's eyes.

Natalie turned and walked away. She wasn't going to say another word. She heard Ruth calling after her, telling her she would be marrying Lucca. Natalie ignored her and kept walking. Even after all this time, the tears rolled down her face, and her heart felt heavy. She vowed she would never hurt someone or let someone do this again.

Natalie was hard to get out of the door for the first couple of weeks after seeing Ruth. She went to school and mostly stayed in her room. She spoke with Rosanne and Rose a lot on the phone. They could tell she was healing. She had started to laugh again. She knew Lucca was not coming back.

A few months later, her dad got her, Rosanne, and Stephanie tickets to the Army-Navy game. It was here at the game that she met the midshipman. He was average height, had broad shoulders, a strong chin and cheekbones, and clear blue eyes. He and two other midshipmen approached them. He singled Natalie out. The other two midshipmen placed themselves next to Rosanne and Stephanie.

He was standing beside Natalie. His smile was sweet, Natalie thought.

"I'm Jackson Coburn. And you are?"

Her voice was small. "I'm Natalie."

"Natalie, after the game, we have a floor at the Sheraton with parents and other midshipmen to celebrate. Would the three of you like to come?"

Natalie let out a little smile. "Will you celebrate if you lose?" She looked him straight in the eyes.

"We aren't going to lose."

"All right, we'll come, win or lose."

Natalie looked at Rosanne, who was driving. There was a broad smile across Rosanne's face as she nodded.

Over the coming months, Natalie, Rosanne, and Stephanie learned what it was like to date someone from the Naval Academy. The school year went by, and Jackson stayed with her and her father for Easter. It was an easy relationship. Natalie learned to have a deep affection for Jackson. They both knew where they were headed in life, but Natalie always kept part of her feelings to herself. She never gave it her all, keeping a part of her at a distance. Never again, she thought, would she let someone hurt her. Deep inside, she knew Jackson was honest and devoted and wanted a future with her. She loved his honesty, and they laughed a lot when together. They wrote endearing letters.

Natalie didn't encounter Lucca for a long time, and slowly he faded from her memory. She mailed his ring back—the only thing she felt good about. She shared with Jackson about what had happened. He promised he would never treat her with such dishonesty. Their relationship grew over the years as he and Natalie made the long-distance relationship work.

She, Rosanne, and Stephanie rented a house down the shore. They worked on the boardwalk and enjoyed themselves. Jackson wrote to her weekly. The Academy sent him on manoeuvres for the summer, and before school would start, he had to visit home. Natalie declined to meet him in Texas. She wasn't to meet his parents. Her years with Jackson were pure, healthy and safe.

She encountered Lucca at the beginning of her last year in college. He stopped as he drove by her new home, the cottage her father promised they would move into. She was startled when he pulled up.

"Natalie!"

A lump came to her throat when she heard his voice. "I'm in a hurry, Lucca. I can't talk to you."

"Natalie, I've called and driven by a few times, but you haven't been home. I have a job in New York. I don't get back here much."

She stopped in her tracks at the steps to the front gate. "Why are you here?" She crossed her arms over her chest. Her pulse was fluttering, and she felt the old pain come rushing in. "I heard you got married. You should get home to your wife."

Lucca hung his head. "Natalie, I've handled this terribly. Marriage to Ruth isn't what I thought it would be. You are my most beautiful regret. I never stopped loving you. When I think of you sometimes, it leaves me aching. I feel an empty space inside myself. I think it's because you're not there."

She swallowed hard to clear her throat. This conversation was toxic, she thought. What sort of game was he playing?

"Natalie, I treated you inexcusably. I was wrong. I couldn't back out of the relationship with Ruth. There was so much pressure from her and Mom that we had to get married. I made too many promises." He stuttered a little. "My mother wanted her, and they get along so well. Ruth always tells her that she just wants to be a mother and give her lots of grandchildren."

Natalie backed away, her voice carrying with strong emotion. "Don't bother to apologize. Your words mean nothing." She just wanted to run into the house. She hadn't thought of him in such a long time, and here he was.

"Lucca, someday, you'll pass through hurt and fragility in some form. I hope it turns to strength, as it did with me. I became strong. Ruth is such a selfish, evil person. She gambled and sucked out her own soul to please herself. Lucca, I wish you the best. Go on with your life. Life's full of painful moments, but we learn from them. There's s no point to this conversation. The past is the past, and let it remain so."

"Natalie, I was just hoping once we talked…" he stammered. "God, Natalie, you are still so beautiful. Your eyes sparkle like stars. I've dreamt of us. I wake up sometimes and think about what I've done. I miss your laugh. Ruth doesn't laugh like you do., There are so many things I miss about you."

She gave him a weak smile. "Lucca, for a time, my world stopped. What you did was like walking on broken shards of glass those first few months. Those edges of the glass cut into my heart so deeply. Let me tell you, it's easy to pick up shards and throw them in the trash where they belong." She stood straight and gathered all her composure. "You had me making myself a prisoner in my own mind for a time, but I moved on. You mean nothing to me now, just a faded memory."

His lips became thin. He looked almost angry. "Yes, I know you moved on to some naval officer. The one time I did drive by, I saw the two of you in an embrace outside your door."

"Yes, Lucca, I have moved on. I would rather have the light in my life than the darkness that you're living with. I was fortunate to find Jackson. He helped me remove you from my memory. He's kind and honest. I know you've already cheated on Ruth. I've run into some of your friends, and they have loose lips. God, I'm so glad you're gone from my life."

Her voice was strong, and he could see in her eyes that she meant every word. It was on the tip of her tongue to tell him about Ruth's old boyfriends visiting her at her and Lucca's home, but she decided not to sink as low as Ruth. Maybe someday, the truths would come out. *What a couple*, Natalie thought.

"One more thing, Lucca. What are you going to tell your children when they ask how you and Ruth met? It's bound to come up."

"Natalie, I wish I could make this right." He went to touch her arm, but she pulled back. Touching him would make her cry. Then, a powerful feeling came over her, and she took a deep breath. She had to say something that might sink into his heart. Her voice was colder than a winter blizzard.

"You married someone with a sickness in her, a woman with no empathy and no heart. Don't ever come around me again. You will never make it right. I waited a long time to tell you. You can have all the success you will have, but in your heart, I truly do not feel you will ever be happy."

She turned and walked into her home. She heard him call her name but didn't look back at him. He was a faded memory, just like the words of her mother had been fading from her. Her mother left her with the gift of knowing how people can hate. She knew how it felt to hurt, and she wasn't going to live with those memories any longer. She thought about this every night as she fell asleep. She smiled to herself as she walked into the living room and sat on the chair. Her cat jumped on her lap and sat for a long time. She shed no tears, and a slight smile came upon her lips.

She was free.

Psalms came to her again.

Psalm 4:8

I will lie down and sleep in peace for you alone. O Lord, make me dwell in safety.

Epilogue

Years came and went. Natalie and Rosanne planned to leave Pennsylvania, maybe. She'd moved on from dating her midshipman as they both finished their college years. Natalie and Jackson knew it wouldn't work, and they parted on good terms. He had asked her to marry him, but she just didn't want to be a Navy wife. He told her he'd never forget her and to reach out if she ever needed anything, and they left as best friends.

In the last year of college, Rosanne met a young man named Mario in the summer. They were now old enough to attend bars down on the beach, and he was in the band. It turned out to be much more than a summer romance. Once out of college, he became a police officer. They were in love by the end of the summer and married that winter. It was hard on Natalie to lose Rosanne after she moved out of state. They were never too far apart because they would not let each other go. Natalie felt honoured to be godmother to her son Tony. They had a friendship for a lifetime, as well as her friend Rose. She would be there for years to come, and Rose suffered from the wrath of Ruth, who separated her from her brother.

Life would forever change for Natalie once she became a flight attendant, which turned out to be her dream job. Sadly, her father died, never finding true happiness again, even though Natalie had introduced him to a wonderful Pan Am flight attendant. Throughout her life, Natalie was convinced the Holy Spirit and its grace guided her through both the wonderful times and the times of heartbreak and agony.

She ran into Lucca three times in her life, twice in New York City and once in Spain. He was standing with Ruth, and she looked as miserable as he did. What were the odds? The first time, she and two other flight attendants were having lunch in Manhattan, and she backed out of the restaurant to avoid him. He was there with someone besides his wife and was embracing the woman in a way that one could tell she was more than a friend. Their kiss was passionate, and she saw him gently touch her cheek. She was a tall, beautiful brunette much younger than he.

The second time, Natalie was on a layover in New York City, and they saw each other in the Marriott lobby. She was checking in, and she felt a tap on her shoulder. This time, she spoke to him for the first time in thirty years. They met at the bar in the Marriot for drinks, and as she listened to his life story, she suddenly felt sorry for him. He'd fallen deeply in love with another woman, but divorcing Ruth would be too costly. Here, he had everything—houses, a company, children—and yet he was one of the unhappiest people she had talked to in a long time.

He told her his life could have been different, happier if he had married her so long ago. Natalie just smiled and told him it wasn't meant to be. In reality, it was just a high school romance, but he quickly said it was more than that. He showed her some pictures of his children as well as the woman he had been involved with for years. She truly was beautiful and looked to be a kind person.

Natalie just smiled as she listened. Ruth lived with his infidelities because she couldn't bring him happiness. She didn't want to lose the big houses, the cars and the money. She was a bitter, unhappy woman. Lucca said he and Ruth lived separate lives. He'd fallen out of love with her and now lived for his children and grandchildren. Natalie wished him well and hoped he would find happiness.

In her life, there were corridors in her heart that would echo with footsteps of memories, especially late at night in some strange country where she felt alone. She never doubted the Holy Spirit, and angels brought her comfort during the most challenging parts of her life.

For many years, her life had revolved around her father. Rosanne, Rose, and her Aunt Jane would be a crucial part of her life in later years. Each family member who died left a hole in her heart, especially her grandparents. Each sorrow was immeasurable for her. Those experiences gave her strength for the years to come. When her first husband, Loyd, died, she felt the world would never be the same again. It was a challenge after his death to move forward. Her cousin Shawn talked her into coming back to the Mountains of North Carolina, where life again turned to great happiness.

Natalie had long left her mother's demons behind. She forgave her mother but had no interest in a relationship and had never tried to find her. She knew Katarina moved from city to city, country to country, always running. Katarina and John's other child did find Natalie in 1992, and that relationship became another lesson in her path in life.

On a visit with Aunt Gertrude, Natalie was told Katarina disappeared for many years. Kat had told Hans that she had regrets, including the way she treated John and all her children. There were times Katarina could feel sadness for what she had done, but her true ache was still from Gregory. Her feelings for him never left her. She'd seen him through the years, and they had several more journeys with

Peter and Louis.

Natalie knew of every sibling out there and kept them in her mind.

Rosanne and Rose were each only a phone call away, and she kept them close to her heart and her sister and family in Germany.

She always pulled out Sister Agnes's letter with each heartache throughout her years and knew she was blessed. She also kept her American grandmother's letters close. Her grandmother had written her a letter every month from the time she returned to the United States without fail. She wrote about life, how proud she was of her, and how she loved being part of her life.

Katarina's and Natalie's story are still to be told as both there life's unfolded, Katarina, she was asked on other dangerous paths during the cold war and Natalie would go on with her own life stories. Natalie will bring stories of laughter and tears as she ventured into the world of airlines for thirty eight years. Natalie would hear from family and read later in life letters and journals of what else her Mother did during the cold war.

THE END

About the Author

The Author retired as a Delta International Flight Attendant, which allowed her to research her books while visiting family in Europe. Living in Rome, Paris and Germany, she was able to do extensive research for her books. She has had the opportunity to travel the world, gaining insights into people's perceptions, their lives, and places. She now lives in Wisconsin with her husband, dogs, cats, and horses, where she writes her books. She has written 2 books previously, "The Star and The Cross" and "Crawlng Out Of the Darkness" that are a part of a trilogy with "The Past is a Dangerous Place" being the third in the series.